DARKNESS
FALLS

DARKNESS
FALLS

JOYCE ANNE SCHNEIDER

POCKET BOOKS

New York   London   Toronto   Sydney   Tokyo

POCKET BOOKS, a division of Simon & Schuster Inc.
1230 Avenue of the Americas, New York, NY 10020

ISBN: 0-671-31173-5

First Pocket Books trade special advance printing April 1989

10 9 8 7 6 5 4 3 2 1

POCKET and colophon are trademarks
of Simon & Schuster Inc.

Printed in the U.S.A.

For Bob, Matt, and Danielle,
With all my love.

DARKNESS
FALLS

1

THE BODY WAS DISCOVERED at 6:10 P.M., on a perfect Sunday in June, with the low sun beaming its pink and golden rays over the town of Grand Cove's yacht basin, and a sunburned family of four bringing in their long white sloop to its mooring. In their tall, slender fairness the four resembled each other: two parents, two children, a Ralph Lauren Instant Old Family that could have been found in any of the hundred or more marinas that lined the coast of Connecticut's southern Fairfield County.

These were not people accustomed to shock. The mother, smiling, looking a decade younger than her years, her long, blond hair pulled back into a simple ponytail; the father, in his requisite polo shirt and shorts and docksiders without socks, ordering his children to their posts in a rather beery, jolly version of a latter-day Captain Bligh; and the children, about ten and twelve, a girl and a boy, sun-streaked and rather bored-looking, moving forward to the bow with coils of thin rope in their hands.

"What's that?" the girl piped, frowning, crouching on the bow and pointing to a spot just ahead in the water.

The boy, standing over her, peered ahead. The closer the sloop glided, the more he could see a large, bobbing, pale object that had become entangled on something. A dead sand shark maybe, belly up? The boy blinked, and looked again.

"Hey, Dad," he turned and called back. "There's something scuzzy wrapped around our buoy. Dad? Hey, cut the motor, we're going to hit it!"

His father, oblivious, was cheerily yelling something to another marina family just coming in, so his mother moved forward, looked for herself, and unconsciously, still staring, reached for her children.

The first thing she felt, as she saw it getting closer, was that creeping, queasy sensation she sometimes got while working in the garden, when she suddenly heard the movement and the *hiss* of a garter snake. Harmless, she'd shakily rebuke herself; yet still, irrationally, there was always that skin-crawling feeling of having brushed with evil, and it was coming upon her now, worse as they came within yards and she saw the froth of a million tiny bubbles clinging to the thing . . . fermentation, she realized . . . and then the boat's motion swirled the water and the pallid, bobbing mass rolled over, and the woman put both fists to her mouth and knew she was going to be sick now, and she screamed.

Throughout the busy harbor and along the docks, heads jerked up at the sound. The blond woman screaming and screaming again and trying to hustle her children back along the gunwales; the husband running forward from the other side, hollering "Oh, God! Oh, Jesus!" and yelling across the water for someone to call the harbor cops; his radio was out. Voices shouted back; people ran; someone in a motor launch set out grim-faced toward them. Word flashed quickly through the rest of Grand Cove. The EMS call heard on the police scanner sent local reporters running, and the local radio station interrupted its broadcast to announce that an unidentified young blond woman had been found drowned at the Laurel Point Yacht Club.

Not until the following day would newspapers coast to coast report the startling identity of the victim.

2

SOMETHING'S WRONG, Amanda Hammond thought, as she turned onto Shore Drive.

Usually this lush and narrow road that wound past the old waterfront estates was quiet; little traffic, sightseers mostly, people slowing down to crane their necks in an effort to see over the ivied walls or through the wrought-iron gates to the graceful, multi-chimneyed mansions beyond. Even the police seemed to respond to the hushed splendor of the area by patrolling at slower speeds than they used in other neighborhoods, which was why Amanda was startled to hear the wail of fast-approaching sirens behind her. Braking her black Jaguar, frowning in puzzlement, she barely made it to the grassy shoulder as two squad cars came hurtling round the curve and sped clamorously past her.

Involuntarily, as she stared after them, her fingers tightened on the steering wheel and she felt the old downpress of terror that had plagued her since childhood. *It's not the other thing,* she stormed at herself, willing herself to be calm, then giving up when another pair of cruisers screamed past with their own nerve-shattering version of sound and light.

"Why . . . ?" she breathed out loud, slumping back in her seat and feeling only half-foolish at the question. What in this sealed-off world of wealth and peace could possibly have produced the kind of cop drama that she associated with the raunchy old tenement street where she had lived for four years in New York? (And wasn't it odd, she reflected, that such things didn't bother her a bit when she was in the city?) A little shakily she reached forward, pulled her Aretha Franklin tape out of the tape deck, and tossed it onto the pile of other tapes that she kept for company on the seat beside her. The Aretha mood was killed. She checked her rearview mirror and pulled back onto the road, but as she drove her sense of panic came and rolled back through her again.

Police patrolling leisurely, after all, was a far cry from police speeding, police arriving hell-bent at your house with their lights whipping the night and their expressions grim. Nightmare images came to Amanda of flashlights sweeping the dark of her family's property; of her father's agitated voice shouting *she couldn't have gone anywhere . . . the cars are all here!* Of the two big uniformed cops *(why two, she had always wondered . . . was the task of confronting a tearful eleven-year-old too heartbreaking for one to go it alone?)* coming up to her room to tell her that they had found her mother.

Stop it, she told herself, trying to wrestle down the old terror that rose up at her at odd moments like this. The trauma had happened long ago, and on this pretty Sunday evening the neighborhood looked its usual untraumatic, overdignified dowager self, *ergo* . . . some old sport must have just got back from his sail to the Vineyard and discovered the family jewels missing, and called the police. Simple as that, right? *Right?*

Amanda guided her car past a line of overgrown rhododendrons, persuading herself. It did make sense, didn't it? Weekend burglaries around here were not exactly rare: so many of the residents in this, the richest section of this affluent commuter town were often away, spending their winters in Palm Beach or Gstaad, their summers on the Riviera or wherever, while their homes, left in the hands of staff who mostly took off on weekends, made tempting targets for thieves willing to tackle the elaborate security systems.

So. Just another robbery, Amanda decided, calming a little as she breathed in the tangy sea breezes coming through the open window. The sky outside was turning a breathtaking dusky rose. Glancing to the right, she caught glimpses of the Long Island Sound through the occasional open driveway, the rare expanse of unwalled, sweeping lawn, the—

—Wait a minute. Four patrol cars for a just-reported burglary that was probably committed like most burglaries on Saturday night? For something so routine they don't go tearing around like that, so what could it be?

Slowing, back to fretting, Amanda turned right onto a graveled drive and pulled up to the cobbled courtyard of an enormous brick Georgian house. What a pile, she thought, pushing back a long strand of auburn hair and turning off the ignition. The front entrance of the house was lighted, plus a few of the downstairs rooms—which only emphasized, she realized, the depressing emptiness of the rest of the place.

Squint, she told herself, leaning forward on the leather upholstery of the Jaguar. It is twenty years ago, and I am eleven, and I'm up there in that high branch of the old copper beech, listening in the dark as my father yells and my mother sobs. Their muted voices are coming from that far window up there, now as dark as their graves. Now unsquint, and breathe deeply, and remind yourself that you're a grown woman now, and that you've managed to come back and live in this place for nearly a year to prove that you can put the past behind you. The irony of the situation did not escape Amanda. If she, of all people, could not turn her back on old nightmares and get on with her life, then who in the world could? And how could she expect them to?

Would it be fair, accurate, and objective to say that I became a psychiatrist because I needed one?

Stop tormenting yourself.

GETTING OUT AND SLAMMING THE CAR DOOR, Amanda noticed that the house seemed unusually closed up tonight. Odd, she thought. On balmy evenings like this Suki loved to throw open the French doors and let the sea breezes waft in from the terrace. Hurrying up the front steps, Amanda was surprised to see the tiny red light on under the hanging ivy: it was the burglar alarm, which ordinarily they used only to lock up for the night. Mystified, she fumbled for her keys in her purse. She turned off the alarm, used a second key to open the front door, and stepped into the foyer.

"Suki?" she called out a little nervously. "You there?"

The warm glow of the wide hall greeted her. Rosy Chinese rugs stretched across gleaming parquet to twin fireplaces that stood facing each other. On each side of the hall graceful arches led into large, formal rooms, and Amanda was reminded of the pictures in *House Beautiful* and *Architectural Digest* of magnificent homes and magnificent rooms with no one in them. She sighed, missing New York; missing the high-voltage energy and good smells and noise of the city; but most of all missing the comraderie that she had had at Bellevue during her years of medical school and psychiatric training. She had gone into the city Friday night for a first reunion of her med school class, had had too good a time and stayed too late, and had driven home feeling lonely and depressed.

Come in more *often,* her old friends had scolded. What is it—a forty-five minute drive?

She had sat at a table for ten with the people who had been her support system—her family, practically—for eight years of her life. Ellie Brown, her roommate in med school and best friend during residency, now happily launched in a pediatric practice; Sam Holzer, engaged to Ellie, still funny and sarcastic as ever and starting a surgery practice; Carole Mayer, who shared Sam's gift for turning stress into wisecracks, almost finished with an extra-year fellowship in cardiology. With the others at the table they had reminisced about the good times, mainly, happy to forget the brutal studies, the occasional nasty resident, the forty-hour stretches without sleep. In Amanda's refrigerator was a huge cheesecake—a jokey gift from Ellie, who after all these years and visits to Grand Cove was still insisting that "you can't get *anything* like this in the Land of Cucumber Sandwiches."

Amanda smiled, remembering. Had it only been Friday night? The reunion already seemed ages ago. She placed her purse and some notebooks on an antique table, and turned, hearing the sound of anxious footsteps rushing down the hall. "Suki?" she called.

Suki Pepper, Amanda's housekeeper, was a nervous but devoted woman of sixty-three, with nearly white hair, a thin, pretty face and alert blue eyes. She usually spent her weekends with her married niece who lived across town, then came running back early on Sunday evenings complaining that she couldn't sleep without the sound of the water lapping outside her window. The real reason, Amanda suspected, was that Suki couldn't bear to see her alone and was still playing mother hen to her after all these years, although— Amanda looked more closely as she approached—her old friend seemed more tense than usual tonight.

"Oh, Amanda," Suki said in a torrent. "I'm so glad you're back. Have you heard what happened? That's why I turned on the alarm. I mean, if it were tomorrow and *daytime* it wouldn't have been so bad, but nights it's just so darn *scary* being here alone!"

Amanda blinked at her, seeing again the clamor of police cars wailing past, and she felt a chill. "I haven't heard a thing," she said. "What happened?"

How strange, she thought, to see this maternal figure of her childhood now running to her as if she were the parent. Amanda had been eleven when Suki, a former school teacher, came to work for the Hammonds six months before the tragedy. She had kept Amanda home and tutored her—with Mr. Hammond's permission—during the next harrowing year when Amanda had refused to return to boarding school. And she had stayed on, tending the lonely little household, until nine years ago when Amanda's father died. Amanda by then was in medical school. They had cried together, gotten (with Ellie Brown's help) through that second terrible funeral together, and then, to Suki's relief, Amanda had closed the house. Just locked it and left it, not ready yet to decide what to do with it. For a while Suki lived alone and quite happily, then agreed to move in and help her niece with her family, and then floored Amanda last July by agreeing to come and play housekeeper for one final year.

Now, feeling a little sad at the role reversal, Amanda put a comforting arm around the older woman's shoulder as they headed for the kitchen.

"Let me guess," Amanda said. "Someone just got back from Marrakesh and reported a stolen Picasso."

Suki rolled her eyes in exasperation. "Just what do you folks *do* at that hospital? You never turn on the radio? You pipe Mozart and Mendelssohn all over the place to further pacify the Thorazine bunch, and you haven't got the foggiest idea what's going on in the real world? No, now don't laugh, it's true." With a mock-indignant sniff, Suki paused to admire the tall, slender beauty her former charge had grown into. Amanda had inherited her mother's patrician features, with large, gray-green eyes, dark hair nearly down to her shoulders, and the same air of delicate, quiet intensity. She was wearing an open-necked creamy silk blouse with a beige linen skirt—the picture of poise and elegance. There was no sign of the tearful, frightened little girl of years ago. In her place was this competent and warm, controlled young woman.

Sometimes Suki worried that Amanda was too controlled.

They reached the enormous, Mexican-tiled kitchen. "Well," Suki went on. "I'll tell you what's happened. A young blond woman was found drowned an hour ago in the Laurel Point Marina, I heard it on the radio. The Laurel Marina, Mandie—that's less than a quarter mile down the shore from us! And *naturally* they said that as yet the police suspect no foul play, which means I'll bet that they *do* suspect foul play. What kid in Grand Cove doesn't know how to swim?''

Amanda felt a sensation of grief that was all too familiar. ''That's terrible,'' she murmured, frowning, deeply disturbed. ''Have they identified her yet?''

''No. Just said long blond hair and nude, and that was the part that scared me. Nobody drowns nude, do they?'' Suki's eyes filled with sympathetic woe, then reverted quickly to the agitation of a moment ago. ''So. Until I hear to the contrary, there's a homicidal maniac hiding right out there under your dock, Amanda, and the *least* we can do is turn on the burglar—''

The telephone rang, and Suki let out a yelp and fluttered nervous fingers at her throat. ''I'll get it. I must calm down, I'm really going overboard, aren't I? *Oh, God, terrible joke!''* She moved to the wall phone behind her, and before picking up let it ring again and said, ''I forgot. See? Hysteria. You had some calls and I put your messages over there on the counter.'' She pointed and turned back and took the phone off the hook. ''Dr. Hammond's residence,'' she announced.

AMANDA CROSSED THE GLEAMING TILE FLOOR, picked up the pink memo slips, and put them back down. No way could she concentrate—hearing about the drowning had upset her deeply. A young woman? *Whose* young woman? Which set of loved ones was going to get that life-shattering phone call from the police tonight? Sight unseen, she grieved for those people, could taste their pain and tears with the power of her own bitter memory. The world's too hard a place, she thought, sighing, looking out the long set of windows over the sink. Terrible things happen, and people we love are taken away from us and we are left all alone. *How can I go on?* her patients asked—how many times had she heard that question?—and she usually said, *You just will, that's all. You will grieve and you will find yourself crying in closets and under the covers but you'll go on. You'll get through one day, and then another, and then another.*

She wondered solemnly who the drowned girl was. One saw so

many of these California-looking kids all over town, flocking to the beaches, or summer-jobbing in the boutiques and restaurants. She thought in particular of the neighbor's daughter who used to jog up and down their private beach; then realized that half the female lifeguards at the town beach perched in their high, white chairs looked like that too . . .

"Hello? Hello? Would you speak up, please?"

Amanda screened out Suki's voice behind her, and looked back out the windows to the Sound. The water was murky-looking now, with the lights of small craft bobbing in the distance. And in the far distance, the hazy, winking lights of Long Island. Her father in his sober moments used to joke about the Sound, calling it the Great Gatsby Inland Sea. He was right, it should be renamed, Amanda thought. There was opulence on the other side, too. Huge homes with docks and deep mooring just like hers, their owners—old money types or members of the new, overnight aristocracy—no different from each other, really, in their conviction that they could buy forever. And . . . oh my, the Sound held secrets, Amanda knew. More boozing, business schemes, and marital infidelities took place on that body of water or in its yacht basins than they did on the land. As a psychiatrist, she saw daily the dark soul behind the genteel upper class. Sick preppies, alcoholic Junior Leaguers, skeletons in Fortune 500 closets.

Money, Amanda thought, exhaling heavily. Too much or too little was equally dangerous. One made people desperate. The other made them careless.

But murder? She turned back to the agitated Suki, who was clutching the phone and wearing a quizzical expression. Maniacs under the dock, indeed. Maybe some people did drown naked; it wasn't so unlikely. They sunbathed nude on their yachts and got drunk or stoned and rolled into the water. Amanda shuddered. It was horrible any way you looked at it.

"I shouldn't laugh," Suki said low, covering the mouthpiece.

"Another crisis?" Amanda smiled. If she was Miss Bowl-of-Jello vulnerable in her personal life, she also had the professional detachment of so many physicians who had learned over the years not to jump every time they heard the word, "Emergency."

Suki grimaced. "It's Mr. Morley."

Morley was one of the patients—and there were many—who

had learned to get past a doctor's answering service by insisting that their crisis was urgent. The answering service, usually staffed by well-meaning and easily intimidated souls, would then put the call through to the doctor's residence. There was one woman who had called Amanda at two and three A.M. to report her dreams. And a man who usually chose around four in the morning to call her and talk dirty. Morley's problem was along those lines.

"He said"—Suki screwed up her features to mimic Morley's voice—"that he tried what you told him and it didn't *work*."

Amanda leaned with her back to the sink and grinned wanly. "Tell him to try harder."

There was something a little funny and a lot sad in the way that Suki resumed a brief and exasperated conversation with the patient. When Amanda was home she was always on top of situations in case anything really serious came in, but the pathetic thing was that the patients knew exactly who Suki was, and *they didn't care*—they struggled to keep her on the phone; they just wanted to talk to anybody. Amanda listened half-frowning to the drift of the conversation, her ears tuned to the slightest indication that she should intercept, when that possibility became quickly mooted by Suki's shrill-voiced, "I *beg* your pardon!" and slamming down of the phone.

She turned, red-faced. "You know what he said to me, Amanda? He said"—she cocked her head lewdly and dropped her voice to hostile, crank-call register—"'I know what *you* need, lady.'"

She had done such a perfect job of imitating a patient she had never seen that Amanda, in spite of herself, gave in to laughter.

"Don't tell a soul," she said, wiping an eye, "but you're the one who keeps the psychiatrist sane."

When Suki smiled, her whole face crinkled. "Well," she said, as if the call had interrupted something else on her agenda. She made a business of crossing to the cooktop center island, turning on the radio, and fiddling with the dial to look for the news. As an Elton John song played softly she straightened, and looked at Amanda with a new and . . . waiting air of expectancy, Amanda realized. "Aren't you going to read your phone messages?" she asked.

"Oh, right." Amanda picked up the pink memo slips again. "Let's see who has to be called back." She looked up and around suddenly, as if only now aware that the place reeked of other women's perfume and men's cologne and the strong scent of Havana cigars. Her last break with the past had been to put her house up for sale. In the three weeks that it had been on the market, realtors with their parades of customers had trooped through almost daily, their ranks including a smattering of European titles and Miami moguls wearing neck chains. "Heavy day while I was gone?"

She scanned the memos with half an eye while Suki told of the day's stream of expensively dressed prospective buyers. *"Terrible* how some of those realtors act like such toadies. I heard that woman from the Global Agency saying that she absolutely agreed that your tiles in the kitchen are all *wrong,* they're passé, they should be ripped out and replaced by Art Deco, oh, yes, much pretentious talk about Making A Statement. And some couple with Phyllis Whatsername from the Chandler Agency came in saying they want to rip out your mother's rose garden to build an indoor swimming pool, and then *your* agent Gordie Maitland was here *twice* with two different couples, one from Palm Beach who . . ."

Suki stopped suddenly. She edged closer to where Amanda stood frozen, her eyes staring stupidly at one of the pink sheets.

"Oh," she said faintly, looking over Amanda's shoulder. "Yes, Peter Barron called."

She saw Amanda flush crimson, and her good maternal heart felt suddenly guilty at having run on so. "Out of the blue, he called," she said awkwardly, coloring herself. "He sounded . . . different, though I must admit, it was nice hearing his voice again . . ."

"Was he charming?" Amanda said tightly. Abruptly she grabbed up the memos and headed for the door. Her heart was pounding painfully, and she couldn't think straight enough to form another sentence. Understanding, Suki called soothingly after her, offering to make something to eat. "An omelet? Sound good to you?"

Amanda stopped, sighed, and turned to smile bleakly. Just seeing that man's name had made her overreact; she certainly didn't want to hurt her old friend. "No thanks, I already grabbed a bite at the hospital. Be my good buddy and eat for two."

Leaving Suki busy at the stove, she walked through the formal dining room and into the library, exhaling gratefully as she entered. This room was a refuge. A place to be quiet, to nurse headaches like the one she had coming on now, to wrestle with the darker thoughts that had been nagging under the surface all day. She glanced appreciatively around at the familiar surroundings: mahogany paneling, the jumble of antiques and plants, an eighteenth-century carved mantel over the well-used fireplace, tall windows that overlooked the water on one side and the front driveway on the other. She sat at the old English desk and got out her logbook. She leaned back in her chair, closed her eyes, and tried hard to think of the day's caseload of patients.

Peter Barron came to her instead.

She saw him the way he had looked that first time she had ever laid eyes on him. Mid-December, the first snow of the season already melting and turning slushy on the sidewalks of Main Street, and there he was, dark-haired and handsome in his ski parka, striding like an athlete toward her with one of those twenty-five-pound bags of Puppy Chow slung over his shoulder. She had tried not to stare and had failed: something about the intensity of those deep-set dark eyes—and the way they turned playful when he caught her looking at him and he . . . Amanda swallowed hard, just thinking about it . . . he *winked* at her and smiled. Amanda had just stood there, dumbstruck and crimson-cheeked, after he passed. *Winked?* she remembered thinking. As in flirt, the way men two generations ago used to do before they had such outrageous habits slapped out of them? Hadn't this guy heard? *What man in today's world still flirts?*

Amanda Hammond, independent, professional, been-every-where-seen-it-all product of the '80s, stood there that day on that slushy sidewalk and realized to her amazement that she had never blushed.

The next day he had shown up at her office wearing that roguish smile of his, and had asked her out. "I knew who you were yesterday," he told her simply. He mentioned a friend in common who had pointed her out a few weeks earlier; and surprised her with not just who he was, but what he was.

"Why didn't you stop and say hello?" she asked, still a little wary.

"I'm shy," he said solemnly, and she had laughed and softened.

Their love affair had been like an intense and hungry fire before it ended, badly, for the same ironic reasons that it had started. They were two of a kind in every sense. They had both come from the sort of super-rich, unhappy families (his owned a pharmaceutical empire) that seem to raise only junior clones and emotional cripples, and they had each wanted to break out: to do hard, substantial, and different things on their own if they were going to be strong. "Two stubborns," Peter had groused one night after a first minor tiff. And later—for the whirlwind had lasted only five weeks—he had come up with an even better analysis. "We have matching hang-ups, *that's* the problem."

He had behaved abominably at the end—there was no denying that—but it was also true that when he had begged for a reconciliation, she had pushed him out of her life like a furious adolescent.

Very nice, she now told herself. Just the mature behavior one would expect from a psychiatrist. *(But he deserved it!* an angry voice hollered indignantly back in her mind—*he's a world-class egotist and I hate him and if I never see him again it will be too soon!)*

Enough, she told herself unhappily, leaning forward again in her chair, trying to clear her mind for more grown-up thoughts. What's over is over. Think sexless. *Try.*

Dispiritedly she turned a page in her medical log, and stared at words like Miltown and Elavil and Mellaril through a film of tears. She blinked her eyes hard, forced the tears back—

(hate him)

—and commanded herself to act halfway responsible and get that damned logbook up to date.

Had today really been Sunday? she brooded, picking up her pen. You'd never know it in this type A lady's life. She had had to go in to Brooklawn, the private psychiatric hospital where she worked, to make rounds and rewrite medication orders. Controlled-drug orders had to be rewritten by an M.D. every day; the small medical staff of five psychiatrists rotated weekends, and Amanda had been up for this one. Still, she had kidded herself that she might be able to zip in and out in under two hours, and that the able staff of psychologists, psychiatric social workers, and nurses could handle the rest . . . but since Fate just loved to play tricks on her, one of the hospitalized—

The phone on the desk in front of her rang. She stared at it, her heart speeding up again, and decided that she'd simply be out for anyone she didn't want to talk to. Suki will get it, she thought, and returned to her notes.

—one of the hospitalized patients had had an explosive crying jag and needed ninety minutes of treatment, and as soon as they had gotten her quieted down, two—

The phone rang again. *Suki!*

—two emergency admissions arrived: one a suicidal actress who had come to Connecticut to get sane (Brooklawn was popular with the entertainment crowd); the other an investment banker who had had a psychotic break at his country club and attacked a fellow golfer with his nine iron.

The phone stopped ringing.

Amanda began to write in her log, describing the day's cases and symptoms, medications and long-range treatment plans . . .

. . . and Suki came into the room.

Amanda looked up. She took in Suki's bug-eyed expression, and uneasily put down her pen.

"What's up?"

"That phone call," Suki said, gesturing incredulously with the spatula she held in her hand. "It's the police. A Detective Somebody." Her eyes blinked nervously as if all that frantic fantasizing about maniacs hiding under the dock had surprised her by coming true. "He says he wants to talk to you."

3

FROWNING, AMANDA REACHED FOR THE PHONE. "Hello?" she said, trying to avoid the unsettling effect of Suki's frightened gaze.

"Doctor Hammond," said a man's voice. "Sorry to disturb you. This is Detective McHugh, of the Grand Cove Police. We think you might be able to help us." The voice was strong, kind, and somewhat muffled. Sounds of a busy squad room were in the background.

Amanda stopped breathing without realizing it. "What can I do for you?"

"We have reason to think that a drowning victim found late today might be one of your patients. I'd like to stop by to talk to you if you're free."

Amanda sagged. "Oh no," she murmured, seeing the patrol cars flying at her again, understanding now her overreaction for the fatal announcement that it was. At her side she heard Suki utter troubled little whimpers and hurry back toward the kitchen. She gave the detective directions to the house and hung up, feeling numb horror rise up in her throat. So . . . it wasn't one of the beach bunnies or the girls working the boutiques and the restaurants; it was someone who *might* (the detective's word, she frantically reminded herself) be one of her patients. Long blond hair? She had two teenage patients who answered to that description. Both of them sweet, vulnerable kids, so motivated to get well, so close to breakthrough in the long struggle back. One of them, in fact, had lived until recently right next door . . .

"God, no," Amanda whispered in a low, husky voice.

She got up and paced. From the library to the long, relentlessly formal living room, back and forth in front of the carved marble fireplace, then out to the wide center hall.

In the hall her sense of foreboding deepened. Disturbed, she climbed the three steps to the staircase landing, and peered out the small, lead-paned window to the property adjoining hers. The Payne house, a darkened, Tudor mansion, empty and for sale now, like her own. One of life's more bizarre, ironic twists.

She had been fourteen when that family moved in. She remembered standing in this very place one summer afternoon, watching the moving trucks arrive, wondering desperately if the new family had any children. Suki, peering out with her, had given her a vaguely worried look, then said that yes, she had heard they had a baby. About a year old. A little girl. Amanda had been ecstatic.

"A baby!" she had exclaimed. "Do you think they'd let me play with her? Emily and I could both go over and play with her, couldn't we?" Emily was Suki's niece, and at the time Amanda's only friend in the world. At boarding school she was painfully shy and kept to herself, but when she came home on weekends Suki saw to it that the slightly younger Emily was usually there for companionship. The two grew up to be very close.

Suki had felt torn on that long ago day discussing the baby. "Well," she had said, looking out again uncertainly. "Your father isn't too keen on that Mr. Payne. He says he's a crook, although I don't know why." She had looked back at Amanda's pathetically hopeful expression and had probably thought, poor child, three years without a mother, a baby would be fun. So she had smiled and said, "Em's coming over tomorrow. Why don't you both go over and introduce yourselves? The baby's probably lonely, too. They might be happy to have company for her."

That was seventeen years ago. For the children began an idyll of two-big-sisters-for-the-lonely-baby, of afternoons of piggyback and silly games and storytime that went on forever. Neither girl took much notice of the parents, because they were seldom there. Mr. Payne was a big, handsome Texan who—if you ever saw him at all—was always just heading for the airport. And Mrs. Payne was what the adults called "flashy," a woman who left her home and child pretty much to the servants.

Amanda stared sadly across at the darkened Tudor, remembering the rest of that family's terrible history.

Carl Payne got even further away from his East Texas boyhood by increasing his fortune from "jest a few million" to hundreds of millions. People (including Amanda's father, begrudgingly) called him a business genius because of his ability to buy dying companies, turn them around, and reap enormous profits. Rumors of bribery and corruption grew along with his fortune. His company went public, he skimmed enough off the top to support a couple of Third World countries, and then the SEC and the Treasury Department closed in. Indictments came hand in hand with the divorce; Kelly's mother took off for good times on the Riviera; and Carl Payne's pilot two years ago crashed their twin-engine Cessna into the Sound. The shattering of the family was complete. The laughing, tiny Kelly Payne who had once been like a little sister to Amanda grew up miserable, drifted away, made her fretful round of boarding schools while Amanda was in college and medical training, and had been living for the past fourteen months in a lonely waterfront condo. Not until eight months ago had she sought Amanda out and begged her for psychiatric treatment. Refused to go to anyone else. *You or no one,* she had sobbed. *It will seem like old times.*

Amanda turned away frowning from the window, remembering the detective's words to her over the phone. *But Kelly's an excellent swimmer!* came unbidden to her mind. Which in turn gave rise to the fear that the dead girl was her *other* blond patient, another kid she adored and wanted to help.

She stepped back down to the hall and began to pace again. *It's neither of them,* she stormed at herself, getting more panicky by the second. *Someone's made a terrible mistake.*

DETECTIVE LIEUTENANT JOSEPH MCHUGH was a powerfully built man in his early fifties, with thick gray-brown hair and a kindly, rugged face. He showed her his identification, followed her into the living room, and looked around quizzically as he sat in an upholstered chair by the fireplace.

"Have I been here before?" he asked.

Amanda, seating herself opposite him, smiled thinly and said, "It's possible." She watched him get out his pen and notebook, and waited.

He got right to it. "Was a girl named Kelly Payne one of your patients?"

Amanda went white. *"I'm alive! For the first time in my life, I'm really alive!"* She heard Kelly's high voice right here in the room with her. Kelly had finished last Thursday's appointment in a rare state of jubilation and had hugged her. She was finally beginning to feel stronger, less desperately depressed and more hopeful about getting on with her life.

I'm not hearing this, Amanda thought. As if from a hazy, faraway distance she heard herself say, "Yes. Kelly . . . is my patient. There must be some mistake."

McHugh shook his head gravely and scribbled a quick something. He looked up and began to speak in a voice that probably never ran out of sorrow. "She had a friend named Susan Weems staying with her for the weekend. She went out on a date Friday night and never came back. Her friend waited until Saturday—yesterday—to call the police, and when the floater was found it matched the description. Miss Weems knew of you, which is how we happened to call." He leaned forward wearily.

"Susan Weems—who is, by the way, hysterical and down at headquarters—says that Kelly was excited and seemed very up about her date. She was also late to meet the guy, and ran out the door barely blurting his name. Weems didn't quite catch it, but it sounded like either Ryan or Brian." He paused, studying Amanda. "Anyone named Ryan or Brian you know of in Kelly's life?"

Amanda's throat closed. She looked away from McHugh and stared helplessly down at the reds and golds of the Persian carpet. Shock number two, she thought numbly, again with that same disconnected, this-can't-be-happening feeling that had hit when she heard about Kelly. *It's Brian, Lieutenant,* she thought. *Brian Kirkley, without a doubt, because Brian and Kelly had discovered each other and were helping each other and you could go so far as to say they were in love. But I can't tell you about Brian, Lieutenant; he's my patient too. You of all people know about doctor-patient privacy. And Brian never harmed anybody. These were just two love-hungry rich kids who ached to be part of a real family. Who envied—are you ready for this, Lieutenant?—who envied the kids who came from what they perceived as normal, middle-class homes. No . . . we won't discuss Brian at all. He's never harmed anyone.*

Amanda realized that McHugh was waiting patiently; she inhaled with great effort and looked back at him. "Both of those names are common in that age group," she said, sidestepping the question. "Kelly might have known one of each." She swallowed and added softly, "How can I help?"

"For starters we need someone to identify her. There seems to be no next of kin around, and her friend, well, she's in no shape." He shook his head. "Can't say as I blame her. We've told her it's not a pretty sight: the victim was floating in warm water for close to forty hours."

"I'll do it. She's in the morgue?"

"Yes." McHugh paused and looked around again, this time studying the tall and gracefully draped Palladian windows, the overstuffed chintz-covered furniture in shades of peach and rose. His eyes came to rest on the huge gilt-framed mirror over the fireplace with its heavily carved white marble surround, and very quietly he said, "I have been here before."

He looked back at Amanda, frowning slightly. "About eighteen years ago . . . ?"

"Twenty," Amanda said. She looked at him without expression. "Yes, it's possible you were here then."

His features changed as something dawned. He leaned forward in his chair, hunched and intent. "Don't tell me you're the daughter . . . that . . . young kid?"

She nodded, willing her voice to sound controlled. "You have quite a memory. I was eleven at the time, but probably looked younger. I was very skinny. Did you . . . see her?"

"Yes." The look of dark pity in his eyes made her feel vulnerable, made her want to plunge stoically on.

"Well, I don't remember you. There were so many police milling around . . ." In her mind she heard the wail of her own tumultuous grief down through the years of struggling alone, and then in analysis, to come to grips with the terrible story. A mother who put on a blue chiffon dress one night and gave a dinner party, who smiled when everyone told her how beautiful she looked, and then, after they left, took a walk down to her beach and drowned herself. And her father . . . who plunged into heavier drinking for the rest of his life, trying to blot out his guilt over his philandering and his wife's hurt. Who became such a spectral, shambling presence at his family's board meetings that they finally told him to get sober or stay home. And who had told Amanda one night, weeping, about his obsession. That her mother had not been drowned but murdered. "There were *marks* on her . . . like fingerprint marks . . . on her shoulders . . . but they were faint, and no one paid attention. No one would *listen* to me!"

And now as Amanda sat there, almost too dazed to think, she was aware of the dovetailing, truly hideous irony: both houses for sale, both families destroyed forever . . . and now Kelly dead . . .

"I'm sorry, I didn't realize," McHugh said softly.

Amanda made a gesture with her hand: life goes on. "Except, if I act a little weird on the subject of drownings, please understand. The hazards of living close to the water instead of the highway, right?"

The detective lowered his head and shook it. "Life sure can be a bitch. Does it help any to be a psychiatrist?"

Amanda gazed at him sadly. "Sometimes I wonder." Cops and shrinks, she thought. We get nothing but the tears of this world. She realized that the tale of her beleaguered history had derailed them from the subject at hand.

"I can go to the morgue now, I guess. Best to get it over with." Sweat sprang suddenly to her hands as she thought of the next question. "I'm assuming the drowning was ruled accidental . . . right?"

McHugh stood as she did and ran his hand across his brow. "Well, there seems to be a bit of confusion over there. One of the Assistant M.E.'s looked at her first and said it was accidental. Then the Medical Examiner himself, Dr. Barron, stepped in and said no, he's not so sure. He's waiting for us now. Do you know Peter Barron?"

4

ONE HUNDRED YARDS AWAY, a man sat in the fading gray light at a dusty window. He sat very still, his spine stiff on the edge of an old steamer trunk. Below, across the darkening sweep of gardens and vast lawns, the adjoining property was well lit. He saw the unmarked police car disappear down the drive, and grunted darkly to himself. A formality, he thought, but his face twisted uneasily and he whispered to himself, "bitch."

He stood and looked around. Early moonlight washed feebly over the floorboards from the attic window across the way, the window that looked out over the leafy tops of trees to the far end of the cove. Only hours before, that window must have admitted the setting rays of the sun—and an unobstructed view of them taking her out of the water.

Pity he had not been here to see it. But he could *imagine* how it must have been—oh, yes—he could visualize the whole inevitable scene from that first thin scream of discovery, to people yelling and running down there, small as toys from this distance. Then the sirens, of course. The arriving police cars, an ambulance, police boats churning the water as they rushed in—*such* heroes, oh my, and not one of them guessing that he was pulling their strings; *he had made it all happen.* Inhaling deeply, he felt a rancid, gloating triumph spread through him. A swooning sense of power.

He had graduated, was how he saw it. If he could murder coolly like that, without the slightest fear of detection, then he could do anything, get away with anything and still be safe. They thought they knew him in this smug, complacent town. But no one would ever guess at this other life of his, this deliciously obscene game, this adrenaline rush obsession that was his and his alone.

He knew how to get into their houses. Locks? Burglar alarms? He could turn them off with the flick of a wrist. Enter while they were sleeping, or having sex parties in their Jacuzzis, and then he would watch, thrilled with his own newfound kinkiness. He had also—and this was secondary, just gravy for a man already rich—he had also helped himself to a magnificent set of emeralds once—these people left their jewels lying around as often as they locked them up—and he had laughed up his sleeve when neither the police nor insurance company had believed the theft. After all, milady must have simply misplaced her baubles—how could they possibly have been stolen when the family's state-of-the-art, sophisticated security system had been on?

Now, as he stood in the cobwebby gloom, Kelly's face came back to him. Those eyes, wide with fear in the darkness, backing away . . . his hot surge of dirty joy when he held her, drunk and struggling feebly, under the water.

He bent, gathered up his things in the near darkness, and pulled on his black kidskin gloves. Shining his flashlight low, he stepped past boxes and piles of old magazines and a sway-backed Victorian settee. He went down the wooden staircase, closed the door carefully, and stepped into the enormous master bedroom.

He flicked the light around, breathing quickly. The beam was a strobe as it picked out a wide four-poster bed, two antique highboys, a fireplace flanked by plushy chairs, and, turning, a low dresser against the wall, still crowded with trinkets that the rich bought for themselves and then forgot: a silver brush and handmirror set; a scale-model mountain range of perfume bottles; a porcelain dog; a silver-framed photo of a blond girl astride her thoroughbred.

With a gloved hand he picked it up and put his light beam on it.

Three or so years ago, but still, unrecognizable. Destiny's darling all got up in her navy riding jacket, jodhpurs, hair pulled back in a pristine ponytail. He frowned. He saw her as she looked two nights ago on the dock, naked, her long blond hair loose and flying wantonly about her shoulders, her high, obscene laughter catching in a gasp when she saw him standing there.

With a stiff, slow movement he put the picture back.

A moment later he was moving down the grand staircase, and

heading through the dark hallway toward the front of the house, where he switched off his light.

In the foyer, thin moonlight streamed in through a tall window on his left—the side facing west, he realized.

He looked out. The chimneys and slate roof of the Georgian manor next door appeared as if painted with silver, aristocratic and haughty even in the forgetful veil of darkness and sea-mist.

He stared at the house for a long moment, a nagging worry making his hands perspire inside their black leather gloves.

What did Kelly tell her?

The thought occurred to him that it would probably be safer to kill the shrink. Quickly. Just to be on the safe side.

Turning, he peered through the front glass to make sure Shore Drive was empty of traffic. He checked his watch and swore. He was late, he had to hurry.

He opened the door, let himself out, and locked up again carefully, using first one key to lock the front door and then another to turn on the burglar alarm. It was an easy matter, getting the keys to people's houses. All you needed was the brains to figure the system.

Stepping back, checking the tiny red light that told him the security system was reactivated, he turned, disappeared hurriedly into the yew hedges lining the drive, and jogged down the road to where his car waited in shadow.

5

THE GRAND COVE HOSPITAL MORGUE was about a hundred years newer than the Bellevue morgue, but the sickly feeling of being there was the same—which did nothing to alleviate Amanda's apprehension or her headache that was beginning to throb. Tensely she looked around at the white tiles, the tilted examining tables with drains at their feet, the large, white sinks and, to her right, the wall of labeled metal drawers. Not since her first year of residency had she been in a morgue, and it felt very strange. She saw a sign hung over the double swinging doors—GOLFERS: NO CLEATS ALLOWED (now *that* was something one didn't see at Bellevue)—and turned balefully back to detective Joe McHugh.

"That somebody's idea of a joke?" she asked.

McHugh glanced wearily up at the sign and shook his head. "Can't tell with these guys. Some of the doctors here are a little strange."

"No kidding," Amanda remarked in a voice that was not quite casual, and the policeman glanced at her curiously. Mercifully he glanced away again, lost in his own thoughts that came with standing around waiting in a morgue.

I'm not handling this, she thought. *It's too much—identifying the remains of an old, dear friend and confronting a man I once thought I could love. My heart is going to burst. I can't do this. I have to get out of here.*

Just then the swinging doors pushed open, and a tall, darkly handsome man in a white lab coat came striding in. Deep blue eyes in a strong, intelligent face. Thirty-four years old still, Amanda remembered. Birthday not until September.

"Hi, Joe." The two men smiled and shook hands like old

cohorts. McHugh, who knew that psychiatrists were the one medical group who seldom came to the hospital and often knew few of the staff, took it upon himself to introduce the two.

"Dr. Peter Barron, forensic pathologist," he said. He caught the glance that passed between them and said, "Oh—you two already know each other?"

"Sort of," Peter Barron said awkwardly, eyeing Amanda, while she managed a stiffly polite "We've met" and then looked away, a different woman from the one who had driven over with McHugh, her features suddenly closed and pursed and tight-lipped. *Uh-huh,* McHugh thought, never one to miss implications, but still picking up on the extra amperage that had registered the moment Peter walked in. These, for sure, were two people on edge. But there was more pain than unfriendliness in the air—he didn't know how, he could just feel it.

The moment passed, and he was relieved when the expressions of the man and woman who faced each other turned restrained but professional again.

"Nasty business, that girl," Peter Barron said. "Needs to be identified, does she?"

McHugh nodded, and Barron's face turned thoughtful. Looking back at Amanda, he said: "It's late. Psychiatrists, um, sometimes forget what death looks like. You sure you're up to this?"

Yeah, I'm feeling just peachy. Pulse rate is already up to 130, and we haven't even gotten to the hard part yet.

A little raggedly, Amanda said, "Either way I'm not going to sleep."

"Suit yourself," said Barron tightly, and led the way to the wall of metal drawers. He pulled open one at waist level, looked in grimly, and pulled it out further.

Amanda and Joe McHugh came closer. McHugh took one look, breathed, "Christ," and stepped away again. He glanced unhappily at Amanda, who was standing, rigid, staring into the drawer. "Well?" he asked her.

She was silent, unable to take her eyes off the tangled matte of blond hair, the deadly white face, still bloated and sagging grotesquely from the effects of the water. A chunk of flesh had been torn from the upper cheek *(damn* fish, Amanda thought), but there was no mistaking the features: the eyes long and upturned-exotic even when closed, the thin, slightly aquiline nose, the high-domed forehead with the small crescent scar at the hairline.

Result of a bike accident when Kelly was five and Amanda was eighteen. Summertime: Amanda home from college, Kelly just learning to ride, Kelly's mother as always silkily latching on to Amanda to be a cross between big sister and babysitter. Not that Amanda, desperately unhappy and lonely, minded. Kelly had kicked and screamed her way through a series of fed-up, short-staying nannies, and it turned out that both only children were more than happy at the chance for real companionship.

And then the accident.

Kelly's strong little legs had pedaled their wobbly way right through the wall of the family greenhouse, shattering thirty square feet of glass. Miraculously, the child had sustained only a few lacerations and a very bruised ego, but to this day Amanda could hear the mother's shrill, infuriated accusations. Where were you, you lazy, irresponsible girl? Lying in the sun? Getting a suntan in your tight little bikini while you should have been taking care of Kelly?

And where were you, you terrible, drunk-face mother? Up in the sack with the latest hunk of a handyman? In her fury, Amanda had thought those words rather than scream them out as she had wanted to, but her expression said it all. From that day on, Kelly had become even more clingy to her, and Kelly's mother had actually turned her back on them both, refusing even to fake affection. Amanda and Mrs. Payne had never again exchanged, for all Amanda could remember, another word after that—although, to be honest, Amanda had gotten busier with college and then swamped by medical school, and had seen Kelly only two or three times a year on brief holiday visits. Then even those occasions dwindled, with Amanda spending most of the year in the city, and the two drifted apart without realizing it. Amanda heard via the housekeeper grapevine that Kelly's parents had gotten divorced; that the growing-up, pretty blond girl was living a life even worse than the one Amanda had lived not too long before: rootless, shuttling back and forth between different prep schools and the lonely, servant-staffed house which offered everything but love.

Twice Amanda had called her at school. Kelly had been

unresponsive in a way that Amanda realized only reflected her unhappiness. But what more could she have done?

So it seemed a cruel irony that Amanda now was remembering those words of long ago, and feeling overwhelmed by angry, irrational guilt. *You should have been taking care of Kelly!* She swallowed, blinked her eyes against the sudden sting of tears, and looked up to the two men who were waiting.

"It's her," she said.

PETER BARRON, who had pulled on rubber gloves, was watching her solemnly from the other side of the drawer. "I'm feeling pretty torn on this ruling," he said. He hesitated, and when her gaze met his and he saw her pale and strained expression, her eyes swimming with tears of shock, he realized that he had never seen this Amanda before. He had seen her passionate, moody, and more damned efficient than a roomful of tax accountants, but he had never seen her . . . vulnerable. He felt some of his edginess drain away, dropped his glance again, and went on.

"Seemed straightforward enough at first: lungs full of water, blood alcohol .15, which is close to roll-in-the-water drunk . . . so an accidental drowning, right? That was the original ruling. A vaginal smear turned up a full house of sperm, by the way, which still doesn't mean a whole lot. She could have had a date, and *then* gone off and fallen into the water. It happens. Boat parties. Everyone else is blotto, nobody notices—"

"But no boyfriend reported her missing?" Amanda asked tonelessly. She was coming back to herself now; looking at him stolidly, almost politely, as if saying: *Okay, truce. We'll set aside the egos. I can deal with you professionally.*

"No boyfriend, nobody," McHugh put in, and then frowned at the pathologist. "Forty hours in the water and there was still sperm?"

Barron nodded. "Right. In a young woman—in any woman who hasn't borne six kids—the birth canal's still pretty tight if the genitalia are closed."

Engrossed, he stared down at the dead girl. "So the accidental ruling seemed okay at first. I dunno. It may change." Reaching in, he put his fingertips on each side of the head and gently rotated it so that the face was toward him. "Amanda"—there was a brisk familiarity in the way he spoke the name—"something's bothering me. Take a look at the top of the right shoulder. By the neck. See anything unusual?"

Woodenly, Amanda bent and looked. Frowned at the indicated area of dead-looking flesh. Then straightened, her face still and frozen. "Gloves. I need gloves. Got an extra lab coat?"

McHugh pulled over a stool and sat on it, while Peter Barron went and got surgical gloves and a white lab coat for Amanda, and a bit awkwardly helped her on with them. *Snap! Snap!* went the pulled-on gloves, and McHugh, watching them, rubbed at his chin in amazement. It was magic: the regal-looking sophisticate was instantly transformed into a doctor. Like in a movie, the two in white had cast off that strange undercurrent of tension and suddenly matched each other, right down to the preoccupied expressions and the practiced, clinical gestures. Well, I'll be damned, he thought.

They went to work. Amanda duplicating Barron's pose with her hands on both sides of Kelly Payne's head; stooping, peering— "See that?" Barron was saying, "and *that?*"—touching the dead girl's shoulders and upper torso with the tips of her gloved fingers before straightening, still looking down, and feeling the room begin to turn on its axis. *Impossible,* she thought frantically, feeling nausea begin to well up. *Just a coincidence.*

Her father's voice, drunk, weeping, chilling her flesh, terrorizing a decade's worth of agonized nightmares. *"There were marks on her, Amanda. Like . . . finger marks . . . on her shoulders . . . but they were faint, and no one paid attention. No one would listen to me!"*

"Yes. Marks," she answered Barron, shaky-voiced and struggling against the faintness that washed over her. She forced herself on. "Same thing . . . anywhere else? You checked her back, buttocks?"

"Yes. Nothing else, only these three on the shoulders and easy to miss . . ." He looked at her and broke off. "Amanda," he said sharply. "Are you all right?"

"I'm fine," she said, avoiding his stubborn gaze as if that would help her maintain her composure.

And brave the rush of memories. Her young, beautiful mother, hours before that final dinner party, seeming almost cheerful in that dreamy, delicate way of hers. "Tomorrow, Mandie," Charlotte

Hammond had promised, hugging her daughter. "Tomorrow we'll go cut the roses and put them in your favorite vase. Isn't it too beautiful? The first roses of summer!"

She had not seemed depressed, although she had scarcely spoken to her husband for days. They had fought again several nights before. Amanda had lain in bed, crying, trying not to hear, but the pillow over her head had done her little good. She had heard her father shouting and getting drunker; heard her mother sobbing, *"You and your women! So why don't you go? Leave!"* They had subsided into one of their miserable silences which lasted until the day of the party, when Charlotte Hammond seemed to perk up again. "The guests were invited ages ago," Amanda heard her saying. "It will be good for us, a little gaiety."

So both parents had seemed to brighten on that day. And Charlotte Hammond had put on her blue chiffon gown and twirled for her daughter, looking a decade younger than her thirty-two years. And looking back to *happy,* which was why, in the darkest hours of the sleepless nights that followed, Amanda had begun fearfully to take on her father's obsession. Especially since . . . and this was the thought that still haunted her . . . what mother promises some wonderful form of togetherness for the next day, and *then goes off and commits suicide?*

Peter meanwhile was watching Amanda, guessing at her feelings. During their affair she had told him about her mother's drowning and her father's obsession. He wasn't sure how much she was identifying, and decided to keep an eye on her.

Soft-voiced, he half-turned and said, "Take a look, Joe. See how faint?"

McHugh came and peered into the drawer as Barron lifted the corpse's shoulder slightly, pointing out three pale-colored bruises, two on the front of the shoulder, the other in back near the top of the scapula. "Finger marks?" Barron asked. "Someone holding her down?"

So that's how it happens, Amanda thought, frozen between the two. *You work so hard for so long to regain your sanity, and you think at last you're there, and then something happens to pop out the fragile linchpin and it slips . . . it slips . . . and time grabs hold of you and slaps you cruelly back . . .*

Dazed, she watched McHugh study the marks, straighten, and

frown in thought. "Possible," he said, in a voice that sounded very far away. "But marks that faint could be from a week ago. From something else. They don't seem to suggest force . . ." He trailed off, annoyed and stumped, wishing prints could be taken off a body as easily as dusted from a wall, a telephone receiver.

"No," Barron conceded. "They don't seem to suggest force. They're not necessarily even finger marks. And if they are from Friday night and she was drunk, she could have gone klutzing into booms or branches or anything else. I also thought of semi-rough sex, and then threw that out—she'd have similar marks on her thighs and torso, and there's nothing." He pursed his lips hard. "So that's it. She's identified, and she's drowned, and we've got three *maybe* suspicious marks on her and not a damn thing else to go on." He hesitated, searching for something else to say, and finding nothing. "Okay if I slide her back?"

Slide her back . . . Those words, Amanda thought, spoken with nearly the casualness of a foreman on an assembly line. She heard McHugh assent and she turned away, sick, disbelieving, blinking back the shock of hearing that drawer scrape its metallic way closed. Groping for balance, her mind flashed desperately to a long-ago day on a breeze-swept veranda, reading a fairy tale to Kelly. ". . . And the prince and princess lived happily ever after . . ." *God, the horseshit we feed these kids. Why? Do we use their innocence to pretend to ourselves?* She turned back to see the drawer closed, blended in with the rest of the now-flush squares of metal, another brick in the wall. Good-bye Kelly, little sister. Good-bye to another link with my vanished past. Good-bye mother . . . good-bye father . . .

She was not even aware that she was crying until Peter Barron came over and offered a Kleenex. "Here, wipe," he said, pulling a nickel pack out of an inside pocket and unceremoniously mopping her cheek. Did that come with the service? she wondered resentfully. Do all medical examiners have hankies handy for those who come to identify the dead?

Muttering thanks, she turned away from him, realizing now that it was herself she was grieving for.

"Come on, kids," she heard Joe McHugh say in a comforting tone. "I need a ruling on this." He pushed the white stool back to its place and walked to the center of the room, where he looked suddenly older and very tired under the glare of the overhead fluorescents.

"Got any coffee?" he asked Peter. "I can't think without caffeine, and I've got a few dozen more questions I want to ask about this girl."

6

A MAID IN A GRAY UNIFORM and starched white apron poured coffee from a silver pot and glanced nervously around. The four people at the dining room table were oblivious to her, just like the people at other houses like this where she had worked. Rich people acted as if you were invisible while you served and they kept on talking, except that the Kirkleys tonight were acting different. They weren't talking at all; they had *been* talking before she came in and had stopped suddenly, and stared rigidly ahead, and were pointedly waiting for her to leave.

"Will that be all, Ma'am?" she asked.

The blond, elegant woman at the foot of the table smiled her iron little smile, and without looking up said, "Yes, Doreen, that will be all. Thank you." Her eyes saw the maid's hands make quick little adjusting motions with the strawberry dessert, and she said magnanimously, *"I'll* serve. *Thank* you, Doreen."

The maid, stepping back, chanced one more peek at the faces around the table—Mr. and Mrs. Kirkley, tanned and stoney-faced; their big-shot guest, an impressive, not-tanned man with a thatch of gray hair and sharp features; and the Kirkley's nineteen-year-old son: handsome, dark-haired Brian, the image of his father, looking more miserable and out of place than he usually did at that fancy Chip 'n' Dale dining room table. Doreen's big heart ached for Brian. He was a nice kid, not at all hoity-toity like his parents. "Want me to help you carry in the groceries?" he'd ask her; or, to Lisl who was the Swiss cook and getting on in her years: "Don't *lift* that, Lisl—here, let me." Now he looked terrible—pale, hunched forward, staring wretchedly down at his plate as if watching some terrible scene taking place on the shiny glare of the china. The others darted quick

glances from him to each other and back at him—as if *they* were the
ones in trouble, Doreen suddenly realized, and were angry because he
wasn't cooperating in fixing whatever the problem was. She hoped
the poor kid wasn't in any more hot water.

She was turning to leave when he surprised her by looking up
suddenly, and giving her a heart-breaking, lopsided smile. "Thanks,
Reenie."

Also the only one who ever said thank you around here. Taking
in the scowling threesome surrounding him, Doreen felt even more
protective. Remembered a word she had seen that newscaster use
on TV. Pulled in a deep breath, sent him her most penetrat-
ing, sympathetic look, and said, "Courage, honey." Then left the
room.

John Kirkley leaned forward at the head of the table.

"And that's *another* problem we've had to deal with," he hissed
low to the man who sat on his right. "Familiarity with the servants.
This boy has *never* known his place—"

"His station," Anne Kirkley corrected him, ever on the alert for
the do's and don'ts of Junior League diction. "You make him sound
like a ditch-digger."

Her husband's aggressive, angular face turned to her in cold
fury.

"Well, maybe he *should* have done some ditch digging. Like I
did, for God's sake, starting on a shoestring, working by the sweat of
my goddamn brow to get into college, get a scholarship—"

"Marry the boss's daughter," she said indifferently to her
wineglass, a little bored, glancing up as if for succor at a picture of an
ugly ship that hung over a sideboard. An oil-tanker. Her father's
oil-tanker, named after her when she was seventeen and planning her
début. The *Annie Lucinda* was now old and rusting and still bringing
oil out of all those bad places to America. Her family had had some
outstanding forbears—she sometimes wondered when she thought
about Brian if her father had been right about bringing mongrel
blood into the line.

"And I've *tripled* the boss's daughter's Strickland Corpora-
tion!" Kirkley exploded. So much for hushed voices. His features
had reddened and he had half-risen out of his chair, as if wanting to
strike her. An unusual display of violence, their gray-haired visitor
noted with casual surprise, leaning forward now as if he had tucked

enough away on his mental Rolodex, and it was time to steer things back to where they belonged.

"Okay, knock it off," he said mildly, folding his well-manicured hands and looking with the familiarity of years from one Kirkley to the other. Brian sought his eyes too, but they flicked almost absently over him, as adults' eyes always had since he was little and they were talking *about* him and not *to* him. Which prep school should he attend? Which riding instructor was best? Which yacht race should he enter?

Only this time it was: What to do about this dreadful business of the Payne girl.

You're damn lucky, Brian, that Ray Herrick is such a marvelous lawyer, and practically a neighbor and one of our very dearest friends. He's coming over tonight for a late dinner, he'll tell you what to do, and for heaven's sake get out of those awful clothes and wear a tie and jacket. Are you listening, Brian? Good God, snap out of it!"

Brian stared into the flames of the cream-colored candles before him, barely seeing the button-downed-and-blazered hotshot who sat in dimness across from him. Trying not to hear Herrick's falsely solicitous voice as it finally addressed him, launching into its Big Speech about the legalities of this and that and the importance of keeping your head down.

"Give yourself up, Brian? What on earth *for?*" Herrick smiled. "It was just an accident. You're under absolutely no legal obligation to put your head in the noose. It was your boat—the police will be only too happy to turn an accident into negligent homicide. The papers will have a field day—society boy accused!—and our very ambitious prosecutor will weave a net of circumstantial evidence around you that will embarrass your family. Do you think any of them *cares* that you were drunk and remember nothing?"

"Couldn't have said it better," murmured John Kirkley, irritably checking his watch; he had already told them he was late for a meeting. And Anne Kirkley, leaning forward with a simpering expression, said: "Her father was a crook, dear, you have to remember. So maybe some . . . gangster snuck up and pushed her out of some sort of vengeance. You shouldn't blame yourself—"

"Her father was *not* a crook!" Brian erupted, his fury and despair wringing pops of sweat on his brow. "Nobody ever proved a damn thing!"

His father glared at him. "Security fraud? Stock manipulation? You don't call that crime? Christ, the SEC and IRS were after his tail like bats out of hell. If he hadn't gotten himself killed—"

"Irrelevant, ir*rel*evant," Ray Herrick cut in, waving a hand in annoyance. It was amazing—all these years and he had never realized how incapable this family was of even talking to each other. He watched them subside resentfully, then leaned back and flicked at invisible lint on his blazer sleeve. "Brian," he said carefully, "do you think you were seen with her?"

Brian was clasping and unclasping his hands. "I don't know. I had had a few before I . . . picked her up at her dock. I don't think there was anyone around . . . not a lot of people *leave* to go sailing at seven in the evening, but . . . s-somebody could have been looking out a window." He stared down at his trembling fingers, which suddenly stilled, and his voice became thick with the tears that were threatening.

"What's killing me is—what if I *did* do something to cause this? You expect me to live with that? With not knowing? Not remembering a damn thing?" A tear streamed glistening down his cheek, and he angrily brushed it away. The others waited, stiff as boards. The last people in the world he would tell that he had really loved Kelly Payne.

"I want to talk to Amanda," he said abruptly, fighting off more tears. "Maybe she can help me remember, or . . . Jesus . . . help me with this . . . this guilt . . ."

The other three began shaking their heads and admonishing at once. Don't talk to *anyone,* they said. Not even your psychiatrist . . . privileged relationship, yes, but she might . . . who knows? Persuade you to clear your conscience? Tell all to the police so you'll have a nice, unburdened psyche in your jail cell while your family name gets dragged through the mud?

Brian suddenly thought he was going to be sick. "That's it! I'm out of here!" he cried, standing up so abruptly that his chair fell over backwards. He heard them calling to him—and his father shouting —as he stormed out of the dining room and out of the house, slamming the front door good and hard to tell them he had no intention of going up to his room.

He hadn't in nearly a year. Not since getting kicked out of prep school, and all those troubles that had sent him to a psychiatrist in the first place. Bad troubles. Fights. Feelings of worthlessness.

Breathing hard, feeling rage that made him want to drive his car into a wall, he hurried over dark, spongy lawn, down an embankment and then down a flight of rough-hewn stone stairs, stumbling as he went, until he heard the softly lapping sound of water and reached the boat house. His boat house.

He stepped into the interior of darkly glinting water, gulped in without relief the familiar, pungent smells of salt water and hemp and boat fuel. Glanced despondently in the gloom at the family sloop moored on the left, the vintage Chris Craft softly slapping the water on the right. Then hurried up the inside stairs to his place in the loft.

He did not turn on the light—the moonlight seemed enough as it lay in bars over the coiled ropes and rigging and piles of life jackets strewn on the floor. He headed for the crowded tool closet, opened it, and took from its dim recesses a bottle of unopened Gallo—*premier cru*—he thought, laughing insanely as he felt the burning tears start to come. He carried the bottle to his bed and sat down, hugging it as if it were his only friend in the world. Then twisted the cap open, and drank deeply.

He hated them. He hated them all, he hated himself. He looked at the bottle again—old friend, old buddy—and took another deep swig. Felt better, felt worse. *I'm sorry, Amanda. Really sorry. You told me to stay away from this shit and I . . . didn't, did I? Just a bum to the core, pretty lady. You were wasting your time.*

It was hitting him now, hitting good and carrying him up and far away from tears to the stars and the moon. Trembling, his face wet, he put the bottle down on the crate next to the bed, and got up to stare out the window that overlooked the water. The moon was flirting with him, he thought—inviting him, laying a bright, seductive path for him from here across the water to the horizon and oblivion, which was what he wanted. Oblivion. Forgetfulness, guaranteed and permanent. He looked down. The rocks below looked like gray, velvet pillows in the shadows. You could do a header into that soft surround and it would be over in seconds, just one bright flash of primal pain, and then . . . peace . . . home at last.

Time, he thought. He had needed to get fully loaded before this moment.

He reached to a place behind where he had put the bottle and picked up a photograph of Kelly. Held it to him, sat back on the bed, rocked back and forth. Then exploded into sobs. His shoulders heaved and lurched. The tears scalded, and his chest shuddered desperately, unable to breathe, and still the sobs came.

"Kelly, Kelly," he wept, pleading desperately to the picture. "What did I do to you? What the hell happened?"

7

"MURDER," Amanda said, her voice dull and neutral.

"Just like that?" McHugh asked almost indulgently. "So sure?"

Peter Barron said nothing and leaned against the counter near where McHugh stood, frowning down into his steaming Styrofoam cup with his lips pursed in frustration. They needed a ruling on this, and there was so little to go on. And, if truth be told, his brain was feeling too paralyzed to think. He was tired—hadn't slept much the previous night—and he was still rather stunned that Amanda Hammond was right here in this place, walking tensely back and forth in front of them as she argued her case. Her beauty, which he remembered from their five too brief, too intense weeks of infatuation, seemed only emphasized now by her emotional upset.

". . . wasn't *that* drunk," she was saying, looking reproachfully back at Barron. "How much alcohol *is* .15, anyway? Four beers? That may be legally drunk in this state—too drunk to drive, anyway—but I wouldn't exactly call it roll-in-the-water drunk, either. Besides, Kelly was an excellent swimmer."

McHugh was listening intently. "But it was enough to slow her reflexes . . . weaken her, is that what you're saying?"

"Yes. She only weighed about 110. A little booze and she'd be easy as a kitten to drown forcefully. Hence the faint finger marks. There was no need for a struggle."

"*Did* we decide those are definitely finger marks?" Peter asked, rebuking her gently. He was surprised at his own restraint. Anyone else stepping on his terrain would get decapitated on the spot, but Amanda . . . *What happened between us was my fault. Go easy.*

She turned to scowl at him, and said nothing. Behind her,

McHugh was telling Barron that the Friday night date was named either Ryan or Brian, according to Kelly's friend. Just for the record, he said.

"What about suicide?" the policeman now asked her. "You were her psychiatrist. Any possibility there?"

From a shelf of test tube racks Amanda had picked up a plastic bottle of Coppertone suntanning lotion, and was looking at it as if trying to fathom its absurdly incongruous presence in a morgue. She held it up to Peter Barron. "Yours?"

He half-grinned and shook his head in a way that said *now you're really getting nasty.* "No," he said without missing a beat. "Why? Want to borrow it?"

Exasperated, she put back the Coppertone and returned her attention to McHugh. "Suicide? No way. Kelly was doing too well in therapy. The first months were rough, sure, but then she started *wanting* to get strong. Became compulsive about doing every little thing right: driving extra carefully, joining an exercise class, drinking *carrot* juice, for God's sake." She shook her head firmly. "Suicide? Never."

"So back to square one." Peter Barron turned and tossed the remainder of his coffee into the sink behind him; thoughtfully watched it trickle darkly down the drain, then turned back and folded his arms.

"Water is our worst enemy," he said. "It washes everything away, except in this case the semen which will be typed but not suspect, since there are no signs of rape." He pushed his dark hair off his brow; inhaled. "Somebody gets murdered on land, all we'd need is a blood sample of the assailant, a speck of skin under the victim's fingernails . . . we're so high-tech these days we don't even need fingerprints anymore. But what do we have with this girl? She wasn't raped, there are three marks on her that could be"—he looked at Amanda—"anything, and the rest is washed clean." He shook his head in conflict. "I'm suspicious but I'm not entirely convinced. Close—but I need more time."

That's it, Amanda thought resignedly. *You do what you can and then you go home.* Feeling drained, she gathered up her handbag, turned to go, and stopped short with a hand squeezing her heart when she saw Kelly's metal drawer across the room. Behind her, she heard McHugh's voice ask:

"By the way, can you tell me why Kelly had no next of kin around for us to call? We couldn't find a soul."

She turned and looked back at him. McHugh was standing there looking solemn with his notebook in his hands, and Peter was going around checking the locks on cabinet doors. She bit down on her lip.

"When Kelly's parents decided to divorce, they bought her a condo on the water as a consolation prize. A $450,000 consolation prize for a busted-up family. You're seventeen, they told her; that's old enough to be on your own; here are the keys. Then they really took off. Her mother took up with some playboy type on the Riviera, and her father private-jetted between his London and New York apartments, his big house in the Bahamas. By the time I started treating Kelly eight months ago, her father was dead—killed in a small plane crash right off the coast here—and she was pretty much out of contact with her mother. Spent her entire first session with me just sitting there crying. Couldn't stop." Amanda inhaled heavily. "How's that for a Gold Coast happy story?"

McHugh shook his head and looked down and wrote. "I've heard similar."

Peter Barron slammed a supply closet door—roughly, Amanda thought—glanced down at his thin, gold Swiss watch, and appeared suddenly as worn out as McHugh. "It's late. What say we get out of here?"

They started to leave with Barron bringing up the rear. Halfway through the swinging doors Amanda forgot herself and abruptly turned, colliding with him and becoming flustered.

"Oh," she said, seeing his tense, unhappy eyes. "I'm sorry. I . . ." Her gaze slid away and traveled past his shoulder to the room behind with the wall of gray metal drawers. "I just wanted one last look."

He nodded, understanding, and stepped outside.

She looked in. Saw the drawer at waist level that held her former young neighbor, her former bravely struggling patient. Felt the stinging glitter of tears and thought, *Good-bye, Kelly, you poor kid, you never had a chance.*

In the hallway, she started past Barron and he put a hand on her arm. "Amanda, wait. I have to talk to you. Just for a second."

For a moment their gazes met, and Amanda flushed in

confusion. Then a look of hurt mixed with mistrust and renewed anger crept back into her eyes, and she pulled her arm away.

"Good night, Peter," she said. "Be well."

And hurried after McHugh.

AND SO HE STOOD THERE, stunned at the turmoil of his feelings when he had convinced himself that there were none. Not anymore. Finished, kaput. *Sturm und Drang* reduced to the lesser hell of a chronic, dull ache. That's how she wanted it, so let her go.

Had she noticed that his hands were shaking?

Cursing himself for his lack of cool, Peter Barron stood there in the corridor staring at nothing as he listened to the sound of their retreating footsteps. He had tried to appear controlled, professional, and had failed, he was certain, on two occasions: the time he had helped her on with her lab coat, feeling his heart go from its miserable thudding to an all-out sickly racket, and then when she had left—just pulled her arm away and stepped past him like that wearing that pursed-up little expression. That was the moment, he realized, when a feeling of real panic set in, and a furious, churning replay of all the self-recriminations he had gone through five months ago. *I'm sorry, Amanda,* he heard himself pleading into the phone. *Jesus, you're killing me . . . Amanda, don't hang up!*

"Evenin', doc."

"Huh?" Blinking, he was aware of one of the night orderlies pushing a sheet-shrouded, laden gurney past him toward the morgue doors. He stepped aside to let the man pass, muttering, yes, evening, and staring at the white mound that was making its final journey. Who? A man? A woman? Life is so goddamned short.

"Cops here," the orderly said brightly. "Some weekend. Lotsa cops. Sure glad it's Sunday night. Give erribody a chance to rest up."

Peter Barron looked at the orderly, a black man of about seventy with gray popcorn hair and a limp and a ready smile. He had pushed the gurney halfway through the swinging doors, and had left it like that to keep them propped open as he stepped back for a little conversation. The deceased, Barron knew, considering the area they lived in, might well have been a tycoon or a corporate exec or one of those Wall Street types—in any case someone who took himself very seriously. In death, this individual was being used as a door jam. *Sic transit gloria.*

He smiled tiredly at the orderly. "Yes, Henry, Sunday night. You'd think it was the city the way things pick up on weekends."

"Sure *looks* like the city out there. In back, I mean. 'Nother patrol car just pull in, lights flashin'. Two cops start walkin' into Emergency and then stop when they seen that plainclothes guy comin' out. With that pretty woman. My, in't she somethin'? I just seen them when I pushed wheelie here through."

"*Just?* They're still here?" Barron realized that scarcely four minutes had passed since Amanda's departure.

"Don't know 'bout still," said the older man, putting both hands back on the gurney, giving it a cheerful shove. "They was talkin' and leavin' at the same time. Probably just revvin' up right now."

Peter Barron bade the man a hasty good-night and hurried down the deserted hallway, pulling off his lab coat and tossing it into a laundry bin as he went. Leaving Emergency through the automatic sliding doors, he went out into the night and the activity of the ambulance bay.

LIGHT FROM THE ENTRANCE washed over a line of ambulances parked by the receiving platform, and behind them, off to one side and in dimmer light, stood two patrol cars, one with its lights still flashing, and the unmarked car of Joe McHugh. It was a scene, Barron thought, approaching, somehow garish and violent and suburban all at once, with blue and red beams strobing over the emergency vehicles, the two cops—one of them baby-faced with high school football still written all over him—conferring with McHugh and Amanda . . . and another pair of cops just yards away dealing with a kid, about sixteen, retching on his Reeboks and bawling—between heaves—"*Puleeze* don't call my father!" A tweedy doctor coming into the building and a nurse just leaving in a track suit walked through the crazy, fracturing lights without so much as a glance. Same old thing, their faces said.

"Amanda."

Four faces turned to him, McHugh and the officers looking nonplussed, Amanda stiffening visibly.

What she saw was a different man from the white-coated colleague she could deal with at least professionally. This was the

Peter she knew better: tennis-shouldered and lean, the body athletic and seductive under the navy polo shirt and lightweight gray slacks. Peter the egotist with that hard, earnest stare for the ladies. Peter who was the prime marital catch in a very rich sea, and knew it.

"We have to go," she said tersely, turning away from him and moving toward the car.

"To Brooklawn for next-of-kin info," McHugh said, looking from Peter to Amanda, taking in both their scowls and thinking: *Oh.* If he had picked up any funny vibes in the morgue, it was clear now what was going on. Barron running out of the building like that, staring after Amanda with the look of an injured ten-year-old; Amanda sounding curt and avoiding eye contact—but not before McHugh had caught the wounded look in her eyes. *Well, well.* McHugh surrendered to the briefest of smiles: all Irish charm and delight for one irresponsible instant, then caught himself, cleared his throat and said awkwardly, "Dr. Hammond's being very helpful."

"Joe," Barron said, coming closer and speaking rapidly. "I'd like to talk to Dr. Hammond for a sec. Okay—thirty seconds. Can you wait thirty seconds?"

"Sure, Peter," McHugh said—much too amiably, Amanda thought. "No problem."

These guys are buddies? Sure, Peter, take all the time you want. Furious, Amanda straightened from where she was fumbling with the door handle. Fixed Peter with blazing eyes, said, too forcefully, "We have nothing to discuss!" Then winced at her mistake. Too hostile. Anger showing. Voice all wrong after McHugh's warmer tone. She felt the startled stares and knew they were all watching her: the two young cops catching on, peering uncomfortably from her to Peter and back again; McHugh giving her a sidelong, sheepish eye; and Peter going into his deepest brooding look routine. Four men, almost comic-looking if one's sense of humor were skewed enough, each in his own way bracing himself for a scene that threatened female wrath.

Which was why Amanda shifted her stance to merely arch and said: "Unless you change your ruling. I believe that particular death needs serious looking into."

They stared at each other, Barron's expression fierce and confused, Amanda's frankly surprised at how quickly she had recovered. The others looked idiotically relieved as Barron muttered, "Conference time," took hold of her arm above the elbow, and steered her determinedly away from the group.

At a distance of several yards, they fought in low tones.

"What's this about change the ruling?" he stormed. "It so happens I *already* decided on homicide, three minutes ago, when I was drag-assing after you out of that hospital!"

"I was *planning*," Amanda said icily, "to put my intense convictions in an overnight letter." She crossed her arms tightly across her chest. "It just blurted out. I didn't want to embarrass them." She indicated the three policemen who had turned to watch their colleagues having a hard time dragging the stoned kid into Emergency.

Peter Barron stepped back, gaping at her furiously. His height—about six feet one inch—and the deeper dark of where they stood made him seem almost threatening.

"An overnight letter," he echoed sarcastically. "Amanda Hammond, the Great Communicator. Just like when you hung up on me three times in a row, sent away the kid with the flowers, refused to accept my most *ab-ject*"—he said this sarcastically— "apologies because you . . . ah . . ." He stopped. He had run into a wall. Could not bring himself to put into words the fact that he had allowed a spoiled, manipulative bitch to bust up a promising relationship.

"And how *is* Melissa, by the way?" said Amanda nastily, biting back the old hurt. "Still riding her precious thoroughbreds? Still co-chairing polo matches and such? A valuable human being."

"Melinda," he corrected her. He was leaning forward. His jaw was set and there was a petulant hurt in his eyes. "It was nothing. *Nothing.*" He straightened suddenly, looking spent and beaten, and shook his head as if now directing his anger at himself. "Christ, Amanda, what else can I say?"

Melinda Pell had been divorced two years earlier, had embarked despite her millions on law school until she found out that it was *hard,* and now played the fashionable social circuit with an energy and guile that escaped men completely. Or almost completely. Peter had known what she was up to. But Peter had also been mad. For the truth, as Peter Barron saw it, was that Melinda's behavior had not been the cause of his split with Amanda, but merely the last straw.

Mid-January. They had been picking at each other all week. Little things that were really big things. Huge things which—Peter later unhappily realized—had a lot to do with what was going wrong between men and women these days. Peter liked his women a little softer. Amanda had struggled for years to build up her rhinoceros skin. Peter had started making cracks about psychiatry (he didn't like it; it made him uncomfortable), and Amanda had retorted that with compassion like that he had probably chosen pathology for its very *absence* of personality. They had argued. For the rest of the week. Pressure building.

Until that damned black-tie gala he had dragged her to with all those Do-Gooder charity phonies who spent fortunes on gowns and bands and food and decorations and netted a few bucks and felt noble. ("I *have* to go, Amanda—it's the Cancer Research Ball, it's helpful if doctors put in an appearance.")

Some appearance. They had arrived already tense with each other. Bad start. Peter overdid the bubbly, and the women (married? hah!) started coming on to him. Melinda Pell saw her chance and seized it, and by 10 P.M. was all over him, with her breasts popping out and her fingers in his hair. *And he, the bastard, was enjoying every minute of it!*

Very quietly, Amanda had left. Just called a cab and walked out into the snow. The next day someone told her that Peter had driven Melinda home, and she had stopped that person right there. Didn't want to know what had happened next. Still didn't.

"I think your thirty seconds are up," she now told him stiffly. She started to walk back toward where the policemen had been, and weren't anymore, because it had taken four of them to carry the thrashing kid in, with McHugh following behind, probably to make out a disorderly conduct report.

"Manda, wait!" He caught up and reached for her arm, which she didn't yank away this time. *Admit it, he's wearing you down.* And he had called her that . . . name. It was a name he had made up for her: Manda the Panda, he would say; pandas are shy and solitary and steer clear of each other even when the female's in *heat,* for God's sake: that's why they're dying out.

He was right, of course. Boy, did he have her number. She sighed.

With a softer expression she watched him hold up both hands in a pleading gesture. "Listen," he said, and then he stopped and frowned and looked stuck again. He had wanted to spew it all out. The thinking he had done during his self-recrimination time about her father, the stories he had heard from his equally social parents about Stanton Hammond, the obsessive philanderer. The sensitivities he had trampled on so thoughtlessly and had suffered over afterward. But suddenly he was tongue-tied. No big speech, just a sorrowful gaze into her eyes, and the hesitant words, "That night . . . I must have seemed like your father" . . . and then he looked away, depressed, vaguely aware of the approaching wail of another ambulance.

He felt her eyes on him. Her voice was sad. "Guess that's it, isn't it?" she said. "I don't want a life like my mother's. It's why I'm so leery of . . . relationships, of . . ." She swallowed painfully.

He looked back and finished for her. "Of marriage, right? And I told you about my parents' unlovely relationship, remember? No violence, true—that's about the *only* good thing I can say about them." He shook his head bleakly. "So maybe we're both the Leery Twins."

A moment passed; his intense, dark eyes probed hers.

"I wanted to comfort you tonight. I just wanted you to know that. It must have been Nagasaki for you. Your patient dying like that . . . like your mother . . ."

"Nagasaki." Amanda mulled the word wearily. "That comes close."

He dared a small smile. "Remember the time you told me you became a psychiatrist because you needed one? I'm beginning to think maybe that wasn't such a bad idea."

They fell silent when the new ambulance came screaming in; stepped aside to get out of the way; were grateful, both of them, for the chance to think and not speak, and to feel, if not comfortable, then not entirely uncomfortable with each other. Tragedy had a way of putting self-pity into perspective.

It was only when the driver turned off his siren that Amanda became aware of her own beeper chirping urgently.

"What . . . ?" she said, looking down at it in surprise.

"Use the ER clerk's phone inside," Peter said. He saw one of the cops standing duty inside the glass sliding doors, and a second one (the high school football face) heading back across Emergency to join him. "Looks like they're finishing up with that kid. You'll have a minute."

THE ER CLERK WAS A PIP.

She was a tightly permed, end-of-patience old hand who was dealing with the usual weekend night crowd scene that she had dealt with for the past twenty years. Telephones rang and white push buttons flashed while she and a not-very-with-it-looking assistant tried to log in waiting patients ("my stomach!" "my ankle!"), and fathom a pair of hysterical individuals who spoke no English. An ER nurse standing behind the counter was loudly demanding something about Blue Cross forms as the clerk looked crossly up at Amanda.

"You on staff here?"

"No, but—"

"Sorry! Phone's for emergency use only!"

Peter stepped from where he was standing slightly behind Amanda and regarded the clerk sternly. "It's okay, Gladys."

The clerk blinked apologetically, and a moment later Amanda's answering service was telling her to call Brooklawn in a hurry. She did, and was connected to a worried-sounding psychiatric nurse. Watching her, Peter saw her go pale, her expression crumpling into the same look of stunned disbelief that he had seen her wear in the morgue. She said something rapid-fire into the phone which he didn't catch in the din, and then he heard:

"Make him comfortable and keep him *upstairs,* above all. Tell him I'm on my way."

She hung up as someone jostled her into him, and reflexively he raised his hands to hold her. She looked at him, reddening; broke nervously away as if needing a few feet of space in which to think. Disappointed, he watched her for a moment; studied the cameo grace of her profile as she stood, turned partly away. He had figured out the call, and went to her.

"The Friday night date, right? The house full of sperm? Showed up distraught after all."

She jerked her head around and stared at him for one, helpless instant. Shifted frantically down the stretch of hall with McHugh and his officer striding toward them. Turned back, her mind racing.

"Peter, will you help me? I've already told McHugh I'd give him info on Kelly at Brooklawn, and now I can't. I need ten, maybe fifteen minutes upstairs. Will you . . . ?"

He nodded. "Take him to your office and open your Payne file to him? Come on, ask me something harder." He touched her shoulder tentatively. "So am I right? It's your girl's Friday night date?"

Amanda looked alarmed. "Peter, you don't know a *thing!* Patient privilege in any case. If you say one blinkin' word—"

"Hey, no need for that. Just give me the key to your file and tell me—oops—in the car. Here they come."

8

IT FELT STRANGE—no, *eerie*—to be back in the passenger seat of Barron's Porsche, as if the last time had been yesterday, and the only difference now was that they were speeding through a warm summer night instead of through snow. Amanda glanced around the car's interior, thinking, *Even the same junk.* The tins of Dunlop tennis balls clunking around on the floor; the scrunched-up white paper McDonald's bags in the leather door pouches; the toppled pile of paperbacks in the trough between the seats. The familiarity of these things dispelled some of the awkwardness Amanda felt. Any remaining unease dissolved fast when she thought of Brian Kirkley.

"You don't think he did it?" Peter asked.

She glanced grimly over at him, then returned her eyes to the squad car moving rapidly ahead of them along the lighted Post Road. The "he" Peter had referred to was still unnamed, nineteen years old, and just another of Amanda's patients. That was all. She had decided to fill him in on some of the boy's case history, if not his actual identity, because Peter was helping, and though he did have his faults she knew of his special sympathy for the troubled kids of the area.

"No," she said vehemently. "I know him, he's just not capable. What I'm afraid he *is* capable of is harming himself. Thinking he was somehow to blame and then . . . going to pieces."

Peter braked, followed the cruiser through an intersection and then up a darker secondary road. It still seemed unreal, having her next to him. *Even the same perfume,* he thought, and he wanted to groan out loud. Instead he pulled in a breath and said: "This boy have a history of self-destruction?"

Amanda sighed heavily. How do you define the subtler forms of self-destructiveness? she thought. Does it include heavy boozing? Would it include Brian's getting into a fight at a truck stop one night when he was supposed to be headed back to school? Would it include pouring lighter fluid under your friend's dorm door at two in the morning, and hollering you were going to *light* it if he didn't get up and help you with a physics concept? (*Just a joke,* he had cried and pleaded when they kicked him out, citing a long list of grievances forgiven and covered up before the lighter fluid incident.)

Her mind came back to Brian's drinking. When he first came to her, he had been a lot worse off than your usual-and-bad-enough teen problem drinker who drank to "let off steam" and wound up throwing up in parking lots. Brian hadn't even pretended to be after release; he was after . . . what was that word he kept using? Oblivion. Yes, that was it. When Brian drank, it was skip Go and skip the party and proceed immediately to Flat-on-Your-Face Oblivion Boulevard. No pain that way, he insisted. No rehashing of heartaches and failures that only went away if you were totally shitfaced.

"Okay," Amanda had told him one day. "But what about the next morning? The whole next day of feeling like your head's been through a Mixmaster?"

"Oh," Brian had allowed. "Yeah, Jesus, that part sure sucks."

He had made good progress during therapy. *Talked* out problems he said nobody had ever listened to. Stayed even further away from the bottle when he met Kelly at a group therapy session. Grinned in sheepish amazement when he discovered that he was actually getting *happy.* Amanda had had misgivings about the two getting serious, and then had set her misgivings aside. What was so terrible? Two horny, troubled kids finding each other and supporting each other to make the progress that counted? The down side, of course, was his snob family and their attitude toward Kelly's father (a dead crook was still a crook), and the newly rich in general. The two had asked Amanda to keep their relationship a secret, and she for the umpteenth time had explained to them about patient-physician privacy.

Well, Brian had finally learned, hadn't he? Gotten himself to Brooklawn to tell her . . . my God . . . *what?*

Peter's question, she reminded herself, glancing out at an illuminated white-columned house that looked a little too George and Martha. She looked back.

"Self-destructive? Yes. This kid has fought, boozed, even *shoplifted* to get attention. No God-forbid razors or driving off cliffs or anything like that . . . yet." She paused, staring straight ahead. "The main thing is that it's all been self-directed. He's never harmed another person or creature to my knowledge. Gets depressed when he passes run-over raccoons in the road. Stands on the lawn at Brooklawn and cries, 'Hey, you stepped on a *flower!*'" She looked down at her clasped hands in her lap. "I tell you. This kid's a real heart-breaker."

Peter stared fixedly ahead. She was aware of his handsome profile dimly illuminated by the lights from the dashboard, but he was thinking, she could tell. Were it not for the zooming Porsche she was sure you could have heard the circuits whirring and clicking in that head of his. One thing about Peter—and one of the reasons he complained that psychiatry was too fuzzy—was his insistence that things should make *sense.* You have a crisis? A problem? You figure it out piece by piece the way you would figure a jigsaw puzzle. That was Peter. She waited, he glanced over at her, and seemed to measure his words carefully.

"Wonder how far apart they were at the time of the murder," he said quietly.

She looked at him, her eyes large and dark in the dimness. "Far apart?"

He swerved, followed the cruiser through a pair of stone columns and up the long private drive that led to Brooklawn. "Well. The amount of sperm in her suggests that she had just gotten up from being with him. Walked a few yards, maybe. The proximity is important. It means the killer knew the boy was there, which next makes me wonder . . . why didn't he kill them *both?*"

"Peter . . ."

"Who knew about that couple's habits? Did they have a favorite lovers' lane? Was there anyone in Kelly's life who had it in for her? Drowning is the upper-class way of murder, you know. Plenty of drownings don't get ruled as homicides when they damn well should."

He pulled into a parking slot next to McHugh's car, and switched off the engine. In the moonlight Amanda saw the silhouettes of perfect flower beds and ancient trees studding a manicured, downsloping lawn that seemed to go on forever. English garden perfection doing not a damn thing for the tormented souls inside. One of those souls was Brian Kirkley. She opened the door to get out.

A moment later the two were joining McHugh and his younger officer as they stood on the gravel of the wide circular drive, staring up in silence at the grand old mansion with its seemingly hundred windows ablaze.

"See that, Joe?" said the younger cop. "There's even a swanky way to go crazy."

In silence the four entered the wash of light from an antique lamp and mounted the steps to the front door.

IN THE GRAND GEORGIAN FOYER at the foot of a winding staircase they spoke briefly, Amanda hurriedly telling the policemen about her patient waiting upstairs as she fished out the key to her files and gave it to Peter.

"What about the door?" he asked her. "The key to your office door?"

"Nobody locks their offices in this place," she said. "What for? The file cabinets *in* the offices lock, and so do the desks although I never lock mine. What's to steal in a psychiatric hospital? Except drugs, which are kept upstairs." The cops were looking at her a little strangely, and so she continued, glancing defensively around at the side tables with their lit, oriental-based lamps, the antique Tabriz rug that covered the foyer floor like a field of exotic flowers. "This place used to be a private residence, remember. I don't think most of the downstairs doors even have locks, and if they do, the hardware is ancient."

She wanted to say more, but bit it back. That Brooklawn wasn't nightmare Bellevue where you had to check them for switchblades, it was—*who are we kidding, gentlemen?*—a for-the-most-part drying out place for the very rich, the deeply but genteelly troubled whose pain had finally broken through decades of determined decorum, and had brought them in terrified mostly of themselves. It was a place that held sedate little Christmas parties with pretty tea cookies, where visitors could come and have lovely chats with patients they mistook for the psychiatrists, and come away exclaiming that they all seemed so *normal* ("the wonders of Thorazine, Suki").

The younger officer, whose name Amanda had learned was Fowler, was looking around, sizing up the place and frowning slightly.

"What about the outside doors?" he asked. "Do they get locked?"

The question surprised her. "No, it's like any hospital. Fire laws prohibit locking any first-floor doors that connect with outside. Some sections of upstairs have locks—which are activated and opened automatically if the fire alarm goes off." She turned, started up the stairs, then stopped and pointed over the curving banister to a mahogany desk by the front door. A small lamp was on and glowing over a stack of patient charts, but the chair was empty.

"That's the downstairs nurses' station," she explained. "The nurse is usually . . . ah . . . there, to monitor who comes and goes, and there's one of those panic buttons like they have in banks embedded in the desk surface in case anyone shows up unruly."

She paused to peer up to the second floor with a look of annoyance. "Wonder where she is? Well, in any case, that alarm button's never been used to my knowledge."

McHugh cast a baleful eye at the unmanned nurses' station. Night staffs even in regular hospitals were small, he realized, and the patients here were sedated as hell, and the nurse had probably been called away for just a moment. Still, the place seemed to be run pretty casually, he thought, frowning, until he realized Amanda was speaking to him.

". . . will only take a few minutes, and then I'll rejoin you and Dr. Barron. My office is down that hall on the right—"

"I was *there*, remember?" Peter complained, looking injured.

She glanced back at him, coloring slightly before she shifted her gaze away. "Yes. Well . . ." Resumed, wooden-faced, mounting the stairs as McHugh told Fowler to wait by the nurses' station, and Peter bounded up behind her intent on a final word.

"Amanda."

She turned to face him, her expression clouded and already emoting over the scene that awaited her.

"*I'm* driving you home," he said, looking for all the world like a kid at a prom riled about his competition.

"Okay," she said faintly, and turned and hurried on up.

9

HE LAY HUNCHED in an almost fetal position on a couch in the second floor visitors' lounge. He was wearing his usual faded jeans and his blue denim jacket that must have cost fifteen dollars, and he was hugging a throw pillow to his face as if he was trying to suffocate himself. From the door, Amanda could smell the booze, could hear the dry, heaving sob that sounded as if it was coming not from a hunky six-footer, but from a thoroughly traumatized little boy.

"Drugs?" she whispered to the nurse standing next to her. "Did he take anything besides the alcohol?"

The graying, sympathetic-featured woman in white shook her head. "No. Just chug-a-lugged a whole, twenty-six-ounce bottle of Gallo Red and drove himself over." She looked horrified. "Miracle he made it in one piece. He's badly agitated. Told the orderly he was doing sixty before he even left his family's property."

My God, Amanda thought. She asked the nurse to bring 25 milligrams of injectible Librium—a safe dose, despite the alcohol—then went in, crouched down and put an arm around Brian's shoulder. With her free hand she gently pulled the pillow away. He let her. He opened his eyes, and she winced at the redness, the horror-stricken pleading in his desperate features. His face was glistening with tears.

"You came," he said in a frail, cracking voice.

"Of course I came," she said gently. She brushed his mop of dark hair from his brow; stared at his pallid, clammy skin, his trembling hand as it reached out to her. She took his wrist and felt for his pulse. 160. Terribly agitated. Ready to blow. She thought her heart would break.

"Kelly," he said a little incoherently, and started to cry again.

"I know," she soothed. "I—"

"*My fault!*" He struggled up on an elbow, gaped at her like a child having a nightmare with his eyes open. "Maybe I . . . *did* something!"

Amanda shook her head slowly, holding his pathetic, burned-out stare with her own steady gaze. "I don't believe that," she said. "Not for one second."

He looked at her uncomprehendingly, his mouth working. Then, as if sitting up would help him understand, he struggled into an upright position with his feet on the floor, and dropped his head into trembling hands. "Gonna be sick," he whispered urgently. "Gonna be sick."

The gray-haired nurse came in carrying an alcohol sponge and the Librium syringe that Amanda had requested. Amanda shook her head worriedly. "Nausea. Change to five milligrams of Compazine. *Quick,* Frannie."

The nurse took one look at the chalk-faced, profusely sweating kid on the couch, said, "Oh, boy," and hurried out. And, competent wonder that she was, seemed back in almost no time with a different syringe which she handed to Amanda.

"Help me get his jacket off," Amanda said.

Together the two women peeled off Brian's blue jacket to reveal a white polo shirt underneath. ("Shit," he kept saying with his face in his hands. "Oh, shit.") Amanda kneeled, swabbed the inside of his left elbow, and injected the drug right into the vein. It worked fastest that way. Thirty seconds, I.V., compared to a whole five minutes if injected intramuscularly. The nurse bending solicitously over her straightened and heaved a great sigh. "What would we do without Compazine," she breathed gratefully.

Sitting back on her heels, Amanda watched the color of Brian's skin change from sickly white to pink and then to almost ruddy. Truly miraculous. The nausea was gone, the drug was doing its tranquilizer job, but he was still very drunk. With a groan he fell back again on the couch and stared into space, that uncomprehending look of hurt and bewildered shock back in his eyes.

Amanda looked up at the nurse. "We'll definitely admit him. Get some pajamas, Frannie. And the admission form and order sheet. He's not going to be feeling good in the morning."

The nurse went. Amanda got up, turned off the glaring

overhead light, and moved the warmer glow of the table lamp away from Brian's head. In the softer light, she crouched again close to talk to him.

"Better?" she asked.

His head was sagging low over the crocheted throw pillow. Whose crochet? A patient? A volunteer? As he looked slowly up at her, she saw the tranquilizer beginning to help the struggling, frightened mind to clear itself. "You said . . . you said . . . ?" he managed, his voice baffled, cracking.

She understood and nodded. "I said I don't believe you had anything to do with what happened to Kelly. Partly because I know *you*, partly for other reasons we'll talk about when you feel ready." She paused, wanting to calm him, but sensing also his compulsion to talk, to ventilate his confusion and sense of horror.

"I feel ready now," he said quietly. Just like that. Sadly. No hysteria. "I have to talk, or I'll go crazy for good."

She stared at him, feeling a creeping foreboding that she tried to control. "What happened?" she asked softly.

He told her, haltingly, painfully, about Friday night. His date with Kelly. Sailed his boat to her condo dock to pick her up, a little after seven. Went night sailing. Had fun, made love, got roaring drunk.

"I did, anyway. Went through two six-packs. We got the boat back to her dock and moored it there . . . I think I passed out . . ."

"Her dock?" Amanda was confused. "You mean, the condo . . . ?" And as soon as the words were out, she knew the answer, and felt her heart drop. *Of course not Kelly's condo dock . . . the other one, stupid. Kelly's family's dock, the one right next to my house!* Of course . . . that would explain how the tide had carried the body the short distance to the yacht basin . . .

Amanda turned her face away, closing her eyes as images reeled. Finger marks on ghostly, pale shoulders . . . a floating, blue chiffon gown . . . She felt goose flesh creep crazily up her arms and back and neck, felt suddenly unsteady, and waited for the lightheadedness to recede. She realized that Brian was speaking again, and a little dazedly turned back to him.

". . . wasn't there when I came to, around five in the morning. Thought . . . don't know what I thought . . . that she had gotten mad and left . . . didn't know where she had gone."

Amanda asked him how he had gotten home. He looked numbly past her, as if seeing through the wall to the murky waters of the Sound. "Just sailed home," he said low. "Hung over, but I made it. Sick . . . all day Saturday, spent the whole day on my bed. Felt lousy . . . Sunday, too, but I tried to call her. Twice. Hung up, though, she had her answering machine on. Didn't know what the hell until . . ." Horror flickered anew in the back of his eyes. "Heard on the radio. Went crazy. Thought I did something. Wound up here."

A rustling sound pulled Amanda's attention to the door, where she saw the matronly nurse and another, younger nurse, standing holding folded pajamas and a clipboard with papers attached. The admission form; the doctor's order sheet. Mechanically she got up and took the clipboard, forcing her mind onto automatic pilot as she planned what she was going to write on the order sheet: *No side rails, no restraints, no locked door; drugs: low-dose Librium if needed . . .*

. . . and then she was aware that Brian, too, had gotten up off the couch and was standing there in the dim light, looking shambly and weepy again, a big, 160-pound rag doll thrown away by its owner and regarding her with desperately unhappy eyes.

The nurse named Frannie gave her the pajamas; then they both left.

"Come on," she told Brian gently. "The orderly will help you if you need it."

He took an unsteady step toward her, pulled in a long, shuddering breath, and let a tear slide down his cheek.

"Can I've a hug?" he cried more plaintively than any Dickens orphan begging for gruel.

She went and hugged him. He dropped his head on her shoulder and bawled like a baby. When the orderly came, Brian followed after him docilely, but only after Amanda promised to come and see him in the morning, first thing.

10

"KELLY'S MOTHER," Peter said dryly. "Would you like her Fifth Avenue number, or her London townhouse, or her villa on the Riviera? There's also a place in Oahu, right on the beach, I'll bet. Feel like calling Hawaii?"

Joe McHugh was writing in his notebook. "I'll start with New York. Save the taxpayers some money."

"*These* taxpayers? You're kidding!"

They were sitting in Amanda's office; Peter at the desk, McHugh in the leather club chair facing the desk. Two men, both used to rougher environs, feeling companionably uncomfortable in the overelegant feminine surroundings. Pale coral walls with an elaborate fireplace and a bow window. A plump couch upholstered in flowered chintz against the rear wall. High ceilings, crown moldings, jam-packed bookshelves interspersed with framed watercolors and Victorian bric-a-brac.

"You *sure* she trained at Bellevue?" McHugh had asked when they first let themselves in.

Peter had mumbled something about architecture from the 1920's, and the fact that the room had probably looked like this before Amanda's arrival.

Now he sat staring at a cream-colored sheet he had pulled out of Kelly Payne's folder, and was reading down a list of global addresses and telephone numbers typed above a long paragraph of clinical observations. It was the *neatness* of that paragraph that bothered him. Kind of like an obituary for a whole family, he thought: seven inches square of neatly typed-by-a-secretary fossilized shrink words to describe the pain and messy disintegration of people who probably started out looking kissy perfect in their annual

Christmas cards. Parents turning absentee or destructive, kids growing up as emotional cripples, unable to fight or to break out of the unhappy pattern.

He read off the information to McHugh with only the superficial part of his mind. The more emotional realms of his thinking could not help but remember the rough waters of his own life and think, *Well, I broke out, didn't I? This little mouse jumped off the family wheel, out of the multigenerational labyrinth with all the matching little scratch marks.* Reading off a thirteen-digit direct dial phone number for Antibes, Peter thought back to the time when he was . . . what? . . . fifteen? . . . and realized intuitively that he would have to get outside and stay outside his family if he was going to be strong. His older brother hadn't. And his older brother who had done everything he had been programmed to do was now Chairman of the Family Bored and approaching his second divorce and going through roughly the same corporate craziness as— lemmesee, Peter thought, peering closer at the cream-colored page in his hand . . . yeah, that's it—as Kelly Payne's father was by line seven of his psychiatric profile.

He looked up. "The mother remarried, by the way. Says here she's already split from the new husband—a young guy I think I met, come to think of it. Some stupid party. Guy was a sleaze. Looked like one of those Vegas piano-bar singers. You want his number too?"

"Definitely." McHugh's pen was poised.

Peter read off the address and number of the man who had been Kelly Payne's stepfather for a heart-warming ten months. Then closed the manila folder, got up, and returned it to its drawer in the tall metal file cabinet. Thumbed over the other folders jammed in tightly, stepped back, counted the vertical line of drawers, and multiplied. *How many other neat seven-inch paragraphs in there? Gee—ain't it a wonderful life?*

He pushed the drawer closed, locked the file, and turned back to McHugh. "So that's it. The girl has one next of kin to notify, and it's her mother who lives in twenty-eight different places. You realize . . . all the numbers in the world aren't going to guarantee that she'll be *home*."

McHugh was leaning hunched forward now with his elbows on

his knees, his creased, high-cheeked face reflective, his thoughts drifting to other times, other people. "Care to guess how many messages we've left with servants?" he said quietly. He stood, paced over to the window, looked down at his watch. "Twenty minutes," he said. "What's keeping our good doctor? I need to ask her more questions."

"Yes, well, she's probably—"

The telephone on the desk rang.

Peter looked down at it. It rang again. Peter looked at McHugh, who broke out in a grin. "Answer it. Say it's Joe's Bar."

Peter picked up on the third ring. "Brooklawn Hospital." Very official-sounding. Listened, frowning, then said: "I have no idea. You've reached the wrong part of the hospital, actually. How old is the patient?"

Listened again. From where McHugh stood, the voice seemed to be getting louder, more insultingly demanding—until Peter abruptly cut it off in mid-sentence, from the sound of it, by saying: "I don't care *who* your lawyer is. He's not a minor and he can do what he damn pleases!" And slamming down the phone.

Joe McHugh stood there shaking his head from side to side. *"Such* a bedside manner, Peter."

They looked at each other. Began to grin wickedly when they heard a sound in the outer receptionist's office, and practically stood at attention when they saw Amanda come hurrying in.

"I'm sorry to keep you waiting," she said with her eyes on McHugh. Beautiful eyes. Troubled, despairing, exhausted eyes. Barron noticed that she seemed a little shaky, and he asked, "Problem upstairs?"

"Nothing unusual." She had stopped by a long, glass-fronted bookcase and was staring dejectedly in at shelves crowded with patient tapes.

"Oh," he said, shrugging, stung by her shortness. "Just your everyday agitated depression compounded by acute alcoholic intoxication crisis."

She wheeled and looked at him. He gave back a look of stunned innocence, then glumly sank back down into the chair at her desk. She glanced quickly over at McHugh who was absently polishing the face of his watch. She inhaled deeply.

"Did you get the information you needed, Lieutenant?"

He looked up. "The next-of-kin stuff, yes." Looked away in thought, and paced a little. "But investigating this is going to be hard, the murderer could be someone from around here or some thief or drifter who's three states away by now. For this end of things, any help you give us just could be key. For instance, was there anyone you know of in Kelly's life who may have wanted to harm her? Any jealous boyfriends? Any patients *here* who might be capable of homicide?"

Amanda was silent, deliberating, while one long, graceful hand played with the latch on the bookcase. Finally she said:

"I'll do everything I can within the bounds of medical ethics." She lowered her head; sighed bleakly. "Trouble is, Kelly must have known a million people. You should check where she worked . . . the Crow's Nest restaurant here in town. Also she . . . ah, partied a lot until a few months ago. Frenzied, directionless, going off with strangers kind of thing. She had simmered down lately, but there's still that past to consider. And—no, I don't believe any patient from Brooklawn is connected to what happened. They're mostly just . . . sad here."

"You two were close," the detective said. "Did she talk about people outside of therapy?"

"Yes. Certain conversations stand out. I'll try to remember."

Amanda turned back to the glass-fronted bookcase and opened it. "See these?" She pointed at the shelves crowded with patient tapes. "Most psychiatrists nowadays tape their patients' sessions. I plan to listen to Kelly's tapes, every one of them. Maybe I'll hear something important." She closed the bookcase and leaned, sagging, against it. "Starting tomorrow, first chance. It's past midnight and I'm feeling . . . wasted."

"Of course." McHugh frowned. "Sure wish I could legally impound those tapes. I know, don't say it—patient privilege, even if the patient is deceased."

She nodded. "You'd have to request permission from the estate, which would take too long. I'll get to you soonest tomorrow and let you know if I find anything."

The policeman shrugged in frustration and glanced over at Barron, signaling that he was finished. Barron came to stand tired-faced by him with his hands shoved in his pockets. "It's been a long day," McHugh said, leading the way to the door, "and I have to reach this poor kid's mother before I turn in." The thought depressed him, and then he thought of something else. "Do you both realize the newspapers are going to be front-paging this tomorrow, coast to coast? Brace yourselves. The town's going to be crawling with reporters."

Peter grunted. "Give 'em all parking tickets."

Together the three walked back to the front of the building, where Officer Fowler stood talking with an attractive, red-headed nurse at the foyer desk.

"Try the Riviera number first," Amanda said dully. "That's where Kelly's mother usually spends her summers."

In a tone of mock-dismay, McHugh remarked that it was early dawn now over there. "Think I'll wake her up?"

And for the first time in the evening Amanda and Peter had identical emotional responses. *"Tough,"* they both said.

IN THE CAR it all caught up with her.

This terrible night. This terrible nightmare, old and black and evil, had come back without warning and with one hellish stroke had respawned itself, sending cracks down the work of twenty years, shattering the fragile, foolish delusion that the present can ever fully escape the past. Exactly where, Amanda wondered, does each human mind reach that point where sanity either saves itself or goes under? Most people manage well enough when their lives remain within the range of what is tolerable—you don't need a psychiatrist to tell you that. But the danger of those benign stretches is that we kid ourselves; we forget or don't realize that in nearly all human experience there is one weakness, one single event or long-term sorrow that is simply there, susceptible to unhappy coincidence, ever ready to leap out at us and trigger the blackness all over again.

Coincidence? she thought, sitting there and staring out the window, seeing the marks on Kelly's shoulders, seeing again her weeping father describing the same marks on her mother. And Kelly drowning right next door? As if some ghastly troll had been living all these years under the docks of one of the two families, and had decided it was time to come out and strike again?

Her heart was thudding so heavily that it made her dizzy.

Peter, driving, had been uncharacteristically quiet. She sensed that he was reading her thoughts—some of them, anyway—and she felt both grateful and unnerved over that. Grateful, to coin a phrase, that someone understood; but also fearful that this man whom she had sworn off for good was beginning to get back under her skin. Something about his thoughtful, somber demeanor seemed to be waiting for her to speak, and suddenly she wanted to. She wanted to hear her own voice to see if it still sounded sane, for one. And secondly, there was something he had said when they left Brooklawn that her overburdened mind was not yet ready to process. She remembered nodding and saying Uh-huh and thinking, *it's okay, he can be trusted.* Now she wasn't even sure that she had heard correctly in the first place.

"Again," she said, turning to him. "About Kirkley."

They were driving through the center of town, down night-empty Main Street balmy and pretty with its reproduction gas lamps, brick sidewalks, and illuminated, trendy boutiques. Anorexically thin, bewigged dummies posed in store windows in their Laura Ashley fluff, or leaned in other store windows on sea captain's wheels or golf clubs or fake elephant tusks. EVERYTHING FOR YOUR SAFARI, said the sign in the window with the elephant tusks. Across the street, in a sports equipment store, an Alpine-looking poster hanging next to all the summer bathing suits and tennis racquets urged everyone to SKI CHILE.

Peter seemed to consider, then nodded imperceptibly.

"Mrs. John Kirkley isn't, unfortunately, quite as sharp as her husband. She called the hospital all worked up, and demanded to know if her son was there. Said the kid got roaring drunk and practically belted her trying to leave the property to come to Brooklawn. Said she was going to call their hot-shot lawyer right away to come and haul him out. Heard of Ray Herrick, the corporate lawyer? I just reminded her the kid wasn't a minor and could do what he pleased."

He slowed and turned onto another street of pretty shopfronts.

"So it was obvious: the Kirkley kid is the nineteen-year-old you were talking about on the way over. And McHugh's 'Ryan or Brian' he mentioned in the morgue. It fits; I know the family; the two probably met because they were both your patients." Peter glanced questioningly at Amanda. "But if he's such a basically good kid, why did he take so long to turn up?"

"He was drunk," Amanda said numbly. "Passed out, sick all weekend. Someone else came along and killed Kelly. Brian remembers nothing." It struck her that something Peter had just said had sounded wrong, off center, and she frowned. "Kirkley's husband usually manages every confounded thing. How come *he* didn't call?"

"He was out. She distinctly said"—Peter's voice rose in mock shrillness—"'if my husband were here he'd tell *you* a thing or two, and as soon as he returns from his meeting I'm going to tell him . . .' Well, that's where I hung up on her." Peter grinned without mirth. "She must think Brooklawn has very rude personnel."

Amanda stared, genuinely perplexed. "He was *out?* His family's into major destruct and he's out? Where could he possibly have been?"

"Who knows. The yacht club or the country club might have had one of their little emergency meetings. We need funds to widen the channel, reseed the greens, build another squash court. That sort of thing. Makes the heart beat faster, doesn't it? Or maybe he went to a political meeting. That would be likely—he's planning to run for Senator, isn't he? Maybe his Campaign Committee gave him a Best Father of the Year award."

Heavy silence ticked between them.

"When Kirkley announced his candidacy," Amanda said in a wan voice, looking out, "Brian became more than just an embarrassment. His dating Kelly was a threat to his father's political ambitions." She exhaled heavily; looked back. "They sent Herrick to talk to her, can you imagine? Twice. He tried every approach. He was friendly at first. Came while she was working and drew her aside. Asked her to cool it with Brian until after the elections—eighteen months from now—for *Brian's* sake. It wasn't good for him to be further estranged from his family, Herrick said. Then hinted that if she played ball, attitudes would soften toward them as a couple."

"After the election—hah!" Peter said. "Did he come to the Crow's Nest the second time?"

"No. To her condo. With a whole different approach. Began

like before . . . more than friendly, in fact. Then, if you can believe this, he started to come *on* to her. Was practically pushing her into the bedroom, telling her he could make her lots happier than some messed-up kid. Kelly caught on immediately. They were just trying to show Brian what a tramp she was. Herrick probably had a recorder right in his pocket, Kelly said. Well, she just laughed in his face. Gave him some wild tale to carry back that she and Brian were going to get married soonest, and invite Ivan Boesky and the Mafia and the whole Medellín coke cartel. She threw him out and called to tell me. This was . . . about three weeks ago." Amanda lowered her head and stared at her hands. "Ruthless, determined bastards," she said softly.

"Right," Peter said. "Only Kirkley's always pulled the strings. He's a cutthroat in the WASP tradition: use other people to do your dirty work; have the arrogance to assume you'll always be able to buy off or cover up." He was silent a moment. "Herrick's been Kirkley's errand boy for years, by the way. I know because my father knew them, knew their tricks. Care to guess how Kirkley expanded the power of Strickland Shipping? Here's how: Herrick's a big shareholder in Strickland; uses his old-boy contacts to bribe government officials to get government contracts. You think they'd be carrying all that wheat and farm machinery and military equipment if highly paid friends in D.C. hadn't arranged for their export licenses?" Peter pushed his dark hair off his brow. "Herrick came to my old man and offered him a bribe directly, because you don't need an export license for pharmaceuticals. Well, what he didn't know was you don't tangle with the head of Barron Pharmaceuticals unless you want to find yourself face down in a company litter bin. Herrick looked mad enough to kill—that's what I heard."

Amanda stared at him, feeling her heart speed up in her chest.

"But *would* he kill? I thought of telling that whole story to McHugh, then decided . . . not yet. They're into dirty tricks, not murder . . . I thought." She sounded torn. "Kelly knew rougher people than that in her bad old days, and I felt I had to think of Brian before making the Kirkleys more hostile."

"You're probably right," Peter said. "But for the record, remember that Kirkley's the more stop-at-nothing kind of guy, while Herrick, well, my feeling is he'd go as far as greed would send him, but wouldn't risk something like murder for anyone. You need a different kind of errand boy for that."

Peter leaned forward, switched off the FM station, pushed a tape into the cassette player. Ray Charles. Singing "Georgia on My Mind." He leaned back, thinking.

"On the other hand, maybe it's wrong to underestimate either of those two. They grew up poor and angry—that's their bond. Herrick likes to tell people he grew up on an eighty-acre estate up in the back country; well, he did—as the son of the caretaker. Spent his whole childhood living over the family's five-car garage. Kirkley had it a little better—his father owned a diner on the Post Road. He slugged his way up the whole ladder: Mr. Ambition in high school, scholarship, borrowed money post-grad to start a little construction company . . . next thing you know, he's calling himself a contractor and subcontracting to the government and engaged to the heiress he met in college. The Stricklands hated him—my mother knew Anne Strickland's mother—but the rest is the usual story of spoiled, rebellious daughter getting her way, and black sheep son-in-law turning out to have the best corporate brains in the family." Peter inhaled. "He strikes me as someone who still harbors a hell of a lot of resentment."

He had stopped at the light, and together they looked across the street at the line of cutesy, night-lit store fronts. A bow-fronted shop named CONN-ETIQUETTE that was having a summer cashmere sale. A cheery-looking delicatessen fronted by geraniums and cafe tables on the sidewalk. A small restaurant with mullioned windows, a designer-nautical motif, and a tub of nasturtiums climbing up an antique ship's anchor. All of it like a stage setting, Amanda thought, evoking pretty surfaces and a sealed-off world of wealth and safety where violence—overt violence—was simply unthinkable. Cheating? Mental violence? If someone drank or beat his wife or embezzled in the big, bad city, it was swept under the Persian rug: facades here were kept as relentlessly polished and crew-neck wholesome as a red Yankee apple.

"That's where Kelly worked," Amanda said in a drained voice, indicating the restaurant with the mullioned windows and the sign overhead that read *The Crow's Nest.* Her thoughts took another unhappy dive; she barely heard Peter's comment that the police would probably start there in the morning with their investigation. She brooded; he drove, negotiating the intersection and heading down the road that led to the shore. Soon they were passing stone walls and moonlit homes of increasingly larger size. The taped music was playing softly. The night air was lush with the mingled scents of honeysuckle and just-watered lawns.

They drove on in silence.

Not until they pulled into Amanda's driveway did Peter see that she was crying a little, and he felt both moved and alarmed. Hurriedly, he switched off the ignition and took her—to his amazement—in his arms.

"Hey, don't do that," he said, pulling her closer, letting his lips brush over her cheek. "I know, it's been a trauma. Your patient drowned just like your mother . . . it brings all the nightmare back—"

"There's more," she said, her voice ragged and muffled in the crook of his neck. "It gets more . . . insane." She pulled away slightly and looked at him. In the bar of faint moonlight coming through the open window, her eyes looked haunted. "I haven't told you everything."

As Peter listened, his expression going from deep concern to one of disbelief, even fear, Amanda told him the rest of Brian's story: that the young pair had been moored at the Payne dock when Brian passed out; that when he came to, Kelly was gone; that the only conclusion to draw was that she had been drowned right there, less than one hundred yards from Amanda's house.

"My God," he said softly. He looked slowly away, shook his head from side to side as if puzzled about his own lapse in thinking. "It just never occurred to me to ask *where*," he said a little hoarsely. "I mean, he was blotto and I assumed she was pushed in . . . somewhere . . . anywhere but—*here?*"

Abruptly he opened the door on his side, and there was almost a crazy calm in the way that he pulled her out by the hand, saying, "I want a closer look."

"Peter, what are you *doing?*" Her voice was frightened, dazed; she let him lead her a few steps and then pulled her hand away. "It's almost one o'clock! What do you expect to see?"

"I don't know," came the even reply.

But he continued to stand there in deeper darkness, yards away from her, staring across the roughly three acres of ground now moving with dark shadows and an unpleasant, black line of weeping willows. Fearfully, she moved closer to where he stood, noticing that his mouth was agape, and that the gusting, salty wind blew through his hair, ruffling it. The sky was eerie with a three-quarter moon racing through clouds.

"Where's their dock?" he said. "I can't see a thing."

She pointed, although his back was mostly turned. "Beyond those willows. This end of their beach."

Unconsciously, they both roamed their eyes over the shadowy terrain spanning the two properties. It was too dark to see much, and the Sound itself looked as black as the bottom of a well. Overhead, leaves rustled and murmured.

Peter turned back to her, looking as tense as a man standing night guard who has heard a branch snap.

"It's not *certain* she was murdered here, have you thought of that? Maybe she got mad at gorked-out Brian and took a walk."

"*Naked,* Peter?"

"No, not naked. She might have taken a walk and run into somebody who . . . did the deed and stripped her. Or—hey, another possibility. Since night sailing's so popular someone *else* might have heard their voices and tied up at the dock to join the fun. She may have gone off with the newcomer. I know people who go night fishing. Tide's high after midnight around now, and the blues'll practically jump into the boat for you." He turned again and stared stiffly out to the blackened Sound, as if weighing his own words to see if he believed them.

Right, Peter. And maybe there's some creep who travels up and down the Eastern Seaboard, stopping in certain unlucky places every twenty years to see if anyone wants to go for a dip. And maybe that creep could still be around here even now, lurking in the bushes and listening to our every word. And if he sees that we're getting wise to him, he'll simply lurch out looking like Arnold Whatsisname in The Terminator *and . . .*

Amanda was suddenly too unutterably tired to exchange another word. She turned and without explanation began to trudge wearily toward the house. Peter caught up to her as she neared the front light and mounted the stone steps. His features were contrite as he saw her rooting for her keys.

"Just trying to help," he protested softly.

"I know." Her voice quavered. "I don't think . . . I would have survived tonight without you." She pushed in her alarm key, twisted it off, then used her second key to open the door. Only then did she look haggardly up at him. She reached out and gently touched his face. "Thank you, Peter. I'm glad that we're . . . friends again, and that you're . . . helping."

He stood there stupidly, searching her face and thinking, *That's it?* His heart sank. Her awkward words, he knew, expressed the confused jumble of feelings that churned inside both of them. He felt crushed. He watched her smile in that sad, tired way of hers, and step over the threshold.

And that's when the unease that had been nagging at him leaped into fear.

"Wait."

She stood with a questioning air just inside the door, a small hall lamp back-lighting her faintly. "Yes?"

He pulled his eyes from her and stepped back a bit, angling his head to peer down the long, dark facade of her house. All the lights were out except those at the entrance. He brought his gaze back to her. "Where does Suki sleep?" he asked.

Puzzled, she came out and pointed. "Over the garage. I wanted her to move to one of the bigger bedrooms, but she insisted. She's got a big apartment to herself, we tore down walls and redecorated—"

"And it's at *least* eighty feet away from where you sleep. Christ, she might just as well be in another building!" He found himself speaking with a haggard earnestness.

Amanda looked at him, then slowly exhaled.

"When I was at Bellevue I lived on East 28th Street off Second. Alone. In a crack neighborhood. Murder, pimps, hookers, and I even got mugged once. And survived. Now . . . I'm devastated about Kelly, but that happened *outside*." She spoke with patient effort. "And as soon as you leave I'm going to turn on this alarm, which is a moat full of water compared to what I had in the city."

Peter scowled at her wordlessly. He darted his eyes to the

realtor's metal keybox that hung on a J-loop from Amanda's front door handle. He stepped closer to it; took it in his hands; looked back at her. "Your house keys are in this? Duplicates?"

She nodded dully.

"I *hate* these things," he said. "Someone's been murdered right next door, and you've got your keys hanging outside your house in this funny little box *that I could open with a goddamn can opener!*"

Amanda blinked at him, and the brilliance of her eyes told him she was near tears again. "Thank you, Peter. I really needed that. It just caps off a wonderfully serene evening." She turned stiffly to go. "And pleasant dreams to you, too."

He stepped into the dimly lit hall after her, and in one mad, impulsive gesture pulled her to him and began to kiss her, hard, feverishly, like a man who was terrified that letting her go would leave him adrift forever.

"Please listen to me," he whispered, his lips searing her cheek. "Hearing that girl was maybe killed next door changes everything. You were her *psychiatrist,* for God's sake! That could make you a target."

He pulled away and looked into her glistening eyes that were as dark and deep as emeralds.

"Sleep with me," he said. "Come back to my place. I don't want to leave you here alone."

She hesitated; looked at him for a long moment of melting resistance, then caught herself and shook her head.

"I *have* to be alone. Can you please try to understand?"

So hurt and frustrated did he look that she summoned her last ounce of energy to reason with him.

"Apples and oranges, Peter." She pushed away tears with her fingertips. "You're confusing the tragedy with the fact that my house is for sale. Two things with no connection at all." Her voice despite its fatigue had that utter certainty of an adult explaining away monsters to a child. And then she surprised him. She raised both hands to his face and kissed his lips. He felt his heart turn over. It was the first time she had reached out to him in the way that she used to.

"I'm going to go now," she said softly, looking into his eyes. "Please let me."

In a turmoil, he stepped outside. She raised her hand to him and he gave an awkward wave back. Then the door closed.

And he stood there, the dark wind gusting more strongly now, watching as Amanda's alarm light came on and glowed red.

He stood there staring at that light for what seemed like a long time.

Then he gave up and went back to his car.

11

NURSE CAROL OWEN sighed with fatigue as she returned to the foyer desk. It was one-forty in the morning and she had just completed her rounds. And such a *hectic* night, she thought, smoothing her wiry, red hair with her hand, adjusting her desk lamp. More patients than usual awake and anxious, weeping and fearful, begging for twice the medication just to sleep. A phase of the moon, maybe? Carol was convinced that it was.

From where she sat, she had two vantage points of the night. She could see across and out one of the opposite windows to where the moon arced the sky. And to her left, through the vestibule and the screened front door, she could glimpse the circular drive and the lawn, glowing pallidly. On a balmy night like this it was nice to have the door open and the breezes wafting through the screen; it had been Carol's idea and the other night nurses had been all for it. The door itself was never locked because of fire laws, so why not? And if the night seemed occasionally spooky, it was still better than feeling all cooped up in this basket factory of locked wards and sedated patients with wire mesh on their windows. It was better by a mile.

Oddly, though, the turmoil upstairs made Carol feel a little better about her own problems. These people, with their cashmere robes and maids bringing cheese baskets, were miserable. Boy, what I could do with their money, she thought. And of *course* I wouldn't make the same mistakes they have . . .

Frowning, she leaned her pale, freckled face on her hand and thought about her life. Thirty-six last week. Two kids, tons of housework, and an exhausted husband with calloused hands and a fledgling landscaping business who needed her to work this two-nights-a-week job, even though she hated it. Both had agreed that with two small children at home, there was no way she could take a full-time job in a regular hospital. Last year they had bought a cottage in a nearby, inland town that was less impossibly expensive to live in, and the down payment had taken nearly everything they had. Billy Junior was wearing clothes two sizes too small ("It's too tight, Mom. It *hurts*."), and little Becky's teeth were coming in all wrong. Carol literally had nightmares about orthodontia bills.

"Stop it," she scolded herself. "Get to work and count your blessings." Sighing again, she got out her nurses' notes, opened charts, and began her night's paperwork. For several minutes she forced herself to write, then gave up, unable to concentrate, and sat staring at the antique oriental rug that stretched across the parquet floor. How much was something like that worth? she wondered.

The phone on the desk rang and interrupted her thoughts. "First floor, Mrs. Owen," she answered.

Then frowned. One of the upstairs nurses was calling to say they were having trouble with a patient and needed help.

"Lord, here we go again," she breathed wearily, hanging up. A moment later she was rushing up the stairs, wondering if she'd ever get her paperwork done.

No one heard the sound of a car approaching in front; of ignition being switched off.

The screen door opened and a man in a business suit carrying a briefcase came striding in. His hair and mustache were graying brown, and he was wearing tortoiseshell glasses. He looked around, confused for a moment. Then restrained the impulse to laugh out loud.

No one at the nurses' desk, after all. No one in *sight*. All that damned trouble over the perfect disguise, the rehearsed speech— "I'm Dr. Michaels. I'm here to pick up something at Dr. Hammond's request. I've been subpoenaed to a commitment hearing in the morning, and I'm having second thoughts." All that fretting over the fact that a sharp eye would realize that doctors never carry briefcases . . . *it hadn't even been necessary.*

He reminded himself that getting back out might be a different story.

Barely glancing at the hospital directory over the nurses' desk, he strode purposefully past the wide, carpeted staircase and down the hall to the right. Stopping at the door marked "Dr. Hammond," he reached out, and turned the knob.

Inside Amanda's office, he worked quickly.

He found his way through the shadows to the desk lamp, which he turned on. Good, he thought, stepping back from it. The small cone of light illuminated just the desk top and left the rest of the room in near darkness.

It was enough to see by.

He looked around, took in the high, book-filled shelves, the file cabinet, the antique furniture. His gaze came back to an English pine bookcase, elaborate and glass-fronted. He stepped closer, opened the first pair of fragile-paned doors, and grunted with pleasure.

He laid his briefcase down and searched, his index finger scanning the backs of little boxes, not finding what he wanted. He closed the first set of doors and moved to open the second. Top shelf . . . yes, he was getting closer. The boxes here began with "L." On the second shelf down he found what he was looking for.

Moments later he had filled his empty briefcase. He snapped it closed, straightened to close the bookcase doors, and checked his watch. Four minutes, the illuminated dial told him. Four minutes to get exactly what he wanted. Piece of cake.

He turned off the desk lamp, made for the door in darkness, and closed it carefully as he stepped into the lighted hall.

The nurses' desk in the foyer was still empty. From upstairs came the sound of a scuffle, someone wailing, and the voices of two or three women piping orders to each other.

He hurried down the steps to his car, a drab little rental he had left in shadow fifty feet from the entrance. Starting the engine, peeling off his transparent surgical gloves—tight, invisible from a few feet—he glanced back at the mansion that looked for all the world like an oversized and dimly lit old dowager. Regular hospitals, with their security guards and watchful night personnel . . . that would have complicated things.

Piece of cake, he thought again, driving away.

12

THE TELEPHONE SHRILLED, jolting Amanda with a cry out of a terrifying dream. No! She jerked awake, her heart pounding, seeing herself not in bed at all but still in some cold, dark lake where hands were pulling her down, and a man with a bloodied face leered at her through the swirling water as she struggled. Help me! The inky waters receded, and she looked fearfully around her bedroom, assuring herself that it *was* her bedroom, and that no man with a bloodied face was in attendance.

What a nightmare, she thought. Where had she pulled *that* from?

The phone shrilled again and stopped in mid-ring. Thank God. Suki. Already downstairs at . . . what time was it?

Amanda held up a trembling hand and looked at her watch. 7:30. She was surprised at having slept so late; then, with a shudder of despair, remembered why.

She closed her eyes, remembering last night. Unbelievable. Unbelievable. Suki had been in her housecoat waiting up for her when she returned, and they had cried together. "That poor child, we knew her as a *baby*," Suki kept saying, until she finally tottered off to sleep, still wiping her eyes, at nearly two in the morning. Amanda had come upstairs and wandered around like a lost soul until four. Back and forth in front of her bedroom window that overlooked the Sound; then out into the hallway and down to the other bedrooms, the smaller ones once inhabited by laughing, boisterous, weekend cousins lost to divorce; then down finally all the way to the master suite, the beautiful, heavy-beamed room with every piece of furniture still in place. A museum, really . . . of a past now up for sale with its owner feeling like the last kid left in the orphanage. She had sat in one of the overstuffed armchairs by the fireplace, turning pages in the old family scrapbook. Pictures of mother, pictures of father, pictures of herself playing with Kelly . . . amazing, she brooded, how much time they had spent together as kids . . .

She had stared for a long time at one picture in particular. She was standing, aged eleven, next to her smiling father before a stand of trees. Further back but in shadow, a young workman leaned on a board and smiled for the camera, too. For the *person taking the picture,* that is . . . you could tell, somehow . . . and that person could only have been her mother. April vacation? Had to be. Two months before the drowning. Amanda had brought the book closer to the lamp and tried to study the workman's face. Young, longish dark hair, the eyes and angles too lost in shadow to see well, but the mouth . . . a slow, flirtatious smile . . . or was that her imagination?

Exhausted, she had finally put the scrapbook back in its drawer, stopping for a moment to blink down, remembering, at her father's old .38 Smith and Wesson. One of the crazier things he had done after her mother's death. Gone out and bought that gun, spent that whole terrible summer at their place in the Adirondacks, target-shooting. Insisted that Amanda learn too—"No, you're *not* too young!" he had shouted—and she had, a little, anyway, although she was terrified. How to load and unload it, check the safety, hold it. And that was all. Never once had she actually fired it, although . . . how much skill does it take to pull a trigger?

She had also peered into the back of the drawer, and sure enough—a small, cardboard box of bullets. Never used, she knew. Her father had quickly expended his furies, and was a broken man by the time he put the gun away for good.

Now in her bed she lay still on her back, grateful to feel her heart rate slowing, watching the shifting patterns of light and leaf-shadows on her ceiling for their sedative effect . . . like staring into a campfire, she thought, or watching water running under a bridge . . . She inhaled deeply, further steadying her nerves (Bloodied face? Where *had* that come from?), exhaled, inhaled—

And the phone on the bed table buzzed. *Jesus!* A short, apologetic zap, which in Suki's code meant unimportant call, pushy caller. For people Suki liked and for emergencies, she practically jumped on the buzzer.

Who could be bugging her this early? With a sick-sounding groan Amanda reached over, pressed the intercom button, and picked up.

"Morning, Suki. Tell them I've left town."

"Morning! Oh, that's what I *should* have said, I'm just not thinking right. It's your realtor, Gordon Maitland, insisting on talking to you. He wants to offer his *condolences,* and I said thank you, I'd tell you, and he said *he* wanted to tell you . . . wouldn't *dream* of bothering you at the office, and, well, we've practically been *fighting* . . ."

"You need lessons on how to get people off the phone."

"Wouldn't work with this one! Pushy isn't the word!"

"Okay, I'll take it. Thanks, Suki. Did you sleep?"

"Badly. You?"

"Same. Well . . ."

"The phony. What do you suppose he's really calling about?"

"I'll handle it. Don't worry."

Amanda pressed the phone's single lit button. Sat up and greeted Call-Me-Gordie Maitland, her realtor, Kelly's realtor. Who launched right into his posh-but-sincerely-concerned-undertaker's voice, a key part of his repertoire since so much of his business derived from death, divorce, and Getting Transferred. She felt suddenly trapped, smothered.

". . . tell you how very, *very* sorry I am," he began. "How sorry *all* of us at Maitland and Company Realty are. This must be very difficult for you."

"Thank you," Amanda said tonelessly. *Yes, it's excruciating.* "It's kind of you to call."

He resumed. Energetically described his shock upon hearing the news on the Today show—"Stunned! Absolutely stunned!"— then told of trying to reach Kelly's mother at the Cap d'Antibes house, where a servant told him that Madame was not at home, and no, could not be reached.

"Can't be reached! That's ridiculous! I'm assuming the police had better luck in notifying her. No one called *me* so I'm guessing the police got her unlisted numbers from you. We're the only two who have them."

Irritable, Amanda pictured Maitland looking more Connecticut than Connecticut in his bogus rep tie and navy blazer covering a slight paunch. Correction—no tie today. Too hot. Under the blazer he's wearing a yellow Lauren polo shirt. Maybe pink. Maybe green. Or maybe he's still at home in his pink and green pajamas.

Trying to flatten the tension in her voice, Amanda told him that, yes, she had given Mrs. Payne's unlisted numbers to the police, and that she was sure they had reached her. "She's probably already in seclusion," she said evenly, "but I'm sure she'll appreciate receiving your message." Maitland knew nothing of the non-relationship between Kelly and her mother. It was none of his damned business.

"Ah." For a moment he hesitated, and when he spoke there was a calculated edge to his voice. Amenities done, he was getting to the point of his call.

"Good. Yes, good. By the way, I don't quite know how to put this but . . ."

. . . but he had some buyers hot to see the Payne house. Serious Tudor-lovers. Did Amanda think, well, under the circumstances, would it be all right to show the place? And did Amanda think that the price might *come down,* assuming Mrs. Payne might now be more anxious to sell—

Amanda's heart leaped. "The opposite," she snapped, hunching up in fury, summoning up the worst possible thing she could think of to say. "She'll probably be so upset she'll change her mind about selling and yank the house right off the market!"

"What?"

"It's possible. It's very possible. As a matter of fact, I have some concerns over the showing of *this* place, and I'm planning to drop in on my way to the office. Hope you plan to be there."

He was still sputtering when Amanda slammed down the phone. She went into the bathroom, furious, heart thudding, reflecting however that the clod had served a purpose of sorts. He had gotten her mad, gotten her moving. And wasn't it better to be mad than depressed? Now . . . if she could only loosen this tight, iron vise around her chest, her stomach. This stampeding of her heart. Okay . . . it's nerves, it's nerves . . . Admit it, she thought, looking at her strained white face in the mirror. Until last night you were fine, just peachy, and now you're coming apart a little. It's to be expected . . . just *hang on* . . . you have to stay strong for this . . .

Abruptly she remembered something else from last night— *Sleep with me, Amanda. I don't want to leave you alone*—and her shoulders slumped. No way, she thought with a shuddering sigh. No way is this day going to be easy, there's too much to deal with and I'm paralyzed. Can't even think . . .

She showered, shampooed, and blew dry her hair so fast that she thought there was something the matter with her watch. Pulled on a cream linen dress and cream pumps, put on a dab, two dabs, of makeup, and went down to where Suki was pacing unhappily in the kitchen.

"I keep looking *out,* Amanda. That house looks so beautiful, so *peaceful* in the sunshine. Who would believe . . . ?"

At the breakfast table they pushed around unbuttered toast and worried about the caffeine in coffee. Suki—*please, no*—was wearing the same woeful, heartbroken look that she wore on the morning after Amanda's mother's death. *She can't help it, hang on.* Suki was saying well-meaning things about how pale Amanda looked, how tense—"Look how fast you're gulping your coffee!"—and Amanda hand-gestured vaguely. Nerves. Both women jumped when the phone rang again, and this time Amanda answered.

"Oh. Hi Emily."

Emily Hagin. Suki's married niece, Amanda's old friend. Crying. She had just heard. The whole town was just hearing. Emily was now thirty, with a little boy of her own.

"Do you remember, Mandie, how we used to cart Kelly around? Give her piggy-back rides? Who could have *done* such a thing?"

They spoke for a few minutes, commiserating, and then Amanda passed the phone to Suki, miming her good-byes.

"So early?" Suki asked, holding the receiver. "You never leave till ten of."

"Nerves," Amanda said again, reaching for her purse. "This house—I just want to get out."

They exchanged wan smiles and see-you-laters and Amanda headed for the car. The inside way, walking rapidly through the kitchen, the butler's pantry, and the old cutting room door to the five-car garage. Her Jaguar was just outside the open garage doors, parked in hot sunshine where she had left it last night. Before McHugh had come to tell her what had happened. Before the world turned upside down.

"Crazy," she said a little frantically, opening the car door, then pausing as if obeying some unseen impulse.

She turned, and walked slowly back into the darkened, cool garage. Looked up at the niche above the window in the west wall. Smiled a little. Found some comfort in the movement she saw there. The reason she hadn't parked inside the garage for weeks.

Sparrows nesting. Babies. Getting bigger now. Ready to fly any day. The mother was there, stuffing food into four tiny beaks that poked up hungrily. Bigger than last time she had seen them. Ready to fly any day.

Life . . . it's not fair but it sure goes on. The words came unbidden to her. Followed by tears. A great, cathartic welling up of grief and anger and fear of what lay ahead.

She stood like that for a few moments, weeping silently, privately, watching the sparrows going industriously about their business. Then she wiped her eyes, and walked back out into the sunlight.

She got in her car and drove away.

13

EMILY HAGIN HUNG UP TEARFULLY, feeling worse after the call than before. She had heard on the radio, the TV, and she had been numb, unbelieving. Only talking to Amanda had confirmed it for her, made the nightmare real, and though her eyes were full she felt suddenly too overwhelmed to speak.

Her husband in his tie and jacket leaned against the kitchen counter, saying, "Unbelievable. That poor kid," over and over, helplessly shaking his head as he stared down at the floor. Russ Hagin had hovered protectively during his wife's call, and now realized that between their dismayed telephoning and their matching, shocked expressions, they probably made a tableau that was being repeated in every home in town. "A boyfriend?" he said, looking up. "An intruder? Who could have done something like that? And *here?* Nice, safe Grand Cove . . . ?"

Emily's eyes swam as she shook her head at him. "Not so safe, apparently," she whispered, brushing a tear from her cheek.

There was the sound of something clunking down the stairs, and she stiffened, reached and yanked some Bounty off the roll, and wiped her face dry. Their son, Davey, was making his usual descent by dragging his schoolbag behind him. And what could be in the schoolbag of a second grader? Two thin, scribbled-in notebooks and his pet stone collection. Russ Hagin straightened from the counter, and like his wife tried to brighten his troubled features. With a melting sensation they watched their elfin-faced seven-year-old run into the kitchen, dragging now his bag and a small braided rug in his wake.

"Am I late for the bus?" he piped worriedly, pushing away dark sandy hair that was so like his father's.

"No, Sport," said Russ as he glanced at his wife and bent to hug the boy. "I'm going to be driving you today."

With Davey looking something between confused and delighted, they got through the usual morning rushing around scene, and Emily soon found herself on the front porch, bending to hug Davey, straightening again to put her arms around her husband's neck.

"Scared . . ." she whispered, feeling some terrible new fear pumping into her to replace the tears.

He pulled back to study her face. "Lock up," he said low. "Stay in, just today. It was probably a jealous boyfriend or something, but still . . ."

"Or a multi-state mass murderer," she said half-seriously, a tremor in her voice. "I'm going to put locks on the locks. And stay holed up all day and use the time to catch up on chores." She shook her head in still-shocked disbelief. "It's just so awful about Kelly . . ."

A moment later she was watching them go, Russ holding on protectively to his son's hand, Davey so vulnerable-looking as he trotted to keep up with his Dad. They crossed the lawn to the car in the long driveway, got in, and backed out waving. She blew a last kiss, and then they were past the overgrown junipers and gone.

For a minute she stood there on the porch, squinting up into the glaring blue sky. Already so hot? she thought. The heat suddenly felt like July instead of June. Oppressive. Troubling. As if even the air around them had gone off its thermostat and out of control. She shivered despite the temperature and went back inside.

Where she closed and locked the door, and tugged on the handle, double-checking. She went around feeling foolish doing the same to all the other doors and windows, then returned to the living room and looked bleakly out.

This house, she thought. They had been thrilled when they bought it, last November, after living for three years in a boxy little rental. But on a young lawyer's income, the mortgage was a killer, and the "privacy" that had been so appealing now translated into an every-two-acres loneliness, with houses tucked into rolling glens, fronted by winding driveways and heavy shrubbery, and separated by thin stretches of woods. She shook her head and looked away from the window. Kelly's death was making her terribly upset and anxious, she realized. If Aunt Suki were here, she could have a good, long cry and then talk it out, but . . .

She wandered into the kitchen, grateful that there'd be no carpenters coming today. A month ago they had finished a small remodeling job of the cabinets and counters: not what she and Russ had wanted, but what they could afford. Funny how things work out, Emily thought, going to the sink, looking out. Kelly . . . *impossible to believe!* . . . has been murdered, and whoever did it is still at large, and no way could I admit carpenters or anyone else today without being absolutely terrified.

She went and turned on the radio, just to fill the silence, then decided to get to work. Any kind of work. Clean closets, even. Anything to get her mind back to where it could function again.

14

PETER BARRON HAD HAD A BAD NIGHT.

It had started when he came home, worried about Amanda, and the phone had rung to tell him that he was needed, fast. A speeding BMW full of kids had crashed on I-95. The State Trooper calling reported two boys killed, one gravely injured, and a fourth—the one who had been driving—insisting that he *hadn't* been driving . . . It was one of the dead kids, he was howling, drunk but barely injured (the only one who had been wearing a seat belt), armed with the legal smarts derived from a long string of DWI arrests, and staggering around the cleared highway ranting obscenities at two in the morning. The cops wanted to charge him with manslaughter . . . and couldn't. Couldn't touch a thing or unsnarl traffic for miles until Peter got there, examined the two mangled bodies, and made a ruling on who was where before the crash.

It had been the usual hellish scene. The escort of wailing squad cars pulling into his driveway, then all of them peeling off together . . . the terrible spectacle on the highway . . . the flashing red-blue lights . . . the blood, oh God, the blood . . .

It was past three when he got back home, heartsick. He showered and somehow got to sleep, then woke with a jolt three hours later, anxious and perspiring, thinking again of Amanda. He had tried to call her twice, once in his bedroom and once here, sitting downstairs at his desk. The line had been busy both times. He dropped his brow into his hand, feeling jittery and very, very tired.

Amanda . . . Kelly Payne . . . the autopsy today . . . Had he ever before done an autopsy which he so dreaded?

He looked up, taking in the room around him.

Long, low-ceilinged, heavy-beamed, it was the front room of

his 1771 Colonial which had served as a tavern during the Revolution. A *tavern* . . . The idea of soldiers and couriers sitting at tables before that very stone hearth over there had bowled him over when he had first seen this house, two years ago, and bought it on the spot. And for a while the warm wood paneling, the beehive oven in the fireplace, the wide plank floors two centuries old—for a while these things had been an antidote to his work world of formaldehyde and test tubes and plastic sheets draped over tragedy . . .

Not any more. He seemed to be sadder these days, lonelier . . .

Crunch crunch crunch crunch

"Hey, Tubbs," he said, hearing the familiar sound of puppy teeth destroying something. He got up, and walked around the desk to where his dog lay happily chewing a rawhide stick on one of the two sofas that stretched before the fireplace. Toby (which was his real name; Amanda had called him Tubbs when he was a fat puppy) was an eight-month-old English sheepdog, a huge, romping mound of white fluff who already weighed over seventy pounds. Seeing Peter, Toby cheerfully relinquished his rawhide and jumped up playfully to get a hug.

Scratching his dog's head, Peter realized that he could never look at Toby without remembering happier times with Amanda. The restaurants and parties they had gone to . . . none of it compared to the pure fun of curling up before the fire and playing with the lovable little ball who scampered back and forth between them. Once, on a Sunday, Peter had brought him over to Amanda's to meet Suki and the Hagins. Emily, Davey, and Amanda had spent half the afternoon on the floor playing with him, with Amanda collapsing into helpless laughter when Davey chased him back out of the dining room squealing, "He *peed*, Mommie. All over the pretty rug!"

And later, after a beautiful Sunday dinner cooked by Suki, Davey had been broken-hearted to have to leave the puppy, which had provided Emily with the opportunity to invite Peter and Amanda to the Hagins' house for next week. Peter had been pleased. He had hit it off well with Russ.

"Can I come without my little clown?" he had asked, smiling.

"*Never!*" they all chorused, making him laugh. He had been twice to the Hagins' before his breakup with Amanda—the word, even now, making him wince . . .

Sighing, he gave his now-enormous dog a final pat. He slung his seersucker jacket over his shoulder and took Toby out to his run, a loamy and now chicken-wired paddock adjacent to the empty, six-stall barn. He stood there a moment with his hands in his pockets, watching Toby charge merrily after a clutch of furious mallards, then turned and squinted back in the hot sun at his house. Weatherbeaten, green-shuttered white blocks marching up and down a grassy knoll—that's what the place looked like with its connected barn, outbuildings, main house, and garage. Remodeled or added to at the rate of twice a century since the time it was built, the place was now a historic hodge-podge that would have looked terrific on a calendar, but was certainly much too big for one person.

"Fill those bedrooms," his realtor's teasy last words to him on the day he had moved in.

Sure, lady, he had thought. *Easier said . . .*

Now he checked his watch and walked back up the short slope to the garage. Opening the Porsche door, he stopped for a second and peered across the garage interior to the closed hall door. Just checking, a nervous habit—the alarm light was on, red and glowing. He had locked up carefully when he brought Toby out.

Satisfied that everything from dog to alarm had been tended to, he got into the car and headed for the office.

HIS SECRETARY, JEAN SIMONDS, was holding the phone up when he walked through the door. Jean was in her late forties, married, maternal, and as funny-sarcastic as Carol Burnett any time. Another antidote to all the heartache around here.

"A call for you," she announced. "It's Detective McHugh. I was just about to take the message and—oh boy!—you look terrible! Don't tell me another night without sleep!"

"Okay, I won't tell you." Peter smiled feebly and took the call in his inner office. McHugh was starting the day sounding tired, too, he noticed.

"Seen the papers yet?" the policeman said without preamble.

"No. I haven't even opened my eyes yet. Drove here in my sleep."

McHugh said he had heard about Peter's night and commiserated, then added, "Brace yourself. Kelly Payne is selling newspapers this morning. Every one of them. Front page."

Peter sank into his chair and looked up wearily when Jean came in carrying a mug of fresh-perked coffee. He watched her bend and peer, dismayed, into his haggard face and then shake her head with concern. *What can I do?* he hand-gestured back, and she rolled her eyes and left.

To McHugh he said, "I'm not looking forward to doing that autopsy, Joe. The poor kid. It's like the final awfulness . . ."

"She won't feel it. But I'm getting the picture of what her life was like. Listen to this final awfulness: We tracked down her mother last night, and it wasn't easy. Called the Antibes house, got the runaround from some servant who spoke maybe six words of English, kept hollering, 'Call London, call London,' so we did—and got some butler character who sounded like Gielgud and gave us more runaround until we told him about the tragedy. Then he came clean. Are you ready for this?"

Swallowing, Peter leaned forward in his chair.

McHugh's voice was dull with sadness. "Kelly's mother has been institutionalized outside of London for the past five weeks. Alcoholism. Acute depression. Now, I don't know if anyone's planning a memorial service or anything, but it looks like the mother is permanently out of the picture. Like she's always been."

"My God," Peter said softly. A stinging mist came to his eyes and he closed them, rubbed them. "Lonely in life, lonely in death," he muttered. "Christ."

"Yeah. This story really is worse than most. Tell Dr. Hammond for me, will you? I called her house a minute ago and the housekeeper said she had already left."

Peter said he'd pass on the message, hung up, and looked at his watch. Only 8:20. Amanda had left the house already? Funny. He had noticed during their five weeks together that she tended to be a creature of habit. Her first patients were almost always scheduled at nine, and she usually left a few minutes before that.

She's upset, he thought, poking disconsolately at a stack of mail.

Last night: *Drowning is the upper-class way of murder, you know.* Had he really said that to her? Yes. Peter the Insensitive had opened his mouth again. But, dammit, there was something about that line that nagged at him and made him think of something else, but he couldn't remember what. With the three hours of sleep catching up on him, he couldn't think, period.

He switched on the intercom and asked Jean to come in again.

Jean was the social historian of the Pathology Department. She had worked twelve years for two Medical Examiners (now retired) before Peter had come to work here, two years ago, and she remembered some of the more bizarre cases as if she had read all about them yesterday.

"Jean," Peter said, as she laid today's crowded schedule sheet on his desk and looked at him questioningly. "I'm trying to remember a case and I can't. From about three years ago, people were still talking about it when I got here. Some Wall Street financier, healthy, middle-aged, drowned in his own bathtub . . ."

"Oh!" Jean's eyes lit up. It was a guessing game, a history quiz, and she was the smartest kid in the class who knew all the answers.

"Gartrell, first name, um . . . began with an 'L.' " She made the connection. "I get it. You're remembering that case because it was a drowning, like the Payne girl. Only it *wasn't* like the Payne girl because Gartrell was an accidental *inside* drowning, not an *outside* . . ."

She stopped in mid-sentence when Jeff Stein, the Assistant Medical Examiner, about age thirty, came into the room balancing three Styrofoam cups of coffee and a bulging bag from Dunkin' Donuts. "Morning," he mumbled, sleepy-looking, systematically laying the coffee and donuts down on the edge of Peter's desk. Peter remembered he hadn't eaten. He put his chin in his hand, appraising the dark, oily stain down the side of the donut bag as Stein peeked in, announcing, "Chocolate covered, chocolate on the *inside* and covered, sugar glazed, apple cinnamon glazed . . ." His florid and freckly face looked up unhappily at Peter. "I had the powdered sugar kind with the jelly on the inside, y'know, but I made the mistake of stopping in the lab and looking at those two kids from the accident last night, and, oh, Jesus, I threw them out, the donuts, I mean. Peter, did you see the one who was thrown *fifty feet?*"

With a sick little whimper Jean ran back to her desk, and Peter gratefully accepted his second cup of coffee. "Jeff," he said thoughtfully, watching as his colleague pried off the plastic lid from his coffee. "Have you considered leaving your body to science?"

"'Course." Stein tossed the lids into the wastebasket. "One lump or two?"

They spent a few minutes going over the day's schedule, then pitched empty cups into the basket and headed out for the lab. On the way, Peter stopped by Jean's desk.

"You'll get the Gartrell file?" he asked.

She nodded, perplexed. "Sure. But what good? It happened inside. It was ruled accidental."

He shrugged. "I know. I just want to read it. There's something I heard about that case and can't remember. It's bothering me." As he spoke, Peter thought of how dark the terrain by Amanda's house had been last night; recalled Bradbury's *Something Wicked This Way Comes* for no other reason than the fact that the title fitted the way he was feeling.

Jean smiled. "I'll have it to you in a jiff. Any others?"

He thought. "Come to think of it, one more. Charlotte Hammond, another drowning, twenty years ago exactly. June. That far back you won't find in this floor's files. You'll have to go down to the microfilm section."

"Lord, in the *basement?*" Jean wailed. "I *hate* it down there!"

"I'll send someone looking for you if you're not back in an hour."

"But Peter, you're *forgetful!*"

He shrugged again, and turned to go. "So? Nobody's perfect."

15

DRIVING WAS NOT WORKING as a diversion: Amanda found that out about two miles down the road when she almost ran a stop sign and had to slam on her brakes.

"Jeez, lady!" screamed a kid on a ten-speed crossing just feet in front of her fender. He pedaled faster to get away from the crazy driver.

Her heart pounding, Amanda sat grasping the steering wheel with white-knuckled hands as she watched him go. She drove on shakily, and found her thoughts slipping morbidly back to the dream. That bloodied face . . . what bothered her especially was the feeling that there was something so damned *accurate* about that dream, but she couldn't remember . . . couldn't dig within herself to find any link . . .

Stop it, she thought grimly. Try to forget the dream for a while. Concentrate on the scenery, this picture-perfect scenery. *Try.*

She tried. She guided her car from one winding lane to the next, the sunlight dappling down on her windshield as she passed white pre-Revolutionary homes, rustic stone walls, gray shingled salt boxes tucked between overgrown stands of lilac. She passed an eighteenth century graveyard with its faceless, tilting tombstones casting their early morning shadows, and she felt her heart turn over. Kelly used to like wandering through old cemeteries. Amanda had told her it wasn't good and Kelly said, yes it is, it's pretty, it's so peaceful, it gives me perspective. But Kelly had also liked a rock group called "The Grateful Dead." Once, when the girl was struggling through a particularly critical phase, she had wondered aloud and tearfully if it was the music or the group's name that really appealed to her. The question was *important,* she told Amanda. It would tell her if deep down she really wanted to go on with the gigantic effort of living.

Well, kiddo, someone took away your choice in the matter. Amanda accelerated again, realizing that the scenery wasn't helping her either, wondering how in the world she was going to get her mind to where it could cope with the day. And then it occurred to her that human contact of a more robust and strictly non-Brooklawn variety might be the answer.

"I'll just go look at the papers," she said out loud.

She stopped in the town center and went into the popular Izzie's Delicatessen, a guaranteed pick-me-up place fragrant with spicy odors, always bustling at this hour with the usual morning crowd. The guys in pinstripes getting their coffee and Danish before hustling to the train; people who worked locally—lawyers, merchants, the artists-and-writers bunch; joggers in shorts, housewives on their way to aerobics . . . on the most dismal of days Izzie's had a liveliness that, Amanda saw as she entered, taking a better look, wasn't there today . . .

They all looked as if they had been hit by a polo mallet.

From the front to the rear, where the tables were, knots of round-eyed people gathered. Heads shook excitedly, incredulously; fingers pointed to newspapers and someone in the group by the coffee urn cried, "Murder? *Here?*" A few troubled glances seemed to flick over her, but she wasn't sure, and hurried directly to the line of newspaper stacks piled across the crowded aisle from the bakery counter. She looked, and caught her breath.

There, from the front pages of the *New York Times, USA Today,* the *Daily News,* and the local papers, Kelly Payne smiled out at her, portrait-pretty, while headlines above her face blared news of the tragedy. HEIRESS FOUND DROWNED, said one. NUDE BLOND HEIRESS FOUND DROWNED, sensationalized another. Amanda jerked up a copy and began high-speed skimming down one of the columns . . . *only child of tycoon Carlton Payne . . . floating in exclusive yacht club marina . . . unclothed body . . . father before his death under indictment . . . Securities and Exchange Commission still investigating . . . had been under the care of a psychiatrist . . .*

At this last Amanda looked up with a dull stirring of anger, and stared at a line of Doritos clipped to a rod. Who are the cold, busy moths of night who find out these things so fast? ". . . just eighteen!" said someone right next to her, and someone else groaned, "So young! My God!" Fingers trembling, she tore open the paper to continue reading on page five when someone touched her arm, and she wheeled, eyes wide.

"Horrible. Just horrible," said a drawn-faced woman in a beige linen suit, and Amanda had to blink, confused, before she realized who it was. Bunny Rosoff, member of the public school system's Board of Education, mother of a former patient. The teenaged Amy Rosoff was lucky: had only suffered through a brief bout of "overachieveritis," the town's junior brand of perfection-seeking where the victim, usually a hard-driving sports, social, and academic star, is sometimes reduced to anxiety attacks, fits of hopeless weeping, and the utter conviction that he/she is miserable. (An irony compounded by the fact that it was middle-class kids like Amy whom Kelly *envied:* "They all come from real families!" she would cry; "No one sends *them* away to school; I see them shopping and things with their mothers!")

Amanda numbly closed the newspaper, at a loss for words. "Out of the blue," came unbidden to her lips, and then, almost beneath the decibel level of the crowd around them: "The pity is, she was doing so well."

"Which is what *I* heard," Bunny Rosoff said mournfully. "Doing well. Getting happy. This is just plain unbelievable!" She had short, stylishly cut graying hair, a beginning-to-line face that was not fashionably tanned, and the hands of a woman who did her own gardening. Amanda liked her.

"Amy told me just the other day that Kelly was looking better," she continued, stepping aside to let a couple in shorts and T-shirts pass. "She—Amy, I mean—had stopped in with some friends at the Crow's Nest and she ran into Kelly, who was working there as a waitress, apparently. More power to her—that's what I told Amy. They'd known each other off and on since childhood, did you know that?"

"No," Amanda said with surprise. "Kelly talked mostly about parent problems and current— Oh! Sorry!"

A man in a dark suit jostled Amanda, apologized, and hurried on. The two were about to speak again when a trio of dressed-for-the-city women and a girl carrying a tray of cheese Danish maneuvered precariously past them.

"Do you have a minute?" Bunny asked her.

Amanda nodded. "I flew out of the house. Beats hanging around and pacing."

"Understandable," said Bunny Rosoff sympathetically. She pointed to the tables in the rear. "It's quieter back there," she said. "Let's find a corner."

THEY SAT OVER COFFEE, talking. Amy Rosoff had known Kelly for years, despite the fact that, like Amanda, Kelly had spent her childhood packed off to boarding schools instead of attending the local and very good public schools. But in the curious way of a town like Grand Cove, the paths of Kelly Payne and Amy Rosoff had crossed at intervals, usually in summer, when the beach and the long stretch of shoreline became a mecca for preppies and upper-middle-class kids alike. Realtors boasted that there were enough town-sponsored programs to keep the kids busier in summer than they were in winter: swimming classes in the Olympic pool; water safety courses in the Sound; sailing school; golf and tennis lessons for all, provided they were—or so people joked—potty-trained.

"It was summer and they were both about eight—yes—ten years ago," Bunny now mused, frowning down at the speckled formica of the table top. "That was the first time I saw Kelly, and boy, what a surprise I got. Amy came to the car after her swimming lesson and said there was another little girl, standing over by the public phone and crying. Nobody from home would come to pick her up, Amy told me. Well, we offered her a ride home, and that kid was in the car faster than you could say animal crackers. So *skinny,* I thought. I had her figured for somebody's latchkey child, and I felt sorry for her. Then when I drove her up to that . . . that chateau, well, the picture changed. Poor little rich girl, right?"

Amanda nodded, sipped coffee, put the cup down. "That about says it. But the two became friends after that?"

Bunny smiled distractedly at a passing acquaintance, looked back and said, "Yes. Oh, cripes, look at the time. I'm supposed to be at Town Hall by 8:30. Well, they can wait a minute."

She sighed. "Friends. Yes. Although if you want the truth—
and I know this is going to sound mean—Amy started complaining
that she couldn't get rid of Kelly. You know how eight-year-olds can
be. There was Amy, already busy with her friends from public
school, and this pathetic child is calling morning, noon, and night.
Pestering Amy to come over and visit, she was lonely, didn't know
any kids in town, hated the new housekeeper . . . like that. No one
ever but indifferent-looking servants around for her, God knew
where the parents were." Bunny paused, shaking her head in
disbelieving pity. This was, after all, the woman who had sat in
Amanda's office weeping at the thought that her own child was
unhappy.

"Anyway," Bunny went on, "I told Amy to feel sorry for her,
not annoyed, and after that Amy took her under her wing, and I
wound up driving her almost every day that summer. And the *reason*
I drove her was because, if I didn't, they'd send some pretty
strange-looking people to get her. A gardener once, in a beat-up
station wagon. A workman in his rusty truck . . . *anybody* . . . get
the picture? Amanda? Amanda, what's the matter? You look as if
you've seen a ghost!"

*Dad hit him; that's why his face was bleeding. He was a workman
lying on the ground and Dad was standing over him, furious,
yelling . . .*

"Huh?" Amanda jolted back to the present. Her throat felt
paralyzed and her mind was reeling with the shock of memory.
"Ghost?" she breathed without thinking. "I've been seeing ghosts
since 7:30 last night. Don't be alarmed if I look a little spooked."

Bunny Rosoff leaned forward, frowning in concern. "You're so
pale," she said feelingly. "You should take some time off. Try to
calm down if you can." She smiled a little, suddenly self-conscious.
"Listen to me, telling a psychiatrist how to cope."

Amanda made a gesture with her hands: Why not? She realized
suddenly that she was cold, freezing in fact, and hugged herself.

"There's too much air-conditioning in here, have you noticed?"

Bunny nodded. "They heard there's the first heat wave of the
season coming, and they overreacted. Pushed the climate control
down to colder than they have it in January." She reached for her
purse. "Want to go?"

They paid at the cashier and went out the back way, into the parking lot that in the space of minutes had turned into a Turkish bath. Their cars, they discovered, were not far apart.

Walking, Amanda was quiet (*There's more. If I don't remember the rest about that bleeding face I'll scream*), and Bunny squinted up with a troubled look at the seagulls wheeling over the cars. They reached her gray Saab first, and Bunny fished out her keys.

"Are you going to be okay?" she asked Amanda as she got in behind the wheel.

Amanda shook her head uncertainly. Sweat had broken out on her brow. "You put one foot in front of the other, you know?" She leaned closer to talk through the open window, and swayed on her feet a little. "Kelly had her problems, but she was such a sweet kid. Who could have killed her?"

Bunny just sat there, hot, watching waves of heat rising like weird emanations from the hood of her car. "Who knows?" she said quietly. Then she looked back, wearing the same strained expression that Amanda had seen on the faces crowded into Izzie's. "The scary thing is that it could have been anybody. Someone from her past or even one of our supposedly upright citizens. You never really know people, do you?" She sighed and started the ignition. "Guess that's what's really frightening."

ON LEADEN FEET Amanda headed for her car. Reached it, got in, and sat there sweltering, immobile, trying to remember. Nothing came. Nothing beyond that flash she had had in the deli, the bloody-face dream enlarged into a recollection of a man sprawled on the ground, with her father standing over him, absolutely furious . . .

She turned on the ignition and air-conditioning and began to back out, abruptly realizing that the picture of the man on the ground had actually freeze-framed in her mind, refusing to go forward like a VCR tape stuck on Pause. Which was odd, she decided, because she had always had a good memory. She remembered detailed events as far back as age three or four, and the things that occurred during that terrible spring, that last, stormy season of her family's fragile history, she remembered in particularly vivid detail. That was one thing that had impressed her own adolescent psychiatrist, in the year following the tragedy. Nothing—not one single thing—had been repressed. It was as if the most mundane word or action of a parent (which normally might have slipped into forgetfulness) had been stored away in precious, obsessive detail, like a final family movie.

Driving, Amanda wondered suddenly if she had ever actually seen that event between her father and a workman . . . or if it had only been described to her. That would explain why she remembered so little; why she had never once in all the years thought again of something so ugly; and why it should resurface now of all times in the form of a nightmare.

But who could have told her that story? Her mother? Suki?

I'll ask Suki later, she thought. When I get back tonight.

Not until she was stopped at a red light did Amanda wander onto the next and inevitable question: how come Suki never mentioned such a thing? Suki made plenty of references to the unlovely past: it wasn't off limits; and, like Amanda, she felt better talking things out. So why not this?

It happened. I know that it happened, and I either saw it or heard about it afterward. Why has it been buried for so long?

She pulled into a slanted parking slot before a brick sidewalk and an impressive colonial-fronted building. *Maitland and Company Realtors,* the sign said over the bow window. She sat for a moment, brooding. Rooted around a little, until the psychiatrist in her came up with an explanation of sorts for the frightening dream, for so much of the crushing anxiety that she was feeling. Kelly's death had dislodged every bad memory that ever was, that was it. The whole unhappy closetful—it's just all come tumbling out onto this poor, ragged psyche, a reaction that will continue for one or two days, and then subside.

Won't it?

In the meantime she had to deal with quite another source of anxiety, building since last night, and owed entirely to *I could pry this open with a goddamn can opener!* Peter, bless his neurotic little heart.

She got out of the car and went in to see Gordon Maitland.

16

"I DON'T UNDERSTAND," Gordon Maitland said in a voice of utter, reasonable patience to the woman who stood across the desk from him, looking frantic. "Thirty thousand dollars, Frances. How could you *misplace* a check for thirty thousand dollars?" The woman named Frances tugged in anguish at her strand of cultured pearls and began to sputter.

"It was just so darn *late* when that couple finally signed. All day long they diddle-daddled and wanted to see more houses before deciding. Then, last minute, the husband said okay, we'll take it, and made out the check. It must have been at *least* seven-thirty—"

"Here? They made it out back here?"

"Absolutely! I was so tired, I *thought* I put it on your desk, but if it's not here it's *surely* in the outer office. We'll turn the place upside down."

They were arguing about a binder check that represented 1% of the house in question's sale price (three million). It wasn't a *major* sale like the Payne and Hammond houses, but still—a sale was a sale. The owners-to-be were a Wall Street couple. The husband was 31 and the wife was 28.

"Well, you just do that," Gordon Maitland said in that same quiet voice. He leaned forward with his knuckles on his desk in a way that made the woman shrink backward. "You turn this place upside down and if you don't by God find that—"

He stopped when the door opened and Amanda walked in. "Why, Dr. Hammond!" His tone switched to posh and hearty. "Yes, you did say you were going to stop by. How nice! Come to keep me company while I wait for my call from Neuilly?"

Amanda hid her annoyance. She stepped aside as the

distraught-looking woman left, then turned to the smiling, slightly thick man in his early forties with the receding, sandy hair.

He was looking as usual. Today it was a yellow (not pink, not green) Lauren polo shirt under his blazer—and the predictable, sweaty rush into his impress-the-customers talk about phone calls from Grosse Point, Marbella, and Beverly Hills the instant you were in the door. He had built his success on such pretentious bluster, widening his network and going around saying such things when they weren't so, and soon—since people tend to believe what they hear—it became so. Gordon Maitland was a realtor of near-mogul proportions. From a small stake he had made a killing in the 70s during the Gold Coast Rush when property values in Southern Connecticut had leaped to ten and fifteen times their worth. He had (and Amanda had heard this from others) the inside track on who was selling/divorcing/dying from Monaco to Malibu. He could pick up the phone and *tell* someone that L.A. would only make him crazy . . . while this new place, twenty baronial rooms, twelve acres, on a deer run and adjacent to the bridle trails, was his if he moved fast. He got phone calls from sweating global execs doing time in Riyadh, Jakarta, Maracaibo, and "backward states," announcing that they were getting transferred back, find me a place. And to all he was somewhere between reassuring and unctuous, probably closer to the former to the poor souls on the other end holding the phone with one hand and slamming at mosquitoes with the other. A modest man, he liked to call his office the Ellis Island back to gentility.

Amanda couldn't stand him, but had felt when she put her house up for sale that she had no choice. In the hands of a more low key agency without connections, her home (like Kelly's and all the other big places) would have risked getting the white elephant treatment.

"You *have* to forgive me," Maitland said urgently, abruptly serious and pacing behind his chair as Amanda approached. "I truly hope you didn't misconstrue what I said on the phone. This tragedy . . . it's awful, horrible . . . but I was simply assuming that the family . . . well . . ." He stopped and inhaled regretfully, solemnly, completing his obligatory speech with all the sincerity of an actor reading his lines.

Amanda waited, saying nothing. The psychiatrist's prod.

His expression changed and he said suddenly, "You weren't serious, were you? About the Payne house being taken off the market?"

Amanda sat in an armchair and, checking her watch, resolved to spend five minutes here, maximum. "No," she answered a bit tersely. "I was speaking of myself, actually. I'd like my house removed from the market as of this evening. I would say this morning, but you probably have appointments already scheduled."

He dropped into his own chair, reddening. "A toy manufacturer, sick of Chicago! A beef tycoon, sick of Argentina! My God, your place could sell this very day!"

"Let's hope," she murmured, looking curiously around. It occurred to her that this was only the second time she had been in his office. The first time was for formalities, three weeks ago, and his expensive furnishings, nautical antiques, and photos on the wall had only been a blur. Now she took a better look, and sat up straighter, surprised.

The wall to her right was crowded with photographs. Mostly Maitland with other sportsmen, holding up a Florida marlin, running in one of the County marathons, racing his sharp-tilted yacht with grinning, spray-soaked companions. Her eye returned to a small, older photo off to the side which was easy to miss. Three beaming men in their early thirties, each bending slightly with his foot on a shovel, breaking ground. She recognized Maitland and one of the other faces immediately, and stood and pointed to the third.

"Who's that?" she asked casually. "He looks familiar."

Maitland frowned. His aggressive-blue eyes had darkened. "That's Ray Herrick," he said. "An old friend and pretty well-known corporate lawyer. You've probably seen him in the papers." For a moment he looked at her, noting the long, slender legs ("limousine legs," they used to call them when he was a kid), the impeccably detailed linen dress. Old money, he knew. Railroads and Manhattan real estate from the previous century, he had heard. He thought of the rotting old house he had grown up in with the clothesline out in back. He was torn between resentment and the desire to impress her.

He leaned back in his swivel chair with his arms folded. "That picture was the ground breaking of one of our first real estate deals, by the way. We've always made a terrific team. I picked the investments; we did well; they taught me how to diversify."

Amanda nodded slowly, feeling a strange sense of déjà vu which she couldn't quite place. She moved her eyes from Herrick in the photo to the man standing next to him, dark-haired, dangerously handsome . . . a man who had sat in her office more than once complaining about her slow progress in fixing his broken product. *How the hell long does it take? We have the school's promise they'll take him back if you'll say he's straightened out. Jesus—just sign the papers and we can make second semester!*

The way he would berate a mechanic late in fixing his Mercedes, Amanda thought. But . . . these *three* together that far back? Old buddies? She rubbed at goosepimples on her arm and turned back to Maitland.

"That's John Kirkley on the left, isn't it? I know the family, and yes, I've heard of Ray Herrick." She paused. "I just didn't realize you knew the two of *them.*"

Maitland nodded tensely. "We knew each other as kids. Three ambitious kids. We worked damned hard and—well, look at us now. I really don't need real estate anymore, you know. I'm getting bored; looking for greener—no pun—pastures. And John running for Senate! He'll be a shoo-in, provided the campaign goes without a hitch. You should see the party enthusiasm, the contributions pouring in." Maitland leaned forward again; raised a brow. "He's named me his campaign manager, did you know that?"

Amanda slowly shook her head. "No, I didn't."

"He's going to make it official this week. Maybe today. I tell you," he mused, "when Potomac Fever hits, it really hits. This is how Reagan's Kitchen Cabinet got started, you know. Just a bunch of old friends, good at what they do, *very* good at what they do—"

"Provided the campaign goes without a hitch," Amanda cut in, stiffening. She had the sudden feeling that she had stepped into a dark hole without knowing how deep it was. Her heart began to thud.

Startled silence from Gordon Maitland. Then, annoyed, almost prim, "I don't see why it shouldn't."

Stop right there, a voice in her mind cautioned. Amanda felt suddenly anxious to leave. She had gone too far, said almost too much without weighing her words first. She remembered seeing Maitland browbeating his employee when she first came in. And in that instant, he had turned to her still wearing the look intended for the employee . . . a look, Amanda realized, just as rough and cutthroat as the way Peter had described Kirkley and Herrick last night.

Diversify, Gordie? You wouldn't also happen to be a shareholder of Strickand, would you? Which, given its subsidiaries, its well-placed friends, its key bribing position in Washington, can only benefit from having Kirkley spread his net wider in the corridors of power. Start up a little company on the side, Gordie; Kirkley will see that you get a multi-million dollar defense contract. You'll be the guy Kirkley owes favors to; maybe you even have fantasies of becoming Presidential Advisor a few years from now . . .

Provided the campaign goes without a hitch. Provided there isn't a breath of scandal . . .

Amanda bent to retrieve her handbag, slinging the strap over her shoulder. "I'm sure you'll do your utmost to protect your candidate's image. Now about my house . . ."

He stared at her. "Surely you weren't serious." Something about him had become silent and watchful.

"My request still stands," she said, and headed for the door.

"This is *ridiculous . . .*" He got up, and hurried through the door after her into the outer office. They strode tensely, without speaking, down the wide, green-carpeted aisle between the desks, which were mostly full now; male and female employees had arrived just after Amanda, and some were already on their phones. The woman Amanda had seen leaving Maitland's office was frantically rummaging through drawers; and another, an overdressed blonde in her forties, was watering plants.

"But what brought this *on?*" Maitland said, his voice stiff with anger. "Just when your sale prospects were so good . . ."

Near the door she stopped, wanting to see his reaction to what she had come in thinking about in the first place.

"Well," she said a trace too loudly. "I've been upset enough about the Payne murder, as you can imagine. Then on top of that someone started me thinking about the keybox on my door, and I must confess it makes me nervous. Duplicates of my keys hanging out there in that little box that any nut could pry open?"

Every head in the office jerked up at her, startled.

Maitland blinked at her. He tried to resume his realtor persona and failed.

"So that's what this is about. And that's *all?* God forbid! Those keyboxes can't be pried open. They're as strong as armor."

Amanda looked at him. "Oh. If you say so." She looked harder at him. "But back to the keybox *system,* because that's making me nervous, too. Let's see: thousands of realtors carry matching keys, like skeleton keys, that fit every box on every house for sale. So I worry: do any of those keys ever get lost? Fall into the wrong hands?"

From his pocket he extracted his car keys, singled out a different-looking one, and held it up. It was fat, short, and ugly. "Dr. Hammond, this keybox key never leaves my key ring. *All* of us keep our keys on our car key rings at all times, isn't that so?" He turned for confirmation from the agents at their desks, and an older blond woman, a brown-haired man just hanging up, and the woman scavenging for the check all chorused, *"Of course,"* like obedient schoolchildren. The overdressed woman holding the watering can nodded vigorously and said, *"Have to."*

Maitland smiled a counterfeit smile. "So you see, Dr. Hammond, I can safely say we are the most careful agency around. You have nothing to worry about."

Amanda opened the door, and looked out at the sun-dappled street. *The Pentagon loses military secrets, and Picassos get stolen from museums, but none of these people ever loses a key.* She looked back at Gordon Maitland for a long, thoughtful moment.

"You know," she said almost disappointedly. "I wish you hadn't said you're the most careful agency around. That means other agencies *aren't* as careful, in your opinion, and all the thousands of keys in the county match, right?"

He started to protest, but she went out the door and crossed the brick sidewalk to her car. Looking back before getting in, she said, "Please have that keybox off my front door by sundown, or I'll take it off myself with a hacksaw."

He stared at her coldly. "I hardly think that's necessary," he said. "You're making a very big mistake."

"I'll be the judge of that," she said. She put the car into gear and drove off.

17

WALKING DOWN THE HALL to her office, Amanda was surprised to see her door widely ajar and raised voices coming from inside. She stepped into her outer office—and stopped short when she saw the tumult: her secretary, Josie, was on the phone arguing; another phone rang as she stared helplessly down at the second lit button; three men and a woman stood by the desk trying to get her attention, and one of the day nurses was in there trying to get them out.

The nurse turned to greet Amanda and threw up her hands. "Reporters!" she cried, in the same tone she would have used if she had just spotted a mouse. "I've asked them *nicely* to leave, but they insist on talking to you—"

"I'm Steve Sands from *The Standard,*" said a brisk young man, leading the group that raced to her. Bright-eyed, they elbowed and shoved at each other, while a flashbulb and then another popped and they all talked at once.

"Any further details on the death of Carl Payne's daughter?" demanded the one named Sands.

"What are your own thoughts on the girl's murder?" shrilled a young woman in a jumpsuit.

The nurse decided with relief that she was no longer needed and rushed out. Josie rolled her eyes at Amanda and reached frantically for the second call. And Amanda winced away, reflecting that the voices (". . . drowned *nude?*" someone exclaimed) were clone-voices of every reporter ever seen on television asking grieving relatives how they felt about the plane crash, the kidnapping of their loved one, the fact that their dying child needed a liver fast.

Feeling a headache coming on, she moved to one side of the door and pulled it all the way open.

"I'm afraid you'll have to leave," she said with icy calm. "This is a private hospital and I have no comment for you." She nodded imperceptibly to Josie, who though still on the phone reached and pressed a hidden button. "The police will be the first to know of any developments. Go back to headquarters and wait there."

"What was Kelly Payne being treated for?" clamored Steve Sands hoarsely without budging; and, from the jump-suited young woman: "Our readers will want to *know!* Ever heard of the First Amendment?"

Amanda stared her down and said, tight-voiced, "Ever heard of criminal trespass?"

Four mouths opened to protest, then snapped shut as a sudden shape loomed behind Amanda. She turned and looked up into the dark, moon-shaped face of Vinnie Lopato. He had shown up so fast it was as if someone else, hearing the clamor, had summoned him before Josie's button.

"Somethin' the matter, Dr. Hammond?" His dark eyebrows furrowed as he took in the hostile-faced reporters. Vinnie's nature was such that he would have tucked a kitten under his jacket in a storm; but, for those who didn't know him, his bull shoulders and hands like prize hams looked fearsome.

"Yes, Vinnie. These visitors seem unable to find the door." Amanda's head had begun to throb. "Would you show it to them and make sure they leave?"

"Okay, *okay,*" snapped Steve Sands, holding up his hands as if giving in to Fascist goons. The others stormed out after him, and Amanda stopped Vinnie by the door to ask him to stay out front to keep other reporters at bay. Then, rubbing her aching forehead, she turned back into her office to say a proper good morning to her secretary.

"SO DAMN SMART," Josie Neal said angrily as she trailed Amanda into her inner office. "Those reporters know all the tricks. Parked in back, entered through the kitchen, asked one of the kitchen help where your office was, and sashayed in cool as you please. You know, this place is too open and vulnerable, I've decided. Never gave it a *thought* until this terrible business, but now . . . Oh, Amanda, you look terrible. Pale as a ghost."

Amanda placed her purse on the desk, and flopped into her chair. "You're looking a little rattled yourself, Josie."

The cute secretary with the short-cropped brown hair slumped into the chair facing the desk, as if, at this early hour, the day had already exhausted her.

"Some nightmare, huh?"

"I'm still in shock. Call all the patients, Josie. Cancel everybody and tell them their shrink is a basket case."

"Right." Josie nodded, straight-faced, falling reflexively into the pair's brand of irony that usually went some distance at saving sanity. But not today. Today every syllable spoken rang with tragedy; Josie's usual gift of ironic detachment was replaced by a look of genuine shock and sadness. Amanda remembered that she had come to care deeply about Kelly Payne.

"I tried to call you last night," Josie went on, absently trying to pat down a cockatoo tuft on top of her head. It sprang up again. "Around ten-thirty, which is when I heard. Bill and I had just gotten back from Litchfield and the sitter told us. Poor kid. Fifteen, terrified, and a sleeping two-year-old for company. I called your private line . . . didn't want to disturb your housekeeper. You were out, so I figured . . ." She shrugged somberly, not knowing how to finish.

Amanda nodded. Hearing the tension in her own voice, she told of her Sunday evening spent in the morgue and with the police. Watched Josie's face turn ashen with deeper shock, then realized with a start that even this moment . . . was wrong somehow. Four minutes past nine . . . Josie still sitting here . . . no nine o'clock patient . . .

"Oh!" Josie read her features. "Scratch Mrs. Bradwick. I'm sorry, I forgot to tell you. She showed up early, took one look at those reporters acting like vultures, and ran out again. Poor woman. They must have set her back five years."

Amanda stared at her, open-mouthed and furious. "Well, that's just great! That's just terrific!"

Lucinda Bradwick—who admitted to an early life of pampered shallowness and a nickname of Muffy—was now a forty-eight-year-old agoraphobic with a paranoid fear of strangers. So great was her terror of open or public places that it had taken her family a year just to get her to walk out of her house. And another year to get her into psychiatric treatment. In a twenty-room mansion, she now lived basically in her bedroom, came out twice a week to see Amanda, and had been making slow but stoic progress—until this morning.

First casualty of the casualty, Amanda thought miserably, resolving to call the patient and reassure her. She rubbed at her temple, glancing unseeingly at the glass-fronted bookcase on the side wall with one of its doors ajar. "Any other cancellations?" she asked, bringing her gaze back to her secretary. The ache behind her eyes had become a steady throb.

Josie stood up.

"No. Just that first session. Those calls bombarding us were all from reporters demanding interviews with you. I gave *them* bleeping what for. Well, maybe they'll go pester elsewhere and things'll simmer down here."

She turned back to the outer office, stopped, and turned again to study Amanda. Her warm brown eyes were worried.

"You really do look . . . drained," she said. "Pale, on edge . . . maybe you should have taken today off. Rest up or something."

That makes two, Amanda thought, remembering Bunny Rosoff's concern. The whole day is going to be like this, the parade barely begun with people wandering in, voicing their sorrow, their distress. And Amanda didn't want to *talk,* that was the thing; to hear again and again the nightmare stuck like a broken record. Maybe Bunny and Josie were right. Was she being strong or stubborn? she wondered. Truthfully she did not know.

She gave Josie a wan smile. "I'll be okay," she said, and added: "Oh, would you call upstairs and ask if Brian Kirkley's awake? He'll probably be sleeping late, but just check for me anyway."

"Brian . . . sleeping . . . here?" Josie looked shocked.

No more, Amanda thought. She craved a few moments' quiet. "He was admitted last night," she said. Left it at that.

Provided the campaign goes without a hitch . . . The words resurfaced in her mind, and with them the blindly missed implication that Maitland must have known about Brian. Campaign Managers are the first to know of any dirt needing damage control; certainly anything so massively negative as the candidate's son being admitted to a psychiatric hospital. *Anne Kirkley said she was going to call their hot-shot lawyer right away to come and haul him out.* Amanda remembered Peter saying that last night, on the drive home. So if they called Herrick, they must have called Maitland, too—and there he sat this morning, phony as can be and acting as if he knew nothing, knowing as he must have known all along that the Kirkleys' embarrassing son was Amanda's patient . . .

Shrewder than I thought, she reflected.

Josie, looking sad, said she'll call about Brian and disappeared back to her desk.

And Amanda, muttering her thanks, realized suddenly why the Kirkley-Herrick-Maitland camp was acting so cool. *Have the arrogance to assume you'll always be able to buy off or cover up,* Peter had also said. Why, of course, Amanda thought, chiding herself for not realizing sooner. They're planning to yank Brian out of here the second he's sober enough to hear their guilt tactics, and before word can leak. Which means this morning, I'll bet—and what are the odds it's that hot-shot lawyer who comes to get him?

Her eyes fell on a folded, cream-colored piece of stationery that sat on her desk. Weeks ago, she had received this invitation to a fund-raiser for Kirkley to be held, ironically, this afternoon. She had held on to it, undecided, thinking that she just might go for Brian's sake.

Now, screwing her face in distaste, she reached for the invitation, tore it up, and threw it into the wastebasket.

FIVE MINUTES LATER, Amanda was standing at a file getting out some finished Rorschach tests that she had promised to one of the hospital psychologists. The phone rang. Josie was on the other line. She reached and picked up herself. It was Peter, sounding grim.

"The autopsy's done. What now? Any funeral home I should release her to?"

Amanda sat down, her throat tightening, her eyes filling with tears at those final, devastating words.

"I'll arrange a memorial service." Her voice faltered. "I don't know what or where, or even who to ask. The kids from the Crow's Nest, for starters."

"Well, I'll tell you who not to expect, and brace yourself. Her *mother,* for God's sake. McHugh tried to reach you around eight, found out during the night that the grieving maternal wonder checked into a clothesline outside London five weeks ago. She is otherwise engaged with depression and alcoholism. Christ, does this story get any *sadder?*"

Amanda closed her eyes and said, "I'm not surprised. I knew that somehow that woman would find a way to be . . . unavailable."

Peter grunted. His silences were more emotional than his speech, she had learned. She could picture him sitting there, moodily pushing around paper clips or drawing sad-eyed little doodles on his pad. The sorrow of his work frequently took its toll. She had seen him slam things and break things. She had seen him turn his beakers upside down and use them for bowling pins. She had—

". . . just so *bugged,*" he was saying, and she came back to him. "What?"

"I said, you know what I'm holding in my hand and I'm so goddamn mad? That invitation to Kirkley's fund-raiser. You must have gotten one. Even the *wording's* enfuriating. A mass-mailing, right? And it says"—his voice became sarcastic—"'To our dearest friends and supporters'—the cloying phonies! The kid they scorned is lying alone forever back in her drawer, and they're going to be over there glad-handing and acting like God's gift to American virtue."

Amanda leaned forward, rubbing gently at her brow. "What are you getting at, Peter?"

A short silence. "Well, ah . . . how would you feel about the two of us going over to that dog show and just observing? You know—look, listen, see what we can see?"

A knot formed instantly in Amanda's stomach. "Not a chance. The thought of even going *near* that bunch gives me hives."

He sighed. "Okay. But what will I do without your special radar?"

"You're going anyway?"

"Yes. It's a dirty job but someone's got to do it. Starts at four if you change your mind."

"No. The dog show's all yours." She hesitated. "Peter, what do you know about Gordon Maitland?"

"Who? Maitland your realtor? Nothing. Except that he's your realtor and he made a lot of money in land speculation. Why?"

"I found out this morning—from him—that he's been cronies with Kirkley for as long as Herrick has. He's also going to be Kirkley's campaign manager, and sounds as if he's in it for some pretty bloated personal ambition."

"What campaign manager isn't? And nine times out of ten they've sunk a lot of their own money into it. Well, so Maitland makes three, and what I said last night about the other two probably goes for him. Birds of a feather, right?"

Amanda's hand tightened on the telephone wire. "Brian and Kelly dating . . ."

"They didn't any of them like it."

She didn't answer, and Peter sounded momentarily irritated. "Okay, so I'll go alone to this damned thing and . . . hey—would you meet me afterwards, for dinner, say, and I'll tell you all about it?" Now he sounded earnest. "Amanda, I really want to see you."

She looked down, coloring, feeling torn. "I . . . don't know. I don't think I'm ready for dinner or . . ." She inhaled. "Give me a little time, okay?"

He was a hard man to dissuade. "Can I call you later? You might feel differently."

She smiled a soft smile in spite of herself, and agreed to speak again later. Hanging up, she gathered together the set of Rorschach tests, and hurried to the office shared by two psychologists on the other side of the building, passing through the front foyer on her way.

"Oh, that's her!" she heard, and turned, and saw a sharp-featured man by the nurses' desk look in her direction. The nurse smiled brightly. "I was just about to buzz your office, Dr. Hammond. Mr. Herrick here was wondering if you were free."

Herrick? Well, well. Amanda stiffened and said nothing, studying him as he approached. He was a hard-bodied man of about forty-four (same age as Kirkley, she remembered), with a politician's thatch of thick, gray hair, and dressed in red golf pants, a white belt, and a white polo shirt. Otherwise, scarcely different from the way he looked in that roughly ten-year-old picture. Hair graying early even then.

He greeted her and smiled: the lawyer wooing his jury. "I'll just take a moment," he said conversationally. "I'm in a hurry myself, actually." He looked pleasantly around. "Is there a place where we can talk?"

Sandbagged, Amanda thought dismally. "All right." She led him to a seating area in an alcove overlooking the garden.

"Yes?" she said, standing stiffly, her hand on the back of a brocaded chair.

Herrick smiled again and folded his arms. He was about an inch shorter than Kirkley and a trace heavier, but even in casual attire he exuded that same aura of arrogant, corporate power.

"Dr. Hammond," he began, "I'm here on behalf of Brian Kirkley's parents. To say how concerned they are that he . . . overreacted last night, and how much they hope he'll return home soonest."

She had to restrain an irrational desire to laugh. He had recited almost word for word the speech that she had expected to hear.

"That he will," she said, recapturing her neutral voice. "When he feels ready and the time is appropriate. Not a minute before."

Herrick turned his head and gazed out the window at an extravagant mass of blue Siberian iris. "We were hoping sooner," he said mildly. "Surely he's sobered up by now."

"Sooner?" Amanda echoed in a higher voice. "Now? Oh—you mean, in time for this afternoon's fund-raiser? Dry him out, dress him up, prop him up for the happy family portrait?"

The lawyer swiveled his eyes back from the garden and fixed them coldly on Amanda. "Doctor, you are being foolish, and, if I must say, unappreciative."

"Indeed," said Amanda, anger welling. "How so?"

"Well, do you *want* the Kirkleys to sue you for malpractice for the way you've handled Brian's care? You knew that he was seeing a girl who could only bring him more trouble. Look at the predicament he and his family are in now." He peered at her with an insulting lift of his chin. "Send Brian home immediately, or I'm afraid we'll have no choice but to take appropriate action."

Outrage flamed up. "You're threatening me with malpractice?" Amanda said low, acidly. "That's terrific, it really is. For starters you know damn well you have no legal grounds. Brian is over eighteen and can do as he chooses. Secondly, the police might not have a whole lot of trouble finding out who Kelly Payne's date was Friday night, in which case Brian becomes a suspect. And thirdly, harassing me might just open a can of worms for *you* folks and your government-bribing operations. I would think very carefully if I were you."

She watched his eyes flash with anger and surprise. "So why don't we just call it a draw," she concluded. "Why don't you just go golfing and accept the fact that not *all* your bluffs are terribly effective."

His aggressive features were frozen. "You're a stubborn woman, Dr. Hammond."

She lifted her chin as coolly as he had a moment before. "Good day, Mr. Herrick."

18

"HERE'S GARTRELL," Jean Simonds said, putting a file on Peter's desk. "And here's Charlotte Hammond from twenty years ago. I had to have that one reproduced from microfilm."

"Great," Peter said, taking a pen from the breast pocket of his white lab coat, pulling the files across the desk to him. "The basement wasn't so bad, was it?"

"Could use a decorator's touch. Gartrell's first name was Lloyd, by the way, and it happened three years ago. A *crazy* case! I'm remembering more about it the more I think of it."

Peter looked at her, eyebrows up. "Grab a chair, Jean. Read it with me and see what else memory jogs."

It was after eleven. He had done another post after speaking to Amanda, and spent the next hour tending to administrative details. The tedious stuff that couldn't wait. Answering correspondence, signing release forms and death certificates, discussing forensic details with an overzealous assistant prosecutor who was trying to change a self-defense case to murder. Jeff Stein was still working in the lab, and Peter's office was quiet. Time at last to get to the file that had nagged at him since this morning.

He turned papers in the Gartrell folder as Jean voiced what he was skimming. "You were right," she said. "It was the year before you got here. This Wall Street financier was found drowned in his sunken bathtub in a mansion that was locked with the alarm on. It happened over a weekend. The housekeeper found him Monday morning, and . . . omigod, talk about one-track minds, I'm blocking the name of the M.E. then."

"Dale Hescock." Peter looked up at his secretary. "Alarm on . . . housekeeper—you've got some memory."

She grinned cute donkey teeth at him. "I also peeked while I was waiting to show it to you. Read on."

He did. The housekeeper had found the body on Monday morning, and Dale Hescock said he'd been dead for two days. Ruled it an accidental drowning . . . because in a locked house how could it not be? Except that the man's relatives—he was divorced, but he had relatives—had come and said that that was ridiculous. He had been a strong swimmer in excellent health with no history of fainting or blackouts. They were furious about the ruling. Hescock and the police countered that he had been drinking . . . there was a half-finished bottle of champagne by his head . . . and there was no sign of forced entry. Therefore . . .

Peter looked up, lips pursed. "Ruled accidental," he muttered. "Firm and inarguable. Case closed."

Jean frowned and stared at the open file. "Creepy-sounding, isn't it? I mean, everything about the ruling makes sense, but it doesn't. The victim wasn't sick or elderly or taking drugs. And he doesn't sound like the type to just slide down in the water—"

"Wait. I just remembered what's been bugging me." Peter flipped a page and continued reading down a paragraph, which he finished, and continued to stare at as if stunned. "Look." He angled the folder so Jean could see and said tensely, "Faint marks on his shoulders, see here? Report says the marks were like small bruises, the size of dimes and barely discernible, probably the result of a workout in the gym two days before." Scowling, Peter rummaged frantically through more pages as if looking for something. Then, as if winded, he slumped back in his chair. "Schmucks didn't photograph the marks," he said. "Not one damned picture!"

They exchanged sickly glances. Without a word Jean reached over and pulled a new-looking manila folder off the top of a pile. She opened it, looked in unhappily, and pushed it to Peter. "I'll never develop a stomach for these things," she said, as he stared down at photo close-ups of Kelly Payne's shoulder bruises. Faint, barely discernible . . . the size of dimes as the Gartrell report might have described them.

He looked slowly up at her.

With a visible shiver Jean said, "But for Pete's sake! Gartrell drowned inside a locked house and Kelly Payne was attacked outside. You know where that leaves you? Back to square one." She raised her shoulders in a shrug. "Maybe one of the Gartrell relatives had a key or something . . ."

"And then complained to the police about the ruling?" Peter asked quietly.

The phone jangled on both their desks. "I'll get it!" Jean almost knocked her chair over rushing back to the front office.

While she took the call in the other room, Peter, frowning, closed the Gartrell file and opened Charlotte Hammond's. Same findings, although in the simplified language of a twenty-years-ago coroner. Forensic pathology had barely existed then. Faint marks were faint marks. They didn't even rate getting measured unless they were mean bruises, especially if the victim was intoxicated and had a documented history of depression. He sighed. Read the part about the victim's husband tearfully insisting that those marks *meant* something, along with the notation that the man himself was seriously inebriated. His sadness deepened. Amanda's parents. Her legacy. Poor kid, what a thing to grow up with.

He leaned back, thinking. One inside drowning, two outside —all three with one thing in common. Those marks. Faint. Intended to be missed.

His mind went back over his conversation with Amanda, and something that Jean had said: *maybe one of the Gartrell relatives had a key . . .*

Doubtful.

He got up and walked around the corner to another room in the suite, where he chose certain pages from both the reports Jean had located and Xeroxed them. Holding the still-warm copies in his hands, he wondered how the police files on these two cases, seventeen years apart, corroborated. Both of them so different: Charlotte Hammond drowning just off her own beach and Lloyd Gartrell in a tub in a locked house . . . and yet . . . and yet . . .

No. It hit him just like that.

These cases *didn't* have just one thing in common; they had two. Both victims had relatives who vehemently disputed the coroner/pathologist's findings.

And Kelly, Peter thought. Whoever drowned Kelly Payne had probably walked away feeling quite safe, never dreaming that anything but an accident would be suspected. Yet it was because of Kelly that he now held these other two files in his hands.

He checked his watch. Eleven-thirty-five. Quiet here. He could go to headquarters, look up a few things, be back in forty minutes. Why not?

Behind him, a red-faced and frustrated Jeff Stein stuck his head in the door. "Pro-blem!" he announced.

Peter smiled wearily. Okay, rooting around in old police files would have to wait. "What's the matter?" he asked.

Jeff was fully garbed: green scrubs, surgical gloves, mask pulled down around his neck. Irritably, he jerked his thumb back. "I've got the healthiest, most physically fit toe-tagger you ever saw out there in the lab, and I can't figure out what killed him. Thirty-eight years old, dropped in his tracks in the commuter parking lot, E.R. doctor made a diagnosis of myocardial infarct which is *bullshit!* The guy's coronaries are clean!"

Peter turned, and with Stein at his heels headed back to his office. "Coke arrhythmia," he said, setting the Xeroxed papers down.

"No it ain't! I checked the septum. No fenestration, no nothing."

"With magnification, you checked it?" Peter asked. "Sometimes when the ulceration's just beginning to show, it's barely visible."

Confused, Stein looked fretfully back through the open door to the lab across the hall.

"Come on," Peter said, clapping him on the shoulder. "Let's go take a look."

19

"OUT THERE," the blond woman said, with the hot, gusting breeze blowing her hair in her eyes. She stood, in her jeans and sneakers and yellow sweatshirt with the word "Maui" on it, at the far end of her dock between McHugh and the young officer who had called him. She leaned on the rail and pointed across the sail-dotted blue water.

"From here straight out about forty feet, and they sounded as if they were having fun. Drunk? Lord, yes. Two happy, howling loons klutzing around out there in the moonlight . . . the boat looked like a good thirty-footer, maybe longer." Her voice became wistful. "Frankly, I thought it sounded romantic."

McHugh cocked an eyebrow at her. "They sounded happy?" He was pleased: a special task force of patrolmen had been door-to-door questioning from the marina to here and—nothing. No one had seen or heard a thing. Until this house. The lady—a Mrs. Anita Goodman—had been about to call when the police showed up.

"Yes, happy," she said vehemently. "And Lieutenant, whoever killed Kelly Payne, *it wasn't that boy*. I am a mother. I have radar about kids, and this one, well, he was drunk and pretty incoherent, but he sounded . . . sweet. Puppyish. The kind of voice you can't even picture being angry, much less . . . hurting someone."

McHugh glanced over at the officer, Jim Dorn, who was struggling against the wind trying to take notes. The pages of his notebook were flapping, and McHugh hoped that he was getting everything down. Time, size of boat, impressions of the witness. McHugh himself had the capability of near total recall and used his small notepad sparingly; but Dorn was still at the stage where he went through four spiral-bounds in a month.

He turned back to Anita Goodman. "And you're sure about the time?"

"Absolutely. It was a few minutes after midnight. I come out here often to watch the stars, although Friday night I started watching Johnny Carson instead. His monologue was terrible, so I switched off, came out, and was here in that chaise longue over there for a good half hour before I heard them. Headed this way from Larcom's Point."

McHugh's brow creased as he tried to picture the scene. "Still, two kids out there at night. Isn't that a little unusual?"

She shook her head, bent, and twisted off a spent bloom from a tub of geraniums. "Not at all," she said, straightening, staring sadly down at the withered flower. "Night sailing is a gorgeous experience and it's popular—especially with the kids—but you've got to be a good sailor and preferably sober. You've got to know your tide and harbor charts cold or it could be dangerous."

"After you saw them," McHugh prompted, "what happened next?"

She sighed and stared out at the water, still holding the flower.

"Well. They were out there about ten minutes, laughing, going around in circles, and then they turned and sailed back that way, west. They passed that beach you see in front of my neighbor's property, and the last I saw of them was when they rounded Larcom's Point." She looked back at McHugh. "The Payne estate is just past that, you can't see it from here. But ten minutes later I *heard* something. Come, I want to show you from higher up."

They followed her back toward the house and up the sandy steps, listening as she described the teen voices that still carried but were more muted now, as if the two had moored and were settling down. There were even a few minutes of silence, and then . . .

She swallowed, peering across the acres in the direction of the Payne property. "I heard a . . . cry," she said softly. "Definitely a girl's voice, sounding more . . . startled than frightened, and then . . . an angry voice, but I couldn't make it out . . . it's two properties and six acres away. Sound carries at night, but not that well." She paused. "Anyway, I was concerned, so on a hunch I walked over to . . . well, I'll show you."

"Hunch?" McHugh asked as she led them past carefully trimmed hedges toward the front of the house, a massive contemporary with an Oriental flavor. Dorn was now trying to walk and scribble at the same time.

"Yes," Anita Goodman said, stopping at the crest of an artful Japanese garden with gongs and stone lanterns. The air this close to the house was scented with the delicate aromas of salt and pine, a vacation resort smell, worlds away and yet only minutes away from the sweltering center of town.

"I mean," she went on ruefully, "part of me wanted to tear in and call the police, but my more rational self—ha!—just figured that it was nothing different. Kelly having a good time with one boyfriend and another comes along and she tells him to get lost. She's had wild parties there before. One of my sons knew her and liked her but, well, backed off. He thought she'd be trouble. *I* liked her, though." Anita Goodman heaved a sigh and looked remorsefully from one man to the other. "That poor child. She used to wander up and down the beach looking for someone to talk to. And I always did . . . if I was around." She shook her head slowly. "I should have done more. Invited her or something."

McHugh wanted to get her back to the main line of questioning.

"When they were out in the boat and horsing around," he said. "Did you happen to hear what the boy's name was?"

She looked at him as if reluctant to answer. "But the date didn't *do* it," she said stubbornly. "He was too drunk to lift his head off the deck."

Jim Dorn said politely, "He may have heard something, Ma'am. We'll have to talk to him."

She looked at Dorn, then switched her gaze back to the Sound, which from this angle was a pale, hazy blue in the heat. "I heard Kelly call him by name," she said in a faraway voice. "It was, 'Brian, get up, Brian! Oh, for God's sakes, you're totally shitfaced!'"

Jim Dorn stopped writing and now both men stared.

She sighed as if terminally disgusted with herself. "And later, when I heard that cry, or shout, or whatever it was, I just figured, well, these kids get so drunk they don't know *what* they're doing. I had practically forgotten about it on Saturday, and yesterday I was in the city until this morning at my sister's. When I turned on the news at ten I . . . Oh, God . . . the shock, the *guilt*."

"What could you have done?" Jim Dorn said comfortingly.

"She was drowned in three minutes and whoever did it left fast. You couldn't have saved her."

"Brian," McHugh muttered, almost to himself.

She turned intently back to him. "Yes," she said. And raised a finger. "But you be sure and write down that he didn't do it. *Murder?* That poor kid couldn't even get up! Someone else must have come along!"

20

"SORRY, PAL, the psychiatrist doesn't intimidate," Ray Herrick told John Kirkley. "Which means that either I'm getting older or *women* are getting smarter." He smiled. "Just can't seem to bluff the way I used to."

"How the hell hard did you try?" muttered Kirkley, glaring into his coffee cup.

They were sitting in the executive dining room of the world corporate headquarters of Strickland Shipping. Nine years ago, Kirkley had moved his key divisions from grime-and-gridlocked Manhattan to Grand Cove; had built his new office park to satisfy the town's strict zoning requirements; and now presided over an elegant sprawl of dark glass and low profile set deep in a pine grove and invisible from the road. The view from the dining room overlooked a sculpture garden built around a reclining figure by Henry Moore, but Kirkley seemed unaware of his surroundings, Herrick saw. He seemed nervous and irritable . . . angry, in fact. Only a minute ago, he had snapped at a waitress for not hurrying over with the coffee. Herrick had arrived scarcely four minutes ago.

"Go back," Kirkley demanded. "Get that kid out of that monkey ranch if you have to go upstairs and *carry* him out, for God's sake."

Herrick sat, silently appraising his old ally. This morning he had been ready to leave for a golf date when Kirkley called, the second time in fourteen hours, brushed aside his lawyer's protests that he had taken this week off for vacation, and in a voice that was sounding more annoyingly than ever like the aristocratic bullies they had grown up despising, had insisted that he hurry over to

Brooklawn. "You'd *better* get over there, we've got more trouble," was how he had put it.

We've got trouble, Johnny-boy?

There was still time to bail out before any of this tainted *him,* Herrick thought. Technically, he didn't need John Kirkley any more; he was hugely successful on his own, with offices in both New York and Grand Cove (to which many of his corporate clients, like Strickland, had relocated), and this farce of a friendship would have played out long ago if Kirkley hadn't seized on the idea of going into politics. The media were going to love him with his dark, craggy looks, his money and sophistication. Senator? For how long with his ego? So continue playing along, Herrick decided. Hang on to these coattails; you could wind up Attorney General.

"You worry too much," Herrick placated, forcing down his irritation. He smiled up at the waitress who was back now and nervously pouring, and when she left, he returned John Kirkley's glare with a look of calm reproach.

"*I worry too much?*" Kirkley was burning.

Herrick nodded reassuringly. "Brian doesn't know a *thing,* and—Jesus—you're acting as if psychiatrists are media informers or something."

Kirkley lifted his cup, glared at it, put it down again.

"Sure," he said sarcastically. "Brian knew nothing and Kelly knew *everything.* Spelled out to me on the phone exactly what she was going to blab to the press if I didn't get off her case. And you expect me to believe she didn't *tell* Brian?"

"Yes." Herrick toyed with a spoon and spoke casually. "She was only pretending to give you an ultimatum. She would have hesitated plenty before . . . ah . . . upsetting him."

"That little bitch . . ."

". . . is dead," Herrick finished for him. "Really an amazing coincidence, don't you think? Some old boyfriend probably just decided to settle a score." He raised his cup and shook his head in wonder. "Talk about timing."

Kirkley slowly let his breath out. His hand clenched into a fist and pounded softly on the fine white linen. "But how do I *know* if she said anything before she was killed? How do I *know?*"

Herrick smiled his most winning smile yet. "True love," he said. "That's your answer and I'm not going to say it again. There's no way in hell that Kelly would have done anything that would hurt Brian. So for once your kid's emotional problems have played into your hands. Be thankful! Come on, cheer up. Things couldn't be rosier!"

21

THE PAIN WAS A DARK CLOUD of haze between his ears. When he turned his head on the pillow, his cloud became angry, hot thunderheads crashing together, sending him spinning, the room spinning, the mesh-covered square of blue in the window spinning as if the whole world were in some crazy kind of free fall.

He closed his eyes and then slowly opened them, a device he had been using for longer than he cared to remember to get the feeling of sick to recede and leave him mercifully with just the bad head, because the bad head he could handle, the throb behind his eyes he wanted desperately to handle, now that Amanda was here, sitting in dimness by the bed with that seesawing blue glow from the window illuminating her patient profile, her thoughtful silence. She had her hand resting gently, just the fingertips, on the upper part of his blue-pajamaed arm and that felt good, it felt reassuring, it was helping him to struggle through the awful weight of memory and trauma to try to remember . . .

"Light?" she asked. Her voice was soft and faintly doubtful as she brought her eyes back to him. "Like a lamp in the window?"

On the pillow Brain moved his head no back and forth, and this time, amazingly, the room didn't spin as much. The medication she had given him was starting to work, thank God. He had been awake and in misery for forty-five minutes when she came in, and smiled at him, and gave him whatever that pill was with a paper cup of water. She had told him it was close to noon, on Monday, and he had felt like Rip Van Winkle with a hangover.

It was so hard to speak. "Not that . . . kind of light." Hard to think. "More like some weird gleaming . . . rectangle, and it was . . . *floating*. Sounds crazy, but . . . I was lying sick in the boat, and . . . I lifted my head and looked back to Kelly's house, and . . . there it was, up there and . . ." His features contorted despondently.

He's getting upset, Amanda thought (*gleaming, floating rectangle?*). He was pushing himself, and the stress of not being able to remember was causing his thoughts to jam and his frustration to mount. She leaned forward and patted his shoulder.

"It will come. Don't push it. Rest some more, and next time you'll—"

"No, I want to remember *now*. I'll go crazy if I don't remember!" Agitated, he tried to shift up on an elbow, then slumped back onto the pillow, white-faced, his eyes in torment. No, Amanda thought: better not to wait for any next times.

Very gently she said, "I could hypnotize you. It sometimes works wonders."

She answered his puzzled frown with explanation, delivered calmly, neutral-voiced. No, it wasn't like that stagey hypnosis you see in the movies, it was more like just relaxing, that's all, and going into your own head, soft and easy. A kind of semi-trance, she said. A feeling of peace.

Her voice lulled him. The pill was working, and the room itself seemed to be darkening as he gave her idea thought. "Hynotized," he half-whispered, intrigued.

"Like to try it?" Amanda leaned forward, watching him, clasping her hands together on the mattress near his arm. "Close your eyes. I'm going to count to three. You'll be asleep but you'll hear everything I say."

His eyes fluttered closed, and he inhaled deeply.

She counted, waited. "Do you see the light again? Do you see anything else?"

Silence, and then: "Yeah. It's moving. The light is moving. I see it."

"Someone carrying a flashlight? Like that?"

"No. A lit rectangle. Floating . . . high up." More silence. He was breathing deeply.

Amanda frowned in the shadowy room, her heart thudding hard. He had definitely seen something, and his story was consistent —that was the eerie thing. An illuminated, floating rectangle. She groped. "Moving through space? Like . . . ah . . . a comet?

Brilliant. A rectangular comet. A billboard? A glow-painted kite?"

Her frown deepened as she watched him, so still on the pillow. His eyes remained closed, but were busy, busy behind the lids, frantically scanning the landscape of a nightmare fragment for the thing that had frightened him, but not finding it, no, too drunk then. Whirling terror. Confusion. A thrashing motion as he raised his right arm up over his head, murmuring, "No . . . no . . ."

A sound from the door. Amanda turned to see a nurse coming in. She made an urgent sign and the nurse, understanding, hurried out.

"What is it, Brian?" She leaned closer, breathing shallowly. "What frightened you? There was something else, wasn't there? Besides the light?"

A soft, unhappy sound escaped his lips. His right arm was still up and covering his face. Amanda waited, and with her heart pounding painfully she looked away, as if that would help her think, looked out the window to the scene beyond. A jarringly bright noon, a sun-spangled tree trunk framed by curtains and somehow distant, as if outside and its rhythms had become another world. She blinked, seeing Brian lying sick and retching on a midnight deck, trying to look back at Kelly's house with the world spinning . . . spinning . . .

"Shadow," came the whisper from the bed, and her gaze darted back to him.

His eyes were open now, blue irises turned to deepest violet as they focused on nothing. "I saw someone," he said weakly. "Someone came . . . Kelly . . ."

Amanda uttered a low gasp of surprise.

She hunched stiffly toward the bed. "Who came, Brian?" she said urgently. "Do you remember? What about Kelly?" Goose flesh rose on the back of her neck. Her mind slipped free of its resolve to remain objective, and she felt suddenly disoriented, dislocated into some other dimension where a blond girl was fighting for her life in black water. She shook her head, blinking away the terrible sight, and heard Peter's voice: . . . *murdered right next door* . . .

Brian was pressing the heels of both hands hard to his eyes. A faint, slow shaking of his head and then: "A shadow came . . . man's voice . . . Kelly screaming . . . something . . . it's a blur . . ." A tear leaked from under his hand and slid glistening down his cheek. The corners of his mouth turned down in horror, and Amanda thought: Enough.

Trembling, she reached for a Kleenex, pried his hands away, and wiped his tears.

"I'm going to count again," she soothed, groping madly for the words that would comfort him, if not herself. "When you hear me say 'three,' you will come to. You will feel refreshed, as if you have slept well. You will feel . . . good, because you are a good person, and have helped." She stopped, desperately weighing her next words, then said: "You will remember everything you've told me. It's all right to remember. It will help you remember more."

She counted. He blinked, and blinked again, and looked at her with bloodshot eyes. "Hey," he said, weak-voiced. "That's it?"

She nodded a little weakly. "That's it."

She watched his eyes as the memory of what he had said in his trance came back to him. But this time his expression of shock and fear was different: it had a name. He had dug it out of the locked-away recesses of his mind for the two of them to know. He had no doubts now that somebody else had come.

"You remembered seeing someone," Amanda said, her face now colorless. "The man who probably killed Kelly."

Brian nodded, his eyes still scared. He frowned, and then blurted the question that with telepathic abruptness had also just occurred to Amanda.

"How come he didn't kill me, too?"

How come indeed? "He was probably counting on it looking like an accident," Amanda said. *Or maybe he wanted to make it look like you did it,* came to her, but she bit it back.

Brian blew air out his cheeks and cursed softly. He surprised her by struggling his way into a sitting position with his feet on the floor, elbows on his knees.

She stood and put a hand on his shoulder. "Feel like taking a shower? Getting dressed?"

With a complaining groan he rose to his feet. As if waiting for their cues, a psychiatric social worker and the same nurse as before came bustling in, changing the atmosphere in the room and making it busy. Crisp, today's-guest piles of towels and a bathrobe were placed on the bed while Amanda spoke briefly with the social worker, who smiled at Brian, spoke encouragingly of a group therapy meeting in twenty minutes (". . . *love* to have you join us"), and left, followed seconds later by the nurse on her soft-squeaking shoes. Both of them so chipper and businesslike: the energy of the healthy imposing its wanted-or-not shove on those who have been out of it.

"Come on," Amanda urged Brian as he stared darkly down at the hospital-issue robe. "I'll show you where the showers are."

22

BACK AT HEADQUARTERS, McHugh bent behind the officer seated at the computer and told him what he wanted.

"First name, Brian," he said. "Age group . . ." He hesitated, frowned. "His date was eighteen, so seventeen through twenty, for starters."

"Felonies?" the younger man asked. "Misdemeanors?"

"Anything and everything," McHugh said. "Just pull out every Brian who's ever been arrested in the last couple of years."

A few minutes later they stood scanning a list of twenty-eight possibles, including more than a few from surrounding towns. There were two Brians who pumped gas, one who had just gotten home from Marine duty, one who was back at college in California, another who was gay, and four who worked in supermarkets. One in particular caught their eye simultaneously.

"Brian Kirkley," McHugh read. "Age nineteen years, two months, arrested six months ago by Wallingford police for punching out some truckers, four months ago here for drunken disorderly conduct in front of a Dairy Queen. Hmm. Released to socialite father—I *knew* I recognized that name!—with promise to return to the psychiatric care of . . ."

The two men exchanged looks, and both spoke at once.

"Dr. Amanda Hammond."

"That's the doctor Kelly Payne was going to, isn't it?" said the younger man.

"Yes," said McHugh. "It fits."

23

A SHADOW CAME . . . A MAN'S VOICE . . .

Amanda made it to her office and then collapsed into her chair, trembling as if from fever. It had taken everything she had to control herself for Brian, to reassure him. Now she let the storm hit, grateful that Josie was still out to lunch so she could sit here alone and try to stop shaking. She closed her eyes, but in the darkness she saw a shadowy figure closing in on two teens in a boat. Her eyes flew open again. Had the figure crossed her property to get to Kelly's dock? Had he come from the other direction?

Would he happen to know another night stalker who committed the identical crime twenty years ago?

With a jerky movement, she poked at the morning's set of not-put-away-yet patient tapes, trying to decide what next. It was only 12:40. For some reason she feared the next twenty minutes. Feared the abyss of sitting here thinking of death and night shadows and staring like a shock case across the room at the empty, beige contour couch. She could almost hear the sound of patients weeping, patients crying out their pain and their furies—

"Stop doing that!"

She stood up in exasperation. What good did it do to go under like this? Be rational! Be stern with yourself!

She paused beside her desk, concentrating, chewing a fingernail. *So okay. You've discovered: a) that Kelly was murdered right next door, and b) that Brian saw the shadow of the man who probably did it. Isn't it time to start sharing a little of this with the police?*

She looked down and shook her head. No way. *Prove a shadow?* There wouldn't be footprints after this dry spell we've been having, and the police would be quick to weave a circumstantial net around

Brian. Which brings it all back to protecting the patient . . . saying nothing.

She paced, thinking: But this guy has to be caught! Peter's words resurfaced again to frighten her: *You were her psychiatrist. You could be a target.*

She stopped pacing; pushed that thought away. *The murderer doesn't seem to operate by day, and I don't walk the beach at night. The keybox will be taken off my door and the alarm will go on.*

No, she did not see her own safety as a factor.

She sighed heavily, aware that she had rationalized much of the problem. But at least the trembling had slowed, and her mind was more or less back in working order. She glanced at the time (*only 12:44?*), and wondered what to do next.

Keep busy, she decided. Put the morning tapes away. Start trying to remember if Kelly ever complained about any particular man.

Her idea grew in the time it took her to cross to the glass bookcase. Instead of beginning later in the afternoon to listen to Kelly's tapes, as she had planned, she would begin now. Why not? There was time at least to get started . . .

She pulled open one of the glass doors and reached in. Slid her fingers over the backs of black, rectangular boxes and . . . stopped at the gaping hole where Kelly's tapes should have been.

Her breath caught in her throat.

She saw her right hand hesitate, then numbly finger the tapes on either side marked Lyon, Opert and Richards. She knocked down one of the Richards tapes as she groped around, more frantically now, for something that wasn't there. Payne was missing. *Every Kelly Payne tape was missing!* A wide, black hole stretched on the shelf where Kelly's tapes had been gathering since last October, soon taking up more space than their neighbors, Amanda remembered, because just a few weeks ago she had had to move things around a little to accommodate . . .

Very slowly, as if frozen, she backed away from the open bookcase with both hands pressed to her face. "What is *this?*" she whispered, her heart racing, her eyes not believing.

The phone on her desk rang, making her cry out.

She ran to answer it. Peter, she thought. Maybe it's Peter.

Instead, it was Joe McHugh. "I'd like to talk to you about

Kelly's Friday night date," he said without preamble. "Are you free?"

Amanda heard him only dimly, through the roaring of blood in her ears.

"Lieutenant, please come," she burst out in a cracking, distraught voice. "I've just discovered that Kelly's tapes are missing!"

THIRTY MINUTES LATER, all afternoon patients had been cancelled and the office was a blur of police and squawking walkie-talkies. McHugh and a detective named Rusk stood conferring with Amanda at the far end of the room, by a small sofa set against the wall, while at the other end men dusted for fingerprints and photographed the bookcase.

". . . must be losing my touch," McHugh said unhappily. "I should have asked you to lock up those tapes last night. In the dispensary or something. Makes sense the killer would want to see if there was anything incriminating on them."

Amanda shook her head helplessly while Rusk looked back from watching the others. "Hindsight," he said. He had brown hair and looked to be about forty. "We're not used to places being this unprotected. Municipal hospitals have security guards, at least."

Amanda was numb. She couldn't get her breathing to slow, and though her heartbeat had eased off to a less frantic 110, roughly, there was still a painful constriction around her chest. Nerves, she knew. Pulling tighter like a band that was trying to break her.

She inhaled raggedly. "Security guards . . . What would they do here? A place like this, you worry about people getting out, not in."

She turned to look through the open door to the outer office, where Josie, poor girl, was arguing again, blocking the entrance to an excited group of staff members who wanted to gawk. One of the round-eyed psychologists was babbling, ". . . terrifying! Right here in our midst!" and Amanda recalled how many times the woman had boasted about her finely tuned professional detachment.

She turned back, dazed, feeling as if she were trying to fight her way out of a confused and frightening dream. "So the murderer was here," she said faintly. "Right here in this room." (Maniac under your dock! Suki's words leaped up at her.)

"Looks that way," McHugh said. He took in the way she seemed to huddle standing up, wrapping her arms around her body. Last night in the morgue she had seemed so vehement about wanting to help the investigation. Was this going to spook her permanently? He thought not, but decided to go easy just the same.

"Ah . . ." he said, studying her. "We've made some progress at our end. Found an eyewitness who thinks she saw Kelly and some boy in a boat Friday night"—Amanda's eyes widened—"and then heard them moor at the Payne dock. She also heard Kelly—we can assume it was Kelly—call her date Brian. That anyone you might know about?"

Amanda whitened. She said nothing and sat down on the small damask sofa.

The two policemen took matching French chairs. Amanda breathed shallowly. She was reminded of scenes in movies where *pairs* of cops take turns at questioning. Yes, she realized—that's what they were doing.

"'Course," McHugh went on, "we'll have to study the tide charts to see if currents could have carried Kelly's body to where it was found, but in the meantime it looks definite about the boy's name. Her friend staying the weekend said it was either Ryan or Brian; this morning's eyewitness confirmed it as Brian." He pressed his lips together, then looked almost regretfully at Amanda. "He's here, isn't he? Sobering up? The boy named Brian?"

Amanda tensed in renewed shock. *How could they know?* She opened her mouth to speak and then closed it abruptly, thinking, No. There was no way she could allow the police near Brian. He was innocent and still too emotionally fragile to be questioned, both of which were irrelevant anyway in the light of patient privilege. At least they don't know his last name, she thought. She groped for a way to hedge.

"Kelly probably knew lots of Brians." Her voice came tight from her throat. "It's a popular name in that age group. And I'm afraid you're overstepping to ask who is hospitalized here."

McHugh gestured with his hand: fair enough. Got to his feet again and smiled thinly. "Sure warms my heart to see a doctor so protective of her patient. Okay, I'll do the talking. You listen."

Rusk in the meantime sat silently, staring at a pattern in the rug. *They take turns,* Amanda remembered.

McHugh stood, hands in his pockets.

"The full name is Brian Kirkley, right?"

Amanda's stunned expression was all the confirmation he needed.

He nodded to himself. "Sorry to pull that out so abruptly, but it's vital that we talk to him. Until we hear what he has to say, he'll be considered a prime suspect."

Oh, dear God, Amanda thought. Her shoulders slumped. She exhaled in resignation. "How did you know?"

"I didn't for sure until I saw that look on your face. Sorry again." McHugh turned to Rusk. *Your turn,* his glance said.

Rusk leaned forward, eyeing Amanda fixedly.

"We've got records—misdemeanors, mostly—on several teenaged Brians down at headquarters. But only one from a socialite family who was under your care. It seemed to fit."

"But—" Amanda said hoarsely, still stunned. "How did you know he was *here?*"

"Added two and two," McHugh said simply. "You got a call last night while you were still upstairs. Dr. Barron took it, but I heard his end of the conversation: 'I don't care *who* your lawyer is. He's not a minor and can do what he pleases!' Like that. I kind of guessed then it was about the Friday night date who took his sweet time showing up."

Amanda leaned forward, forgetting herself. "It wasn't that way at all!"

"Then why don't you tell us how it was," said Rusk quietly. "You know his story, do you?"

Her eyes flashed at them both. She was cornered; felt suddenly like a captive forced to the end of a high plank. She took in the rest of her office: every surface and piece of bric-a-brac now covered with ghostly police powder; men still working, moving things. Everything had been thrown out of her control, she realized. If she maintained professional silence, they'd simply get an arrest warrant and come back for Brian. She'd had a patient once at Bellevue who had killed himself in his cell . . .

She leaned back, drained. "All right," she said in a low, intense voice. "From the beginning."

She told them Brian's story. The wild drinking. Getting sick, passing out at Kelly's dock. Waking at five A.M. to find her gone.

Hung over but somehow sailing himself home. Hurt. Confused. Not knowing what had happened until Sunday night. "Under hypnosis," she continued, "he was able to remember more. He saw a man's shadow. Heard Kelly scream." Her eyes became troubled. "He also saw a light. He says he saw . . . a rectangular, glowing light. Up high. Floating."

Silence. Several long seconds of it. McHugh stood, hands in his pockets, and Rusk sat: both of them trading looks that were entirely without expression.

"A floating rectangle," McHugh finally said, too deadpan. "Glowing."

"That's correct," Amanda said, and her eyes dared him to challenge her.

Rusk rubbed wearily at the corner of his eye and looked away.

The others were leaving. *Good, go.* The photographer, the print people and the other officers filed out with the air of business as usual, one stopping to speak briefly to McHugh and then nodding, turning. Amanda pictured Josie sitting like a stone at her desk, watching the procession, silent and scared. A few excited staff voices still carried from the hall.

She looked back to see McHugh studying her cautiously.

"Dr. Hammond, I'm sensing antagonism from you and I hope that's not the case. You've been helpful. Much of what you've said has corroborated with the eyewitness's account. But there are still gaps. Questions. For example"—he inhaled; paced a little—"Saturday to Sunday night is a long stretch . . . why didn't Brian try to *call* Kelly?"

"He did," Amanda said wearily. "Twice. Her answering machine was on. He hung up both times."

She caught the look that passed between the two policemen; the nod; the sense of some new tension coming off them in waves.

Rusk looked at her. "We've heard those two hang-ups on the tape. Plus an older man's voice. Sounding angry. Recorded first, which had to be Friday night. Kelly's friend had gone out to sub for her at the Crow's Nest and left the machine on."

Amanda tensed. "An . . . *older* man?"

"That's right," Rusk said; and McHugh still watched her intently.

"Have we . . . has all *this*"—he waved at the room—"given

you a headache, or would you be willing to come to Kelly's condo? I'd like you to listen to that tape, see if the voice sounds familiar." He took a step toward the door. "Also, the prints and fiber people went over the place this morning, but maybe you'll see something they missed. Say—your patients are canceled. Why not come over now?"

Amanda stared woodenly down at the floor. No more, she thought; make it stop, please.

She took a deep breath, looked at McHugh, and got shakily to her feet.

"All right," she said.

24

THREE MILES AWAY, Emily Hagin caught herself staring nervously out her kitchen window again. *Don't,* she thought quickly, swallowing, reminding herself that there was nothing to get frightened about out there. Just the yard with swings, the red Weber barbecue set at the edge of the patio, and the woods beyond. Everything looked as it always did, and still she stood there, biting her lip, unable to shake her creeping sense of apprehension.

Being alone wasn't good, she realized. She was thinking and thinking about the murder, and succeeding only in making herself more frantic. Apprehensively she glanced over at the wall clock, counting the hours until Davey came home from school and Russ came home from the office.

Sighing, she went back to washing and cutting the vegetables in the sink. She put them in a Baggie and then in the fridge, slammed the door (*I luv Mammy,* said a magnet-attached crayoned heart) with a thump that startled her, and ran to the front door to check the lock again.

This is ridiculous, she thought, twisting the knob to verify its rigid-lock position, just as she used to do in the days when they lived in Manhattan. She almost wished for the slide bolt and the double swag of door chains that they had had back in Russ's law school days . . . but this wasn't 116th Street anymore, and they had moved to this 'burb they couldn't afford for the *safety,* hadn't they? Had laughed then at the thought of bolts and door chains.

She rechecked the back door, went around for the umpteenth time rechecking the locks on all the first floor windows, and then told herself, Enough. Calm down. She picked up the laden laundry basket, and headed for the washing machines in the basement.

She opened the door to the cellar stairs, and looked down. So dark, she thought as fear pricked. Balancing the basket on her right hip, she reached out with her left hand to turn on the light. She heard a movement behind her, looked back over her shoulder, and froze in horror.

A figure lunged; gloved hands seized her slender back and pushed.

She fell forward, screaming, arms pinwheeling, plunging down to the cement cellar floor.

The figure hesitated, staring down in silence at the crumpled figure below. Then he calmly considered the light switch. Turn it off? No, better to leave it on. She would not have gone down a darkened stairway.

He hurried to the back door and let himself out, using his keys on their labeled ring to lock up again carefully. He checked his watch, and grunted contentedly to himself.

The deed had taken barely fifteen minutes. He knew he would not be missed.

25

KELLY'S JEEP WRANGLER was still parked in front of her condo. It was a heartbreaking sight, with its No Nukes and Have You Hugged Your Child Today? bumper stickers.

Twenty or so somber neighbors stood behind the taped-off area, watching the policemen on guard, the squad cars parked quietly next to the Jeep. Amanda parked her car behind McHugh's and surveyed the rubberneckers as she headed for the door. They were what one would expect to see at a luxury condo park at not quite three on a Monday afternoon: older, sportsy-looking types, very comfortably retired. The younger, two-career couples living here would be still at work; not due back until the evening rush of Pin Stripe Specials down at the station. Two age groups: one dreaming of moving up soon to The Big House; the other thrilled to be done with Maintaining the Monster; both paying plenty to live in this upscale, "dockaminium" version of what to Amanda was oppressively Levittown On the Water, 1980s style, with its thin-walled car ports and connected rooflines and poured fake brick sidewalks. The trees were all same-size saplings; the flower beds were too perfect; and the boat slips beyond were laid out like the keys of a very long piano. Years ago, Amanda remembered, this place had been a salt marsh with tall grasses and sea birds. Poetically beautiful. Brine-scented magic. Now, built up and dolled up, it seemed about as uplifting to the soul as a trip to a shopping mall.

She followed McHugh inside and greeted the policeman standing guard in the living room. Then looked around.

It was a tri-level, the most expensive category, with a wall of glass overlooking the docks and the mouth of the river where the condos were situated. From the large, barely furnished living room you could see up to the second and third floor balconies with their two master bedrooms and an extra bedroom/study at the top. Kelly had told Amanda that she hated this place. The most depressing room, she had said, was that top one, empty and totally useless, a reminder that a condo this size was really for a family. Only twice since she moved in had she gone up to that top room. Its view of the rest of the condo park had made her feel desperately isolated and small and forgotten: a throwaway piece in a Fisher-Price toy village.

"Ever been here?" McHugh asked.

Still looking up, feeling the terrible desolation that Kelly must have felt, Amanda shook her head. "No. I was on the point of telling Kelly to move out, in fact. She was miserable here."

In low tones McHugh said that Kelly's friend, Susan Weems, was upstairs and resting. She had changed her mind about going back to her place in Vermont, in case there was going to be a funeral. "I want you to see a few things before we talk to her."

They walked around the living room, taking in the unloved, garage-sale appearance of the single couch, the steamer trunk turned into a coffee table, the old, upright piano to the right of the fireplace. Amanda felt her stomach roll as she realized that everything was covered with the same ghostly fingerprint dust that covered her office. Atop the grungy piano stood a line of photographs in fine silver frames: souvenir of another life, another household. Half the homes around here had similar pictures in similar frames, usually gracing the tops of grand pianos or the lower shelves of paneled libraries. Depicting stock social events and intended for display, they were often indistinguishable from one house to another. The lovely daughter astride her thoroughbred; the smiling parents gazing out to sea from their boat (the father frequently wearing his captain's hat and looking very nautical); the group shot of several couples whooping it up at last year's Republican shindig.

Amanda wondered: had Kelly's parents, upon deciding to divorce, simply said the hell with the whole facade and dumped the pictures on their daughter?

"Know any of these people?" McHugh asked, nodding at the array on the piano.

Amanda bent and peered into the face of a grinning, broad-shouldered man holding up a trophy. "Kelly's father," she said, straightening, guessing the picture to be about ten years old.

Other photos were same-age variations of the Happy Family Together: an eight-year-old Kelly with her parents dressed for a party; Kelly with her glamorous, dark-haired mother waving on their dock; Kelly leaning against a tree before somebody's sprawling pre-Revolutionary home. There were a few framed snaps that included people not in the family, but no one Amanda recognized.

"Probably fair-weather friends who disappeared long ago," she told McHugh. He nodded, turned, and gestured to the patrolman, who started up the flight of stairs. "Susan Weems," he explained. "Come see more while we're waiting."

He led the way into the starkly furnished first-floor bedroom, with its WE ARE THE WORLD and David Bowie posters and its bare wood floor strewn with M&M's. Over the bedside table a piece of blue construction paper was taped to the wall with some of John Lennon's lyrics copied over in Kelly's back-tilting scrawl.

As Amanda read, McHugh picked up something from the small table top and held it out.

"We found this telephone book in the drawer. Glance through it. Recognize any names?"

Amanda thumbed slowly through the pages. In the same back-tilting scrawl was a series of haphazardly listed, unfamiliar first names and telephone numbers. She saw her own name and number ("Amanda" on the "A" page), plus "Maitland Realty" on the "R" page, and—she pulled in her breath—Brian's number on the "K" page. Quickly she turned to the next page and looked up at McHugh.

"I'd need more time to go through this."

"Of course. We've already photographed the contents. I'll get a Xeroxed list to you and you can go over it more thoroughly." The detective paused, measuring his words. "The kids at the Crow's Nest were interviewed this morning, by the way. Everyone from the manager, who's all of twenty-four, to the waiters, waitresses, and dishwashers. We're checking all their alibis, and no one seems to know much, except for two waitresses who say they heard Kelly arguing on the pay phone Thursday night. They came around a corner and heard her telling someone to go to hell, and then she slammed down the phone. When they asked what the matter was, she just threw up her hands and hooted. Said she had some big shot over a barrel and he was mad. Trying to intimidate her."

Amanda stared. "Some . . . big shot?" She felt a chill. "That means . . ."

"It means an older man. Which brings us to the voice on the answering machine. Come on, I'll play it for you."

In the kitchen, small and glass-fronted, McHugh was about to turn on the machine when they heard approaching footsteps, and looked up.

A girl, about eighteen, came uncertainly into the kitchen with the uniformed officer behind her. She was thin, with long, straight brown hair and large, mournful eyes. Her white jeans and T-shirt looked as if she had slept in them. McHugh introduced her as Susan Weems.

Feeling a terrible tightness around her chest, Amanda said, "I'm very, very sorry about the loss of your friend."

The girl seemed lost in a fog. She averted her eyes, her head, and after a hesitation spoke in a whisper, "I still . . . d-don't believe . . ."

Her voice caught, and the bright track of a single tear spilled down her cheek.

They got her to sit, crying quietly, in one of the kitchen chairs. Amanda poured her a glass of water and then sat opposite her while McHugh remained on his feet. Above the kitchen table was a poster showing a frightened kitten hanging by her claws from a high branch. The caption read, "Hang in there, pussycat."

With her eyes still glimmering, Susan Weems tried to smile at Amanda and said, "Kelly really loved you, do you know that? She talked about you all the time."

Amanda leaned forward and gently touched the girl's arm. "I loved her too, Susan. Help us find out who did this to her."

Susan raised her head and looked at McHugh, who encouraged her to describe again the last time she had seen Kelly. She looked back at Amanda. In a faltering, cracking voice, she spoke of Friday night. Kelly was excited—yes, feeling really "up," she said—and ran out waving good-bye just before seven. No, Susan didn't see the date: Kelly's sundeck overlooked the line of docks, but Susan had been rushing to dress, and hadn't gone to peek.

"We were *both* in a hurry, that was the problem," she said sorrowfully. "I had promised Kelly I'd sub for her at the Crow's

Nest, and I was late. I left in her Jeep about five minutes later, and didn't come back until almost one." She swallowed as if it hurt. "Kelly wasn't here when I woke up the next morning . . . not that *that* was unusual . . . but I was worried that she'd lose her job. She had told them she'd do the Saturday lunch shift, so I ran over and subbed again for her. Left the machine on."

Amanda glanced up to see McHugh fiddling with the answering machine that sat on a counter near the wall phone.

"Susan," he said. "I'd like you to listen to this again. And Dr. Hammond, maybe you'll recognize the voice. The recording was probably made Friday night after Susan left."

He pressed the play button. There were two first calls on the tape: one a hang-up, and then a man's voice. An older man's voice. "Kelly?" (Silence.) "Kelly, dammit, are you there?" The second time the voice was stiff with anger . . . and, Amanda thought . . . an undercurrent of fear?

McHugh waited until they heard the next two calls that Amanda had identified as Brian's. (Both times: "Kelly? You there, Kelly?" Definitely the feeble voice of a hungover young man.) The policeman glanced significantly at her and then turned the machine off. "Well?" He looked at Susan Weems, who had reached with a trembling hand for a salt shaker and was turning it slowly in her hands. "Any second thoughts, Susan?"

She shook her head. The salt shaker stopped turning. "Never heard that voice in my life."

He looked at Amanda. "Anyone you know, Dr. Hammond?"

Amanda sat, suddenly straighter in her chair, and stared at the poster of the frightened kitten on the wall. She fixed on the anxious eyes, the all-too-human expression of desperate terror. Part of her thought, *Can't be sure.* But something in her deeper mind argued back, *The hell you can't! You know that voice!*

Her thoughts flew back to a scene in her office, five months ago. Her first meeting with the overbearing, snobbish parents who were horrified that their offspring was continuing to give them trouble. The mother's voice phony-ingratiating as she urged haste in "fixing" the problem. The self-important father demanding that Amanda "Straighten him out! Knock some sense into him!"

Anne and John Kirkley, demanding the overnight repair of their broken product.

John Kirkley. The voice on the tape came close . . . very close, to sounding like his.

But Amanda wasn't sure. She had only spoken with him on that and one other occasion. *"Kelly, dammit, are you there?"* Her mind whirled. Other men could sound like that; those nasal, preppy vowels were something they all cultivated. And Kirkley might not be everybody's idea of a terrific guy, but you can't go pointing your finger at someone unless you're a little more certain . . . she exhaled in defeat . . . than this.

She turned to McHugh with an expression of desperate confusion in her eyes.

"Sounds . . ." she said, and then shook her head. "I don't know. I just can't be sure."

26

TIMMY STEFFINS CROUCHED in his treehouse, peering fearfully out between the leafy branches to see if the coast was clear. He was hot and miserably sticky with sweat, but still he waited, watching the back of Davey Hagin's house, just to be sure that that creepy man wasn't coming back.

He wished he were old enough to tell time, because if he were he'd be wearing a watch like the older kids, and he'd know how long he'd been up here. But he had counted to one hundred so many times he had lost track, and the scary-looking guy hadn't come back, so he figured it was probably safe now to come down and make a run for it.

He poked his head out the rough-hewn door and looked nervously around his tree. Nothing. Quiet except for the rustling leaves and the high-chirring sound of a million cicadas. Too hot for the birds, even.

And that was the weird thing about that guy, Timmy thought, as he scrambled down the heavy branches and swung to the ground. He had been too long-sleeved and covered for this icky weather. Wearing over his regular shirt a dark windbreaker just like his dad wore in the fall, but *not even looking hot,* as if he had just stepped out of an air-conditioned car. He had also worn dark sunglasses, and had looked over his shoulder a couple of times as if he was afraid of being seen. And then . . . Timmy stopped by a thicket and frowned and thoughtfully scratched his head. This was the reee-lly strange part, as his friend and co-treehouse builder Billy Jakes liked to say.

That guy, who sure acted as if he didn't belong in that house, had reached into his pocket and pulled out keys and used them to open the door!

Timmy bit his lip and started to feel more scared than before. He had heard the adults talking about that murder. It scared him to see *them* scared, especially when they said things like "Who could have done it?" and, "Nobody knows! Keep your doors locked!"

A branch snapped nearby. Timmy howled in fright and took off at a run, crashing through underbrush and scratching himself on prickers without even noticing.

"Good Lord!" Miss Wrenn the housekeeper said when he burst into the kitchen. "What on earth happened to you?"

He blurted out what he had seen in a worked-up, little-boy torrent, and she raised her chin to him, her horsy face an English mix of reproval and child-indulgent sympathy.

"Poor Timothy," she said, ruffling his light reddish hair. "That terrible thing has grown-ups jumping at shadows too."

"But Miss Wrenn! . . ."

He felt his usual frustration with this woman coming on. She had primly told him once that English children were *much* better behaved than American children, because they didn't have such frightful imaginations, and knew it was their place to be seen and not heard. He wished desperately that his parents weren't both away on business trips this week. His Mom and Dad listened to him; they thought he was smart and never failed to answer his constant barrage of questions, while Miss Wrenn showed only annoyance at his curiosity and occasional flights of fancy. ("I'm *sorry* I said there were alligators in the sewer! I was only joking!") Deep down, Timmy suspected her of being stupid. To his friends he called her The Bird.

She smiled her prissy smile, and from the counter handed him a small pile of clean clothes. White shorts, white Polo shirt, white socks and underwear.

"It must have been one of their carpenters," she said. "Those people just moved in a while ago, and they're having work done on their house. Besides—what bad man would be creeping around in broad daylight?" She cocked her head. "Now step lively, please, shower and change quickly. Have you forgotten about your tennis lesson?"

Timmy's freckled face was a storm of childish, conflicting emotions. "But that man looked *mean!*"

He saw her purse her lips and heard her voice turn impatient.

"Timmy, you've been watching too much television again.

Now, I *forgave* you for pretending to go to the schoolbus this morning and then playing hooky, but if this continues I'll have no choice but to tell your parents. And you're making matters worse by refusing to get ready—"

"I *hate* tennis!" Timmy was starting to cry.

"Tennis is *important*." The Bird raised her finger to him. "Your mother and father want only what is best for you. Now hurry, please, or your pro will be most disappointed in you. You wouldn't want that, would you?"

With his lower lip quivering, Timmy took the clothes, turned, and stomped sullenly to the bathroom, deciding to do his crying in the shower because it was useless trying to get The Bird to listen.

27

THE VOICE ON THE TAPE haunted Amanda as she drove.

And "haunted" was indeed the word, she thought with a shudder as she replayed it in her mind. Disembodied, strange and yet somehow familiar, mocking the three of them in that sad little kitchen as it called a dead girl to the phone. *Kelly, dammit, are you there?* The chilling part was the irritated familiarity in the voice. Kelly had definitely known that man.

That *older-voiced* man, Amanda thought, and then a sense of panic hit her so hard that she had to pull off the road and onto the soft, loamy shoulder. She thought: *older-voiced, maybe, like the smooth night operator who stole Kelly's tapes? And older-voiced, maybe, like the dark figure Brian saw accosting Kelly at the dock? I thought I had it there for a second, thought I recognized the voice as John Kirkley's . . . and then I wasn't sure . . .*

Besides, if John Kirkley had been bothering Kelly, wouldn't Brian have known about it?

Amanda closed her eyes as the answer came to her unbidden: maybe not. Brian was supersensitive about his estrangement from his parents. Kelly may have *wanted* to tell him something and then hesitated, not wanting to upset him . . . especially . . . Amanda lowered her head, thinking . . .

Especially if Kirkley or whoever that voice was had just *started* to bother her. McHugh said that she was heard arguing with someone on the pay phone Thursday night. *Thursday night!* Had hung up, hooting naive confidence that she had "some big shot over a barrel." And had wound up murdered the very next night . . .

Amanda raised her head. Stared bleakly up the leafy road, tried to concentrate, couldn't. Too shaky, too tired. The painful tightness around her chest had never really let up, and just sitting here struggling to think had gotten her heart back to pounding with a force that frightened her.

Don't push it. Just float. It's peaceful here, at least.

She had stopped with the engine running in front of a gray-shingled saltbox framed by laurel. Eighteenth century, calendar perfect in the late afternoon slanting light, the kind of house people bought and then refurbished with skylights and Jacuzzis and St. Charles gourmet kitchens. Out of sight on the woodsy property was a tennis court, Amanda knew, because she could hear sporting voices and the sound of the ball getting lobbed back and forth . . . *pop . . . pop . . .*

McHugh. Standing before the condo saying good-bye to her; urging caution. Kelly's tapes, he said. Whoever took them knows who you are. Be careful. Lock up and stay in tonight. You have a security system? Good.

Amanda sat back and deep-breathed slowly several times. *Tension letting up? No? Okay, now try music.*

She reached for one of her favorite tapes, pushed it in, listened for a minute, and found that for once, Vivaldi only made it worse. She yanked the tape out, tossed it back onto the pile of other tapes on the seat, and slumped back in despair.

. . . pop . . . pop . . .

The sound of an approaching car caused her to look up. An attractive couple in a red Mercedes convertible passed her, and slowed at the stop sign just ahead. They looked happy. Impulsively the girl, her blond ponytail bouncing, leaned over and kissed the man at the wheel. They laughed and drove off, and Amanda felt her heart turn over.

Peter, she thought.

Peter clamoring to come back into her life on top of—no, she corrected herself—*because* of all this was another source of torment . . . the simple, unavoidable fact being that were it not for the tragedy, she would not have wound up last night in his car, in his arms. *Sleep with me, Amanda. I don't want to leave you here alone.* Oh really? Would he eventually have started calling again if all this hadn't happened?

She caught herself, ashamed of her stumble into self-pity. Swung the other way. Reminded herself that what she really wanted was to help, which meant trying to recognize that voice on the tape, which meant—

(Ohhh no! I'm sick! Deathly tired! Going to go home, get some sleep!)

—that she should crank herself up yet again for the hardest confrontation of the day, and join Peter at the Kirkleys' political fund-raiser. Just slip into the crowd; listen to Kirkley's voice; act as if nothing with Anne Kirkley. Malpractice? What malpractice? *It's a dirty job, but someone's got to do it.*

Amanda took a final look at the old saltbox, grateful for the serene and pastoral setting that had restored her spirits somewhat.

A man's shout: *"Deuce!"*

Another man's shout: *"Schmuck! It was in!"*

She sighed; put the car into gear. Fighting the rise in her throat, she pulled back on to the road and drove off as if to war.

28

AT THE BREAK IN THE TALL HEDGES, the line of expensive cars arriving entered the estate and headed up the drive to the house, a sprawling Norman mansion fronted by a large brick courtyard.

Getting out, looking around, Amanda experienced a strange sense of déjà vu from the few times Brian had described the place. The steep slate roof above lead-paned windows and the turreted entrance: "like Ivanhoe," he had said. And the manicured hedges and hollies and gardens that his mother The Controlling One liked to walk around and *inspect,* as she did her china.

A little anxiously, Amanda searched the crowded courtyard for Peter's car, didn't see it, and fell into step with the well-dressed people already glad-handing and backslapping as they headed for the door. Peter's here, she told herself. He's probably parked in his usual "emergency exit": way down the driveway and furthest car from the house.

By an old-fashioned coach lamp she stopped for a moment, mulling the irony. Only last night she was still bitter about Peter, convinced that there could never again be anything between them. Now, with everyone entering this house—hostile territory—in smiling, laughing twos and threes, she was surprised to find how much she wanted his company, his support.

He has to be inside, doesn't he? He said he was coming!

It was the only thought that got her through the door.

Stiff, she followed others through the hall and living room, festive with laughter and beaming, well-bred voices ("Haven't seen you since *Nassau!*" "We've bought a new horse farm!"), then through two more guest-filled rooms (the library and solarium), and out French doors to the grand terrace, breeze-swept, overlooking the Sound, dazzling under its yellow-and-white-striped party tent.

She spent a moment standing there, surveying what looked like a huge and overdressed tailgate party with uniformed maids and waiters moving through the sea of blazers. Scarcely twenty feet away, John and Anne Kirkley were circulating among their guests and looking—Amanda gaped—as smooth as any veteran party givers, kissing cheeks, shaking hands, beaming and laughing in exactly the same clone-voices that Amanda had heard in the other rooms. "Thank you!" John Kirkley was saying; "Glad you could come!" And, in swooping, cheery tones from Anne Kirkley: "Brian? He's gone sailing with friends to Nantucket!" She had her hard-candy smile turned up full voltage; looked cool, blond, and old-money-understated in yellow linen and afternoon-length pearls.

Neither of them had seen Amanda yet, although there were others who seemed to be watching her; she couldn't be sure.

"Well!" boomed a voice. "Decided to be friends after all?"

She was startled to see Ray Herrick approach her, smiling, with a drink in his hand. Old-style chic in his navy silk blazer, tan slacks and a foulard inside his open shirt collar. Where had he appeared from? It was as if he had been standing near the terrace door, watching who came out.

Amanda took a step back and smiled warily. "Whoever said I wasn't friends?" Her voice was dangerously calm. She thought frantically: *Where's Peter?* and her heart sank as she realized: *Something must have come up.*

Herrick hand-gestured good-naturedly, his drink sloshing a little. "So true. Forgive me. This morning . . . I guess we were both just doing our jobs, *n'est-çe pas?*" He signaled to a waiter carrying champagne on a silver platter; lifted off a glass and with a flourish handed it to Amanda.

She thanked him, watching as he raised his highball in the form of a toast. "To the candidate!" he said jovially. "Can't tell you how happy I am to see you on the right side of the fence!"

She raised her glass, smiling. A bit too sweetly she said, "I've always believed in supporting the right candidate."

He laughed loudly, seeming to delight in her clever equivocation, but at the same time attracting attention. She glanced up, tensing, just as John and Anne Kirkley looked over and saw her. The naked hatred in Anne Kirkley's eyes made her blood go cold. But John Kirkley just stood silently, hostile but startled, seeming somehow to stare right through her. The exchange had taken scarcely an instant, and then quickly they looked away and resumed the roles of genial hosts.

Amanda's hands were trembling. She looked at her watch. It was 4:20; wasn't it time for the speeches to begin? She wanted to get out of here!

"Dr. Hammond! Well, Hell's Bells! Fancy meeting you here!" She and Herrick turned to see Gordon Maitland bearing down on them, red-faced from heat and alcohol, looking like a yachting pennant in a tomato red blazer, white slacks, and blue polo shirt. He was waving a martini and looking . . . Amanda blinked . . . as friendly as Herrick. This morning's tension also seemingly forgotten . . . *We were just doing our jobs, n'est-çe pas?* Amanda reminded herself that smiling faces meant zip with such people: that the truly skilled practitioners of the corporate-hearty facade could party it up convincingly with you on Saturday night and stab you dead on Monday.

She looked from one man to the other and said, "Well, one more and the picture would be complete."

They looked at her questioningly. Maitland stopped his martini halfway to his lips, while around them knots of people laughed, talked loudly, and clinked their ice cubes.

"Picture?" Herrick asked.

"Yes, the one on the wall in your office, Gordon. Both of you and John Kirkley breaking ground?"

They both said "Oh!" and nodded and smiled. Maitland, becoming serious, said, "Real estate's what's really done it for us. All of us. We were young and needed capital, so we bought, pyramided, bought, pyramided—" He jerked his thumb at Herrick. "I still can't keep these guys out of my office!"

Herrick shrugged modestly. "John spots the deals. I figure— gravy is gravy, what the hell?"

Someone called to Maitland, and he drifted off to a nearby group. Amanda, left alone with a thoughtful-looking Herrick, said, "It's hard to picture John Kirkley *ever* needing money. When you look at him now . . ." She shrugged, not too stagily, she hoped, wanting him to continue.

He stopped a waiter, exchanged his empty highball glass for two new champagnes, and gave one to Amanda. She sipped, thanking him, watching beads of sweat form on his brow. It was getting very hot in the tent.

"John started so small," he said, "he had to borrow money for his shoestring. He was successful every step of the way, but always had to borrow money for the *next* step—get my drift? It's the American way." He sipped, pressing his lips together as if the champagne tasted bitter. "Capital? Listen—I was a lawyer just starting out, just when John was looking good but owing big and getting killed by his in-laws. He needed to get golden on his own. Emotionally, it was important."

Amanda stared down into her glass, trying to imagine the anger, the drive and the hangups, that such a background would foster. Her attention was diverted by Gordon Maitland, back again and nudging Herrick.

"Look who's here," said Maitland. "The Commodities King."

"Who?" asked Herrick. He was sweating harder and beginning to look irritable.

"The Commodities King," Maitland said low. "You remember, I told you—name's Sandy Clees, he bought the Simon place on Country Club Lane last year, showed up for the contract signing with three, um . . ." He looked awkwardly at Amanda while Herrick said, "Oh, *him*," and looked over to see. "Christ," he said, turning back. "He's headed this way, and look what's with him."

The heat was getting to Amanda, too. If they don't start the speeches in a minute, she thought, I'll die.

Sandy Clees, ginger-haired, overweight, and dressed for either Wall Street or a funeral, wandered over with a grinning, flashy redhead on his arm. "How're ya doing?" he smiled nervously. Not the best opener for these parts. Amanda was embarrassed for him. He said something eager to Maitland, who smiled and answered, and Clees, delighted, relaxed and introduced his girlfriend, the famous actress.

"Vicki Linford!" she said twice, too brightly, looking with raised brows around the group. "You haven't heard of *Coral Gables?* It's a hit TV series!"

Three blank stares and one "Oh, I *think* I place it." The actress looked miffed at the indifference. Amanda told her that she had seen the show a couple of times (true: the patients had been watching it in the Commons Room), but it didn't placate whatever Vicki Linford's insecurities were in this particular crowd. Angry, she put on her own show, wrapping herself seductively around Clees, laughing in high squeals and opening her décolletage another two buttons.

Amanda saw both Kirkleys look over in fury.

She also realized suddenly that she was feeling ill. The tent was hotter than a greenhouse in July and smelled of gin. Her legs felt weak and she wanted to sit down, but couldn't, because suddenly the guests were being summoned toward a makeshift podium at the far end of the terrace.

At last the speeches, she thought, relieved. She broke away from the others and stood toward the rear of the crowd, waiting.

A plump, smiling woman went up to the microphone and made the introduction. John Kirkley, she intoned. Friend, neighbor, supporter of worthy causes . . .

Appreciative applause. *You left out devoted father,* Amanda thought.

". . . and devoted husband and father, a shining example to us all. I give you, therefore, my dear friend and yours, John Kirrrkley!"

Wild applause, the sea of chiffon and blazers emitting cheers more appropriate to a drunken football rally than to a political event. John Kirkley mounting the podium, smiling, reaching the mike and making a pretense of two-handed hushing gestures.

Finally, the crowd subsided, and he began, "How humble I feel to see your enthusiasm as I seek to serve the state that I love."

Amanda stood like a stone, her face draining of color. The cheers this time sounded distant to her, and she began to back away, her hands hanging loosely at her sides. Because—she blinked—she had heard what she had come to hear, and now she was certain: *Yes. It's the same voice. John Kirkley is the man's voice on Kelly's tape!*

". . . federal deficit, our number one problem!" Kirkley thundered. "And do you know what solution I propose? Would you all like to know?"

The chorus of "yeses" unexpectedly had to wait for the answer, because in the very pregnant pause, the steaming, damp-collared silence that Kirkley had used to utmost oratorical advantage . . .

. . . Amanda's beeper went off.

The high-pitched squeal filled the tent and bounced off the candy-striped canvas, and caused every face to turn away from Kirkley to her in curiosity.

Dead silence reigned as Amanda reached to a side-pocket of her purse to turn it off. "Ah . . . sorry," she said, her voice thin with embarrassment. Anne Kirkley was glaring pure venom at her. And the look on John Kirkley's face made him look capable of murder right here and now.

A maid in a gray and white uniform touched Amanda's arm. "There's a phone in the kitchen if you like." Her voice: lilting and gentle. Jamaican? Barbadian?

With the feeling of a hundred pairs of eyes on her back, Amanda followed the maid from the room.

IN THE BUSTLING KITCHEN Amanda called her answering service, who told her that Dr. Barron had been trying to reach her. Hanging up, she dialed the number they gave her and heard Peter's voice after one ring.

"Manda? Where are you? God, don't tell me you actually *went*—"

"Yes. I'm here at the dogshow. Alone. And I think I am going to die. Where are you?"

At his end, two towns away, Peter looked around the pathetic little apartment with the hilly, cracked linoleum and the walls splattered with blood. The room was filled with busy cops, the police photographer, and the fingerprint expert. Morgue attendants only feet away from him were loading two corpses into body bags and zipping them closed.

He ran a hand through his hair and turned back to the phone.

"In South Bridgeton, upstairs from a laundry, just finishing up with a double homicide. Looks like a drug hit. Hey—do those swells at the party know the crack problem's getting worse in Fairfield County? The next stray bullet might just plug a paisley tie."

Amanda looked at a teetering stack of soiled silver trays on the counter. "Leave this address pinned to the door," she said testily. "Free snow. Supply limited." She sank limply into a chair and rubbed at her brow. "I'm sorry, Peter. I shouldn't have complained." She caught the glances of two maids working near her—one the

Jamaican-or-Barbadian, the other older, more maternal—and thought she saw them smile.

Peter said feelingly, "Of course complain, you've had a terrible day. Are you leaving now? Can I meet you someplace?"

She sighed. "'Fraid not. Sorry again. I just want to go home and collapse . . ." And then she hesitated, suddenly noticing a pattern among the busy kitchen personnel. Most of the waiters and food-preparers zipping around her wore black and white uniforms: they were from a catering company. Whereas the two maids who had smiled at her wore gray and white—and avoided the others.

They work for the family, she realized, and sat a little straighter. "Correction," she said impulsively. "I've just thought of a reason to stay an extra few minutes. As long as I'm here . . ."

"Fine. And I can be there in fifteen minutes." Peter's voice was urgent. "It's on the way. Don't leave. Wait for me!"

Amanda started to protest, but found herself speaking to a dial tone.

IRONICALLY, IT WAS THE WOMEN in the gray and white uniforms who approached her first. Scarcely had she hung up when the older, darker-skinned of the two came over and smiled worriedly.

"Dr. Hammond? We heard you identify yourself on the phone. You're Brian's doctor! My name is Doreen, and this here is Mary."

The younger woman looked sad. "How's Brian doin'? We knew he was better off at your hospital, but we was still worried."

"Brian's gone sailing to Nantucket with friends . . . la-de-da . . ."

Amanda stared at the two women. She didn't know why—maybe it was exhaustion or the awful tension of keeping that face among the phonies—but her shoulders slumped and release flooded her so strongly that tears smarted. "You . . . know where he is?" she said, looking from one to the other, hearing the thickness in her own voice.

"'Course we do," Doreen said, lowering herself tiredly into the chair facing Amanda. Her kindly eyes took the measure of the person she had heard Brian rave about. She nodded to herself.

"Do you know how much that child worships you? I brought him his lunch on a tray on Saturday, and he was already cryin' 'bout wanting to come to you. He was just . . ."

"Too sick," Mary supplied. She began toying with a gold sword swizzle stick. "Had to get better to get drunk again, so's he could do it." She shook her head; sat down next to Doreen. "Lord, what a scene it was out there last night."

Amanda leaned forward. "Last night? You were both here?"

Doreen nodded. "I never left, even though I had Sunday off. And Mary is usually back around eight. My husband—he's a handyman here—was in Utica visiting his sick brother, so I figured, where am I going to go? We live above the caretaker's cottage."

"And I live just off the kitchen"—Mary turned; pointed— "down that hall there. Same side of the house as Mr. Kirkley's apartment, matter of fact. He still calls it the guest suite but he lives there. Nobody's supposed to know. He had it done over nice." She went back to spearing olives onto her sword.

Amanda stared in uncomprehending confusion. "Mr. Kirkley's . . . *apartment?*"

They both looked at her uncomfortably.

Doreen leaned forward in her chair. A waiter from the catering service said "'scuse," and reached over her for a stack of doilies. From the tented area two rooms away, Amanda could hear Kirkley's speech still droning, and she tensed, afraid that someone she'd prefer not to see was going to come walking in.

"They're secretly separated," Doreen said in a near whisper, glancing quickly over her shoulder as Amanda had just done. "Lisl—that's the Swiss cook, she's not here today—Lisl says they were all set to divorce when Mr. Kirkley decided to go into politics. And that suited Mrs. Kirkley just fine, she's real ambitious, so she went along. Pretended things were fine to the outside world, and inside this house they're living in separate wings, just like enemy camps." Another peek to make sure no one was listening. "Mrs. Kirkley lives upstairs, way on the other side of the house. They practically never see each other."

Amanda was dumbstruck. "But . . . this is incredible! Brian never mentioned . . ."

"Brian doesn't know," Mary said, getting up, clearing away crumpled party napkins. "He's been livin' in that boat house for a year. That kid doesn't know *anything* 'bout his parents." She looked sharply back at Amanda. "But you wanna know who *did* know? Kelly. Because *I told her.* She was over here an' cryin' once, his folks was away, and when Brian went upstairs for something, I told her. I jes' felt so bad 'bout the way they was treating her. And that's not *all* I told her . . ." Mary stopped, looking warily over at Doreen, wanting to continue but afraid to.

Doreen seemed abruptly to remember something. "Dr. Hammond, does Brian need more clothes? Sweatshirts? Jeans? He's got drawers full of things he hasn't used in ages." She raised a brow at the watchful Mary and said, "Don't worry. I'll tell the rest. Hurry upstairs and get Brian a nice pile of things for the doctor to take back."

Mary went. Doreen turned back to Amanda and slowly shook her head. "Mary's got a heart that suffers for others. And when she saw Kelly crying, she told her something she maybe shouldn't have told, 'cause we don't know for sure if it's true . . ."

Amanda waited, staring.

Doreen frowned. "Mary and I chanced to hear one unholy screaming match one night between Mr. and Mrs. Kirkley, and"— she swallowed—"Mrs. Kirkley accused him of having prostitutes . . . prostitutes on an expense account, no less, and all kinds of goings-on with young women over at that big shot lawyer's house." She clasped her hands and looked down at them. "He's divorced, you know, that lawyer. And he's got housekeepers and such who aren't there nights, weekends, so . . . that's where they have their parties. Sex and a lot of wild stuff, that's what Mrs. Kirkley was screaming. Said she'd kick that lawyer out of her house in a second if they didn't need him to keep Mr. Kirkley's nose clean." She shrugged. "So Mary told Kelly both things: they're separated, he sees prostitutes. The thing is, I don't think that girl would have told Brian in a million years. She wouldn't have wanted to hurt him, y'know?"

Amanda, pale, slumped back in her chair, trying to absorb what she had just heard. From the tented area came the amplified voice of Kirkley wrapping it up ("honesty and old-time values!"), and the sound of thunderous applause. No good, she thought frantically. They're going to be milling again.

"Truth is," Doreen whispered, leaning closer as if sensing the same new pressure that Amanda was feeling. "I believe that story. Mr. Kirkley sometimes comes in at weird hours, I hear his car. He's got *some* kind of secret life, lemme tell you. His private entrance— it's next to the garage—real convenient."

Amanda looked up and froze as John Kirkley walked into the kitchen.

"Well!" he said, eyeing Amanda. He curved his mouth into a smile. "What have we here? A little tête à tête? Something more interesting than listening to a political speech?"

Heart pounding, Amanda got to her feet. Doreen beside her looked stricken. Fortunately, her back had been turned to Kirkley; reflexively, she had reached for a pile of paper napkins and was stuffing them into their box when she turned to face him.

Amanda regarded Kirkley's face, so craggy-handsome and yet so . . . cold, she thought, with his hard, narrow mouth, his eyes without emotion. She hesitated, then made herself walk toward him. Reaching him, she braced herself lightly on a chair; her legs felt weak.

He smiled again. "No, really," he said in that same quiet tone. "I'd be fascinated to know what's so interesting for you in this kitchen. You heard some sort of story, perhaps? Something you couldn't tear yourself away from?"

An aide appeared behind him, urging him to come back to the gathering. He ignored the young man.

With utmost control, Amanda pretended surprise. "Interesting?" she said, and smiled sweetly. "Hardly. I'm just waiting."

"Waiting! Now what in the world could you possibly . . ."

Mary in her uniform ran back into the kitchen carrying a pile of Brian's clothes. Amanda took them from her, smiled gratefully at the girl, turned and smiled affectionately at a frozen-faced Doreen.

"You are both most kind," she said. "Thank you." She turned back to see Anne Kirkley just arriving, and a second young aide rushing in behind her.

She held up the pile of jeans and sweatshirts and smiled at them all.

"Nights in Nantucket can get chilly," she said pleasantly, and made her way past them and out.

PETER BARRELED HIS PORSCHE up the crowded drive all the way to the house. He saw Amanda just as she was coming out, careened to a stop, and climbed out of the car. Her face as he approached her looked so strained and haggard that he took her in his arms without a word.

She buried her face against his shoulder. "It wasn't fun, Peter. No fun at all."

Still clutching Brian's clothes, she leaned against Peter's car and shakily told him everything. The voice on Kelly's tape. A definite match to Kirkley's voice, she was certain. "And there's more," she said, her fingers rubbing her throbbing brow. She related everything that Mary and Doreen had told her, including Kirkley's comings and goings at strange hours of the night.

Peter's face went slack. "Wonder what his alibi is for Friday night," he said low. "I think McHugh might be interested in talking to him. Hey—why don't I call Joe now, ask him to come over for a questioning during the fund-raiser? Maybe some of Kirkley's dear friends will vouch for him."

Her red-veined eyes looked at him for a long moment, then closed. "I'm going to bed now," she said. She turned and began walking to her own car.

"A restaurant first," he said, in step with her. "You'll feel better and you have to eat anyway. A glass of wine—"

She stopped and thrust Brian's clothes into his hands. "I don't need a restaurant. I need a drugstore and something for a splitting headache. Do something for me, Peter? Drop these clothes off for Brian at Brooklawn. I'd appreciate that more than anything." She sighed heavily; attempted a smile. "I'm sorry I'm so out of it. I haven't slept. If I don't get some peace and quiet, I'll go stark raving."

He looked rueful. "I understand. I'll tell Joe everything you said." He accompanied her to her car, carrying what looked like a small load of folded laundry. As she opened her door, he said, "Tomorrow night? You'll be rested—will you promise to spend the evening with me?"

She got in behind the wheel and smiled wanly up at him. "Okay," she whispered.

He kissed her full on the mouth, and stepped back as she closed the door and started the engine. He raised a hand to her, and stood alone watching until her car was out of sight.

29

THE NURSE, after calling around, said that Brian was swimming in the Olympic pool, so Peter asked her to deliver the clothes, and then asked to use the phone. A minute later he had McHugh on the line.

"Funny you should call," McHugh said. "There's something I want to talk to you about, too."

McHugh sounded . . . what? Off key? Uncomfortable? "You have a lead? Give me a hint," Peter said. He knew he couldn't tie up the foyer phone and planned to keep it short.

McHugh hesitated. "Meet me for a bite. Dante's in twenty minutes, that okay? I'm not going to know *what* I think until I get some chow in me."

That's odd . . . Joe was never one to hedge, Peter thought, hanging up. He dashed out to his car and was at the restaurant across the narrow street from the train station in less than fifteen minutes. It was still early and he got a table by the window, where he sat, intrigued, watching the rush-hour commuter trains roar in, disgorge, and move out at the rate of every few minutes. It was amazing, he thought. There were people in suspenders and pinstripes who got *off* the train still frowning, checking their watches, hurrying. The day was done and they were still hyped up. Once, he thought, just once, he'd like to move through one of those trains, car by car, taking blood pressures . . .

McHugh arrived with a muttered salutation and the two got down to business.

"I've got a bad feeling," McHugh said, pulling his chair in, "and I want you to talk me out of it because it's crazy. It has to be crazy."

Other people were coming into the restaurant: most of them

carrying briefcases and looking as if they had just gotten off the train. Dante's for many was the stop after the stop on the commuter line. A waitress came and both men ordered—veal scaloppini for Peter, chili for McHugh.

"Chili in an Italian restaurant?" Peter grimaced.

"It's the best. You should try it." McHugh folded his arms on the red and white checked tablecloth and looked down, troubled. Peter waited.

"All lab reports are back from Dr. Hammond's office," the policeman said. "And you know what?" He lifted a brooding gaze to Peter. "Not one fingerprint that didn't belong to Dr. Hammond or her secretary *in the vicinity of the bookcase,* the one place we can assume patients and other staff members wouldn't go."

Peter seemed unconcerned. "So the thief wore gloves, what's so unusual about that?"

McHugh nodded. "I know. Of course, but there's more." He thought, looked out the window as another train roared in. The glass vibrated; the restaurant seemed to rock on its foundations. He inhaled and looked back.

"So the guy wore gloves. I've got no problem with that. The problem is, what kind of intruder just walks into a staffed place like that at, say, two in the morning with no apparent fear of being *noticed?* Something's just a little too casual about that. Unless . . ." He hesitated, pursed his lips. "Unless it was someone who *belonged* there . . . who had no concerns about being seen."

The veal and chili came, but Peter did not take his eyes off McHugh. When the waitress left, he said uneasily, "Go on."

McHugh took a spoon and fiddled with the chili. He seemed suddenly to lose his appetite, and put the spoon back down.

"You like Dr. Hammond a lot, don't you?"

Peter looked at McHugh, surprised. Something icy began to creep through his veins. "Yes. Are you trying to say Amanda stole her own tapes?"

"I don't know what the hell I'm trying to say. But I'll tell you what I was *thinking* this afternoon. I've asked around. This Kirkley kid is supposed to be quite the, uh . . . what the women call a hunk. Dr. Hammond's fiercely protective of him, and he's, let's say, emotionally dependent on her . . . or *was,* until a pretty eighteen-year-old came along . . ." McHugh shook his head slowly. His expression was dark. "The murder happened right next door to Dr. Hammond's house. Is that a coincidence, or what?"

Peter, staring, dropped his fork into his veal—*plop*. He stared at McHugh with his mouth open.

"That's off the wall! It's just plain nuts!" Some people at a nearby table looked at him strangely.

"She's a beautiful woman," McHugh said low. His face was actually reddening as he forced himself on. "Anything is possible, and it's my *job* to consider every damned, far-fetched, off the wall thing that comes into my head." He looked unhappily down at his chili; pushed it away. "Hell, if it hadn't been for the way the tapes were stolen *and* the murder happening right next door, I never would have thought of Dr. Hammond. But both things together! How can I *not* think of her?"

Peter frowned at McHugh. Thought. Remembered other times, other cases, where they had had similar differences of opinion, where police thinking had seemed to be grabbing at every straw. He leaned forward, elbows on the table.

"I can understand your doubts about someone just coolly walking into Brooklawn in the middle of the night. But before you go jumping onto theories about Amanda—have you interviewed the rest of the staff? The other psychiatrists, the psychologists?"

"Yes. There's one we're looking into," McHugh admitted.

"Plenty of people there must have known Kelly," Peter went on. "Including where she used to live. Anyway, you said yourself that the idea of suspecting Amanda was crazy."

McHugh looked at him glumly. "Let's hope it is," he said, in a way that told Peter he wasn't convinced. He seemed to sink deeper into his chair, frustrated, the picture of a detective anticipating a tough investigation. Peter watched him brood for a moment, then said, "Amanda for her part has a bad feeling, as you call it, about John Kirkley, Brian's father. Care to hear?"

McHugh put his curled fist to his mouth and nodded.

Peter laid it out for him. Kirkley and his cronies angry that Brian was dating Kelly. Amanda's certainty that it was Kirkley's voice on Kelly's tape. The story of Kirkley's secret separation and odd night-time hours, as told by the two maids.

McHugh leaned back in his chair, looking as glum as before.

"So we'll have him questioned about Friday night, too. And you know what's going to happen? The same thing that always happens with people like that. They *always* have an alibi. They were at the country club, where none of two hundred people saw them slip out for a few minutes. Or they were home alone with the wife, who, even if she hates his guts is going to vouch for him, for appearances." McHugh waved a hand in disgust. "So he's secretly separated and screws around and didn't like his kid dating Kelly—and called to say so. It still doesn't make him the murderer. And it's *exactly* the sort of point you made about Dr. Hammond. Something that sounds so good when you first think about it, and then turns out to be circumstantial evidence. *Maybe.* Figuring that's the hard part."

Peter didn't like that emphasis on the word "maybe." He realized that McHugh was probably still picturing the tape thief as someone more familiar around Brooklawn than the father of a patient.

"You'll look into Kirkley?" he said.

McHugh nodded. "I'll take it as far as I can. He may refuse to talk to me altogether—it's his right. Big shots are sometimes afraid it's going to leak that they're 'being questioned.' "

"What about other possible suspects? Kelly's supposed to have known a lot of people."

McHugh restlessly tapped his fingers on the tablecloth. He looked as if his mind was racing down a dozen paths, measuring hunches, exploring probabilities and possibilities.

"She had a telephone book," he said. "I gave four men the job of tracking down those names, checking their alibis. They're not done, yet, but so far nothing." He paused; looked up at Peter. "Care to guess who had the best alibi of everybody? Her ex-stepfather. Nevada police tell us he spent Friday night in a Tahoe jail. Narcotics possession."

He sighed heavily and pulled back his chili. "People lie, Peter. And people cover for each other, which means that we have to be smarter, dig deeper, go back and start at square one with our thinking." He shook his head almost angrily. "Solving this one is not going to be easy."

Peter looked at him thoughtfully for several moments and then nodded. "Because it's a drowning," he said. "There's nothing harder, is there?"

30

AMANDA PULLED INTO A PLACE in the crowded parking lot. She got out and hesitated, frowning suddenly, before heading for the drugstore.

Had she been locking her car today? Odd, the thought had never even occurred to her. She didn't remember locking up anywhere, but such had been her turmoil since this morning that she had blanked out on most of the automatic, little things.

So . . . shall I lock up here or not? she thought, feeling foolish. Somehow the question seemed terribly important, seemed in its stupid and absolutely trivial way a measure of her sanity at this moment. There was a running joke in Grand Cove that there were two groups of people in town: those who always locked their cars and those who never did. Even now, Amanda noticed, looking around, despite the pall of fear that hung over the town, plenty of people were pulling into this very public lot and ambling away from their unlocked cars without a second glance. And why shouldn't they? The murder had happened at a lonely spot in the dead of night, not in a sun-baked, nearly 6 P.M. parking lot crowded with tired-looking shoppers, kids eating ice cream, and the first wave of commuters just off the early trains.

A little late in the day to start acting paranoid, she decided. She slammed the car door but didn't lock it, and headed for the line of stores.

AT THE COUNTER she filled out her own prescription form for Percodan, one of the bigger-gun pain killers that had to be used prudently; they could be habit-forming. She caught the druggist's curious glance, and thought, *tough.* He knew her; she had forced herself through the usual pleasantries; and he was probably wondering why she wasn't helping herself to the chock-full closets at Brooklawn instead of putting down good money here. Reasonable question, she conceded, and in that moment she realized the real reason she was standing at this counter. She didn't want to *talk* to anyone, that was the thing. Didn't want to run the avid-eyed, isn't-it-horrible-do-the-police-know-anything conversational gamut that she had agonized through all day. Her strength was gone. She had an urgent, crying need to be alone. To try to think, if that was possible. Try to sort out the strange and puzzling fragments that had come to her during the day—

"Here ya go, Dr. Hammond."

She blinked. The pharmacist in his white coat was smiling at her as he put the plastic, cylindrical bottle on the counter. She smiled wearily back, thanked him, and picked it up to examine the label. *Be careful with alcohol.* Thank you very much. *Refillable only during MD's office hours—Ha-hah! Don't you love it? Well, the doctor is in, friends and neighbors. The doctor is in terrible shape and is doing something about it, and can you think of a better reason for going to medical school? As they say, better living through chemistry, the well in this valley never runs dry, eat your heart out, Jackie Susann.*

"Thanks, Charlie." She gave the bottle back and he began putting it into a small paper bag.

"Nothing else?" He seemed surprised. Usually when Amanda came in here she got fistfuls of the kind of impulse items women bought in expensive pharmacies: good shampoo and good cosmetics and Fiber Trim thrown into the same bag with the obscene-sized Toblerone candy bar. This time, just the pills and make it quick, please. She knew that she appeared very tense, and there was nothing she could do about it. The druggist was staring at her with a look of real, avuncular concern and she groaned inwardly, thinking, *please, don't.*

"Y'know, you don't look too good, Dr. Hammond. I hope you don't mind my saying that but . . ." His face fell. "Well, I guess you've got good reason. It must be pretty hard on you."

Was there *anyone* in town who didn't know that Kelly had been her patient? Although come to think of it, Amanda recalled, this was where Kelly used to come to get her prescriptions filled. She smiled bleakly at the man. "Does it show that much?"

He seemed at a loss for words when a woman came up behind her to pay for a bouquet of nail polish bottles. A teenage assistant wrote out Amanda's charge as the druggist took care of the nail polish lady, and Amanda stepped unobtrusively to her left to glance into the mirror on the sunglasses turnstile.

Her jaw dropped. There were dark crescents under her eyes. And in a town full of fashionably tanned and sporting women she looked white-faced, strained and anxious. For just an instant, standing there and looking into the mirror, she felt like Alice in *Through the Looking Glass,* and wanted to climb into that little window and come out the other side, into some sort of Twilight Zone where it was still last week and none of this nightmare had begun.

". . . *was* your patient. See, Trip, I *told* you." The nail polish lady stood there now with a polo-shirted man at her side, her round, bright blue eyes gaping at Amanda. "We're *devastated!* Do the police know who did it yet? Do they have any leads?"

Stiffening, Amanda scanned every expression watching her: the druggist; the teenaged assistant; the woman and her husband; other people drifting over to listen. Their eyes, she thought. The same grim-but-fascinated eyes that you saw watching a building burn.

Muttering something that she hoped sounded reasonably composed, Amanda took her purchase, and fled.

SHE DROVE HOME, parked outside, and went up the steps to her front door. She was relieved to find the keybox gone. One of Maitland's realtors must have stopped by, unlocked and popped open the iron loop, and taken the ugly little clunker away.

It wasn't until she had entered the air-conditioned house that a feeling of unease set in. The place was too deathly quiet. She turned in the hallway, looking around, and called: "Suki?"

She frowned. No Suki. No footsteps hurrying toward her, no radio sound from the kitchen, no sounds of busyness carrying from the various points of the house.

In the kitchen, Amanda was even more bewildered. The house was beginning to fill with shadows: the time Suki usually went around turning on a few lamps . . . but—nothing. Amanda flicked on the copper-hooded light over the center island, then the light over the sink and the colonial chandelier inside the breakfast room. There, under the arched alcove, she turned slowly back and stared across at the cook top with its sparkling blue-and-white tiles, thinking that by now it was usually the scene of pots and pans flying and Suki happily launching into her Julia Child bit.

Nothing.

What had happened? The clock on the wall said it was 6:40. Could Suki be out shopping at this hour? Unlikely—for Suki— although lots of people did it, the stores were open late and it was a way to beat the heat. Confused, a little alarmed, Amanda went to the sink and turned on the tap, grateful even for the sound of running water to fill the silence. She fished in her purse, took out the vial of Percodan, and hesitated, remembering the drug's side effects.

Potent stuff, it eased the kind of pain that over the counter remedies couldn't touch. On the other hand, it could impair mental and physical abilities . . . affect perception . . . The exact wording in Amanda's hefty Physician's Desk Reference came back to her, a somber voice, reminding caution.

But I'm not going anywhere. I'll be locking up and staying in and I'm not planning on operating a vehicle or dangerous machinery.

She filled a glass half full, and took one tablet.

Then she turned, and headed back down the long central hall to the foyer, where she fished out her keys and turned on the burglar alarm. The little red light embedded in the foyer wall came on, and she felt both safe and imprisoned. When Suki came back *(from where?)*, she'd simply use her own set of keys to turn it off.

Back in the kitchen, pacing, Amanda was almost relieved to remember she had a call to make.

Sitting in the breakfast room with pencil and notepad, she dialed Brooklawn and got a floor nurse who up-dated her on several patients. She made troubled little doodles as she listened; then she asked to speak to Brian Kirkley.

"He's watching television," the nurse said blankly.

"He *hates* television! Tell him to come to the phone."

There was a clunk on the other end, and for several moments Amanda waited and heard the muted commotion of the upstairs nurses' station. Then a muffled, unhappy male voice picked up.

"Hullo?"

"Hi, Brian, it's Amanda. How are you feeling?"

"Not wonderful." He pronounced it "wonnerful" and sounded like someone who had been locked in a closet for a year.

"Have they kept you busy?" Amanda asked, prodding gently. "Therapy and such?"

The word struck a nerve. "I'll say. They've got more kinds of therapy here than I ever knew existed. Individual therapy, group therapy, family therapy . . . provided you can stand the *sight* of your family . . . occupational therapy, recreational therapy . . . I made an Eiffel Tower out of toothpicks. I swam three miles in the pool, you know why? 'Cause swimming's the only damned thing you can do around here without having to *talk* to anybody! Hey—thanks for sending over the clothes, by the way."

Amanda smiled. "Thank Doreen. She's thinking of you." On her notepad she doodled a rectangle with glow lines radiating out from it, and asked, "How are you feeling otherwise? Physically?"

A silence. A sigh. "Well. That stuff you ordered for me? Sounds like tough . . . ?"

"Tofranil."

"Right. Well, it's working . . . okay. I mean, I'm not feeling so depressed anymore, I'm more . . . up, but I feel . . . jittery. Anxious. My heart's beating too fast and the nurse tells me I pace too much."

In front of the glowing rectangle Amanda sketched the outline of a man as schematic as the dummies in a police target line-up. Furiously she filled in the figure with dark lead as she reassured her young patient.

"Bri, I'm going to switch you to something called Triavil. It's a mood elevator and a tranquilizer combined. You'll feel better, that's a promise."

He actually sounded a trifle cheered as they said good-bye. Amanda waited a moment, then called back, got the charge nurse, and changed the order. "Triavil," she said. "Three times a day, starting now." The nurse protested something about Brian's having had his last Tofranil less than three hours ago (Amanda could see the woman scrutinizing her medication sheet), and Amanda said, "No problem. Give it to him now. No, *now* now, not bedtime. Sign my name."

She hung up, felt the silence of the big house close in again, and wondered what next.

No *note* from Suki, that was another thing. One of her many caring little touches was always leaving notes—I've dashed out for milk, I'm up in the attic, I'm outside with the tree surgeon—and what did she always say when Amanda kidded her about overdoing it? *I didn't want you to worry, that's all.*

Which could only mean that now, with no note in a darkening house which had been this close to murder . . . a terrible feeling began to dawn in Amanda's mind that something was very wrong . . .

Trying to be calm, she got up and followed the phone cord around the corner to its source on the kitchen wall. She put the receiver in its cradle and stood there staring at it, as if the phone were some sort of sentient being that could give her answers or advice. Should she call someone? Who? And what would she say?

It rang so suddenly that she jumped.

"Hello?" she said, yanking it off the hook.

Suki, in tears. Suki at the hospital, where Emily Hagin lay gravely injured and in intensive care.

". . . horrible," Suki wept. "Russ came home and found little Davey on the front steps crying, and together they went in and . . ." Her voice caught in a sob. ". . . they *found* her, two hours ago, at the foot of the cellar stairs. She had been carrying down the laundry and must have fallen. She has a fractured skull and a concussion and . . ." Suki's voice dissolved into another torrent of tears.

Amanda stood frozen, feeling a sick wave of horror roll through her. She closed her eyes and swayed on her feet. Part of her mind insisted frantically that this had something to do with her, but her thoughts were tumbling too chaotically for her to do more than groan and try to offer comfort.

"Stay over there," she managed. "Help all you can and . . ." The words blurted out. "I'll be right over. Give me fifteen minutes."

"Amanda, no! You've had too much already! You barely slept last night!"

"I'm coming," she said, heartsick. "How could I not?"

With a trembling hand Amanda hung up. Involuntarily, she backed up a step, pressing both hands to her mouth, shaking her head back and forth as if denying what she had just heard. She remembered the fragment of her thought that Emily's accident had something to do with her, and shook her head again. Impossible. *The whole world is just going crazy,* she thought hysterically. The Percodan was starting to work now. The headache was easing up a bit, but she felt dizzy . . . terribly upset but in a disorienting, three-feet-off-the-ground kind of way.

Which was why she cried out when the phone rang again.

That's right, scream. Eight years of training on when not to emote, down the drain in a day.

She moved forward jerkily and picked up. It was Peter, calling from a crowded-sounding Dante's. When she heard his voice she nearly crumbled.

". . . trying to get you," he began, then caught the tremor in her voice and stopped. "Amanda, are you all right? What's going on?"

In a tearful rush she told him about Emily, then announced that she was headed for the hospital.

There was a stunned silence at the other end. She could picture him, staring in shock at the restaurant pay phone before him, trying to absorb this latest bit of horror while commuters piled noisily into the place and the din rose at the bar.

"You're not going to the hospital," he finally said, and she could tell he was leaning closer to the mouthpiece. "I'll go back. McHugh doesn't want you out after dark and . . ." His voice sharpened. "What did you take for your headache?"

"Percodan. Five milligrams." Amanda brushed at a tear.

"That settles it. No driving." He inhaled. "What about that damned keybox? Is it still there?"

"No. I made them take it off. They think I'm neurotic."

"Screw them. Got the alarm on?"

She let out a long, trembling sigh. "Yes. It feels like being locked up after hours in a museum. You'll explain to Suki?"

"Of course . . ." Peter's voice was very somber. "I'll call later and tell you what the prognosis is."

Amanda closed her eyes as tears of strain stung anew. *Prognosis,* the most awful word . . . She opened her eyes, and the thought of hanging up into silence again filled her with terror. "Th-thanks, Peter, and . . . good-bye."

She replaced the receiver. Dropped her face in her hands; cried. *Emily in intensive care. Kelly dead. Me cooped up in this oversized mausoleum and rapidly going to pieces. What is happening? Oh, dear God, what is happening?*

She raised her glistening face; stared blankly at a burnished ray of light that angled in from the window. Sunset, she thought. Last warmth of the day. Last comfort before the darkness comes.

She went into the dining room and looked out the locked French doors to the western sky. And caught her breath. The setting sun flamed its final glory through the clouds and shattered in restless, darkening ripples on the waters of the Sound. Amanda wanted time to stop. Right here. A brilliant-hued, Arctic dusk to last through the night.

"Stay," she whispered, as the last rim of crimson dropped away, and night began.

She turned her back, hugging herself as if she were cold, and left the room with weary steps.

31

"DAMN, THE ICE MELTS FAST IN HERE!"

At eleven o'clock Sandy Clees hauled his chunky, naked body out of the water, reached for his robe tossed onto a chaise longue, and told Vicki Linford in the hot tub that he was going for more cubes. She said something back and laughed—a high and liltingly drunken laugh—then went back to soaping herself all over. She seemed to enjoy her own touch, you could tell even from this distance. Didn't push her dripping, strawberry-colored hair from her face, her shoulders, as she moved the bar of soap across her breasts, back and forth, tilting her head back slightly with her eyes closed in pleasure as she rubbed, now in pressing, getting-whiter circles, one breast at a time. When Clees came back with more champagne and his silver bucket newly full, she stood up in the water grinning lewdly and shimmied her chest from side to side.

"See?" she giggled wildly. "Marshmallows!"

Yards away, the dark figure sat and watched. They had turned off all but the amber-filtered lights over the hot tub, leaving the rest of the plant-filled, curved glass room in steaming shadow. The figure sat at the end near the recirculating waterfall; had chosen one of the decorator-fake stones to sit on, and now peered through the fronds of an elaborate, potted mini-jungle.

Hot as Purgatory in here, he thought, sweating, watching as Clees got back in the water and began to give orders to the girl. Sweated even more profusely as he saw their newest variations of kink—and the docility, the amazingly turn-on *obedience,* of women with rich men.

But that was why he was here, wasn't it? To watch? This house on Country Club Lane was the best show in town, the admission was free, and the Commodity King's ever-changing cast of new, nubile women was a draw in itself. This week it was the actress. Other times, girls reported to the hot tub and the exercise mats along the side in groups of eager twos and threes.

Definitely a place to clear the mind ("Oh . . . *Ohh,*" cried the girl in the pool), although tonight the entertainment wasn't quite working for him. He was preoccupied, he knew. He had to decide how he was going to kill Amanda Hammond.

It had to be fast—before the cops could really get their investigation going—but it had to be original, it had to be *very* original, and that was the problem. Already he had killed four people: two outside, two inside. Three of those four had passed for accidents (and Payne *would* have, if he hadn't been so damnably clumsy); but to get rid of Hammond it would be too soon, too obvious, to use the same methods. He had listened to the tapes and found nothing, which *meant* nothing, he knew. Hammond might still remember something that had never gone onto the tapes. About Kelly . . . about her mother . . . Even if she didn't think she knew, she would begin to connect more and more . . .

Damn, he'd have to be clever in her case.

It began to bother him that he was wasting time, sitting here watching (they were now grunting away on the mats), when he should be out tending to business. He pondered for another moment, and abruptly sat straighter, smiling to himself. He had the glimmer of an idea . . .

Love to stay, folks, but I have another stop.

He pulled on his gloves and crept silently away, passing through dark showplace rooms on his way to the front foyer.

There he took from his jacket pocket the labeled keys to this house. Just two—one for the alarm, one for the door. He studied the tiny red light embedded in the wall that meant the alarm was on, and grunted in the darkness. The security systems around here all cost a fortune and weren't worth a nickel.

An instant later he was outside, relocking the door, then pushing the alarm key into its slot embedded in the house's massive cut stone. Twist it a quarter turn, watch the red light go back on, done.

He had a collection of keys to many houses in the area. He could get into or out of any of these houses in under fifteen seconds.

Hurrying past tall rhododendrons, he reflected for the hundredth time what a perfect setup he had going. Most of the houses he had chosen were in triple-A zoning, which meant that they were acres apart and behind landscaping so dense that he could have hid a regiment.

TEN MINUTES LATER, he was in another dark place, using his flash to swing open a rectangle of wide mahogany paneling on its secret hinges. Inside, a shallow space about five inches deep, four feet wide, and three feet tall, lined in soft, navy velvet. He shone his light on his gleaming treasures, and sucked in his breath at the rush of power they gave him.

Two hundred labeled sets of house keys, each hanging on its shiny little cup hook. And under each set in precise handwriting was the matching address of the house, and the name of its current owner.

He returned this evening's keys to their place and took out another set, which he put in his pocket. Carefully, he shut the faintly creaking door, and watched it disappear into the aristocratic, paneled wall that surrounded it.

He switched off his light and hurried out.

32

AMANDA LAY RIGIDLY AWAKE, eyes open, staring at the darkened ceiling and seeing faces. Emily, unconscious, her head swathed in bandages. Kelly, alive again, her gaze helpless and pleading, "Save me, Amanda. Save me . . ." The thought sent new tears down her cheeks. She rolled onto her side, as if that could bring comfort, and her foot felt the old scrapbook she had left at the bottom of the bed. More faces lit in her mind. Mother. Father. Others, gone, drifted away . . . and, sailing above all their heads, that young workman, leaning in mid-distance on a board, his face lost in shadows.

Why him? Since that crazy dream this morning she had thought several times of his picture *(the man with the bloody face?)*, and had managed to push it down. But now that it was night and she was alone, his image had come rushing back at her. She was frustrated that she hadn't had the chance to ask Suki about him . . .

She tossed, reviewing what she had done with the evening. She had called Josie and asked her to reschedule patients for the morning only, so she would be free by noon to rush over and see Emily. She had showered, changed into a creamy silk nightgown, and then, as if pulled by invisible magnets, had gone back to her parents' bedroom for the scrapbook. Until nearly eleven she had sat on her bed staring at page after page; had turned back, puzzled, so many times to that photograph of the half-smiling, flirtatious young man that she had memorized the shadow-filled angles of his face.

She had turned off the light more than an hour ago, but the darkness had snapped her back into panic, and sleep was impossible.

A scraping sound made her jerk her head on the pillow and gape out at the night. "Oh . . . !" She held her breath, then sighed.

Crazy. It's nothing. Leaves brushing the window in mild, balmy darkness. Nothing else. Get some rest. Try.

Instead she flicked on the small lamp and got up, her mind careening as on naked feet she padded across to the window seat that overlooked the front property. The house is so quiet, she thought, turning her thoughts back again to Emily.

Peter had called at 8:30; updated her.

"Four centimeter depressed skull fracture, no blood in the spinal fluid, but there's still the danger of cerebral edema, neurological damage, paralysis. The next day will tell."

Paralysis, God . . . no, Amanda thought miserably, turning and trudging in to the bathroom.

She splashed cool water on her face, feeling headachy again, but deciding against more Percodan. The throbbing wasn't as bad as before, and she wanted to avoid that faintly sedated feeling that came with taking something so strong. Patting her face dry, Amanda looked in the mirror and pictured the vial of pills, filled to the top, sitting right there on the bed table. Well, she thought. If this headache gets worse I may still take some, but hold off for now . . .

She hung up the towel and went back to bed, where she propped herself up and tried to read. Actually got through a page when she glanced up in puzzlement, dimly aware that she had heard a muffled sound.

What . . . ?

She listened for a moment: nothing. Just the house settling. Went back and this time got through two pages before she heard a creaking noise outside her bedroom, and froze.

Not the house settling, not imagination . . .

Heart leaping, she lay there motionless, straining her hearing; but the hall was silent and she began to suspect that her overwrought mind was playing tricks, until she heard another sound, and focused frantically on the bedpost, recognizing yet refusing to credit what she was hearing.

It's not possible.

You're hearing it, aren't you?

With her pulse throbbing sickly she got up, and made her way back through the bedroom door into the bathroom, where she stood, staring in mute shock at the water running full blast into the sink.

But I turned that off!

Yes, you did.

She went and with a jerky motion turned off the faucet again. Leaned, breathing rapidly, with both hands on the cool blue porcelain. Then noticed a draft. Looked up at the second door leading out to the hall.

Odd. She was sure she hadn't left it at that angle, half closed. She *never* left it at that angle; she either closed it all the way or left it open.

Well, tonight I just might be losing my mind.

With a badly shaking hand she rechecked the tap, opened the door wide to the hall again, then returned to her room and got into bed, trembling. She tried to focus on the still-open page; couldn't. Impossible to concentrate.

She sighed. Let the book drop. Looked over to the mist of dew clinging to the windowpanes. Fog rolling in? Probably. From the Sound came the soft, low song of fog horns. Gentle song, amplified by night. Lulling. Other sounds, too. Lonely whistle of the 12:07 headed for New York, clattering down tracks a mile away . . . tree toads piping . . . some faint, shuffling sound in the attic . . .

She flicked a quick glance to the ceiling. *Mice? Good thing I locked up or I'd be imagining things.*

The faint shuffling turned abruptly into distinct, measured footsteps right over her head.

She leaped up with her pulse rocketing, hand to her throat and eyes to the ceiling. Omigod—someone's up there walking! But how . . . ? *The alarm's on!*

She tried to scream but it froze in her throat. With a convulsive jerk she rolled off the bed, bruising her knees, and crawled back toward the phone on the table. Grasped it, hands fluttering in terror, saw it fly out of her hands and onto the floor. Her heart was bursting out of her chest. Above her, the creaking, walking sound stopped, as if hearing her commotion; then resumed in a hurrying tread as she gaped up in horror and followed it across the ceiling . . . to where the top of the attic stairs led down to this floor . . .

This can't be happening!

Crouching, she scrabbled the phone into her wildly trembling hands and this time managed to punch 911.

"Hang on, we'll be right there," said a reassuring officer's voice.

Footsteps racing down, or only her pulse pounding in her ears?

She crouched rooted to the floor, frozen, her eyes wide and staring in the direction of the old staircase that opened into the hall. In a second that thin door just yards down from the master bedroom was going to burst open and . . .

Dimly, approaching fast, the sweet, high wail of police sirens. Help is coming, help is . . . *Move, for God's sake!*

She grabbed her robe and bolted. From the room, down the hall *(Don't look back don't look . . .),* down the long flight of stairs.

In the vestibule, she stared in mad confusion at the tiny, still-glowing, round red light. Still . . . *on?* She shook her head. *I don't understand, it's not possible.*

Squad cars crunched the gravel; men's footsteps hurried to the door. She rushed and got a spare security key from a hall drawer and, heaving relief, opened up for the police.

They came in, two pairs of them, four big men in blue filling the vestibule. Behind them in the night a third car roared into the driveway, dome lights flashing. The driver and his partner got out and ran to check the outside of the house.

"Your alarm was on?" asked the first officer, puzzled, as the others shouldered past. He was thirty or so and sweating. They had all seen the exterior alarm light just go off.

Amanda nodded and swallowed. She leaned on the hall table and suddenly felt ill.

"All evening," she managed. "Turned it on j-just . . . after seven and . . ."

"Your call was logged at 12:19," he said, quick-glancing into the interior. Another policeman, blue-eyed with black lashes, stepped back to listen. "You heard an intruder?" he asked intently.

With difficulty she told them. The creaking noises, the unmistakable sound of footsteps in the attic. Peripherally she saw the other two cops running up the stairs; also caught the glance exchanged by the pair standing before her, and felt suddenly defensive, embarrassed.

"And you're sure the alarm was never turned off during those five hours?" asked the first officer.

"Absolutely." She was still shaking uncontrollably.

Another glance exchanged, and then, from the blue-eyed one: "We'll go have a look."

They checked everywhere. Upstairs, downstairs, opened closets, looked under beds. Two checked the basement while Amanda followed the other two up the old staircase off the second floor hall to the enormous attic. They turned on the feeble overhead lights and swung their flashlights back and forth on the floor.

"Dry as a bone up here," said one. "No dust. Can't tell if anyone's been here in five years."

They poked under trunk lids and piles of old-fashioned quilts and swept their flashes under an old Victorian sofa. Nothing. One found an overturned floor lamp just feet away from a squirrel's nest inside a hole in the eaves and said, "There's your problem. Jeez, they make a mess." The other policeman, coming to look, pointed out the additional fact that old houses creak and, after all, the alarm *was* on the whole time.

Stupefied, Amanda followed them back down to the first floor central hall. Where the four, regrouped and exchanging notes, were soon rejoined by the two who had reconnoitered the outside. Nothing, reported the older of the outside pair—almost apologetically, it seemed to Amanda.

He said, "We checked every door, window, the back terrace, the sides and rear of the house. Saw two raccoons and a hoot owl and that was about it." He had dark crescents under his eyes and looked very tired. All six of them looked tired and suddenly deflated: a late-night cop's expression that said, Well, that's it. Just another false alarm. They started to head for the door.

Amanda fought her mounting feeling of desperation.

"Wait," she said, her eyes imploring them. "There's more. Something *bizarre* I didn't mention before but . . ." She groped. "A water faucet that I remember quite clearly having turned off came blasting on minutes later, full force. Not dripping but *blasting* . . . violently, as if someone had deliberately opened it all the way."

She waited. Saw the sheepish looks pass between them before the one with the blue eyes and dark lashes spoke up.

"Ma'am, we've searched this house from top to bottom and there's nobody. Now, faucets can sometimes act kind of funny, so maybe it would be a good idea to . . . uh, call a plumber in the morning."

She stared at him, her gaze helpless.

"Plumber," she echoed tonelessly.

Mortified, she saw them to the door and thanked them; stood

there with her arms folded tight as the blue-eyed one filed through last.

He stuck his head back in and looked at her, his face strong, sympathetic. "I'd get jumpy in a place this big," he said. "Get that alarm back on."

She nodded, resigned and infinitely weary, and said, "Right."

IN THE SQUAD CAR, the blue-eyed one sat at the wheel as his partner got in and slammed the door.

"Whew," said the other man as they drove away. "Is that lady flipping out or what? Think we should have left her like that? I mean, maybe she needs a doctor."

The man who was driving seemed deep in thought. "She is a doctor," he said. "Name's Hammond. She's a psychiatrist. She's the one who—"

The other one slapped his brow. "The Payne kid. Of course! That's *her?*"

They continued in silence for a moment, and then the man in the passenger seat voiced what they both were thinking. "You see that overturned bottle of pills in her bedroom?" The blue-eyed man nodded solemnly as he guided the car. He was feeling sorry that a woman that pretty should be alone and upset with pills strewn all over her bedroom floor.

"We'll have to put it in the report," said the other one.

"Yeah," answered his partner. And stepped on the accelerator.

WHAT'S HAPPENING? was all she could think. What is *happening?*

Shaking, Amanda lay in bed with her hands over her face, wondering if she was having some kind of breakdown. In the reddened darkness behind her lids she saw the policemen searching the house: *Nothing, ma'am . . . just squirrels . . . your alarm was on.* She opened her eyes, and the police were gone. Now she saw the water blasting full of hate into the sink basin. Heard—yes, goddammit, *heard*—the muffled, hurried footsteps heading full of purpose across the attic floor toward the stairs leading down.

"Squirrels," she said aloud, laughing a bit hysterically, then feeling the sting of tears. If the police were right (and all logic pointed to the fact that they were), then why was her heart continuing this terrible, lurching beat, as if it knew the unknowable and was staging its own frantic form of protest?

With a rustle of bedclothes she twisted onto her side, stared out at the night, and thought about that fragile thing that people called sanity. Thought about trauma, and the way it weakens our psychic defenses as a dreaded virus weakens our physical defenses. Makes us strung up and suggestible and even prey to . . . *say it* . . . hallucinations. False perceptions. Hysteria.

She thought back to patients she had had who were utterly convinced that they had seen and heard what wasn't there. One at Bellevue—an intelligent man beset by sorrow—had sworn to her that Jesus spoke to him from the radio . . . except that it had to be a particular station. And another patient, a woman ad executive undergoing intolerable pressure, had been brought in screaming one morning that she had opened her desk drawer and seen flames leap out at her.

There was no persuading these people that their experiences were not *real,* and that was what terrified Amanda. Not specifically the water blasting or the footsteps in the attic anymore *(all old houses creak, Ma'am),* but simply the helpless, grinding worry that she might actually be losing her mind.

"Please," she wept, pressing tight fists to her eyes. "Not that."

For just a moment, it occurred to her to wonder if someone was trying to *make* her lose her mind, but such was her turmoil that she was unable to focus, and the thought slipped quickly away.

She opened her eyes and lay there staring despairingly into darkness, knowing that there would be little sleep for her tonight.

AND HALFWAY DOWN THE NARROW, winding old back stairway that connected the former servants' quarters to the kitchen, a newly broken floorboard gaped, as if someone in a big hurry had come crashing down on it and broken through. Had the police known about this stairway, they would have had no trouble finding fibers of ripped sock, torn, rubber-soled shoe, and blood, plenty of blood, as if the deep scrapes inflicted by the needle-sharp, dry wood splinters had come when the individual yanked his foot *out* of the hole. And the fact that the blood was now already drying in the darkness would have no bearing. Forensic pathologists could blood-and-tissue-type an Egyptian mummy from the most minute scraping dissolved in saline solution.

But the stairway had not been used since Amanda was a small child. She had not forgotten that it was there; she simply never thought of it. And on this dreadful night, as she lay there weeping into her hands and fighting to keep a grip on her sanity, her mind was in no shape to think of a musty old childhood staircase, where—of all things—she used to play a pretend game that monsters were stalking her.

33

JOE MCHUGH'S PHONE RANG AT 12:47. He had been sitting, brooding, at his desk in his dark bedroom when his wife Peg picked up behind him, and greeted one of the men on night duty in a voice that was only a little groggy.

"Hi, Tom," he heard her say as she turned on the lamp. "No, don't be silly. No apology necessary."

He turned in his swivel chair to look at her, marvelling as he always did that she could still wake like a shot and be gracious even for a four A.M. call. Twenty-six years of being a policeman's wife, he thought. Some wives showed strain after a few *months,* but Peg? There she was, her cheeks flushed from sleep, propped up on pillows and reassuring the caller that no, Joe hadn't gone to bed yet, and, yes, if it concerned *that* case he was interested. She took more than an interest in his work; she was a participant, a sounding board. And had told him plenty of times that she wished she had gone into police work years ago instead of the administration job she held at the Town Hall.

"Trouble at that Dr. Hammond's place," she said worriedly, holding the receiver out to him. "Talk to Tom."

He got up and crossed to sit next to her on the bed. Took the phone, grunted hello, and listened.

On the other end Tom Renke relayed the report of Officers Camp and Abruzzi. Told of Dr. Hammond's highly emotional state, and her insistence that she had heard an intruder although her alarm had been on. "They searched and only found signs of squirrels in the attic and a floor lamp that looked as if it had just been knocked over, but they radioed in anyway."

McHugh looked blearily across to the dark window and gave a

tired push to his logic. He felt his wife's gaze on him as he said, "Okay. For now add it to the Spook File. She claims she only heard the intruder?"

"Right. But said he was making noise *deliberately,* which is the part that doesn't fit."

"You're right. Well, add it anyway, we'll have a better look in the morning." McHugh hesitated. "She's all right? They felt okay about leaving her?"

"Yes. Abruzzi said he felt sorry for her, but she seemed better when they left."

McHugh hung up, his frown deepening until his wife leaned over closer on the pillow.

"Spook File? You've got to be kidding."

He shrugged. "So named by the men. We've got a bunch of cases we didn't even *think* were cases until someone noticed a pattern recently." He shook his head. "Filed complaints far apart and spanning years, all sworn statements of people insisting that someone had been in their homes while their alarms had been on. And that's *all.* No assaults, just people insisting they had felt watched." He sighed. "Most of these complaints were given the little-old-lady-reporting-her-nightly-prowler treatment until two happened that were . . . different."

His wife looked at him, coming more awake now. "How different?"

He got up and pulled open his pajama drawer.

"One woman reported her dog was barking at two in the morning. She went down to investigate, and found him nearly dead from a savage blow to the head. Another couple reported an emerald necklace stolen, and couldn't collect from their insurance company because how could jewels have been 'stolen' from a house where the alarm had been on? The police had nothing, absolutely nothing, to go on. There wasn't even proof that the woman hadn't beaten her own dog, or that the emerald couple hadn't attempted an insurance scam. Anyway, the detectives would be more likely to think of this than the patrolmen. Camp and Abruzzi called in on Hammond because she was Kelly Payne's doctor."

McHugh pulled out blue pajamas, and stood there clutching them with a faraway, troubled look.

Peg McHugh plumped up the pillows and sank back down sleepily.

"You know," she said, "I think some of the security systems these people have are worthless. I hear stories all the time—they put in expensive alarms, then hire help who come and go and don't give a damn. Couldn't, say, a former housekeeper or caretaker make copies of keys before they quit or get fired? Even *sell* copies of keys if they're afraid to actually rob?"

He nodded and sat on the bed again.

"Sure it's possible, we've already thought of that. And found that these homes have also had everyone in them from decorators to delivery men and workmen who could have filched and copied keys. Suddenly you're trying to investigate hundreds of people and you're not even sure why." He pressed his lips hard together, turning his thoughts uneasily back to Tom Renke's call.

"Something about Dr. Hammond's claim just doesn't wash. This so-called intruder sneaks, if he exists at all. He's never been described as *deliberately* noisy. Could she have heard one of those stories and decided to mimic it? Pretend . . . oh, hell, I don't know what. My mind's going around in circles."

"You need sleep," his wife said firmly, gathering up the pajamas and pressing them into his hands. "If you're tired and upset you won't be able to think, and maybe what happened at Dr. Hammond's tonight . . . well, *means* something."

34

THEY SAILED THE NIGHT SKY, two kids laughing, in a boat that was a wooden shoe, on a wind that sped them high over the safe and sleeping town. "Never afeared are we!" they called happily to the old moon and the stars, who wept as their rushing cloud stream turned into rapids and plunged them, wailing, into the water off the coast of her home. Oh God! She saw them sinking, leaving nothing but a froth of bubbles and a blue chiffon gown floating on the surface. She reached for the gown, her tears streaming, and lay on her back in her bed in the pale light of dawn.

A dream, she realized. She lay there trembling, wishing away the terrible sight. Then remembered. Kelly, so many years ago. Begging for another reading of *Wynken, Blynken, and Nod*.

"Again, oh pleeese?" she'd beg in that high, three-year-old voice. Especially in times of stress. Out of a book crammed heavy with poems and nursery tales, she had picked that most exquisite of childhood sedatives for her favorite.

"Okay, once more," Amanda would say, only pretending to be stern. Sixteen years old and unhappy, she had discovered for herself the mesmerizing comfort of those magic lines, had memorized them, practically . . .

Wynken, Blynken, and Nod one night
Sailed off in a wooden shoe,
Sailed on a river of crystal light
Into a sea of dew.

She got up and went shakily into the bathroom, where she stood staring for a full minute at the blue porcelain sink. The water. Emily. Running footsteps. Police.

She came back into the bedroom, brought her watch up and

squinted at it. Six-twenty, she thought dully. Could have slept till seven.

Ashamed, she bent and gathered the mess of strewn pills into their vial. Then she got back into bed, and lay and thought. Outside, the sky was fogged and the color of gun metal. She reached out, turned on the clock radio, and heard the weather report for Fairfield County: overcast and sultry with dropping barometer; rain later. How dismal. Just the ticket for a depressed person. Well, that finishes me, she decided. I do not want to face this day. I'll call Josie and tell her to cancel the morning, too.

"Never afeared are we!"
So cried the stars to the fishermen three,
Wynken,
Blynken,
And Nod.

Maybe I'll get dressed, at least.

She got up and showered, which made her feel a little better. She brushed her teeth; pulled on her shoes and a cap-sleeved beige linen dress, and limply congratulated herself. Truly despondent people can't even tie their shoelaces; at least she was *moving.*

And in the lonely kitchen, standing waiting for the toast to pop, another notch of strength came from a source she never dreamed she'd use, the Alcoholics Anonymous credo: Get through one blinking day at a time. She found herself buttering the toast angrily, under full power now, thinking of Kelly, of the fact that a murderer was walking around free. Had she really thought of canceling and hiding away? *Get through this day,* she stormed at herself. *That's what you tell your patients, isn't it?*

She carried her toast and coffee into the breakfast room and sat. The phone rang, and she spilled the coffee jumping to get it.

"Hello?"

Peter. Sounding tense.

"How's Emily?" she said in a rush. "Are you at the hospital?"

"Not yet, I called in. Emily is stable. The question is, how are *you?* McHugh just called me. What happened last night?"

Amanda gripped the phone tighter. "I don't know. I thought I heard noises. Got scared and called the police." She swallowed painfully and added, "Maybe I'm just going a little crazy."

"You're not going crazy, don't talk like that. Just tell me: McHugh says you heard *footsteps* in the attic?"

"Yes. Don't remind me. The police came and found a squirrel nest up there and pointed out that the alarm had been on the whole time. I'm not really sure *what* I heard now. Maybe it was all a bad dream."

"No." She caught fear in his voice. "Amanda, I don't like the sound of this. Whatever it was, you shouldn't be alone. Not one more night in that house if I have to drag you out of there."

She closed her eyes; pressed her fingers hard against her brow.

"I don't even want to think about tonight. First I have to get through the day. Call me later, okay?"

With an ache, she hung up. Sat and stared at her breakfast; played stiffly with a spoon. Across from her in the small room, the television lodged in the crowded bookcase looked too blank, too unspeakably lonely and still. Wouldn't hurt to hear a few minutes' worth of sprightly voices talking, she decided.

She got up and turned on NBC's "Today" show. Stood there with her hand on the knob, open-mouthed with surprise as she watched Jane Pauley interviewing Vicki Linford, of all people. Looking very glamorous, with her wild, red hair, her elaborate makeup. And announcing that she was planning to quit her TV series to attempt bigger things. Broadway. Feature films. The actress was incredibly affected, Amanda noticed. Sat there, declaring her oh-so-sensitive distaste for Hollywood, and her plans to move to Connecticut. ". . . just *surrounded* by history," she was gushing.

Amanda made a moue of distaste. *Half of Hollywood is already here, you ninny.*

She turned off the set. Gathered together her things, including the old scrapbook that she wanted to show to Suki. Do I have everything? she thought to herself. She remembered McHugh telling her yesterday: *Whoever took Kelly's tapes knows who you are. Be careful!*

Yes. I'll be very careful, she thought.

She ran back up to her parents' bedroom, and got out her father's old .38. She turned it in her hands for a moment, wondering just how crazy a thing this was to do. *My father would tell me to take it. Definitely.* Quickly, she opened the gray cardboard box of bullets, pushed six into the revolver's cylinder, checked the safety, and slammed the cylinder closed. Then she looked at her purse. Too small. The gun would bulge.

In her room she made a switch. Transferred everything—wallet, keys, cosmetics, and gun—to a large, floppy shoulder bag. She hefted it: the gun disappeared to the bottom of what looked like any woman's bulging carry-all. For extra camouflage, she stuffed a T-shirt and some jogging shorts on top, then pulled in a long, deep breath, feeling safer, and finally left for Brooklawn.

AND A MAN, dressing in his bedroom, had the same TV show on and stopped to stare. The actress! he thought, astonished. He came closer, limping, touching his hand to the screen. He was seeing her *again?* The sex kitten in the hot tub!

He dropped onto his bed, still staring. Oh, look, she's saying she's moving here for the *history,* the little phony! It's too much! Gold digging, Hollywood trash!

Her posturing was making him sick. *Only one posture for you, bitch.* He zapped off the TV, and with a groan stretched his leg out and examined his ankle. Still throbbing, the puffiness showing even through the sock, and that wasn't good. He had been seen walking normally yesterday. People would wonder what he had been up to last night.

Last night. He stiffened as he thought about it, smiling to himself.

She had been easy, a marionette on strings without knowing it. Even called the cops as he had hoped . . . good, she's told the world she's overwrought; her end will look like a suicide.

If only he hadn't gone through that damned stair in his rush to get out . . .

Painfully, he got to his feet. Cursing, limping, he went into the bathroom and took a painkiller. A strong one. He would need more tonight, when he would have to carry her . . .

And then? To celebrate? He laughed out loud, anticipating his favorite hobby.

He left his home hoping that the actress would be back on Country Club Lane tonight. He thought he knew how to find out.

35

THE PHONE RANG shortly after Amanda's first patient left, and Josie buzzed in to say it was someone named Susan Weems. Amanda picked up and greeted the girl.

"Is everything okay?" she asked. "Did you manage to get through the night?"

"Yes. It went okay." The young voice sounded shaky, depressed, Amanda thought. "That policewoman they had stay with me was nice. We . . . talked. It was nice to have c-company, but now . . ."

Silence. The voice had choked up, and now whimpered softly, trying not to.

Amanda said feelingly, "It must be so lonely in that place. You shouldn't spend the day alone . . ." She had an idea and leaned forward. "Susan. I know someone else who's lonely. Dying of loneliness, in fact. It's Brian. Why don't you come over here and visit him? It would be good for both of you."

The silence on the other end became startled. "Oh, I couldn't. I don't even know him. What would I *say*?"

"It doesn't matter. Just visit him." Amanda smiled into the phone. "Listen, you've put a bug in my bonnet and now *I'm* asking *you*. Would you come and visit Brian? Really—you'd both feel better. Wait . . . let me check his schedule."

She pulled a stapled stack of papers to her and scanned. "Here," she said. "He's free today from three o'clock on, and if I know him he's going to be sighing and pacing the place like a caged tiger. Will you come?"

192

Susan's voice wasn't depressed any more; just shy. "Okay," she said.

THE SECOND SURPRISE came when Amanda was standing by the private rear door saying good-bye to Lucy Renwick, and Josie came in. There was someone to see her, Josie said.

"Who?"

"That Detective McHugh. He says he only needs a few minutes." Josie looked shaken by the returned presence of the police.

And Amanda felt her stomach muscles tighten. He's here to ask about last night, she thought. Wants to see for himself if I've gone round the bend.

But McHugh surprised her by coming in wearing an uncomfortable expression and taking the previous night very seriously. "I read the report," he said, sitting down in the club chair facing the desk. "But I wanted to hear for myself. Footsteps overhead and splashing water—that's what you heard?"

Amanda looked stolidly at him as she lowered herself into her chair. She noticed that his question had sounded a little rushed; rehearsed, almost; something to be gotten through quickly before coming to the point. She sat very straight in her chair, and shook her head.

"Heard the footsteps, *saw* the water. Blasting as if someone had spun open the tap all the way."

His gaze was as stolid as hers. "Where? The blasting water was where?"

"In the bathroom, right next to my bedroom. Then came the footsteps, in the attic above my head, loud, deliberate."

"Deliberate," he echoed, engrossed in the carved mahogany front of her desk.

"Unless," she sighed with weary but unmistakable sarcasm, "it was all a bad dream. A delusion, perhaps."

He raised his brows and gave her a long, considering silence. "No. Your story's too consistent. I've sent men back this morning to see if they can find any footprints. The daylight might help."

She looked at him. "After this drought? The ground's hard."

"You never can tell." He glanced at his watch and cleared his throat, as if now getting to what was really on his mind. "Six before eleven," he said. "I figured you'd be free for a bit, since psychiatrists' hours are really forty-five, fifty minutes. That right?"

She nodded, hands clasped before her. Timed to the minute, she thought.

"Well." He shifted his weight. "I had a couple of questions more I wanted to ask you. Purely routine. We're going back to quite a few people to fill in some gaps."

"Such as?"

"Such as, for starters, the purely ridiculous fact that I never asked you on Sunday night what time you got home Friday night. From New York. An oversight, of course. Heat of the moment."

She picked up a ballpoint and turned it in her fingers. "Of course. It was a little after one when I got back. I was at my med school class reunion and I'm afraid I stayed too late. Left around midnight for a trip that should have taken forty-five minutes, but there was a traffic tie-up. An accident ahead, in . . . Rye, I think; had traffic stalled for about twenty minutes."

"Ah. You were on the Merritt Parkway or the Turnpike?"

"The Merritt." Amanda stopped turning the pen and stared at it. He'd be checking on that accident, she realized angrily. Then sighed. Stay objective. Just routine, he says.

McHugh got up and walked thoughtfully over to the glass bookcase. He stood eyeing it for a moment, then turned and looked reluctantly back at her.

"The only prints found on this thing were yours and your secretary's, I'm afraid. It's not surprising. We can assume a thief would be wearing gloves. But, gloves or no gloves, he—assuming it's a 'he'—has told us a lot about himself, hasn't he? Like the fact that it's someone who knew Kelly and also knew about you, your office, the fact that the tapes would be here. Can you think of anyone who might fall into that category? Someone who knew"—he raised his shoulders—"well, as much as you know."

Assuming it's a "he?" Amanda felt her anger come back red-hot. The little routine questions had become an interrogation, she realized, and she was furious to be put on the defensive.

"All my patients know where the tapes are kept," she said tartly. Her hands clutching the ballpoint were trembling. "And Kelly could have told anyone else what her sessions were like."

"But something still seems wrong." McHugh held up a finger.

"I mean, who of all those people would have had the nerve, the absolute cool, to just come walking in here plain as day and help himself? Not knowing whether or not he'd be seen, and not seeming to *mind,* apparently." His eyes probed hers. "I frankly find it hard to believe that such a cool customer exists, unless of course he, or she, felt they *belonged* here in the first place."

The only prints found were yours, I'm afraid. Struggling for control, Amanda rose stiffly to her feet.

"It's an interesting theory, Lieutenant. Why don't you talk to every psychiatrist in the county? They *all* come and go, own gloves, and feel they belong."

By the half-open door, McHugh's heavy features were somber. His voice dropped low so Josie could not hear. "You've taken offense, Dr. Hammond, and I'm sorry for that. But it's my job to consider every possible angle. Such as: tapes stolen by someone who knew he wouldn't attract attention. Such as: a girl murdered next door to you less than an hour before you claim to have come home Friday night. Such as: a handsome young patient who's emotionally dependent on you until he falls in love, and then—what? Jealousy, maybe? It's not within the realm of possibility?"

Amanda's face went dead white. "It is time for my next patient, Lieutenant." She opened the door wider for him. "I'm sure you know your way out."

FURY, HORROR, NUMBNESS—they collided in her mind like birds unwilling to settle.

Clutching her old scrapbook, she walked on weak knees across the foyer. Moved down an opposite hall till she came to an open door where she stopped, caught Brian's eye, and exchanged nods with the group therapy leader. Brian bounded from his seat in the circle of chairs like a big kid let out of school; she had told him earlier she'd try to get him out of his 11:00 meeting, and he had been waiting. He was wearing a navy T-shirt and jeans.

"Outside," she said, when he was at her side with questioning eyes. "Feel like some fresh air?"

He followed her out. Down the lawn and into a shaded English garden with brick walks and crowded flower beds. Most of the early fog had burnt off; what remained was hot haze and a blurred, white sun with the palest rims of thunderheads in the distance.

They sat on a stone bench under the shade of a wide-spreading copper beech tree. Brian had sensed Amanda's tension immediately: that clipped, uncharacteristically hurried way she had spoken in the hall; her rushed, slightly jerky stride as she headed for this tucked-away place. Something was on her mind, he knew. He waited.

"Brian . . ." She placed the scrapbook on her lap; clasped her nervous fingers on it; inhaled. "Something's bothering me. Yesterday, after you told me about Friday night, something came back to me that just didn't seem right. Didn't fit. Only I can't remember what it was. Could we go over it again?"

He nodded; ran his hand thoughtfully through his dark hair. His expression was still solemn, but he had his grip back, she could see.

"Sure. I think I remember more today, in fact. Got some more circuits reconnected." He looked at her, leaning forward with his elbows on his knees. "Listen, do you have, um, one of those things women use to powder their noses with?"

"A compact?"

"Yeah, that's it. Give me yours for a minute. I'll go back over Friday but I also want to show you something."

Amanda dug in her shoulder bag (picking her way carefully around the gun), and gave her compact to Brian. He opened it, checked out the small circular mirror, and peered up for a second into the light-dappled branches. "Good," he said. "This'll work. Okay . . . Friday."

As if in a long sigh, he forced himself again through the nightmare. The desperate feeling of being sick drunk; the eerie light; the man's shadow; hearing Kelly scream—

"Wait," Amanda said, tensing. "That's it. Kelly's voice. Something about Kelly's voice. Tell me again what you heard."

Brian dropped his head; shook it. "That part's still a blur. I've tried to remember what she said but . . ." He shrugged helplessly. "I just can't be sure."

Amanda looked at him. She felt something—something frightening and coming closer to the surface and yet undefined. "Brian," she said quietly, "try to remember. Maybe she screamed her assailant's name, or something that could be . . . important."

"Maybe," he said dubiously. "But she'd had a lot to drink, too. Maybe her speech was slurred. People don't talk so good when they're baked."

And people don't hear so good when they're baked, either. Amanda sat there, staring at him. Tried to catch at her thoughts of a moment ago, but couldn't.

She opened the scrapbook and pointed to the photo where the young workman was standing a short distance behind her and her father.

"Twenty years ago," she said, showing it to Brian, angling it on her lap so he could see better. "Does that face look even remotely familiar?"

He looked; peered at the longish dark hair, the angular features. Shook his head. "Can't make him out. His face is in too much shadow. This guy was working on your property?" He shrugged. "It could even be my father."

Amanda caught her breath. It was getting hot, even here under the drooping-branched tree, and she was feeling suddenly feverish and trembly.

"Your . . . father?"

Brian gestured ambiguously. "He's hollered at me plenty about how easy I've had it. Told me how he used to work for rich people, every odd job he could get to make ends meet. Vacations, summers during college, he dug swimming pools, did carpentry, built decks and cabanas—"

Vacations, Amanda thought.

Brian looked back at the old photo, pondering. "Twenty years ago? That would make him twenty-four then, out of college, but still doing carpentry and stuff 'cause he wanted to save up money to start a business. Then realized he already *had* a business." Brian shook his head in reluctant wonderment. He had opened Amanda's compact again; was tilting the mirror in his hand to catch dappled beams of sunlight. "Such a hustler, he always was. My mother had been smitten with him since their senior year, and her family was horrified. What? A carpenter? So he went and gave a name to this bunch of guys he had working for him. Called it Kirkley Contractors. It sounded better."

Brian's voice faded as Amanda's heart sank . . . *bunch of*

guys . . . The young man in the photo could have been any of them . . . or none of them. She blinked. Brian was droning on. Triavil had a tendency to make people talkative, she remembered.

". . . by which time her parents *had* to let them get married, 'cause she was already two months pregnant with me. She admitted it: I had figured it out from my birth date and their marriage date. See? A hustler to the core. He got her knocked up. I was his ticket, no more." Brian's pursed expression was bitter.

He twisted around on the bench, faced the tree trunk, and used Amanda's compact to refract a thin ray of light onto a stretch of smooth, gray bark. "The light from Kelly's house," he said softly. "I was wrong. It looked like this instead."

Amanda twisted around, too. Watched him move his beam about three inches, from left to right, across the texture of the trunk. "A short arc," he said, "'cept the light was huge."

Amanda looked at him, her heart thudding. "A *short* arc? Not floating free, like you thought yesterday?"

"No. I was still out of it yesterday. I'm sure now this is what it looked like." He turned back, closed the compact, and put it back in her lap. Sighing heavily, he repositioned his elbows on his knees and hung his head. "Just can't figure what that damn light means," he muttered.

"A short arc," Amanda prompted, and now it was a struggle to keep her voice even. "Like something, ah, getting thrown a short distance?"

"No. More like . . . I dunno . . . a windshield wiper arc. You know those TV computer graphics? Geometrical shapes that flip around?"

She stared at him, pops of sweat springing to her arms, her back, her brow. "Wait. A windshield . . . you mean, the shape turned on the same *pivot?* The same . . ." A devastating thought came to her. "The same *hinge?* Brian, could it have been a door—one of those glass French doors off Kelly's terrace?"

He lifted a look to her, his features disturbed. Then he dropped his head again.

"No. Too high up. What I saw wasn't on the first floor."

"But you were drunk! Was the world spinning, Bri? Topsy turvy? And it was high tide. Was the water a little rough? What about the moon? It was a three-quarter moon last weekend. That much moonlight can shine pretty brightly on something, say a *door that's being pushed open,* it can"—the hairs on her arms stood straight up—"it can make it *glow,* Brian!"

He paled. "Jesus," he said softly.

Involuntarily she stood up. The space under the tree seemed suddenly suffocating, claustrophobic. "Let's walk," she said tremulously.

He hurried out after her and up a brick walk. "Someone was . . . *in* the house? And came *out?* It's not possible! The place was locked up!"

"Right," Amanda said in a low, intense voice. Her throat. Tight as a vise. She stopped by a sundial surrounded by miniature roses. "Just like *my* place was locked last night, only listen up, Bri, because either I am losing my mind or someone was creeping around in my house, too. *After* I had locked up and turned on the alarm. I thought it was footsteps in the attic, the police came and said it was squirrels. So I made a fool of myself."

He stared at her in unblinking incredulity. *"Both* houses? Someone's been getting into *both* houses?"

She looked down almost despairingly. "I could have rationalized it if not for your windshield wipers."

Brian stood there dumbstruck, feeling the first surge of adrenaline he had felt in what seemed like a century. Had she, his *psychiatrist,* actually just said *I am losing my mind?* And her red-veined eyes . . . her look of haunted vulnerability . . . He realized that some sweeping sea change had just taken place in his life that made him feel like the stronger one. Protective. Worried about somebody else.

She turned away and started heading up the lawn. "I have to visit a friend in the hospital," she said, distracted, jittery. "Walk me to my car."

"What?" He grabbed her arm; stopped her. "Aren't you going to go to the cops? We've just discovered that someone—*has* to be the same guy—was in Kelly's house the night of the murder and your house last night . . . and has the keys to both places! And you're going to go visit a friend in the *hospital?"*

She looked at him for long, troubled seconds. Cards on the

table, she thought. "I don't think the police are in the mood to listen to anything I have to say." Her voice became sarcastic. "They think I'm . . . unreliable."

Brian slapped his forehead and howled derisively. "Those *ass*holes!"

Then became serious. Leaned closer, looking worried and surprisingly . . . older . . . she realized, as if somewhere back in the last three minutes he had crossed the invisible line into adulthood.

"Footsteps sound like footsteps," he said, very patiently, the way she used to talk to him. "They don't sound like squirrels. And your story plus my story don't sound like squirrels, either. Now, are you going to tell this to *somebody,* or do I have to haul my little Datsun out of Patient Parking and go to the cops myself?"

Peter, Amanda thought.

"The Medical Examiner," she promised. "He's . . . a friend. I'll tell him."

BRIAN SAW HER to her car, where he acted like a teenager again.

"Power door locks!" he cried. "I *hate* power door locks!" He bent to look through the open window as Amanda sat at the wheel.

"Never gave it a thought until a friend told me how dangerous they are. People have been drowned in their cars because they skidded off the road into the river, and the water shorted out the electrical system and they couldn't get their locks open. Hell"—he straightened, looked around frowning—"we're surrounded by water, ever think of that? Like, you're driving to the hospital, you'll probably take that road that runs along the Mihonquit, then cross that damned bridge the governor says is about to fall down any day . . ."

Amanda put the key in the ignition and looked up at him warmly. "Something else to worry about. Thanks, Bri. Just when I thought my list was complete."

He stepped back and grinned sheepishly. "Always something new." He glanced at his watch and made a face. "Hey. It's only 11:35. Do I have to go back to that idiot group therapy? Can I *leave* this place if I want to?"

She smiled, revving the engine. "Yes. From here on, it's okay for you to come and go. If anyone asks, say I gave you permission. I'll sign the order later."

He nodded, relieved; waved as he watched her go.

And in her car, driving, Amanda flicked down the automatic locks, felt suddenly and distinctly uncomfortable, and flicked them back up again.

"For God's *sakes,* Brian," she said aloud.

She reached the main road and headed for the hospital.

36

PETER STOOD SHOULDER TO SHOULDER with Detective Sergeant David Rusk and peered up at a solid wall of manila folders. With its crammed, floor-to-ceiling shelves, and its identical, folder-crowded aisles beyond and behind them, the room reminded him of a medical records library.

"There it is," Rusk said, reaching, pulling down one of the folders and checking the code number on the back. "Yup. Gartrell, Lloyd, that right?"

Peter said that it was and took the folder. He opened it, impatient to start reading.

"You know," Rusk said, reading along over Peter's shoulder, "when you first started describing this case, I thought you meant the *other* one. Norwin, I think the name was." He shook his head. "Boy, I'll never forget that one. It was the same kind of thing—someone dying accidentally in a house locked with the alarm on, relatives in an uproar saying such a thing couldn't possibly have happened. That's the one that gives *me* the creeps."

Peter stopped reading and stared at the detective. *I heard noises, but the alarm was on.*

"Norwin?" he asked.

"Yeah. Some lady fell down a flight of stairs and broke her neck. That's all I remember. Want to get that file, too?"

It took them a few minutes to run back to the computer, find the name and number, and be back at the stacks in a different aisle. This time Peter reached up, opened the folder, and started flipping pages.

"Norwin, Jeanette," he said very quietly. He pointed. "Notice

202

the date of her death. Gartrell was drowned almost three years ago; she died four months later. Kinda close, wouldn't you say?"

Rusk looked, and frowned. "Yeah, I'd say."

Peter stared somberly down at the three files he had gathered. Gartrell, Norwin, and Charlotte Hammond. Now what? he thought dismally. Could anything further be connected between these three, or had his feverish mind worried up something that wasn't there. He thought harder: Gartrell and Hammond had the finger-marks-on-torso link; Gartrell and Norwin had died alone, bizarrely, and chronologically close inside locked houses. And what would the police reaction to *that* be? A tub drowning and a stair fall four months apart in a town of heavy drinkers? He had the sudden feeling that they'd see no connection at all; wouldn't *want* to see a connection and open closed cases with so much that was current bogging them down.

He looked up. "You realize what these three have in common? Angry relatives insisting that something was wrong."

Rusk nodded. "I was just thinking along those lines—that the problem in someone's dying alone is they can't speak for themselves. A case gets ruled accidental, it gets filed away and that's that. Unlike *live* complainants who say they saw or heard . . . well, we've got a file that's just heated up again, maybe, and you jogged my thinking on something."

He angled his head and looked down the busy Headquarters hallway. "I think most of the detectives assigned to the Payne case are here, and I know Joe McHugh is here. What time is it? Twenty to twelve? Care to stay for an impromptu meeting?"

Peter nodded and put the three files under his arm. "You're on," he said.

IT WAS JUST AFTER NOON when Joe McHugh, four detectives, and Peter Barron got their meeting underway. They sat at a longish table in a cream-walled room lined with legal books, gray file cabinets, and a counter with coffee on to perk. In the center of the table were two stacks of manila folders. Runaway ivy climbed up the windows that overlooked the police station parking lot.

"These," Rusk said, looking across to Peter and pointing to the taller stack, "are what we've started calling the Spook File. Sworn statements of some very scared people insisting that someone was in their homes while their alarms were on. And *these*"—he pointed to the smaller stack and looked around at his colleagues—"are the fatality file that Doctor Barron has put together. One suicide, two fatal accidents. All cases closed that we should maybe have another look at."

Tapping the smaller stack, Rusk switched his gaze back to Peter. "The men aren't familiar with all of these. Care to give them a rundown?"

Nodding, Peter reached grim-faced for the smaller stack and slid it toward him. Opened the folders and, thumbing quickly, reviewed out loud the main points of each case. "Gartrell, Lloyd," he said. "Forty-eight years old, a Wall Street financier accidentally drowned almost three years ago in his tub in a locked house. Norwin, Jeanette: aged thirty-six, a wealthy housewife who thirty-one months ago fell down a flight of stairs and broke her neck, again in a locked house. Hammond, Charlotte: thirty-two, whose drowning twenty years ago at her shorefront estate was ruled a suicide, despite the presence of small bruises on her shoulders similar to those found on the bodies of many forced-drowning victims, Kelly Payne, for example."

He looked up, taking in the thoughtful expressions of the men around him; the steaming, Styrofoam cups of coffee before them that were going untouched. McHugh at the other end of the table was rubbing his chin, remaining silent.

"Cases like these," he resumed, "stand out more in the M.E. files than they do in police files, because Pathology people remember the *relatives* coming in to argue about the ruling, insisting that the death was horribly out of character. Gartrell's relatives, for example, came and were incensed at the ruling. Said the guy was an excellent swimmer in excellent health and spirits who *hadn't* had that much to drink. They brought a physician friend to confirm that his blood alcohol level of .07 was low; that's just two glasses of champagne; the police found the rest of the bottle near the tub mostly full. Bottom line: if the maid who found him hadn't said that the house had been locked all weekend, there might have been an investigation."

One of the detectives pushed away his coffee and looked unhappy. "First time I've heard of this case," he said.

"You weren't here three years ago," said another.

McHugh raised his brows at the second man and said

defensively, "And if he was? We have to go by the M.E.'s ruling."
He looked down the table at Peter. "Hescock, right? The M.E. back
then?"

"Right. Dale Hescock. A good man with a stubborn streak."
Peter had opened Charlotte Hammond's file and was staring at the
photo on the first page, a woman so beautiful and so eerily similar in
appearance to Amanda that his throat tightened. He flipped more
pages: the coroner's report stating the victim's history of depression;
her high blood alcohol level at autopsy; her husband's tearful
insistence that despite everything, his wife could not have taken her
life . . .

With an ache, he closed the file but kept his fingers possessively
on it.

"And the Jeanette Norwin case," he continued from memory.
"She hadn't been drinking at all. She was athletic and agile. Her kids
were away at boarding school, her husband was away on business,
and she had just locked up, apparently, and was getting ready for
bed."

"Peter," McHugh cut in, tired-voiced, shifting as if he ached in
his chair, "that lady's husband was away a *lot*. She did the bar scene
like a regular and had a list of boyfriends with some pretty flimsy
alibis." He paused. "Although nobody needed alibis since she was in
a locked-up house."

"Exactly," said Peter. "Okay, I'm done. Who's going to tell
me about these other cases?"

"The Spook File," Rusk said, shaking his head. "Weirdest
damned thing you ever heard of."

The taller pile was slid down to McHugh, who put his big
hands on it and looked as though he didn't know whether to laugh
or get angry. He began to sift through the folders one at a time.

"Nine here," he said quietly. "Sworn statements filed over the
years by people whose only complaint was that they felt *watched*.
Always at night; always when the burglar alarms were on; kinda like
the bogeyman. A man wakes from a sound sleep and thinks he sees a
dark figure. A woman in bed with her husband looks up to see
someone standing over them in the dark. Another woman's dog is
bludgeoned, she swears she was alone. Two instances of jewels stolen.
A woman taking a bath, a couple skinny-dipping in their darkened
indoor pool . . . Well, you get the picture. They heard *maybe* a soft

sound, a thud, they *think,* but they're not sure. The pattern's always the same. They call the police, the police come, and don't find a damned thing: no prints, no sign of forced entry . . . although that would be impossible, forced entry, since all these houses are wired to headquarters and if they go off, we know about it."

McHugh looked at Peter, and then almost peevishly around the table. "It's a damned Chinese puzzle if ever there was one. We tried to investigate, and found that all these houses had recently been on the market. You see the link immediately, right? Wrong. Because then you notice that all of these people had musical maids, servants, workmen, decorators, you name it, coming and going." He frowned over at the pile of manila folders. "Then you notice more. Like, how many of those people admit to having been drinking before bed? Or having taken sleep medication? They wake up—they're still out of it. Add to that the fact that this is a small town. Scare stories spread. Scare stories *get copied,* it's contagious. People are nervous, impressionable, especially if they're alone at night."

He shook his head and pressed his lips thin. "And the real estate angle? How much does that really help us in a town where executives get transferred in and out every two, three years? Where some houses are back on the market before the owner's had a chance to hang the drapes?"

"Speaking of which," said a dark-haired detective sitting next to Peter. The man leaned forward and held up the file he had been reading. "Says here Gartrell had only bought his house the year before. Only used it for weekends, in fact. Lived in the city during the week."

McHugh gave the man a weary nod. "So that either means something, or it doesn't, right?"

"Right." The man shrugged. Rusk, sitting opposite, and the detective next to him both nodded.

McHugh brought his attention back to Peter and seemed almost reluctant to continue.

"Finally," he said. "And I really *hate* to be a stickler for pattern, but Dr. Hammond's claim about an intruder last night seems shaky on a couple of points. First, the guy we've been hearing described, *if* he exists, is quiet. He's a sneak, a sick but shy voyeur, maybe. He doesn't go stomping around in people's attics and blasting their water faucets. Also, Dr. Hammond's always had the same, trusted housekeeper. Sure, her house was closed up for a few years, but it still wasn't the musical maids and caretakers kind of thing you see in the other cases."

Peter considered him, his expression dark and dull with frustration.

"Her house was on the market," he said with deliberate slowness. He leaned forward and gazed fiercely into McHugh's eyes. "And this quiet, shy voyeur, *if* he exists, is one hell of a smart mother, have you factored that in? To get into these houses, however he does it, and be gone without a trace by the time you get there—he's a freaking master! Oh, but we can *depend* on him to stay quiet and shy and not pull any Jekyll and Hyde stuff, can't we? Just a quick peek, Ma'am, and I'm outta here. Listen, he acted the way he did at Amanda's for a reason, we don't know why, but for God's sake, the woman's not a liar. You have to take her seriously!"

McHugh stared at him, remaining calm. "But we have taken her seriously," he said mildly. "Which is not to say we as yet believe her."

Peter scowled at him. *"What?"*

McHugh reached out and pulled the stack of folders to him. He took the top folder off and put it on the table in front of Peter, who stared down at it, mute. Amanda's name was on the cover.

"If someone makes a complaint," McHugh continued in the same mild, reasonable tone, "of course we have to file it. Believing and proving are separate issues." He pointed. "See that? Dr. Hammond makes ten."

37

ON IMPULSE, Amanda had stopped for the local paper which she knew would have a picture of John Kirkley in it. It did. Front page. The dashing candidate addressing his supporters at his lavish shorefront estate.

She tucked the paper inside her scrapbook and hurried to the hospital, where, before going upstairs, she tried to find Peter.

"I'm sorry," said his pleasant secretary. "He's just stepped out. Is there a message I can give him?"

"I'll leave a note," Amanda said.

She went into his inner office, where she found some paper and scribbled in handwriting she scarcely recognized as her own. *Brian remembers: Saw murderer come from INSIDE Kelly's house!* With emotional, childlike stabs, she underlined the word "inside" three times. Then scrawled: *Whole story when I see you tonight. Dinner on. (You're the only one I can tell. Cops won't believe me.)*

For a long moment she stared at those last words she had written, feeling her delayed reaction catching up. McHugh and his rotten theories . . . she had controlled herself for the whole time she had spent with Brian, even bit back her fury, her sense of hurt, on the drive over. Now, standing and blinking down at the note in her hand, she felt hot tears welling at last. Impossible . . . this turn things had taken . . .

The secretary came in, carrying lab reports, and looked at her with round eyes.

"Oh! My dear, what's wrong? Is there anything I can do?"

Embarrassed, Amanda collected herself and demurred. "Thank you anyway," she managed. "Would you see that he finds this note?" She placed it under a paperweight in the middle of Peter's desk, and rushed out fighting back more tears, reflecting that the secretary, kindly though she seemed, was probably quite accustomed to seeing people weep in that department.

AND JEAN SIMONDS STOOD THERE, concerned, wondering what to do.

Her gut feeling told her that that visit had to do with romantic problems. Poor Dr. Barron—forever mooning about things he refused to talk about. And the young woman hadn't mentioned any particular Department case; hadn't come brandishing documents or weeping about anyone dying. Besides, there were different *kinds* of weeping, and the look on that lovely young face was . . . hurt . . . definitely not grief.

So. A lovers' quarrel, Jean decided.

Still, she was tempted to take a peek at the note left on the desk. She advanced and bent closer, inclining her head to get a better look—

—and one of the phones in the front office rang.

"Damn!" she said, more out of irritation over the ever-clamoring phones than not getting to read the note.

She hurried to answer; sank heartsick into her chair as she listened to the cop on the other end reporting a hit and run fatality: a jogger, twenty-six years old.

The tragedy was at the far end of the county, a forty minute drive each way.

Hanging up, Jean remembered how exhausted Dr. Barron had looked this morning. It never ends for him, she thought sadly, as the visit of the emotional young woman slipped to the back of her mind. She punched the button for an outside line and dialed police headquarters, where an officer said he would go and inform Dr. Barron immediately.

SUKI WAS HORRIFIED by Amanda's appearance.

"You look white as a sheet!" she cried. "Thinner I *swear* than when I saw you yesterday, and . . . oh, Amanda, you're trembling."

It seemed crazy, but there they were in the hospital room, Suki and Russ, his face wan and spent, making a fuss over *her* as she headed toward the bed to see Emily. Amanda took one look at her old friend's pale, unconscious face, her head swathed in bandages, and felt the horrendous freight of the last thirty-six hours come crushing down on her.

"I have to sit down," she said weakly.

They got her, still clutching her scrapbook, into one of the visitors' chairs. Russ poured her a glass of water from a plastic pitcher while Suki sat and spoke rapidly, soothingly, explaining that Emily was doing reasonably well, not conscious yet but not in a coma, either. The doctors had been reassuring.

"Last night was *our* time to fall apart," Suki said. "They took three hours to get all the lab tests done—three hours!—and, so help me, I died a thousand times. We feared she was going to be paralyzed, or brain damaged—"

"One doctor," said Russ quietly, leaning on Suki's vinyl chair, "admitted that accidents like this can be fatal hours later . . . the brain swells and it's really the pressure that kills . . ." His voice wavered and his eyes filled. "She's alive. God, we're so lucky."

Amanda exhaled tremulously as she wiped at her eyes with her fingertips. She set her scrapbook aside and peered over again at Emily, who lay scarcely four feet away. Chest rising and falling in normal rhythm. A miracle, she thought prayerfully. An absolute miracle.

She got up and went to the bed; picked up Emily's hand and held it while, behind her, Suki babbled away in the voice of a nervous wreck. ". . . poor Davey just cried and cried. But when the doctor called this morning with better news . . ."

She couldn't help herself. She knew that every neurologist and neurosurgeon in the place had probably been in on this case, but dammit, this was her *friend* . . . and, involuntarily, her fingers stole around to feel the pulse, which was strong, thank God (". . . just marched off to school this morning brave as can be . . ."); then raised the wrist several inches above the mattress and let it drop, noting with joy how it drifted down, muscles in control, instead of flopping down like a dead person's . . .

". . . feel terrible," Suki was saying. "I had been planning to go marketing for us yesterday, and procrastinated, and then that dreadful call. Amanda—" There was sharp alarm in the voice. "What have you been *eating?* There's no food in the house!"

Amanda turned, distracted, shrugging. "There's milk in the

cards one day. The gazebo was half up, and he lured her behind it, and apparently started trying to kiss her . . . just as your dad came round the corner, drunk and *mean,* Mandie—you remember how he used to get sometimes." Suki's eyes suddenly widened. "I came running when I heard the commotion, and there was your dad, standing over this bleeding young man on the ground, yelling that he was fired, get off the property before I kill you . . . like that. Your mother was hysterical . . . she had been trying to push him away, apparently . . . and your dad of all things turned on the *other* men—there were only two that day—standing there just as stunned as I was, and he hollered at *them* and made them start tearing down the gazebo with their bare hands." Suki winced at the memory. "A horrible day. Just horrible."

There was a sound and they looked up to see a nurse come in and head for Emily. "Have to check her vital signs," she told them brightly.

They went out into the corridor, eager to stretch their legs, to escape the smothering clutch of the past. Further down, Amanda saw Russ Hagin talking earnestly with one of the neurologists. Her trembling hands clutched the scrapbook.

"But where was *I?*" she pressed. "Did I see this happen?"

"No. You came home from school the next day, and your parents were still fighting. You must have heard about it."

They headed on slow, heavy steps toward the elevators.

"The name," Amanda said, drained. "Would you remember the young man's name?"

Suki ruefully shook her head. "Probably never knew it. These work crews, they advertise in the paper and come and go, and if you want them again they're already out of business. It was the same then. Your dad called them gypsies." Suki's brow creased in concentration. "Although come to think of it, the name of the outfit was something-something construction, or contractors . . . something like that."

"Kirkley?" Amanda asked, and held her breath.

Suki stopped, and turned and stared at her. "Well, my word, that does sound familiar. Kirkley . . . Kirkley . . ." Something dawned. "Amanda, where else have I heard that name?"

Out came today's newspaper from inside the scrapbook cover. With trembling hands Amanda held it, pointed to the face of John

Kirkley on the front page. "Add twenty years," she managed, her voice thin. "Although this man has probably changed very little—"

"That's him?" Suki snatched the paper from Amanda's hands and stared at it incredulously, examining every feature, tilting her head to be sure. She looked back at Amanda, round-eyed. "But they're big shots! This can't be the same . . ."

She trailed off in astonishment when she saw Amanda nodding. Returned her gaze to the picture and slowly sagged with surprise. "I can't believe it. Yes, this is him all right, I'm sure of it. And look at that! Handsome as ever! Practically hasn't aged!" She shook her head in more amazement as she read the caption under the photograph. "Running for . . . *senator?* Shorefront *estate?*"

A feeling of icy Novocaine spread through Amanda as she took the paper back. *John Kirkley . . . the man with the bloody face.*

"I have to go," she said abruptly, kissing Suki, reaching out to press the "down" button. She saw the confusion on her old friend's face and used her eerie new sense of calm to diffuse it. "Watch over Emily," she said. "I'll call later to see if there's any change."

"But what about—"

Amanda shrugged, a little woodenly, she realized.

"I told you. This awfulness of Kelly and Em just had me spooking up the past. But now that I know who that young man became—such an upright citizen—I'm feeling back to normal. Thanks, Suki."

The elevator arrived, and the doors hissed open. Amanda waved good-bye to Russ, still in earnest conversation a few yards away, and got on. Suki started to babble something about going to the supermarket, but Amanda seemed not to hear. The doors hissed closed before Suki could finish, and then Amanda was gone.

38

FUNNY. She wasn't trembling anymore. The feeling of calm begun in the hospital had spread, like an anesthetic, muting her emotions and sharpening her wits. Her hands were cold, though; that was the only thing she noticed as she walked into the busy library and headed for the microfilm section.

Blinking under the fluorescents, she passed half-full library tables and shelves packed with magazines and turnstiles crammed with a hundred years of the *New York Times* in little boxes.

She found an unused microfilm viewer. Hung her shoulder bag on the wooden chair before the machine (her gun at the bottom clunked the chair leg), and went to a wall of drawers.

Near the bottom, she found what she wanted. Not much call for old hometown papers. Stooping, she located the five-year drawer she needed, pulled it open, and found the right box. Went back and turned on the machine and threaded the tape.

They put ads in the papers . . . two other young men . . . Kirkley? Sounds familiar . . . She started in March, winding the tape slowly forward through the classifieds of twenty years ago.

She wound through three pages of Help Wanteds and Full Time Openings and Happy to Trains. (Amazing—the minimum wage back then.) She saw ads for carpet cleaning, paving contractors, masonry work, landscaping, catering/entertaining. In the carpentry section she scanned very carefully, reading through some pages twice. Nothing.

The wheel whined in protest as she turned rapidly to the next issue (nothing), and the next. Then, in the issue dated March 10, she stopped with her hand on the winding wheel, and stared as if frozen at the screen.

KIRKLEY CONTRACTORS. Decks to Docks! Additions. Custom work. Remodeling. Superior Craftsmanship. Call 935-4713. Ask for John, Ray or Gordon.

Her hands were shaking so much she could barely get out the dime to make the copy.

John, Ray, and Gordon. The world's three most determined social climbers. *We've certainly come a long way, the three of us.* Why, Gordie, you never said you had worked on my property twenty years ago! Never once even mentioned it! And Ray Herrick, were you the "Ray" in the ad, hmm? Or might it have been some other old-buddy Ray—a twin!—who had also grown up angry, ambitious and starting his nest egg with John Kirkley?

She remembered Peter saying on Sunday night: *They've been co-connivers since they were kids. Protecting each other's tails every step up the ladder.*

But on Sunday night Peter had only been talking about Kirkley and Herrick, and only knew about their shadier side from something he had heard from his father. Gordon Maitland, with his glad-handing pretensions and his fake-hearty facade, had been the silent partner all along . . .

Amanda pressed a curled fist to her mouth and leaned forward to think. She had some questions she wanted to ask, and knew that only one of the three had to at least *pretend* civility . . .

She took her shoulder bag and her white-paper copy of the microfilm, got up, and started to rush so blindly from her place that she collided with a man browsing the magazine rack.

"Oh! Sorry!"

"No problem," the man said, smiling easily, turning back and reaching up for a copy of the Gardener's Almanac.

GORDON MAITLAND STARED AT HER, and said, "Well, of *course* I never mentioned it."

Amanda remained silent.

He turned his palms up, injured. "It would have caused you pain! To say, Gee, I knew your mother; to mention her in *any* context would have been insensitive and not my place—you don't see it from *my* viewpoint?" The phone on his desk rang. The flashing button went off immediately. He had told his secretary to hold all calls for the ten minutes Amanda had requested.

Amanda looked down, slowly folding the microfilm copy in her lap into halves, then quarters. He had been visibly embarrassed when she had first brought it in. Then had quickly recovered and was now the picture of sincere and injured innocence.

He clasped his hands earnestly on his desk.

"Doctors and realtors," he said sadly. "We know of more heartaches that happen to people than anyone else, isn't that so? Lord, the tales I've heard of nasty divorces and every other kind of debacle . . . you meet these people months or years later and they're *grateful* when you don't mention them."

Amanda leaned her elbow on the chair's arm rest. She held up the folded square of paper between two fingers and said, "Was it just the three of you, working on that gazebo?"

"No," Maitland said a little too quickly. *Bang!* First glimpse of nervousness peeking through.

"By that stage," he continued, "there were two or three others who'd come and go. Journeymen, really; extra men as the need arose and John would pay them by the day." He became garrulous. "The need arose plenty, let me tell you. What happened with John is, he started out alone, doing odd jobs for cash even before he finished college. He got to be in demand, making more than anyone he had just graduated with—no kidding!—so he asked Ray and me to join him. I didn't know the first thing about carpentry"—*Superior Craftsmanship!*, Amanda remembered—"but I needed the money. And Ray had taken a year off to work before going to law school. Well, the jobs poured in faster than we could handle them; that's when John started hiring an occasional extra man or two. And don't ask me if I remember their names, because I don't. Never got past first names anyway."

Amanda sat still, watching him. Already one glimpse of stress and one inconsistency. He had said there could have been as many as six men working that day, and Suki had said there were only two—in addition to John Kirkley. Amanda inhaled, rethinking it. But Suki would have been inside the house (*"I came running when I heard the commotion"*); and, sharp though her memory was, Amanda could not automatically assume that Maitland was lying.

She watched him toying wistfully with a gold Mark Cross pen: a convincing picture of a self-made man not ashamed to reminisce about his early, hardscrabble days. She leaned forward and decided to catch him off guard.

"Tell me what happened between John Kirkley and my mother."

His busy hands froze. Something about him became quieter, more watchful. "You really are raking up the past, aren't you?" he said. He waited, and thought. "Nothing happened. Not really. Good God, that was a million years ago! This is uncomfortable for me!" He sighed; watched a phone button light up and switch off again. "John told us later that your mother had been crying. I guess . . . he was attracted to her. It"—he looked warily at Amanda—"might have been mutual. Anyway, he tried to comfort her, your father caught them in a clinch, and all hell broke loose."

Amanda sat still, waiting. Nothing like silence to prod people on.

"All I know," he continued, "is I was in the driveway with one of the other men getting boards out of the truck, and we heard the ruckus, and came running to find John on the ground with his face bleeding, and your father standing over him yelling."

The gold pen started to twirl again, angrily. "Your father was drunk," Maitland went on. "But even drunk, you know what he was really mad about? Not the fact that he thought his wife might be cheating on him, but that she had chosen *one of the help*. That's what he kept yelling at us. All of us. As if we were dirt." His lips pressed together in a hard, vengeful line.

He looked up; gestured brusquely around his impressive office. "You know, it's people like your father I'd like to bring back for a day. Show him what *the help* have accomplished; tell him . . . tell him . . ."

"So *there*, you bastard," Amanda finished for him, reading his thoughts, smiling sympathetically.

Maitland looked at her, his expression startled.

She smiled again. "I'll bet you'd also like to show what you've accomplished to my mother, wouldn't you? Did you consider her beautiful, too?"

Something—was it jealousy; fear?—flickered behind his eyes, then scuttled back behind his well-practiced facade. He forced a smile. "Of course I considered her . . . pretty. If I considered her at all. She was the lady who hired us, that was all."

Amanda stood up, thanked him for his time, and took her shoulder bag.

Maitland stood up, too.

By the door she stopped, as if suddenly remembering something. "Incidentally, where was Ray Herrick when all this happened? Do you remember?"

Maitland raised his shoulders. "Hard to say. He was already standing there looking shocked when we arrived. But he couldn't have seen what happened between John and your mother because, well, nobody takes a woman he's attracted to and kisses her right in front of—"

"I get your drift," Amanda said tersely.

She thanked him again and went out.

39

PETER GOT BACK TO THE HOSPITAL around four and went straight to Emily's room, where he stood at the foot of the bed conferring with her neurologist, an older attending named Ned Finley. By the head of the bed, Suki stood gripping the siderails over her still-unconscious niece, while Russ Hagin slumped down into one of the chairs and put his face in his hands.

"She's still so pale," he said despairingly. "So pale."

Peter glanced up for a second, aching for the man, then returned his attention to what Finley was saying.

". . . pupils continue to be equal, and there's still no sign of paralysis." Finley shook his head of curly, graying hair in wonderment. "Just can't get over this girl's luck," he said in hushed tones. "Someone else would have wound up dead or with a broken neck."

Peter recalled the family's description of the laundry basket: soft plastic, round and bulging full. There was no question it had broken Emily's fall. "It's incredible, all right," he said in the same low voice. "What I was worried about was a subdural hematoma starting small like hers and *then* swelling, causing damage as much as . . . what? Forty-eight hours later? When do you relax about a patient? Forty-eight hours and they're out of the woods?"

Finley nodded. "Yes. If they make it that far without change you can usually—"

Both men turned quickly as they heard Suki gasp.

"Omigod, she's coming to!" Suki burst into a torrent of joyous tears. "Emily's lips moved! She was trying to say something!"

Russ Hagin jumped up from his chair. The two white-coated doctors hurried to opposite sides of the bed and let down the

siderails, Peter wishing desperately that Amanda were here
now instead of hours ago to see this. Suki had said that she had
cried . . .

"Emmy," Russ Hagin whispered hoarsely, bending, cradling
his wife's face in his hands and pressing his cheek to hers. "Oh,
Emmy, Emmy . . ."

From behind, Peter saw Russ stiffen, then pull away in
confusion as he watched his wife's face. Her eyes were still closed but
busy, agitated; a tear emerged and slid streaming down her cheek;
her lips moved, as if she was trying to speak.

"S-Someone . . ." she whispered.

The four looked at each other. The room became very still.
Peter felt the first faint pulse of fear go through him.

Suki bent anxiously and put her hand on the young woman's
arm. "What is it, dear? You're going to be all right. Russ is here,
Aunt Suki is here . . ."

The pale lips struggled to form words. "Someone . . . pushed
me."

Stunned glances flicked up at each other. Suki clutched a fist to
her chest and Russ Hagin froze. Emily's eyes fluttered and opened.
Cloudy. Swimming with tears. Seemed trying to focus on Peter's
white coat. He stood tense, heart pounding. *McHugh's report says you
heard footsteps?*

Shaken, he saw Suki gape across the bed at Russ Hagin.
"Pushed?" she breathed.

Saw Hagin shake his head No. His face was colorless. "She had
the house locked tight. She'd been nervous about the Payne murder.
Even said when I left that she missed the slide bolts we had in the
city."

*Gartrell, Lloyd: forty-eight years old, Wall Street financier found
accidentally drowned . . .*

Disturbed, Ned Finley had been watching Emily with an
intense clinical eye. He looked up; exchanged glances across the bed
with Peter; switched his gaze to the patient's husband.

"Mr. Hagin, has your wife ever fallen before? Been accident-
prone in any way?"

Hagin winced at the question. "Never." Emily's tears were
streaming down her face now. He had grabbed a Kleenex from the
side table and was tenderly wiping her cheeks. "She's never *ever* been

accident-prone. She's the one who's always cautioning others. Be careful, be careful."

Norwin, Jeanette: a wealthy housewife who plunged . . . locked house . . .

A sense of cold terror slipped into Peter. Suki knew nothing of Amanda's fearful night. And no one in the room knew about his meeting with the police. He saw Finley eyeing him, thoughtful and alert.

"Well now," the neurologist said quickly, looking back to Suki, Russ Hagin. "I don't think I like the sound of this. In a supposedly locked house, the patient has a near-fatal fall, and regains consciousness to say she was pushed. You know, Mr. Hagin, people just regaining consciousness have a hard enough time getting their minds to start functioning again. It is beyond them to invent."

Russ Hagin was gripping his wife's hand. He stared at Suki, a haunted look coming into his eyes. "My wife doesn't invent," he said hoarsely.

"Ever," Suki exclaimed, her features tight with horror. "She *downplays.* Doesn't like people to get upset!"

Finley turned expectantly to Peter, who was already backing up and heading for the door. They exchanged glances; read each other perfectly.

"Have to make a call," Peter muttered. Finley nodded, and Peter bolted from the room with a terrible sense of things coming together.

HE TOOK THE ELEVATOR down to his office to call McHugh, and had the receiver in his hand when he noticed the small stack of messages waiting for him. Absently, impatiently, he ruffled through them: a call from the First Selectman; a call from the State Forensic lab; five calls from news reporters asking about the death of Kelly Payne; and, at the bottom, like a war dispatch hidden under debris, the painfully scrawled note from Amanda.

"What . . . ?"

Still holding the receiver in his left hand, he picked up the small sheet and read it, frowning.

Brian remembers: Saw murderer come from INSIDE Kelly's house! Whole story when I see you tonight. Dinner on. (You're the only one I can tell. Cops won't believe me.)

Payne *and* Hagin? He stopped breathing. He felt ill. He felt as if the worst kind of nightmare had just slipped into fast forward.

"Jean!"

His secretary came rushing in, startled by his tone. He held out Amanda's memo and said, *"This* you could have paged me for. What time was Dr. Hammond here? It doesn't even say."

Jean Simonds looked flustered. *"Doctor?* She never said she was a doctor. And there's no time on it because it wasn't a call-in, she wrote it herself . . . around noon." Flustered gave way to hurt, defensive. "Besides, she never said she was here about any case, so I figured her note was . . . private."

Peter thought feverishly. *You're the only one . . . cops won't believe me.* What in leaping hell had McHugh said to her? He rubbed at his brow, calculating the four and a half hours since Amanda had been here, and fought his rising sense of panic.

"You couldn't have known," he said tightly. "Did she say where she was going to be later?"

"No." Jean shook her head and looked distinctly uncomfortable. "I'm sorry," she said in a faltering voice. "I *should* have had you paged. I . . . she was crying."

Peter looked at her; she looked away and turned disconsolately back for the outer office.

He inhaled; punched for an outside line; and called Brooklawn. Amanda had checked out for the day around noon, they said. He tried her at home: no answer. He thought some more, chewing his lower lip, then punched out the four digits for the fifth floor nurses' station.

It seemed to take them forever to get Suki to the phone.

"Did Amanda say where she was headed after she left?" he asked in a worried voice.

"Peter, no, and it was the strangest thing. Remember how upset I told you she was when she first saw Emily? Well, toward the end of the visit she was . . . different . . . almost wooden. We had been reminiscing, looking at her old scrapbook—"

"Scrapbook?" Alarm pricked.

"Yes. These terrible things—Kelly, Emily's accident—had her . . . well, obsessed about the past. In particular she wanted to know if I recognized a workman, and I said yes. Someone who was at the house building something just two months before her mother died. It was John Kirkley, *the* John Kirkley, can you believe that?"

His heart pounding, Peter promised to keep posted and hung up.

He thought for a moment, rubbing his hand across his mouth, then made his call to McHugh. The detective came on, sounding tense.

"Have to admit," he said in a rush, "we're sitting here going back over some of these files. It's crazy—I'm feeling more spooked about them. Even sent some men back to requestion a few people."

"Which people?" Peter's voice was stiff.

"The lady whose dog was bashed and she got blamed. Lloyd Gartrell's maid who still lives in town. The people who swear their emeralds were stolen in a locked house—"

"Swell. You ready for more? It just got worse."

McHugh became very silent as Peter told him about Amanda's housekeeper's niece coming to after a fall in a locked house, insisting that someone had pushed her. About Amanda's note saying that Brian had seen someone coming from inside Kelly's house on the night of the murder. "Looks like you've got two more names to add to that file," he said. "Hagin and Payne. Someone had keys to their houses." He waited through more silence as his words penetrated. Finally McHugh said:

"I'll send someone to the hospital to question the Hagin family. Did they ever have maids? Any kind of help who might have had their keys?"

"I doubt it. Carpenters working—but I can't imagine them being given keys."

"What about Dr. Hammond? It's plausible she could have had a key to that house."

"Joe, for God's sake!"

"Sorry. I had to ask that question to see how it felt. It felt lousy. Listen, you think I like having to look at every crazy angle?"

"Well, how 'bout the angle that someone could have *staged* that young woman's accident just to get the housekeeper out of Amanda's house? Did you think of that?"

"Of course." There was a tense silence. "Someone staged something, Peter." McHugh moved imperturbably to the next subject. "And what's this about the Kirkley kid? Did Dr. Hammond's note say who he saw? Did he hear anything?"

Peter sagged. Talking to McHugh was sometimes like talking to a claims adjuster on the morning after the hurricane. *Emote and you'll have two problems.* Where had cops learned that better than doctors? He pressed his palm against tired, burning eyes.

"Amanda might have written *volumes* if she hadn't been upset," he said. "She was here around noon—in tears, my secretary says. Joe, what in hell's name did you say to her?"

Defensive. For the first time. "What we discussed at Dante's. About that tape theft being fishy. Someone who knew right where to go, who had no fear of being noticed as an outsider. Who . . ." A weary sigh. "I said my bad-cop thing, too. Just to get a reaction. The maybe-somebody-was-jealous theory, Brian being such a good-looking—"

"Well, that's just great! Jesus, you went too far!"

"You put yourself in my place and tell me what too far is!"

Sullen silence stretched between them, punctuated at McHugh's end by phones ringing and men's voices arguing almost as heatedly. McHugh was the first to cool off.

"Listen. We both have to do our jobs in the best way we know, agreed?"

Peter maintained his moody silence.

McHugh continued as if nothing. "Which means now I'll have to go back to Brooklawn. Hear what that boy has to say."

"No," said Peter irritably. "I don't think he's ready for your delicate touch. I'll go." His head ached. He remembered what he had saved for his parting shot.

"Incidentally, Amanda's housekeeper has remembered positively that John Kirkley worked on the Hammond property twenty years ago. As a carpenter. Two months before Mrs. Hammond's death."

"John . . . the *father?*"

"None other. He knows Amanda's office well. Has been seen there before. Besides, night staffs of these places don't know one face from another. They're mostly part-timers."

"Why didn't you say that *before?*"

"I just thought of it. I'm used to regular hospitals."

"Oh, for Chrissakes." For a moment, the detective was silent, and when he spoke there was genuine conciliation in his voice. "Believe me, there's nothing I'd like better than to wind up apologizing to Dr. Hammond."

"That sounds real nice, Joe." Peter looked out his window. The air was getting darker and storm winds gusted. "But first, you'd have to find her. She's upset, and no one knows where she is, except maybe the murderer who's already managed to find two of her friends."

40

BRIAN HAD PULLED ON SHORTS and a different T-shirt and mapped out a track for himself, starting behind the back of the pool building, sloping down the acres past and around the stand of old pin oak, and rising again on the far side that crested near the parking lot. It was the second, uphill side of this oval that hurt: he was out of shape, he pushed himself, he *punished* himself to run, to pound the meters, to force his stinging chest and leg muscles to help him forget the pain that gripped his heart.

Ten laps . . .

Easing up a little.

Eleven . . . maybe I'll sleep without medication tonight.

Twelve . . . With thumping strides he reached the high, grassy turn when he noticed a man, leaning on a car, watching him. Imagination? No, the guy gave a tense wave; began to approach him. Tall, athletic-looking himself. Another runner, *here?* Naw, not possible.

"Brian?" the man called to him. "Brian Kirkley?"

Not a cop, either. The car he had been leaning on was a Porsche. Brian nodded, slowing to a panting walk as he pressed both hands to his splitting sides. He reached the man, beckoning him to continue moving with him. "Gotta walk it out," he panted. "I'll cramp."

"One week," the other said, pushing his hands into his slack pockets, falling easily into step. "You'll be back in shape in no time."

Brian looked at him, and Peter put his hand out and introduced himself.

"Hey," Brian said. "The Medical Examiner . . . Amanda's friend?"

227

"The same. She's mentioned you a lot, too."

"Her favorite screwball, huh?" Still breathing heavily, Brian reached for a towel he had thrown over the chain edging the parking lot. Wiped his flushed and perspiring face, and took another look at Peter. A very handsome guy. Nice expression, too; maybe a bit worried-looking. "You two just professional or . . ."

Peter shrugged. "We're in love. She just doesn't know it."

Brian laughed for the first time since Friday night. Then his expression turned somber. He tossed the towel over one shoulder, put his muscled hands on his hips. "She was upset a few hours ago, did you know that?"

"Yeah, that's why I'm here." Peter explained about Amanda's sketchy note; about having no information further than that, and not knowing where she was at the moment.

"She doesn't pick up her page?" Brian asked, frowning.

"No. Just signed out. I'm betting she's alone and brooding someplace—I've tried her at home—but I wanted to talk to you before I went looking for her." Peter glanced worriedly up at the darkening sky; the lifting leaves; the anxious, darting birds. "Could you take a few minutes and tell me what you told her?"

"Jesus, of course. I'll tell you everything."

They walked slowly back toward the main house, Brian laying it all out. Friday night, Kelly's blurred scream, the light Amanda had figured out was a first floor French door being pushed open. "From *inside,* no question about it. Somebody had been inside Kelly's locked house while we were docked. Then, Monday night, Amanda heard someone in *her* house, also supposedly locked, alarm on, the same thing, therefore had to be the same guy. Pretty scary, huh?"

They had reached the stone steps of a side veranda, still talking, when they became aware of someone behind them. They turned, and standing on the grass they saw a forlorn figure: a pretty, brown-haired girl in jeans and a T-shirt clutching white paper bags that were bulging with something. She approached and introduced herself shyly. Susan Weems. Kelly's friend. Dr. Hammond suggested she come over because, she said, "I've been climbing the walls. So lonely . . ."

Peter recognized the name immediately; smiled, shook hands and introduced himself.

"*Two* wall-climbers," said Brian, introducing himself.

The bulging white bags began to slide from the girl's grip. "Oh . . ." she said. Both men helped her, and Brian, turning one soaked-through bag around, whooped with joy.

"McDonald's!" he cried. "Real food! Omigod, I don't believe it!"

"I brought you two Big Macs," the girl said earnestly. She looked at Peter. "See, Kelly and I spent just one semester together at college, but that was enough to turn us off institutional food forever. So I figured Brian must be turning into Starch City by now—"

"Coke!" he was yelling, peeking into another bag. "Orange soda!" He motioned to the veranda behind them with wicker furniture. "We can have a major feeding frenzy up there," he said. He looked up; made a face. "Hell, it's starting to drizzle. Guess we'll have to."

Susan actually started apologizing to Peter for not having brought him anything. "I didn't know you'd be here . . ." she began awkwardly. He smiled and held his hands up. "You're very sweet. I have to run anyway."

He said good-bye and watched them head up the stairs to the enclosed veranda. The rain suddenly got heavier, the wind stronger. Both of them turned and gave him one last wave, and then he hurried back to his car.

41

AMANDA PACED THE SHORE'S EDGE. She moved in a fitful, serpentine fashion as she dodged the waves that were coming in, going out, reaching further up the sand each time as if the incoming tide were trying to catch her.

She headed past occasional knots of kids with Frisbees and ghetto blasters for the jetty at the far end of the beach, beyond which, a short walk down grass-tufted dunes, the water stilled into a sheet of sky-colored, grassy marsh. There was no place, *no place,* better for thinking than a salt marsh, with its tall reeds and sea birds going about their business; and after an hour's aimless driving around it was this place that Amanda had remembered and decided to come back to. A childhood refuge where she used to bring her watercolors; her pain. And a secret place, still: a little too rugged for most people to want to spread a blanket.

She hesitated at one point where the dunes were low enough, and looked back across the sand to where she had parked her car. A small parking lot for this small beach at the end of one of the coastal roads. The hot, humid air had turned suddenly darker; thunder rumbled. She heard shouts and curses and saw kids grabbing their sneakers and six-packs and heading for their cars. The wind around her stiffened, and a high, buzzing noise drew her eye to the Sound, where a small launch was pushing its motor too hard in its rush to safe haven.

Pushing its motor too hard. Spinning its wheels . . .

The frightened little launch had given her an unexpected feeling of comfort, of companionship. Now, if she could only calm down enough to think . . .

She dropped into a hunched position on the sand, locked her

arms around her knees, and wrestled for what had to be the hundredth time with the fact that she wasn't sure of anything. Not any more. Not like two hours ago, when she had been convinced that John Kirkley had killed her mother and Kelly. She had added it all up then and it made such sense; *still* made sense, except for a few nagging details that had wormed their way into her thinking, eroding her certainty enough to make her pull back. Two hours ago, she had even cooled off enough of her anger toward McHugh to see things from his viewpoint; to visualize herself actually walking in to police headquarters with no hard feelings and calmly presenting her own set of suspicions.

The thought that tormented her was the simple fact that she wasn't one hundred percent sure; and running to the police with anything less than that, she feared, ran the risk of hurting Brian all over again.

Groaning, she reached for some burnt driftwood and banged it on the sand, like a gavel, as she groped through it all again, dividing her thinking this time in two: the prosecution; the defense.

Prosecution: Overjoyed with the symmetry, the inarguable web of circumstantial evidence. John Kirkley had had the hots for her mother. Oversexed, handsome, turned on by money, he probably never got "no" from the ladies he worked for, and Suki said that her mother had been trying to *push him away*. Bad enough for an ego like that. But along came Amanda's father who made it worse by clobbering him, and . . . what had Maitland said? *Made us feel like dirt.*

So okay. Who was Kirkley really mad at? Both her parents, for sure; but especially her *father*. And what more maliciously clever way to destroy her father than to . . . destroy his wife? A woman known for her depressions and her midnight walks along the water? The ruling of suicide was practically guaranteed. As well as a life of scandal and devastating guilt for the man so savagely hated.

But, continues the prosecution, forensic medicine has come a long way from the days of near-sighted little coroners. Kirkley's kid undoes all his social climbing by getting serious with Miss Wrong, plays into his father's hands by conducting his love life at water's edge . . . and here the attorney turns, stern-voiced, and points to the defendant, saying: you didn't plan on the easy kill not working the second time, did you, Mr. Kirkley?

Amanda looked up, aware that a drizzling rain had begun. Thunder muttered, and a pair of frightened herons rose in a white blur from the reeds.

She got to her feet, turned and walked, heedless of puddles beginning to crater in sand pockets, lending her thoughts now to the Defense.

Loopholes, your honor.

Such as?

Such as Maitland's assertion that there had been other men building the gazebo, besides the core three. It was plausible, despite what Suki said: no different today when work crews swelled and shrank, depending on the season and the demand. Sometimes six men would show up in the morning, dwindle off for lunchtime or "trips to the shop," and you'd be left with just two or three at day's end. And who could say with any certainty that they hadn't *all* had a crush on her pretty mother? And have felt jealousy upon hearing of Kirkley's interrupted romance, whether they had been there to witness it or not? Maitland himself, Amanda had realized, made a good case for the jealousy angle.

Did you consider her beautiful, too, Gordon?

He had recovered quickly, but she had caught—no fooling *her* eye—that fleeting look of fear and envy, that smile forced onto his face while his hands clenched into fists of anger.

And his gray, sullen look of resentment when he had spoken of her father. *One of the help. That's what he kept yelling at us. As if we were dirt.*

Could Maitland have hated Kelly and Brian for being spoiled, rich kids who had never had to struggle? Kill one (who was a political threat anyway), let the other suffer the same devastating guilt that . . . oh, God . . . Amanda closed her eyes . . . had destroyed her father? . . . It was possible . . . It was possible . . .

He's named me campaign manager, did you know that? This is how Reagan's Kitchen Cabinet started, just a bunch of old friends . . .

I don't need real estate any more. I'm getting bored, looking for greener—no pun, ha!—pastures.

John running for Senate! He'll be a shoo-in, providing the campaign goes without a hitch.

Amanda stood still suddenly, the soaking wind whipping her

hair, her dress, and allowed her imagined voice of the Defense to muscle in with the one question she didn't want to hear. *But what established evidence proves that it was the same killer both times?*

And from the judge: *I'll allow that.*

Until today, and her talk with Suki, Amanda had never known that her mother . . . flirted. It wasn't a surprise, when you really thought about it: her mother had been beautiful; had felt unloved and unhappy, and the men *would* smile . . . but what if she had been involved with others? And what if Oh Dear God those others had even been guests at that fateful dinner party, or *anybody* else . . . leaving no twenty-years-apart connection after all between the two murders? No Avenging Angel sense of being so sure, as she had been since Sunday night . . .

She hurried on, the rain coming harder now, great pelting drops that hurt and glazed her face, and wondered if her obsession had blinded her from the beginning; if, after all, some complete stranger could have come upon Kelly and Brian and . . .

No. *The tapes,* she remembered. Someone who knew Kelly and me and the workings of my office. Someone with the ultimate arrogance to come in like that and help himself, not knowing who he'd run into . . .

But they're all arrogant! Every last one of them! And maybe some I don't even know about!

Go to the cops with the whole story, she decided. Every detail. Let them decide. I can't even think anymore.

Wet through and through, she covered the empty beach in seconds and reached her car just as the real rain exploded. A great tropical downpour that streaked white before her hand unlocking the door; streamed the windshield in blinding sheets as she tried to drive, squinting, her eyes smarting from lack of sleep. The road she knew so well was slick; in a few low places, three or four inches deep in water. She skidded badly and panicked; slowed to about thirty and watched in alarm as the wipers battled futilely with the obscuring rain.

To calm her nerves, she took a tape from the pile on the seat next to her, and pushed it into the tape deck. The rain pounded like marbles dumping on the roof as she waited, driving twenty-five now, expecting Aretha or Brahms or she didn't know which tape she had picked, until, blinking, incredulous, she felt a bolt of horror rip through her heart as she heard *Kelly's voice in the car,* pleading with her: "Save me, Amanda . . . only you can . . . save me . . ."

Terror made her press down harder on the accelerator. The car lurched forward; fishtailed. "No . . . !" She gripped the wheel and tried to ride it out, but the brakes were wet, the brakes were useless; she strained her eyes to make out the road just as a shape loomed up, a tree; and she felt her body flung forward in the sickening crunch of metal.

Then . . . pain. Throbbing pain in her knee, her head, sharp as the shards of broken glass in what was left of the windshield. Rain sweeping in. Darkness enclosing her like fog. From somewhere, approaching sirens.

Police. Strong hands, yanking open the door, touching her arm, her face; voices trying to talk to her. Another siren. An ambulance, yes. My turn. And Amanda makes three.

"Hey, you see this?" A man's voice.

The crash had knocked open her glove compartment. She fought the blackness; tried to focus.

They had the passenger door open, too. Cops, leaning in, glistening wet, examining the still-spilling contents of the glove compartment; one of them, brown-haired, holding up a handful of tapes and frowning at them. Reading one label after another: "Kelly Payne . . . Kelly Payne . . . Kelly . . ."

It was as if the roar of the storm had suddenly stopped and hushed as they all stared at her.

"Dr. Hammond?" asked one cop, leaning in, baffled. "You remember me? I was at your office when you reported these tapes . . . stolen."

Amanda, barely conscious, could only manage to stare stupidly at him, at the tapes. She was aware of blood trickling down the side of her face, and the world growing grayer, and some man's voice on her left giving orders to others to move in the stretcher.

After that, she remembered nothing.

42

IT WAS THE RAIN, pelting her face, that brought her to as they wheeled her in. And the pair of cops, staying on in the emergency room the way they did for criminals, that cleared her head and made her furious. She could see their uniforms just outside the thin curtain of the cubicle, and the doctors tending her were having a hard time getting her to lie flat.

"The knee first," said the younger doctor. Red hair. Trying not to sound exasperated. "Just let me get this suturing done, *please,* and then you can throw IV bottles at their heads, if you want."

Amanda fell back, weak, her mind still in turmoil. Her pale beige dress was torn and blood-splattered—a sickening sight, her own blood—but when they had offered her a johnny to pull over it, she had refused, horrified at the thought of losing her identity, of becoming just another patient.

She closed her eyes; fought tears. "Dr. Barron?" she asked in a whisper.

"He's been called," said the second doctor, a pretty black woman who was gently swabbing her head wound. She saw Amanda wince in pain as her colleague's gloved hands made a few more passes with his suture needle; then looked up as the nylon curtain was flung aside and Peter Barron stood there, chalk-faced, his tan lightweight jacket only glazed with rain as if he had run from his car. "My God," he said softly.

He crossed to the exam table where he took Amanda's hand, bent, and kissed her, saying nothing, just listening, as she began to cry softly about tapes and someone who something'd her glove compartment and the police who were outside.

Annoyed, he straightened; looked out at the uniforms; looked back at the intern. "Rand, go tell them to wait by the exit."

The red-headed young doctor went out and told the cops that they were making the patient more agitated. They moved along and he came back, by which time Peter, holding Amanda's hand in both of his, was listening to the second doctor describe Amanda's injuries.

". . . no fractures, a six centimeter knee laceration, some nasty bruises, maybe 50 c.c.'s of blood lost, no more . . ."

Amanda closed her eyes and let it all wash over her. Their voices, droning the old familiar jargon . . . impossible to believe they were talking about her. She hurt so much, all over. Except for her knee, which she couldn't even feel. The Procaine they had given her. It would be wearing off soon. She took a shuddering breath, not wanting to think about it.

The intern finished applying her gauze dressing, smiled tiredly and gave her a thumbs up sign, and left—colliding in the door with a rumpled and very gloomy-looking (but not *wet,* Amanda noticed) Joe McHugh. She closed her eyes and looked away.

"Hell of a thing," she heard McHugh mutter. Peter said something back, but she willed their muted voices to the fringe of her awareness, not wanting to hear, wanting only peace, escape . . . until, from Peter, heated, moving closer to the side of the exam table: "No, Joe, *planted*—that's what caused the crash! She put in a tape thinking it was Bo Diddley or something, and got hysterical. Just as whoever mixed it with her other tapes *knew* she would! Jesus—you don't see this as attempted *murder?*"

Amanda opened her eyes; stared dully at the wall; at nothing; heard the second doctor finish restocking the sterile table and go out.

Then silence, heavy and waiting. Peter taking her hand, prodding gently. She stiffened, turned her head, and looked past Peter to McHugh.

A human stormcloud. Standing there trying to decide whether or not to erupt. He said quietly, "You're not in the habit of locking your car?"

She shook her head very slowly back and forth.

Peter squeezed her hand and cut in to clarify the too-precise answer. "Habit means *all* the time. Amanda sometimes rushes off and leaves the car unlocked. Public places, that sort of thing."

McHugh studied her for a moment, and said, "Your glove compartment? You don't lock that either?"

She blinked. Inhaled. "Usually," she whispered. "I . . . don't remember."

He stepped closer, his gaze suddenly haggard, intense. "And you don't think that maybe, just maybe, you had those Payne tapes all along?"

"Hey!" Peter complained.

Amanda stared at the detective, white-faced.

"Which brings me to the next thing," he pressed on. "Your friend Emily Hagin's awake. They let me talk to her for a few minutes, and she insists that she was *pushed* down those stairs, and that her house was locked. Now, her family says there were only three sets of keys: one for Emily, one for her husband, and"—his expression hardened—"one for your housekeeper. Which means that only you would have had access to those keys outside of the family, isn't that right?"

Peter stared at McHugh with his mouth open. "Joe, come off it," he protested. "Suki's purse has been in a house for sale that's been traipsed through daily by prospective buyers. For God's sake, enough!"

Amanda had been gripping the edge of the exam table, her knuckles white, her face deadly calm. Painfully, she tried to raise herself up, with Peter catching her as she faltered, and helping her into a sitting position.

"Peter," she said faintly, as if McHugh weren't even there. "Would you get me a lab coat to cover this? I'm going up to see Emily."

Peter stared at her while McHugh turned exasperatedly away . . . until he felt her eyes blazing at him, and looked back.

"*Such* sagacity," she said, her voice trembling in offended fury. "Sure. I had the tapes all along, and hid them in the unlocked glove compartment of an unlocked car to save you the trouble of having to get a search warrant. Wasn't that *nice* of me?" She felt lightheaded; forced herself on. "And then I appropriated the keys of someone who's been like a *mother* to me to harm a person who's been like a *sister* to me. Well, I've got news for you—*I'm* family, too!"

Unsteadily, she started to climb off the table. The effort and her outburst caught up with her, and a wave of dizziness hit like a sledgehammer. She crumpled to Peter's chest as he braced her up with comforting hands.

"You don't think you should stay awhile?" he asked softly.

"No." She shook her head to clear it. "I'm just minor-banged up. I'm going to discharge myself and visit Emily and get the hell out of here." She glared at McHugh. "I don't think you have probable cause, Lieutenant. So why don't you give your officers out there a break and send them home?"

McHugh leaned on the doorjamb watching her, his eyes moody, uncertain. "I already have," he said. He stepped aside as, limping, with Peter gripping her arm, Amanda made for the door. "And Mrs. Hagin's too weak for more visitors," he said to her back. "All banged up like that, you'll scare her."

Amanda turned, catching the look that passed between the two men: *I'm stumped,* McHugh's said; and Peter's said, *What did I tell you?*

McHugh got off the jamb and his expression changed.

"What you said about the tapes being maybe a murder attempt . . ."

"She'll be all right," Peter said firmly, his arm around Amanda as he guided her out. "I'll see to it."

43

LIKE A FRIGHTENED SMALL BIRD, Suki darted across windswept puddles through the darkening parking lot of the supermarket. She wasn't dressed for this weather; felt chilled to the bone as she hugged her goosepimply arms and hurried through the automatic doors.

Taking a cart and beginning to push it, she scolded herself again for not having left the hospital earlier. Not that Amanda would *mind,* but that was the trouble with Amanda. Always worrying about others and neglecting herself. Amanda would have said, "No, Suki, stay with Emily. Don't worry about anything so mundane as shopping."

Except that Emily was completely out of danger now, thank God. Still dreadfully pale, which was to be expected, and still upset and anxious in her insistence that she had been pushed. Suki stopped in her tracks, feeling stinging tears of worry when she thought of that. Did this mean that anything psychiatric was wrong? Emily did sound so certain, but the house had been locked! The poor child, she must have been so terribly nervous . . . and nerves can work mayhem on the imagination, can't they?

After Peter left, Dr. Finley had tried and failed to get Emily to calm down, and then that detective had walked in and Emily had calmed almost immediately. Been happy, relieved, to tell him what she was sure had happened. The doctor had only let him stay a few minutes, and he had talked to Russ and Suki, too, but Emily had seemed better after that. Better enough for Suki to have left for a while then, but it was time for Russ to go and get Davey from the sitter who picked him up after school, so Suki had waited.

Which brought her up to now, just after six. Suki checked her watch and felt terrible, visualizing Amanda wandering around alone in that big awful house, opening kitchen cabinets and finding not much more than a few cereal boxes, while suppertime at the hospital found Emily surrounded by bustling staff and her loving family. My word, talk about *reverse guilt!*

Well, Suki thought, sighing. That's what it is when you love, isn't it? You fret about one, then you fret about the other. Never a moment when you aren't at least a little worried, deep down, thinking . . . Dear Lord, what next?

At the deli counter she got an already-barbecued chicken, then raced around the rest of the place getting milk, juices, eggs, and, *most* uncharacteristic for her, a stack of microwavable entrees.

44

MINUTES AFTER THEY HAD LEFT THE POST ROAD, Amanda looked through the rain-soaked windshield and said, "Wait—this isn't the way to my house."

He looked over at her and nodded. "I know. You're going to spend the night with me." His eyes went back to the road. "You don't want another go with those squirrels in the attic, do you? In your shape?"

She stared at him, not breathing, the terrible images rushing back. Had that just been last night . . . ? His Porsche slammed through a flooded area, sending up booming double arcs of spray, and her heart leaped as she saw her bathroom sink, the water blasting. *Call a plumber, Ma'am.* She lowered her head, breathing shallowly from fear, from pain. Saw her fingers go to Peter's jacket that he had thrown protectively over her shoulders. Scent of aftershave. Sense of comfort, I'll take care of you. She trembled and pulled the jacket tighter around her; looked back at his profile, dimly illuminated by the lights from the dashboard.

"It's been so long," she said quietly.

"Yeah. Too long."

They lapsed into silence as he took a dark turn, and guided the car up a winding lane of wind-whipped foliage and old stone walls. Each of them back to thinking about Emily; it was something Amanda could feel. The questions, the answers, the fact that there *were* no answers. Only implications. Dreadful, terrifying implications that they now had to grapple with.

"I've been thinking," Peter said, and she looked over at him again.

He kept his gaze straight ahead; inhaled deeply. "Why do I

keep getting the feeling that Emily wouldn't even be in the hospital if I had ruled Kelly's death accidental?"

"Peter, that's . . ." She groped.

"That's what? Crazy? Okay, listen. Just listen and tell me if this makes any sense." He squinted against oncoming headlights; waited until the car had passed, and said, "The killer's having a run of bad luck, that's what I think. Kelly's murder was probably supposed to have looked like an accident, and Emily was supposed to have died. Neither came off. Pretty stressful if you're an amateur. Now what I'm wondering . . ."

"But there's no proof that Emily was pushed! And how do Kelly's death and Emily's accident tie in?"

"Because you and Emily tie in. Humor me. Make a leap with me and let's see what we've got. Such as: Killer freaks when Kelly's death is ruled a homicide, then worries about what *you* know, then gets Suki out of the house by staging Emily's accident so he can . . . well, last night . . ."

"Wait." Amanda's heart was thudding. "The key to Emily's house. How do you figure that?"

"Who knows? But someone *could* have gotten at Suki's purse when your house was on the market, or, don't forget, the Hagins were having work done, and maybe *Emily* left her purse around. Somebody somehow gained entry to her house and pushed her. I believe that, and I know you do, too. You said yourself that she's super truthful and doesn't exaggerate. So. Can we come back to my original question, which is: assuming things are going badly for this killer and he's under a lot of stress, what can we expect from him next? What's his behavior going to be?"

Amanda looked down, watching her clasped fingers twitch nervously in her lap. For long, troubled seconds, she was still.

"It depends on his disorder," she said softly. "If he's manic he could spiral out of control, flip out completely and . . . make mistakes. They're easier, the manics. As opposed to paranoids . . . well, they're the smart ones, in their way."

"Their way?"

She watched the windshield wipers battling the rain for a moment. Frantically busy, achieving nothing. "Yes," she said in a strained, low voice. "Most paranoids manage to live with their affliction, in some ways even benefit from it. But strain intensifies their irrational resentments, their fears of conspiracy. Their behavior becomes increasingly erratic and . . . daring, by their old standards. They'll move on from pet targets to new ones. And still be able to fool you by appearing perfectly normal. But that's what makes them the classic psychotic, isn't it? No concept of guilt or self-limitation."

"Wild . . ." Peter had turned into a driveway, his headlights illuminating his sprawling old white-with-green-shutters colonial as they approached. It seemed strange, Amanda thought, considering the fact that this was a tavern once frequented by Revolutionary soldiers with their horses and muskets, to see him press a switch and activate the side of the former old barn by making the electric garage doors whir up. The Porsche roared inside, to a world of dry concrete floor and automatic lights and grungy white sails hanging from the rafters. Behind them, the automatic door whirred back down with a *thump*.

And Peter sat, staring ahead without expression through the still-glistening windshield, as if lost in another dimension. "You know," he said quietly, still staring at nothing as he picked through his words. "I think I've been seeing a bigger pattern than meets the eye. The cops aren't convinced but . . ."

He turned, his solemn, dark eyes probing hers, and told her. About Jeanette Norwin . . . and Lloyd Gartrell . . .

Amanda was shocked. "Gartrell, the Wall Street guy? I read about that in the papers when I was still in New York! It was ruled accidental!"

He looked away. "Some people opposed that ruling. He had the same . . . bruises, two or three, very faint, on his neck, his shoulders. People tried to point that out, but were told no, it was an accident, the house had been locked, same as Jeanette Norwin's house was locked when she took her header down the stairs."

Amanda stared at him mutely; then dropped her face in her hands. He pulled her to him and held her, telling her don't, wait, he wasn't sure, they had to find out more.

"Let's get inside," he said, kissing her, smoothing her hair.

He helped her out, and with an arm around her braced her up as they headed for the door. "Ohh," she said mournfully. They had stopped before his Jeep Wagoneer, parked next to the Porsche, a reminder of the ski trip they had never taken because they had broken up the week before.

He tugged at her hand. "It's still waiting," he said. "Come on."

HE THREW OPEN THE DOOR and they moved through the hall into the dark kitchen. Lightning flashed outside a near window as Peter leaned against a wall, and pulled her to him and kissed her mouth. Her lips parted, and she returned his kiss, putting her arms around his neck as he kissed her again, trembling, squeezing her so hard to him that it hurt and she cried out softly.

"Oof, sorry," he whispered, loosening his grip, his lips grazing her cheek, her neck. "I'll make it better."

He began to kiss her again, and the door on the far side of the room whammed open and thumping sounds headed toward them from the light in the front room, and seventy pounds of furry love jumped up on them.

"Toby!" Amanda cried, forgetting herself. "Omigod, so big!"

She turned stiffly to the leaping, wildly happy Old English sheepdog, petting him and exclaiming, "He remembers me!" as Peter helped her off with the wet jacket. He hung it on a wall peg near the spare keys to the Wagoneer that his maid, Evelyn, used for errands. He stared at the keys for a moment and then turned back to the commotion.

"I don't believe it," Amanda was saying. "What is he now—seven months?"

"Eight last week." Peter gave his dog's head a friendly scratch, but seemed preoccupied in the dimness. He went and flicked on the lamp over the table, came back to where Amanda, bending, was making a fuss over Toby, and said, "I'm going to go lock up."

Fishing in his pocket, he pulled out his keys and retraced his steps through the hall. At the end, just before the door to the garage, he pushed one of the keys into a round metal slot in the wall, and activated the alarm. Then he turned and went back to the kitchen, where he found Amanda seated—painfully, he realized—at the table with the phone to her ear.

She sat very still, waiting, listening, and her face was pale as she looked up at him.

"Suki doesn't answer," she said, dismayed. "That's odd."

"Could she still be at the hospital?"

Amanda frowned a little. "Maybe. Although she said she was planning to head home earlier today to catch up on some rest. She barely slept last night. She—" Amanda's hand went to her brow. "Oh, no. I'll bet she's at the supermarket. She insisted she was going to go, we needed restocking . . . oh, Suki . . ."

Peter called Toby to his side. "Try her every ten minutes. I don't think she should even *be* in that house. I'm going to let Tubbs here out for a while."

He disappeared down another hall with Toby galloping happily ahead. Amanda watched them go and then dialed another number. When Josie answered, she tried to keep her voice friendly and controlled as she told her about the accident, and asked her to arrange for coverage and cancel all patients for tomorrow.

"An accident?" Josie wailed on the other end. "Oh, no! *How?* Are you okay?"

"Mostly okay." Amanda closed her eyes; opened them. "Bumps and bruises and one nasty laceration. I'm very lucky."

A groan on the other end, more commiseration, and the two said good-bye with Josie promising to take care of everything. Hanging up, Amanda stared for a moment at the receiver neatly back in its cradle, so quiet, so *finished,* as if, electronically, she had shut the final door on that fragile thing that until Sunday night she had called normalcy. Outside, the storm continued. The wind shifted and rain pounded like bullets on the window near her. She shivered; felt the pain in her knee growing worse; tried Suki again—no answer—and looked out, feeling wretched.

"Let's go upstairs."

She turned to him. He was standing a few feet away, tall and brooding, as if somewhere in the last minute or so it had dawned on him that the trauma was past, the patient had been spirited to safety, and now had to be looked after. She glanced down at herself and realized what a sight she made. Her dress was torn, and the bloodstains down the front had turned brown. She rose slowly, painfully, from her chair and went to him. Felt his arms enclose her again, and buried her face in his neck.

"This dress is a fright and a half," she murmured.

He kissed her, and kissed her again. "Yes," he said. "Let's get it off."

HIS BEDROOM LOOKED EXACTLY, eerily, the same. Books everywhere: on the floor, jamming the floor-to-ceiling bookcases, piled onto the upholstered chairs pulled up before the fireplace. Medical journals lay in stacks on the old captain's desk and overflowed onto the queen-sized brass bed, and Amanda looked up to the heavy old beams, free of clutter because they were simply out of reach.

Behind her, the sound of Peter rummaging through a drawer. "Ah! A clean one!" He straightened, holding a navy-colored T-shirt, which he tossed onto the bed, saying, "It'll be too big for you, but it's dry."

Then he stared at her, a long moment stretching between them. In the soft glow of a bed lamp he looked yearning and suddenly . . . shy, somehow, as if the two of them were meeting for the first time. "You're just so damn pretty," he said softly. She came to him. Her arms went around his neck as he gripped her to him, kissing her impatiently, breathing hard. The room reeled. She thought that her heart would burst.

In bed, he held her tight and felt her flinch. "You okay?" he whispered, pulling away. "Pain . . . ?"

There were tears in her eyes. "Yes, dammit. Everywhere. The damned leg . . ." She reached out for him and pulled him back to her, held him to her as if she didn't care, as if nothing mattered but this moment and having him back . . . back . . .

"I'll be careful," he promised.

Rain pounded down on the eaves and the whole house seemed buffeted by the storm, but Amanda heard none of that, felt only the old dream of Peter folding her into his arms and loving her, gently, carefully, then not so gently, his face plunged into the softness of her shoulder as if he would never let her go.

Time spun out in the drumming of rain. Somewhere the old house creaked gently, like a ship tossed and holding. At last they were quiet. Amanda lay, feeling his arm across her breasts, his lips brushing her cheek, and as their breathing slowed she could hear the storm again. It seemed to be subsiding.

Peter inhaled; held up his watch and said quietly, "We should make that call."

"Yes." Her eyes were luminous on his.

Groaning, he reached for the phone and punched the familiar numbers. Amanda maneuvered over on the bed and lay her head on his shoulder. He came awake fast, seemed almost surprised, in fact, when the line was picked up on the other end and he heard the familiar voice.

"Hello, Suki?" he said. "It's Peter."

45

SUKI HAD ARRIVED HOME AT 6:25, had peered from her car through the rain at the darkened house, and felt the first stirrings of alarm. She had brought the groceries in through the garage and, leaving the bags on the counter, had gone around turning on lights, calling, "Amanda?"

Trying not to be frightened, she had gone back to emptying the bags and putting the things away, her ears straining for the sound of a car arriving, a key click-turning in the door, and that familiar set of footsteps heading toward her down the hall. *See you tonight. Early for both of us, we didn't sleep much last night.*

I don't understand, Suki thought, beginning to fret as she put away the last thing and slammed the refrigerator door, too loud, the sound frightening her and seeming to reverberate from the darker parts of the house. Good grief! Being alone in this big old place was like being locked in a mausoleum . . . under *ordinary* conditions, but with all these terrifying things that had been happening, it was enough to make one a nervous wreck . . .

She swallowed. Her heart was beginning to thud a little faster. She glanced up at the wall clock and checked the time with her watch. Both correct. 6:41. She paced, wondering what to do next.

Turn on the TV to fill the silence? No. Because with the television going you wouldn't be able to hear *other* things . . . like . . . Suki nervously glanced over her shoulder into the dark hall leading to the foyer, wondering seriously for the first time if someone really had crept up on Emily and . . .

The phone rang, and she cried out.

Rushing to answer, she sagged with relief to hear Peter's voice.

"Amanda's not here!" she blurted as soon as he said his name. "She said she *would* be, early, and now I'm worried that—"

"Everything's okay," Peter said soothingly, slipping into the old med school dictum of getting everyone calm before delivering the mildly upsetting news. (You should never, NEVER, begin with: *A terrible thing has happened!* He could still hear one of his third year profs intoning that one.) "Amanda's with me," he continued in his modulated voice. "She had a slight accident in her car, so I've—"

"Accident! Accident! Oh, my God, no!"

It never worked. "Suki, calm down. Amanda's okay. A few nasty bruises and one laceration, but she's okay. Now listen, there's something I want to tell you . . ."

Lying in the crook of his arm, Amanda could hear Suki's piping dread and felt terrible. We should have called ten minutes ago, she thought, and wondered how long her old friend had been waiting alone. In a minute she would talk to Suki, too, and reassure her, but first things first. Peter was quietly telling her to get out of the house . . .

"Yes, noises. She had a frightening night there last night, then thought it might have been her imagination." He paused, deciding not to bring in his feelings about Emily's accident. "We just have a bad feeling about the place," he went on. "Maybe the fact that that damned realtor keybox was there until yesterday is making it worse, I don't know. Just make us happy. Don't stay."

There was a silence as Peter's words sank in. "There have been a lot of strangers traipsing through," Suki said worriedly; then dropped her voice suddenly to a hushed foreboding. "And . . . Peter . . . there was a keybox on *Emily's* house too, until November when they moved in!"

There. She had made the connection for herself. Connection enough, at any rate: what he had really wanted was for Suki to take action without getting unduly upset.

"Everybody's had a keybox who's ever bought a house," he reminded her in a neutral voice.

Suki's voice rose in pitch. "Oh, but now that I *think* about it . . . I'm going to tell Russ we should all go to a motel. There's a Marriott right near the hospital. We can tell Davey it's to be near his mom!"

Peter glanced down at Amanda; winked and squeezed her. "A

motel," he said evenly. "That's a good idea. You'll rest easier for sure."

They said good-bye and Peter passed the phone to Amanda, who raised up on an elbow and spoke with Peter's hand on her arm. "Yes, yes, I'm okay. No, I only heard noises, but I'd still be happier if you got out. Fast, Suki. Promise."

"I'm on my way," Suki said.

"Kiss Davey for me," Amanda said, and hung up.

She slid back down and looked at Peter, her face anxious and uncertain. "Motel," she said moodily. "Maybe the whole town should sleep in a motel. The whole *county*—one keybox key fits everywhere, doesn't it?"

He stared without blinking at the shadowy ceiling. Sighing, he turned his face and gave her a troubled look. "We're not certain this has anything to do with keyboxes," he said. "I just said that to get Suki moving. Get her—them—to stay clear of *both* houses."

There seemed nothing left that either of them could say. Gently he pulled her to him and kissed her forehead. And then they lay together in silence, worried, listening uneasily as the rain outside drummed on.

I'LL MAKE IT QUICK, Suki thought. I need fresh nightgowns and an extra tube of toothpaste and a change of clothes for tomorrow.

She had left her overnight bag in the car, and rather than waste time running for it, she reached into a low cabinet and pulled out a green plastic Benetton bag. She turned, heading for the foyer and the front stairway, then stopped.

It was too roundabout to go that way, she decided. The stairway was wide and elegant and well-lit, and normally she did not mind the fact that it was double the distance to her rooms—like walking down half a football field and then turning and walking back.

Now it mattered. She decided to take the shortcut to her room, a musty, winding old staircase that opened into the butler's pantry. Ordinarily she hated it, never used it because it was creepy, but now . . .

It would be more creepy. She stood in the kitchen doorway, vacillating, torn between the desire to save time and Amanda's frightening report of having heard noises. She looked up; around. The house was very still. Too still. Not a sound except her own thudding pulse in her ears.

"You're wasting time just *standing* here," she whispered angrily. She squared her shoulders and headed for the butler's pantry.

The narrow door creaked as she opened it, and peered up into darkness. "Mercy," she muttered. She fumbled for the light switch, flicked it on, frowned, flicked it off, and flicked it on again. She swallowed hard. The light was out.

Back to the kitchen she rushed for the big flashlight they kept handy for power outages. And back she came to the staircase, training the light on the old wooden steps as she ascended. Her heart was beating fast. That's no good, she thought fearfully: her blood pressure! The flash in her shaking hand cast weird, moving shadows on the turning, circular wall, and she stopped, suddenly stunned to see that one of the stairs wasn't there.

Imagination? A trick of these leaping shadows? Trembling, she brought the light closer. Sure enough. A gaping, black hole. With fresh, pale-colored sharp splinters encircling it like daggers, and pointing slightly *up,* she realized, as if someone's foot had gone through and then been pulled out . . .

Amanda heard frightening sounds in the house . . .

She almost fell in her headlong rush back down the stairs. At the bottom a knee went out, and she tumbled forward, twisting an ankle, wailing in pain.

Heart attack time for sure, she thought in terror, her fingers trembling uncontrollably as she tried to punch Peter's number. A finger slipped on the last digit, and she was sure she had dialed wrong and was going to die right here and now, on the kitchen floor all alone in this place, with no one to find her or know what had happened until—

"Hello?" from the other end.

A miracle. Peter's voice.

She heard herself half sobbing as she told him what she had found.

And in his bed, Peter sat bolt upright, with Amanda pulling up in shock next to him, both hearing the terrified, hoarse cries coming over the line.

Peter's voice was firm. "I'll call the police. They'll be there fast. Hang on, Suki, and open up for them!"

An instant later he was dialing and Suki was tottering frantically toward the front door.

The first patrol car arrived in the drive exactly ninety seconds later.

46

"SQUIRRELS," Peter muttered, hanging up two calls later. Two brief calls. Hurried conferring. The prints and lab people were heading over to check out the broken stair. Peter was going to join them, then return with them to the police lab. He was pulling on his clothes faster than a fireman.

Stunned, Amanda sat up in bed, her hands tightened painfully on the sheet she held to her chest. Her face was very pale. How long since she had even thought of that old, back staircase to the butler's pantry? How long since *anybody* had thought of it?

The answer came to her and she went cold.

Why, your visitor thought of it, obviously. And, more to the point, your visitor seems to know your house awfully well.

The second thought was more devastating.

"Who could it be . . . ?" she whispered hoarsely. Again. Her heart was racing painfully.

Peter glanced up at her. He had thrown on old chinos and a gray sweatshirt, and was now tying the laces on his running shoes. One look at the sick horror on her face and he stopped what he was doing, crossed to the bed, and put his arm around her.

"Two questions, really," he said low. "One: who could have known about that staircase, and two: if he's a killer, why didn't he even come near you?"

"But he *did!*" she burst out. "The faucet turned on full blast in the bathroom? The bathroom's right next to my bedroom—well, *you* know that—and it was *after* that that I heard him up in the attic!"

Peter pulled back to look at her. Saw the numb horror in her eyes give way to an expression of dawning, frightened comprehension. He swallowed, nodded tensely, and looked away.

"The guy had some sort of plan," he said dully. "It almost looks as if . . ." He groped. Got up and paced.

"As if he was just trying to scare me," she said weakly. "But *why?*" She reached for his navy T-shirt and began to pull it on.

He stopped pacing and watched her, feeling a flash of warmth as he remembered other times she had worn his tees.

"Because he's probably the same guy who killed Kelly, and he's *very* clever. He drowns Kelly, steals her tapes, and plants them in your car. Why? To make you crazy, drive into a tree, *self*-destruct." He felt his skin prickle on the back of his neck. "Much more convenient that way. You can't murder two next-door neighbors only days apart—it's too obvious."

Amanda shuddered visibly. He glanced nervously out at the night as if the people waiting for him were right under the window. Then he looked back.

"The tapes were stolen Sunday night," he said softly. "It's possible you were driving around all day Monday with them in the car, and his scheme didn't work, and he got impatient. Dropped in Monday night to hasten things along. Hell, he probably even *wanted* you to get so scared you'd call the police. Show the world how overwrought you are." Peter pressed his lips into a grim line. "This guy's in a hurry, whoever he is."

He turned; grabbed his wallet and keys off the old rolltop desk and said, "Forensics is waiting. We're going to find some scrapings and try to identify this bastard."

She looked up at him, her eyes welling with tears of fear, frustration. She *hated* feeling helpless and immobilized. "Oh Peter," she said miserably, not wanting him to go.

He came back to the bed, held her, and felt the pounding of her heart through the closeness of their chest walls.

He stroked her hair. "Let me leave Toby with you. He's a terrific watchdog. And . . . medication. That Procaine's going to be wearing off."

A minute later she was watching him line up bottles of Percodan, Darvocet, and Demerol next to a glass of water on the bed table. "A smorgasbord," he said. "Take your choice."

She looked at the array. "I want morphine," she said.

And two minutes later he was back with Toby, who leaped happily onto the bed and started shaking himself.

"He's not even wet," Amanda said, surprised, rubbing his head.

"He has a house. Used to be an old woodshed just off the back door. If it rains, he goes in there."

He glanced at his watch, bent and kissed her, and that was when the real fear hit.

"Peter—" Her eyes were wide.

"Rest," he said, easing her back down on the pillows. His face clouded. "The panic buttons—do you remember where they all are?"

His security system was actually better than hers, with silent alarm buttons like the ones in banks and at Brooklawn installed at several points in the house. She nodded at him numbly.

"Where's the one in this room?"

She pointed: on the wall by the bedside table, easy to reach.

"If you hear *one* sound you don't like, press it. Don't hesitate!"

He kissed her again, then straightened and headed for the door. He turned for one last look. "I'll be at the police lab if you need me." Amanda rose fretfully up on an elbow and Toby raised his head questioningly.

"Stay," he said softly. They both put their heads back down, and then he was gone.

HE HAD A PLAN all worked out in his mind. But it had to go perfectly, it had to be timed *right down to the minute.*

Pulling on his gloves, he rushed across the darkened room and with trembling hands opened the door in the mahogany paneling. Swinging it wide, he shone his flashlight on his collection of keys, two hundred gleaming sets of house keys, all neatly labeled and hanging on their hooks. Quickly, he reached in and began stuffing the special ones into his pocket . . . six sets, seven sets, yes, that ought to be enough—

A *noise?* He snapped his head around and peered down the dark room to the dark hall; listened; shook his head. It was nothing, just the sound of water still glugging down the drain outside the window. Loud, though. Runoff from the roof, the still-wet branches overhead.

He closed the door, locked it, watched it disappear back into the paneling around it, and switched off his flash. Then stood in the darkness, reviewing his plan again. Kill the main threat, fine, he would be safe. But to be even *safer* . . . he smiled to himself . . . kill a second person, he knew exactly who, and then in the same, easy stroke *frame someone else with all of it* . . . every impulsive, too-dangerous act . . . wipe the slate clean once and for all. It could be done. And a prime suspect practically gift-wrapped for the police. They'd be so happy, and he would be free. He could relax and resume his top-drawer life and put all of this stress behind him.

Hurriedly, he returned the flashlight to its place in a different room, and went out to his car.

And the drainpipe glugged on outside the room he had left. And a branch, weakened, snapped off and clattered its way down outside the window. After-the-storm sounds, insignificant, barely perceptible to someone agitated, too focused in his thinking to have noticed himself dropping a set of keys to the lovely old floor beneath their hiding place in the wall.

Veils of opalescent fog drifted past the window, casting a feeble luminescence on the metal surface of the keys, and, indirectly, on the round, cardboard label that was attached to them.

"Hagin, E.," the label read.

IN THE DENSE SHORELINE FOG the front of Amanda's house looked like a hellish carnival, with squad car lights flashing and radio voices squawking their eerie static. Peter parked behind an un-marked car and hurried in, showing his ID to a young cop at the door, bumping into Suki in the crowded hall.

She looked ill and he hugged her. "Oh Peter," she moaned. "There *was* someone, you should see it, and poor Amanda *alone* and thinking she was *imagining* . . . !"

He glanced toward the interior; cops milling in the kitchen. "You saved the day, Suki. Why aren't you out of here and resting?"

"Russ is coming for me. I'm too nervous to drive. I told him everything and he says *definitely* a motel . . . Oh, there he is!"

Russ Hagin was in the foyer agitatedly explaining his identity to a pair of cops.

"It's okay," Peter called to them, and Russ came in, looking like a man who had just stepped off a plunging elevator.

"Stairs," he said almost stupidly, staring past them into the kitchen. "Like Em. Do you think . . . ?"

"Yes. Someone has the keys to both houses." Peter put a hand on Suki's thin shoulder. "Our prize detective here is done in. Get her to peace and quiet." She was trembling, he noticed. "Have you taken something to calm down, Suki?"

"A Valium. It didn't work."

"Take another one. And Russ—don't bring your family home until you change the locks. Come to think of it, maybe you should have a police escort when you go home to pack."

He made arrangements for two officers and a squad car to accompany them, and when they left, he hurried toward the rear and the commotion surrounding the butler's pantry.

Shouldering his way up the narrow stairs, he saw a tumult of men in the claustrophobic space. Wally Burke and Dan Rosen, of police forensics, were reaching down for more glassine envelopes and hollering for elbow room. Above them stood policemen training lights on a stair that was blocked from view. Rosen's cherubic face caught sight of him and looked glad. "Hey, reinforcements! Look what we got, Peter!"

He stepped between two uniformed men (". . . feel *awful*," one was saying. "We told her it was squirrels."), and a plainclothes, sports-shirted back that moved away. Rosen pointed, and he saw the stair, crushed through and gaping, nasty with splinters sticking up like a bear trap. He pulled out a ballpoint and came closer; leaned with one foot on a higher step and nodded.

"Fresh," he said, poking a splinter with the pen. "Wood's unoxidized, pale compared to the surrounding surface. Except here"—he tapped—"and here. This has to be blood."

"Blood and *skin*," said Burke on the stair above him. "We've already vacuumed and dusted the whole flight, but this is the bonanza."

Rosen, from a crouching position, held up a pair of closed glassine envelopes. "First samples. Can't wait to see these Kibbles and Bits under the microscope. Wanna scrape, Peter? You like a scalpel or a Swiss Army knife, sterilized?"

"I'll take a scalpel," Peter said, crouching next to Rosen, who from a supply kit handed him first a pair of surgical gloves that he snapped on, and then, handle first, the glinting, slender knife.

He pushed up the sleeves of his sweatshirt, and realized that his hands were shaking.

Feverish, he poked at a shard and made his first cut.

47

"WHAT IS IT, TOBY?"

Amanda turned her head on the pillow and sat up painfully to check on the dog. He had jerked up suddenly from a companionable sprawl by her feet, and had started to growl. Amanda tensed, glad that she had left the bed lamp on. She watched him turn his head toward the window and bark nervously at the night, and she followed his gaze, straining her ears to hear what he had heard.

Outside, a soft, creaking sound. The wind had shifted, sending branches scraping against the window panes.

"Oh, Toby . . ." She felt her shoulders sag. It was the third time the sheepdog had gone all tense and growly like that. Was he merely sensing her apprehension? Probably, she decided. She glanced at her watch and then at Peter's bedside clock in a one-two sweep that had become an anxious habit. Only nine o'clock, she thought, exhaling. This terrible night was dragging by like drops of Chinese torture.

"It's okay, Tubbs," she said. "It's just the wind." Such irony, she thought, reassuring the dog when she herself was a bundle of nerves. Toby looked back at her, his dark brown eyes dubious. He woofed softly, she reached out to give him a good pat, and he put his head back down on the blanket.

She sighed. At least his jumpiness had gotten her into a sitting position, which a few minutes before she had doubted she'd ever achieve again. Forty-five minutes ago, roughly an hour after Peter had left, the medication had worn off and the pain had come back like a tidal wave. Her leg mostly, but the throbbing in her back and arm came in a close second. She had groaned and reached for the Percodan and lain there staring at it, wondering why she was hesitating. Then she had replaced the bottle on the night table, understanding, and rolled back on the pillow deciding to tough out the pain.

She remembered last night, the single pill she had taken, the blissful relief that had come hand in hand with that slightly fogged-out feeling. No, not tonight, she thought, feeling sharper already in her thanks-to-Toby sitting position. Her injuries hurt dreadfully, but there had been too much that had happened and was still happening, and she wanted to keep her mind clear to think about them.

Unsteadily, she slid her legs over the side of the bed and put her feet on the floor, testing the pain. Bearable, so far. Now for the big test. She got creakily to her feet, wincing, and took a step, then another. Then was limping unaided for the first time since the accident, past the dresser, across the wide braided rug, and through the door to the dressing room.

She did not turn on the light. Carefully, she eased her good knee onto the window seat, leaned forward, and looked out at the night. Peter had left the garage lights on, and she could see the glistening wet of the driveway, the strands of fog that floated like ghosts. She drew back suddenly, afraid, reminded of that face in the shadows in her scrapbook . . .

Her scrapbook! What had happened to it? She hadn't given it a thought since the accident, and now realized that it was probably sitting in her wreck of a car on the sodden lot of some service station. Or maybe some kind soul had seen it and brought it in? She hoped so. With luck, it was waiting right now on somebody's desk next to an empty Coke can and an ashtray full of butts. Fingers crossed . . .

She turned, remembering this room. Long and thin, used two hundred years ago for storing straw mattresses. To her left, the door back into the bedroom and the wall with the long cedar closet. Ahead, another door out to the lighted hall, and to her right, the bathroom.

She went in, drew the shade, turned on the light. The mirror over the sink reflected her own white-faced image, and she looked away. Looked down, not really thinking, as if propelled from outside herself, and turned on the water. Full blast. Stared down at it, remembering. Footsteps rushing across the ceiling above her and down the attic steps. *He's clever,* Peter said. *He's very clever.* And malicious, Amanda thought, frowning, still staring down at the mad, crashing water. Like one of those animals that toys with its doomed prey before it finally kills . . .

She blew air hard out her cheeks, turned off the water, and realized that the phone was ringing.

"Oh!" Peter. He said he'd be calling. The lab. Test results coming back.

She hobbled back to the phone. Toby lifted his head, as if wondering who it was. "Hello?"

"I didn't wake you, did I?"

She eased herself down on the bed. "Hardly. Find anything?"

There was an excited tension in Peter's voice. "Lots. Tell me first—how's the pain?"

"Bearable." She didn't want to complain and she didn't want him to tell her to take medication. "What's happening?"

At his end Peter glanced at the busy lab, so much like his own with its white counters, high stools, microscopes and slide trays. He had just handed a reagent bottle to Wally Burke, who was carrying it back to Rosen and another man bending over a slide. They had all pulled white lab coats over their grungies.

"What's happening is," Peter said, turning back, "this guy left enough blood and microscopic skin bits to make it easy. Other stuff, too. Listen to this." He read from a printout sheet. "He's a white male—the chromosome analysis confirmed his gender—and that hole he put in the stair puts him at about 170 pounds. His blood type is B positive, and we originally thought he had dark brown hair, 'cause that's what they vacuumed. But no, turns out under 440X magnification that the hair was dyed, and *from a wig.*" He paused, gulped air.

"He wears a wig for his little sorties, Amanda. That's how he could have been so brazen about walking into Brooklawn in the dead of night. Probably wore horn rims and dressed like a psychiatrist, and had some cock and bull reason all thought up for being there, and lucked out anyway—the nurse was away from her desk."

Amanda gripped the phone, staring into the shadows of the bedroom. "Fingerprints," she said tonelessly. "Why weren't there any fingerprints?"

"Probably wore gloves of some sort. Anyway, who needs prints when you've got all this other data? And more being tested: fragments of his sock fabric, the sole of his shoe, and some funny kind of shoe polish, maybe the kind people use for their riding boots. Those tests will take longer."

Amanda was silent for a few seconds, then let out a long, shaky breath. "So," she said. "You have this man's whole biological profile. All you need now is to put a name on him."

There was the sound of someone's voice talking to Peter, and of Peter hastily answering: something about saline solution. He came back to the phone, and his tense excitement was gone. He sounded grave.

"I know. But from here the cops go all out. McHugh was here until a few minutes ago, then left like a bat out of hell for his office. I . . ." His voice dropped. "I have to stay, too. We're going to get out old files and try to find a common thread."

I have to stay, too. Amanda's spirits sank.

"Of course stay," she said. "It's . . . important." She bit her lip and hesitated. "I only wish I could get in that Wagoneer of yours and drive down to join you. The keys are hanging on that peg—"

"*What?* You're *injured!* You're supposed to be resting!"

She could picture him, torn, with his brow furrowed and his fingers drumming. And she realized suddenly that she was making it hard for him. He had to keep at it. Stay down there all night if that's what it took.

"You're right." She sounded sad. "I'll stay put and try to rest. Tomorrow, maybe . . ."

"And tomorrow night." There was a reedy exhaustion in his voice. "I may collapse of fatigue in your arms . . ."

She smiled softly into the phone as they said good-night. Hanging up, she leaned gingerly back on the pillows, and looked over at the snoring Toby for a silent, almost frightened moment. She was alone. The child she once was had suffered from a terror of being alone; had figured out at some point that the flip side of loving meant fear of loss, terror of separation. Too big a price, she had figured for years, until January, until tonight. She put a hand to the side of her face, still love-sore from being sandpapered by Peter's bristly cheek.

I wish he were here, she thought with an ache. She turned her head and looked out at leaf-shadows, pressing the dark panes, mournfully lank in the heavy, damp air. She thought of fragments. Kelly. Emily. McHugh *(like a bat out of hell)*. Files, Peter? Who? Gartrell? That woman . . . Norwin, her name?

Tight as a bow string, she lay staring at the ceiling, having no intention of letting herself sleep.

48

Yes, they're sharing a drink they call loneliness,
But it's better than drinking alone.

Susan Weems leaned out an open window that wasn't really open, because of the mesh, but she didn't mind since the rain had stopped and the damp night air smelled like spring water. Behind her, in the second floor commons room, Julie Andrews was climbing every mountain on the VCR before a group of people whose drawn expressions matched those of the group at the bridge table, and those not far away who were just sitting and talking, but she didn't mind that either. It was just so nice not to be alone. And this group . . . well . . . it wasn't so bad . . . there was the feeling of a fellow-suffering, no-threat-no-BS collective in this room . . . kind of like sitting with the sloshed-but-still-company regulars around a bar. Once again, those aching lines from the Billy Joel song, *Piano Man,* came back to her, and she sighed deeply. Bars and psychiatric hospitals: for some people they were really on the same path. One was just a few doors further down from the other, that was all.

She turned back, pulling a leg up under her, and resumed her seat on the couch next to Brian.

"Any luck?" she asked.

"No. Shh. I'm concentrating."

She looked at him a little helplessly. How she wished there were something she could do. He had showered and changed and now there he was, staring out into the room with his chin in his hand, wearing the same troubled, bewildered look she had first seen on him when he was talking with Dr. Barron. And gnawing on his nail, too.

That wasn't going to help anything. Very gently, her touch like a dove, she reached out and pulled his hand from his face.

He looked at her, and tried to smile. He drew in a deep, ragged breath and said, *"Damn,* I can't think in here."

She lifted a shoulder. "So why don't you get out? You said your doctor said it was okay to leave. Maybe you'll remember better if you just get a change." She saw his eyes muddy with fear, and realized that he had been thinking the same thing that she had, and was terrified. Gently she added, "The dock? Why not? The rain has stopped. I'll bet sitting on that dock would bring back *everything.*"

He blinked, and brushed at his cheek. His fingertips came away moist. "Scared," he whispered. "Just the thought of that place . . ."

She smiled at him. "You won't be alone. We'll be together. And we're both sober and I've got my Mace and it's nine-thirty—visiting hours are over—so they'll be kicking *me* out anyway—"

She stopped when he rose to his feet, his face pale but resolved.

"Okay," he said shakily. "Let's go."

49

PETER BARRON SPENT AN UNPLEASANT HALF HOUR waiting for the others.

There were more detectives around the table this time. McHugh wanted the ones who had been absent before to familiarize themselves with the files, so they sat, reading like speed demons and passing folders back and forth, while the others argued theories and frowned down at their copies of the forensic printout. Peter paced and brooded out the window and ended up at the counter making bad coffee. He was very tense. The excitement he had felt in the police lab was giving way to a growing sense of letdown.

"Sit," McHugh said. "You're making me nervous."

Peter saw that McHugh was looking just as tense. He sat at the head of the table with his broad shoulders hunched, his face scowling, and his hand gripping his chin in concentration. The detectives flanked him on both sides of the table, with Peter resuming his place at the other end.

McHugh watched the last man close his folder, then looked around the table with the expression of a man who has just been awakened from a bad dream.

"Well," he said. "It looks like our spook exists."

Somber faces nodded, pale.

McHugh's fingers nervously tapped his copy of the forensic printout. "And where does this guy decide to fall through a stair? At the house most recently on the market of all those files, Dr. Hammond's. The house that *didn't* have musical maids, caretakers, decorators and you name it coming and going. Which kind of narrows things down to the real estate angle, wouldn't you say?"

"*Narrows,*" murmured one of the detectives, in his early forties with strawberry-blond hair. "There's about six hundred realtors in this town alone."

"And in the county, more like six thousand," said another detective, dark-haired. "Every fourth housewife has a license, I'll bet."

"We're not looking for housewives," muttered a third detective. "We're looking for a one-hundred-and-seventy-pound white male."

"Christ," said the man opposite him. "*I* answer to that description! You realize how many guys do?"

A grim thought came to Peter and he leaned forward. "Wait." He looked at McHugh and said intently, "You don't know for sure if tonight's man is the *same* man from the other complaints. Did one person in those files give a description? I didn't see any. How do you know you're not dealing with a ring, or accomplices? And by the way, I've remembered something since the last meeting. Amanda *has* had workmen in her house: last fall, she had her housekeeper's apartment redecorated. They must have had everyone from plumbers and carpenters to wallpaper hangers in there. The housekeeper might have left her purse around . . ."

"Oh, great," said the dark-haired detective. "So we can't even *narrow* this—ha!—to real estate."

McHugh rubbed slowly at his brow, as if his head ached. He thought for a long moment before he looked back at Peter.

"Go back to this 'ring' or more-than-one-guy theory. What's your gut feeling?"

Peter was silent for several seconds. "I think it's a loner," he said, and that wrenching sense of letdown returned when he remembered the detective's words, *It could be thousands,* and Amanda's sobering voice on the phone: *"So you have this man's whole biological profile. All you have to do now is put a name on him."* He peered anxiously at his watch, worrying about getting back to Amanda, and then went on. "I think it's a loner and without doubt a psychotic—to wit, the bludgeoned dog, the Gartrell maybe-forced drowning, the Norwin maybe-stair-shove . . . and Emily Hagin, the only victim who lived to describe what happened."

Psychotic . . . the word hung in the air as each man thought of Kelly Payne, drowned four nights ago, only yards from the house where just last night a stair had been punched through by an escaping intruder. Same guy? How could it not be? But *who?* Anyone from the commonest handyman to prospective buyers trooping through houses for sale to someone more directly connected to real estate. And if not from those giant categories—what then?

"The worst of it," Peter said, tapping a pencil, "is that this guy feels safe. He's probably too smart to have a record, and he knows that looking for him is like looking for the proverbial needle in a haystack. He must be some arrogant son of a bitch."

"We're chasing our tails," said one of the detectives.

McHugh shook his head. "No. Go back to the beginning," he said. "There must be something we're missing."

THEY HAD ENTERED THE PAYNE PROPERTY via the spruce-lined drive, and had pulled around to the back where they got out. They had walked down the sloping lawn to the dock, where they now sat at the far end, their arms locked around their knees, their eyes peering up through the eerie fog to the house.

"*Had* to be the French doors," Susan Weems said. "The upstairs windows are small, not big rectangles that move."

Brian inhaled the damp air deeply and held it in his lungs a moment, as if it were the most exquisite of drugs. He exhaled, thought, and said, "Yeah. Amanda had it figured, but I had to see for myself." He heard the water lapping softly, and inhaled again. "*God,* it's good to be out."

Susan hugged herself and rubbed her arms with her hands. When they had left Brooklawn, Brian had given her one of his sweatshirts to wear, but the downy layer of cotton was no match for the dampness. Still, what they were doing was important, and she didn't want to complain. Brian had come back to this terrible place; he was beginning to remember things that he had buried, even under hypnosis; she was beginning to get excited.

In the darkness she turned her face to the left, scanning the area of higher ground that met the dock before dropping to blend with the shore. It was hard to see. The night was totally socked in, and if there was a moon up there somewhere it was casting only the most feeble light on the surface of things. She pointed.

"There? The shadow was standing there?"

Beside her, Brian nodded. "And Kelly was walking *toward* him . . . I don't know how I remember—"

"That and the scream."

He nodded again. Thought. "Only it wasn't really a scream, it was a . . ." He dropped his head, stymied, guessing. "It was more like she was angry—yeah, that's right. She was angry as hell and telling him to . . . to . . . oh, Jeez, it's coming back . . . she was telling him to Go '*way,* that's what it sounded like!"

Susan looked at him, frowning faintly. "Go '*way?* But Kelly didn't talk like that. Little kids talk like that. Wouldn't Kelly have said, "Go away?"

His arms were still locked around his knees, and he laid his head down. "She was pretty baked, don't forget." A silence, then: "But you're right. It's crazy. It doesn't sound like Kelly, but it sounds like what I *heard.* Hell, that's the closest I've come since Brooklawn and the time when—"

"Brian, what are those lights?"

"Huh?"

"Those lights over there." Susan pointed. He looked. And in the spaces between the border of trees separating the Payne and Hammond properties, he saw. Light beams bobbing. An occasional red-blue flash. The sound of men's voices.

He stood up stiffly, his mouth open. "What in the hell . . . ? Hey! That's Amanda's house! What's going on?" For the first time he craned in that direction: noticed that the part of the house visible above the trees was very dark. An odd counterpoint to the barely seen activity at the front of the house. Foreboding chilled him as he knew—just knew—that something else bad had happened. Something involving Amanda Hammond.

He reached down, seized Susan's hand, and pulled her up. "Come on!"

They ran. Up the dock and over uneven terrain through the wide border of trees, where branches whipped their faces and Susan stumbled over a stump.

"You okay?" Brian asked, steadying her.

She nodded, just beginning to feel the sting of a nasty scratch on her cheek. From where they stood, they had a clearer view. "Look, Brian. Police."

They ran across lawn and driveway to the front of the house, where two squad cars were parked one behind the other, and four policemen standing in the wash of the front light turned to eye their approach.

"Can I help you?" said one warily as he pushed away from his car.

Brian seemed heedless of him; was looking up and around the dark house with an air of baffled fear.

"What's happened?" he demanded in a voice surprisingly firm. "Where's Dr. Hammond? Why is her house dark?"

The policemen looked curiously at the boy. He knew the homeowner's name and seemed genuinely upset. Ditto the girl. Questionable characters don't usually come running *to* the cops.

Another officer, older, thicker, came down the steps carrying a big flashlight.

"There's been an incident," he said guardedly. "Dr. Hammond isn't here. Would you two care to identify yourselves?"

"*What* incident?" Brian blurted his name and Susan's, who interjected, "We're friends of Dr. Hammond. Is she all right?"

Dread fell as they watched the cops exchange somber looks. The older one took pity on them. "She's had a car accident," he said. "She's not seriously—"

"A *car* accident!" Susan wailed.

"—injured, and I'm afraid that's all I can tell you."

Brian pummeled them with questions: was Amanda in the hospital? If not, where? Who could he talk to? And while the cops shook their heads, saying, sorry, we can't divulge more, Brian's mind whirled. Who *could* he call? He suddenly slapped his brow as if he were the prize village idiot.

"Dr. Barron!" he cried. "We can talk to him! Can we use your car radios? Or at least let us in the house so we can use the damn phone!"

The effect was magic. Every policeman stood a little more alert, looked at the kids with a whole new expression. One, who didn't look much older than Brian, said with surprise, "You know Dr. Barron?"

Brian was getting angry. He *hated* being stalled. "Yeah, I know him," he said tersely; and Susan said, "We *both* know him!" She turned to Brian and looked past him to the Payne property. "Let's just go back to the car. We'll *find* a phone and call him, wherever he is."

The young cop followed their gaze and frowned. "You're car's over there?"

"Yes." Susan looked back at him. "We were Kelly Payne's friends, too."

These weren't two ordinary kids, that much was apparent. The thicker-set officer spoke up. "Dr. Barron happens to be at headquarters now, as a matter of fact." In the dim light he peered at the scratch on the side of Susan's face. "Do you know you're bleeding, Ma'am? Now why would you want to go running back the whole five acres and maybe scratch yourself again, when you can get a lift with Officers Fenton and Dorn, here? We're all just leaving, matter of fact." He looked back at one of the men. "You're going straight back, aren't you, Jim?"

Jim Dorn and another man answered at once and headed for their car, Dorn opening the rear door and beckoning to Brian and Susan. "Hop in," he said. "We'll radio ahead that you're coming."

50

THE DROPS WERE FALLING, and the creases of the paper puddled, fuzzing the images, dissolving them into water of pale sepia that overflowed the scrapbook page and dripped like tears onto the floor of the demolished car. She climbed up in the rain, ignoring the shrill alarm, and with her body tried to cover the gash in the roof; but the metal cut her and the page below her on the seat was now blank as an old tombstone, and so she cried, and lay hunched on her side trying to shut out the alarm, in a bed in a shadowy room. Peter's bed. Light from the hall. Toby snoring. *Phone ringing.*

She jerked up, perspiring and shivering, and grappled for the phone. "Hello?" Peter, she thought. It must be Peter again.

Silence on the other end. Still trembling, she pressed the receiver closer, furrowing her brow as she realized that someone was there. "Hello?" she said more timidly. The line was open, she could tell that much. Groggy or not, she realized that the absence of a dial tone, and the sense of faint breathing, of enormous space at the other end meant . . . yes, the line was open. And the feeling of hate coming over the phone . . . It was something that she sensed as plain as if there were someone hateful right here in the room . . . Her breathing turned shallow and her senses sharpened. *Listen,* she told herself. Any giveaway sounds in the background? Sounds of traffic? Of a public place? This could be just a crank call or—

The line went dead.

With a slow, shaky movement she put back the receiver and stared at it, her heart thudding.

Call Peter and tell him? No, let him work. It probably was a crank call; this was, after all, the residence of the County Medical

Examiner. If the kids got hold of this number they'd have a field day.

But that bad feeling she had sensed coming over the phone . . . she couldn't shake it. Steeling herself against her body's protests, she got up, crossed to the window, and looked out. Below, the lights Peter had left on illuminated the property in a circle of reassuring light, and she found herself exhaling with relief. Now she admitted to herself that the call had frightened her.

She stood silently for a moment, then decided that pain or no pain, a little more reconnoitering was in order before she could calm down. She hobbled out into the lit hall, where she stopped to peer worriedly down the flight of stairs, then made an "L" turn toward the back of the house and one of the rear bedrooms. She entered the first, looked out, and exhaled in relief again.

In the fog, a pearly wash of light bathed the back of the house, too. And all exits were locked; an alarm system worthy of Fort Knox was in operation; and a dog big enough to knock down Arnold Schwarzenegger was a friend of hers and lying on the bed.

She limped back to Peter's bedroom, noticing that the pain was much worse now than when she had first gotten out of bed. Like an invalid, she thought bleakly, groaning faintly as she lowered herself back onto the pillows. A short walk and you're wiped out.

Involuntarily, she glanced at Peter's bedside clock, hoping that her watch might be wrong. No such luck. It was only 10:15. She had no memory of having dozed off; must have slept for barely thirty-five minutes when the phone woke her. "A little nap," she breathed ironically to herself, wondering if, sleep-wise, that was it for the night.

At her feet, Toby stretched and rolled over.

She practiced reaching for the panic button by the bed, then lay, staring out at the night, wondering who the crank caller might have been.

AND, FOUR MILES DOWN THE ROAD, a sleek car glided under the dark, leafy canopy at an almost jaunty speed. Inside, the driver was reviewing in his mind the sound of Amanda's voice as it had come to him over the line. He smiled, pleased with himself. He had passed her house, seen the flurry of police, and known that she wouldn't be there. Then—how clever he was!—he had remembered seeing her with Barron yesterday. In the courtyard, after the fund-raiser . . . he had picked just the right moment to spy out the window. So he had passed Barron's house and from the road seen the outside all lit up: a giveaway, a common, foolish ploy of homeowners designed to make people think that everyone was home, when usually the opposite was true. But if the owner was out—attending an emergency meeting at the police station, for example, where he had seen Barron's Porsche parked—then why was that small lamp burning in the bedroom?

As if he didn't know.

Still, he had wanted to be sure. Had stopped at a deserted pay phone by a nearby school and dialed.

Because his plans had to go like clockwork. How long would the police meeting last? The illuminated dial on the dashboard said it was 10:20. Would the meeting end sooner than eleven? Doubtful, it would probably last half the night, which was irrelevant in any case.

Forty minutes was plenty of time to kill both targets.

He stepped on the gas, heading for Country Club Lane. Better to hit the Clees house first, he had decided. It would be easier.

TWO MILES AWAY, Timmy Steffins wasn't sleeping. He had gone sulkily through the motions when Miss Wrenn had put him to bed, almost two hours ago. He had barely spoken, hadn't even complained as he usually did that all his friends got to stay up until nine, and she hadn't noticed that he was different. Or if she had, she was glad. She wanted to watch her favorite TV show that started at 8:30, Timmy knew that, even if she did chatter on about how nice it was that he'd be getting a good night's sleep tonight, his mum would come home tomorrow and find him rested and be *evah* so pleased.

But it was for the TV that she was making all those rushing, tucking-in motions. The Bird was bananas for American TV.

He had lain there tossing for an hour. Had tried to shake his bad feeling by looking around at the prettiness of his pastel bedroom, but the images of that creepy guy with the keys, and the police car he had seen in the Hagins' driveway tonight kept coming back to him.

Why would a police car *be* there if everything was okay? Miss Wrenn, driving him home from swimming class, said that the police were always checking people's houses, but that just didn't sound right. No way!

Finally, feeling troubled and having no one to tell, he got up, went to his mostly-closed door, and peeked out. Coast clear. He crept down the hall a bit, crouched, and looked through the balustrade to the living room below. He couldn't see The Bird, but he heard her and the television two rooms away. The den. She preferred the den TV to the one in her room; it was bigger. She had the sound way up and was laughing her head off. Ha ha to you, too, Bird.

He turned, and with lifting spirits hurried back to his parents' bedroom, burying his face in their pillows and wriggling himself under their covers. He always did this when they were away. It made him feel less lonely.

After a few minutes he stopped his wriggling, and blinked. It wasn't working this time. The bad feeling had followed him *in* here, and was getting *worse,* making his chest feel like a big, hot balloon that was going to burst any moment and make him cry his heart out. He squirmed up in bed, tight-mouthed with his lips pressed into an upside down "U." He reached for the remote thingie and zapped on the television; zapped again every five seconds—*pow! pow!*—because there was nothing good on, nothing at all until he hit a cable station with *Down and Out in Beverly Hills* just starting, just showing the scene where the homeless guy jumps into the rich guy's swimming pool and the rich guy comes running out screaming, "Call 911! Call 911!"

Timmy pulled closer. On the screen, the people all running and screaming trying to save the homeless man were good people. They were doing what Timmy's father was talking about when he said you have to *help* that old lady who just dropped her bundle, because that is your *responsibility,* to show that you are a caring person . . .

Timmy suddenly realized what a very little boy he was. His lip quivered as he felt fury welling up, because he had let someone talk him out of what he knew he should have done all along, and should really do right now, except that he was scared, he was just so honest-to-God scared . . .

Were they going to *scold* him for not telling sooner?

He zapped down the TV volume. Slowly, he squirmed around

on the blue sheet and faced the phone on the bed table, just as he always saw his dad do when he had to make an Important Call. Had his dad ever felt this terrified when he was a kid?

Concentrating, noticing that for the first time in his life his hands were shaking, just like big people's, he began to dial . . .

51

THE MEN IN THE CONFERENCE ROOM were tired; Peter could see that as he pulled up the rolling blackboard and chalked out two words on its surface. He pointed to them.

" 'Go 'way'?" he said. "Just the two syllables?"

In the chair they had pulled up for him Brian nodded solemnly, and Susan sitting next to him said, "We agree it doesn't *sound* like Kelly, but that's what Brian *heard*. It just came back to him when we were sitting on the dock."

Brian leaned forward with his elbows on his knees, his expression earnest; grave. "It's what I think I heard," he amended softly. "It was either that or something damned close." He looked up despairingly at Peter. "I'm just not sure."

McHugh at the head of the table got up and came over. Gazed ruefully down at Brian and said, "But she was drunk. Drunk people get sloppy with their speech. You may be remembering correctly."

Brian looked at him stolidly, then looked away. "Maybe. So why do I have this feeling of only being half right?" He leaned back and blew out breath.

Peter and McHugh stared grimly at the blackboard, while the men at the table started talking at once. The exact words didn't *matter*, said one detective, Kelly was obviously telling *someone* to beat it; and probably someone she *knew*, said another detective, since Brian had said that she sounded more angry than alarmed. Which brought heated reminders of going back through Kelly's telephone book, while someone else said, *"My* speech doesn't get sloppy when I'm drunk, just ask my wife—"

They froze as a buzzing noise called their attention to the intercom just switched on from "out front," the Communications

Center, and to the clamorous, ringing sound of a small child bawling his head off over the loudspeaker.

"Now calm down, son, calm down," they heard from the speaker on the wall. Dave Manchek's voice. Manchek was one of the two men doing the Communications shift tonight.

"*What?*" Joe McHugh said. Peter held up his hand, intently eyeing the speaker.

"You saw a bad man?" the Manchek voice prodded gently, as the little voice stopped to gulp air. A silence, a sound halfway between a sob and a hiccup, and then, "Yes. He had *keys* to Mrs. Hagin's house, and"—another sob-hiccup—"I saw him go in the day Mrs. Hagin fell! Only Miss Wrenn, she's our housekeeper—"

Chairs scraped and there was a mad scramble out the door, down the hall, and into the brightly lit, computer-banked, glassed-in area where Manchek was sitting, listening and scribbling like mad.

". . . same street," the kid was saying between air gulps. "Thirty-eight Indian Lane. I'm Timmy Steffins and Davey Hagin is older than me. He's in second grade and—"

There was a cry of surprise and the clunking sound of the phone being wrested away. An adult throat was heard imperiously clearing itself, and the glassed-in area boomed with a voice straight out of Masterpiece Theater.

"See heah. Who *is* this at this hour?"

Manchek glanced up at McHugh and flipped a switch on his console. McHugh leaned forward and boomed right back.

"This is Joseph McHugh, Chief of Detectives of the Grand Cove Police. Timmy has information concerning the attempted murder of Mrs. Emily Hagin, and wants to talk to us. You can come if you choose, but we'll have a car there for him in three minutes."

HE ACTUALLY SET his stop watch. He had it planned down to the last detail, and eight minutes, maximum, was all he gave himself. These two were cake.

The dark figure moved through the huge, dim house toward the sound of splashing and drunken laughter. He stopped by the shadowy entrance to the Jacuzzi room, and watched, mesmerized.

Backlit by the steam, the amber-colored Florida lights, she was massaging his white-lathered back and laughing, begging for more.

"Bitch. I'm exhausted," Sandy Clees complained, and then they both laughed.

The figure turned, went down a long, dark hall, and into a lavish study.

He approached the cluttered desk, emptied the gleaming, clinking contents of his pocket into a ginger jar, and left the top off. Then with his gloved right hand he picked up one of the two phones, and used it to dial the number of the other. Scarcely had he placed the receiver to one side when the second phone began to ring. He ran out, hearing it ring again, and hurried back up the hall to watch the reaction.

Sandy Clees was standing up in the water, not enjoying his massage anymore. The phone rang a third time. "Shit," he said, frowning.

Answer it, dammit!

"Aw, let it ring, honey," Vicki Linford cooed. The phone rang again. From behind she hugged Clees's neck and began licking his ear. "Who could be calling at this hour?"

Sandy Clees cursed again and reached for a towel. "Tokyo," he said.

He got out of the water and headed predictably through a different door to the kitchen. Predictably because the kitchen was closer, and tiled, and a man dripping wet isn't about to traipse down a long hallway floored with expensive oak parquet. Still, the figure watching grunted with pleasure. How easy it was to fool people. All of them.

He heard Clees in the kitchen—"Hello? Hello?"—as he rushed into the steamy room, hunched low, and approached the actress from behind. She was floating on her back, with her eyes closed and a drunken little smile on her lips. He knelt and grabbed her by the shoulders. Had her suddenly horror-struck face below the water before she could emit a sound, and held her, squeezing roughly, until she stopped struggling. Elapsed time: ninety seconds. She had never even been able to grab a breath.

And in the kitchen Sandy Clees hung up and stood scowling at the wall phone. Damndest thing! He hadn't had so much champagne that he didn't realize it was a crank call. *Had* to be. He had two phones. One was unlisted and the other was *more* unlisted: only a few key overseas brokers had the number . . . oh yes, and one ex-wife. Jesus! Could *she* have pulled a stunt like this? That would be just like her. Call from California and get him to fuck up the overseas line, just when the Tokyo and Hong Kong Exchanges were opening . . .

Nah, he thought, rethinking it, turning away. Just kids making up numbers. They'll hang up when their fun is over so they can bother someone else.

From the refrigerator he extracted a new bottle of Dom Perignon. He thought he heard a soft thump somewhere, like a door closing, and looked up. Nothing. He shrugged, returned his attention to a defective corkscrew, then headed back to the Jacuzzi.

"Vicki?"

From ten feet away he knew that something was horribly wrong. She was half-floating, face down in the water, her arms and legs limp and . . . you could see it from here . . . turning blue.

"Vicki! Oh, Jesus!"

The champagne slid from his hand and smashed against the sweating tiles, sending shards flying. In a frenzy he rushed to the edge, pulled at her hand, and flipped her over, recoiling in screaming horror at the blue face, the lolling tongue.

Heart attack? he wondered frantically. At twenty-*eight?* His own heart was whamming too fast to think clearly, but he could have sworn that, in the instant he had pulled her toward him, he had seen dark bruises on her shoulders, as if . . .

And what was this water splashed by the side of the pool? Too far away from where he had dropped the champagne . . .

Trembling with shock, he rose to his feet, remembering the soft thud he had heard. *Like a door closing,* he remembered thinking. No! Crazy!

He ran in a frenzy to see. The tiny red light glowed; the alarm was still on. *What the hell . . . ?* He paced in shock and panic in his front hall, wondering frantically what to do. He didn't want to call the police, didn't *need* this kind of publicity. Jesus, his reputation!

IT WAS THE CALL that did it, that made her understand, Amanda realized as she stared into the flames. She had found a halfway bearable position to sit in before the bedroom fireplace, and now shifted her weight, heedless of the dull throbbing in her leg. She felt a most peculiar calm, as if things were somehow going to end soon . . .

Her little fire was going out. Quickly, she balled more paper and tossed it in; watched the glow flare up again; concentrated.

She had been unable to shake the mounting and probably irrational feeling that that call was no crank call. That feeling of hate coming over the line . . . maybe the product of an overwrought imagination, but other crank calls . . . kids giggled, drunks garbled, there was always *some* sort of sound instead of complete, heavy silence, intelligent, listening. *Thwarted, their behavior becomes erratic,* she had told Peter. *They become daring and overconfident by their old standards.* And to herself she thought: *Overconfident, such as making a call that in less agitated times they would never dream of making, just checking to see if the next victim was in . . .*

It had occurred to her that she had been seen with Peter in various places around town: Brooklawn, the hospital, after yesterday's fund-raiser—that nest of nasties where anything having to do with Kelly was concerned. Peter's house would be at the top of the list for anyone trying to locate her.

The killer is coming . . . the thought refused to dislodge itself from her mind.

He's not only coming, but *the police are never going to catch him*—another thought that had seized hold of her and refused to let go. He gets in and out of locked houses, he slips away in seconds before the police arrive . . . it's going to be the same as last night, only this time I may be dead . . .

She balled more paper, threw it in, blinked at the flickering light.

When it had all first come to her she had gotten up, put on Peter's blue terry robe, and looked around. She had taken a yellow legal pad from the desk, matches from the mantel, and eased herself down before the hearth. She had lit a single sheet first, and then another. The warmth and the mesmerizing little blaze had helped her to concentrate. She felt her breathing slow; her mind begin to float free, deciding what to do . . .

Am I sure?

No. Far from sure.

So? What next? Call Peter at headquarters and say you've had the most convincing hunch?

Forget it.

She waited. The last tongue of flame died down, and she got painfully to her feet. *This guy's in a hurry,* she remembered Peter saying. She looked over at Toby, who was groggily watching her from where he sprawled at the foot of the bed, his chin resting on one of his forepaws.

She looked at Toby for a long time, until she realized what she was going to do.

Does Connecticut have a death penalty?

No, they usually cop an insanity plea or spend a few years in the pen. Ten years? Fifteen? What kind of punishment is that? Besides . . . there was something she had to know.

You've really snapped, you know that? You've dreamed up this whole scenario that isn't going to happen . . .

Right. Just taking a few precautions, that's all. Gives me something to do.

"C'mon Toby," she coaxed. "You have to change places."

Limping, she led the dog into the dressing room, where she pulled some blankets off a shelf and arranged them on the floor like a bed. He went to them and curled up. "Trust me, Tubbs," she said, patting him, scratching behind his ear. He put his head down, still looking questioningly at her. She hobbled to the door leading out to the hall and closed it, then quietly passed him again and closed the door leading back to the bedroom. Tightly.

Then, still eerily calm, she crossed to the chair near the bed, and picked up her shoulder bag. She opened it, and took out her father's gun. How strange, she thought. Like Poe's purloined letter, it's been here all along. In the crash, in the hospital, only feet from McHugh, from Peter when we made love. She had nearly forgotten it herself, and no one had dreamed of looking.

Methodically, her breathing as regular as if she were in a slight trance, she pulled open the cylinder again, rotated it, counted the bullets. Six, same as this morning.

She pressed the cylinder closed. Looked up, took one of Peter's medical books from a shelf, and got back into bed. She opened the book, and put the gun under it, with the muzzle facing the door.

Sitting there, listening, watching the door, she asked herself for the umpteenth time if she had indeed taken leave of her senses.

Only this idea is crazy, a voice in her mind said. *Put the gun back. Nothing's going to happen.*

We'll see, she thought, and sat and waited. We'll see.

52

ROUND-EYED, looking worried, Timmy Steffins seemed impossibly small in the group of tense cops who ushered him down the hall. McHugh met them halfway, bent and talked to the boy, exchanged greetings with the bewildered housekeeper. When they reached the conference room, one of the detectives pulled out two chairs.

Timmy gaped at the indicated place at the big table in the middle of the room, and felt even more vulnerable. He looked around; saw extra chairs lined under the windows at the end of the room, and three people he liked right away standing near them. A tall, dark-haired man with a nice face smiled at him. And two teenagers—a boy and a girl who reminded him of last summer's camp counselors—were looking at him as if they knew exactly how he felt.

He raced past a green blackboard to them; was overjoyed when the girl hugged him and the man and the boy ruffled his hair. "I'll sit here," he told McHugh and some detectives who were on his heels, and plunked himself down between the man and the boy.

His cheeks burned as he realized suddenly what a baby he must look like. The police car had come almost right away. There hadn't been time to do more than pull on his old jeans and sneaks and leave on the top of his G.I. Joe pajamas. Now he fingered them, wishing he had at least put on a sweatshirt, like the sweatshirts his dad wore on Sundays and his three new friends were wearing now. He looked up at the dark-haired man who had ruffled his hair and asked tremulously, "What's your name?"

The man smiled again. He leaned toward him with a foot up on one of the chairs and said gently, "My name's Peter. Think you can answer the question, Timmy?"

"Huh?"

He looked back at the others. Oh. The man who had said his name was Detective McHugh had asked him something. He had pulled a chair away from the table and now sat facing him, leaning forward. A bunch of guys were behind and around him.

"Timmy," the Detective said, in the same unhurried, gentle way that Peter had talked, the child noticed. "You saw a bad-looking man go into Mrs. Hagin's house?"

Timmy's eyes widened. *"Mean,"* he said. "He had this mean look on his face and I could *tell* he didn't belong there 'cause he kept looking over his shoulder!"

The room became very still. "Do you think you can tell us what the man looked like?" McHugh asked.

"He had brown hair."

The wig, they all thought. That was no help. "Anything else?" McHugh said. "Do you remember how tall he was?"

Timmy looked around at the men, thought, and then pointed to David Rusk. "Like him."

Rusk straightened, nodding. "I'm 5'11"," he said.

"And the man's face?" asked McHugh, still in the same gently prodding tone. "Did you get a look at the man's face?"

"Yeah, he looked like . . . um . . ." Timmy screwed up his face. "He looked like *Voltron.*"

"Voltron," McHugh repeated quietly. Questioning glances were exchanged all around until Brian pushed himself away from the window sill.

"Voltron's a kid's robot show," he said. He stepped closer to Timmy; bent and peered into the little boy's eyes. "Voltron's face is kind of square, right?"

"Right!" Timmy brightened. "And he has a chin that kind of . . ." He hand-gestured. "Sticks out—"

"A jutting chin?" Brian asked.

"Yeah! Jutting! Not as *much* as Voltron's but still . . ." Timmy's eyes slid self-consciously over to Miss Wrenn, who was sitting off to one side with a disapproving look on her face. "I haven't watched Voltron all *week,*" he said in a high, thin wail. "Honest!"

Brian slowly straightened and looked questioningly at the detective standing next to him.

"Brown hair?" he asked.

"Wig," the detective said.

McHugh and another man resumed talking to Timmy, and Brian stepped away, blinking, his heart feeling as if it had just leaped into his throat. A little jerkily, he walked over to the blackboard and stood there, reading and rereading the words that Peter had scrawled. The voices around him receded, and he heard the nightmare girlish scream again, still blurred but loud, as if someone had turned up the amps in his head.

Susan was suddenly at his side. "What's the matter?" she whispered.

His lips were slightly parted. He shook his head slowly back and forth. "Wasn't 'Go 'way,' he said huskily.

She looked at him.

Still staring at the board, he said in a faraway voice, "How common do you think a description like that is? Five-eleven, square-faced with a jutting chin?"

She said solemnly, "I can think of a few people who sound like that."

"Yeah?" Brian said. "Well, I can only think of one." He was staring desperately at the board; reached up with a finger and made a damp, shaky track through the chalk dust. "But 'Go 'way' isn't right, I'm sure of that now. God, Susan, help me remember—"

They both turned, startled, as a uniformed officer rushed in to tell two of the detectives about something on Country Club Lane. ". . . just called," they heard. And, "first patrol cars already at the scene . . . looks like the Gartrell thing."

There was a flurry of agitation and men leaving the room. Two or three stayed, but seemed suddenly and furiously engrossed in a pile of manila folders that sat in the middle of the conference table.

Brian and Susan returned their attention to the board.

AND ON COUNTRY CLUB LANE, the cops were acting funny.

Sandy Clees, still pale and shaking, had given in to civic duty and sheer terror and called them, and in a panicked torrent was now telling them what had happened. That he didn't *know* what had happened, that was the thing. She was just fine and sloshing around one minute, and then he came back from some fake phone call and found her like that . . . he pointed in horror . . . floating, dead . . .

And the cops, frowning, tight-faced, were casing the place as if he weren't even there . . . as if they knew it wasn't his fault. *Could this be possible?*

One of the older cops now asked, "You're sure your alarm was on the whole time?"

"Yes! *Yes!*" Sandy Clees cried, his eyes wide and his skin going suddenly from pale to an overwrought red and blotchy. His Yves St. Laurent robe was hanging open without his realizing it. He had the thumb of his left hand gripping the wrist of his right hand and was taking his own pulse, the cop noticed.

Uh-huh, was all the cop said, turning when two younger cops came in from another part of the house.

One of them said, "I'd like to hear about that fake phone call again."

Depleted, Sandy Clees sank down onto a chaise longue and dropped his brow into his hand, shielding himself from the awful sight in the pool. He inhaled and exhaled as if it were his last. Without looking up, he went through it all again.

"We were in the water, having a good time. I heard the phone and had to get out and answer it—"

"*Had* to?" one of the cops asked.

Clees nodded dully. "Half my business depends on the Hong Kong and Tokyo Exchanges. It's a twelve hour time difference." No one interrupted, so he continued. "The phone rang and I went into the kitchen to answer it. There was no one there, but the *line* was open, as if someone had called but wasn't talking. I figured a crank call."

"Did you notice anything else? Anything out of the ordinary?" asked the first cop, the older one. A few feet away, other policemen were bending and examining the splashed water by the side of the Jacuzzi.

Clees looked up bleakly. "As a matter of fact, I was getting some champagne out of the fridge, and I thought I heard a door being closed someplace. It was like . . . a soft thud. Then I figured I was crazy. The alarm was on the whole time."

The second of the younger policemen spoke up. "You have two phones, correct?"

Clees blinked at him. "Yeah. One of them, there's maybe five people in the world who know the number—"

"And in theory," continued the same cop, "one of those phones could be used to call the other, *right here in the house,* is that right?"

The color drained from Clees's face again. "I don't understand."

The cop held his hand up and showed the older officer what he had been holding by his side. Five glassine envelopes: four enclosing sets of ordinary house keys, labeled; the fifth holding a single small key, fat and ugly. A realtor's keybox key, immediately recognizable to anyone who has ever moved.

Clees shot to his feet. "Jesus Christ, what the hell is *that?*"

"The labels say Hammond, Payne, Gartrell, and Norwin," the cop told his colleague quietly.

Nodding, the older officer turned and went to call headquarters, while Sandy Clees gaped apoplectically at the man's retreating back, not knowing what to make of it.

53

A BOARD CREAKED near the top stair, and in the bedroom, Amanda jerked her head up. *No! Oh no! Press the panic button!* She controlled her breathing, and pulled the gun out from under the medical book, and pointed its muzzle toward the door.

Feeling her blood turn to ice, she waited until a man in a jacket entered the room, limping slightly, and she stared at him, confused, because she didn't recognize him . . . until he smiled, and reached up and pulled off his dark wig and eyebrows, just peeled them off the way they do in movies, and stood there changed back into . . . not Kirkley, not Maitland or some stranger, but Ray Herrick. Amanda was stunned. He looked bizarrely delighted about something.

"Why, you didn't even *try* for the panic button," he said, stuffing the wig into his pocket. "And the dog. I was planning to kill him—ah, good—you've confined him." His eyes went to the closed door to the dressing room. On the other side Toby was whining and beginning to bark.

She stared at him, not breathing. "I don't remember leaving the door open."

He sighed and shrugged modestly. "No door is closed to me."

He saw the gun that she pointed at him and came closer, curious. "Your father's .38?" he said conversationally. "I know that gun. It was in the drawer in your parents' room with the old scrapbook." He caught her expression and smiled. "Oh, I've been in your house *lots* of times, looking around. Did you see the page with Kirkley's picture on it? Your mother adored him. She was really taking the picture of him, you know, not you and your father. I saw her take it. I knew what was going on." He turned his head and seemed very interested in the fireplace . . . in the *poker* by the fireplace, Amanda realized.

She was suddenly breathing too fast. His manner was too casual about the gun, and the awful realization struck that she was probably going to have to use it. She gripped it tighter, began squeezing the trigger.

"How?" Her voice shook, but the questions that would not rest pushed her on. "How did you get into my house? And here and . . . Kelly's? You were there, too, weren't you?"

He looked back from the poker and seemed pleased with himself. "The same way I got into your friend Hagin's house. Others, too. Too numerous to mention. Do the names Gartrell and Norwin mean anything to you? Probably not. Norwin was a woman who was two-timing me. With Gartrell. But that's all in the past." He sighed philosophically and stepped closer. "This is a satisfying moment for me, can you believe that? I was afraid I'd never get the chance to brag to *someone,* so I'm going to tell you, because I value your intelligence, and because in a minute I'm going to kill you." He smiled. "Can you guess how I got into all those houses? Can you *begin* to imagine?"

She stared at him, silent and frozen-faced. *I'm going to kill you?* But she was the one holding the gun. She struggled for control. He's insane, she reminded herself.

He unzipped a small jacket pocket and extracted a key. A realtor's keybox key. Amanda recognized it immediately. He held it up.

"I had a pair, but I just gave one away," he said mildly. *"So* easy to steal, these little things. One realtor biddie I followed one night to the parking lot. Stole her whole purse like candy from a baby. She never even reported the theft—it would be bad for business. And Maitland, that moron. Left his keys in his pants pocket when he went in to the showers at the Club." Herrick laughed. "If he noticed it was gone later, he never breathed a word. They never do, these realtors. I've had *plenty* of chances to take keys from their offices, but two was enough, I decided."

Carefully, he put the key back into his pocket and zipped it closed again. Toby barked; whimpered.

Amanda winced in pain. She had been sitting up so stiffly that her back and leg were beginning to throb.

"You should see my collection," Herrick sighed regretfully. "In my house behind paneling, where no one would find it in a million years. I steal keys and duplicate them when the house is on the market. Then I save them for later enjoyment. The husband's away? I sneak in and watch the woman bathe, or cheat on him with another man. God, the bored, oversexed women you get in this town. Hagin, of course, was a different matter. What luck when *she* moved! I knew her key would come in handy someday." He blinked at Amanda; took another step closer. "There are other things I do, too. Would you like to hear more before I kill you?"

Amanda stared coldly at him, gripping the gun. "I'd like to hear why you killed my mother."

He looked at her; shrugged defensively. "I didn't *mean* to, that was the irony of *that* kill. I just wanted her to know how *angry* I was with her." He nodded. "Because she rejected me. She was the most beautiful woman I had ever seen, and she flirted with me, and then turned her back and fell for . . . for Kirkley, which was a very bad move on her part. She picked the one man who's *always* taken *everything* from me. Football trophies to women, he always took, always won, damn him. I was *happy* when your father hit him! I wanted to punch in his conceited face myself! But then, God! He marries into millions and what final slap do I get years later?" He raised his voice. "Kelly. I *wanted* that little morsel! I was obsessed— but she must have told you that. That I came to her condo and she laughed at me? Threw me out?"—Toby barked and bumped— "Kept insisting how she loved Kirkley's *son,* of all people!" Toby began scratching furiously. "It was too much. John winning your mother and his son screwing that little bitch every night. She deserved to die!"

He stepped closer and Amanda raised her gun at him. He waved at it dismissively and scolded, "Stop being dramatic. I've examined that old clunker. It doesn't *work!*" He laughed brightly. She stared at him, stunned.

"It's jammed!" He advanced another step. "You shoot that gun and you'll just blow off your hand!"

Amanda's blood ran cold. She hesitated, frozen in fear, as he lunged for her. She screamed—not hearing the door thumping, the wild barking—screamed again as he dragged her from the bed. She hit his face with the gun; saw blood; cried out in pain as he fought her, yanked it away; heard the door throw itself open—*wham!*—heard dog howls, thudding paws, snarls, a shout. She gasped, rolled free; looked up, screamed, "No!" Herrick. Gun in hand, beating Toby—"No! No!"—Toby jaw-clamping Herrick's free arm, eyes wild, tearing. . . tearing . . .

Sobbing, her heart bursting in her chest, she tried to crawl from the room. Pain lanced her leg, her back. She reached the door; pulled herself up; felt pain rip through her chest. She looked back. Herrick had broken free; was coming after her. She forced herself out. Heard Toby catch him, snarling, leaping, by the door.

She hurried. Down the stairs, gripping the rail, shaking in pain, in mindless terror. She reached the landing, gasping. Leaned against the wall and closed her eyes. Where could she go now? Nowhere. The pain was too great. She couldn't go on.

Above, the sound of an angry yell and a dog-shriek, a whimper, a spreading thud. Then footsteps coming.

Her pain exploding, she half-stumbled the remaining steps. And remembered. Under the stairs, the old-fashioned closet. Closed, it looked like the woodwork.

She made it to the wrought-iron latch; lifted it and opened the door. Dragged herself into a darkness of hanging jackets, pulled the door closed, and heard the latch drop outside.

Gasping against the wall, she let herself slide down, hurting, crying.

Above her footsteps pounded, hit the landing, and headed toward her.

54

SUKI WAS ANXIOUS. Still dressed, she sat on the bed on her side of the motel room and watched Davey sleep in his cot. Thank God. He had finally dropped off a few minutes ago, giving her the first chance to think that she had had all evening.

He knew that something upsetting was still going on, and hadn't stopped barraging the adults with questions all evening. Why was the policeman there while they were packing their overnight bags? Why is Aunt Suki so nervous? And, in the hospital room: if Mommie's feeling better, why is everyone still looking so worried? *Hey, Mom, what are you and Aunt Suki whispering about?* They had all hugged him and tried unsuccessfully to appear more relaxed. But none of them had ever lied to him, and were too wrung out to invent anything even plausible that would satisfy him.

Finally, Russ had sat him down on his bed on the other side of the cot, and more or less given it to him straight. "Davey, it's Amanda we're worried about. She was in a car accident today, and we're afraid that some bad person made her have the accident, and may still be trying to hurt her."

Davey's brow had furrowed, and his mouth had formed itself into a little "O" of concern. But the truth—or that part of the truth that Russ had told him—had proved to be the best approach after all. He spent the next half hour asking more questions—why isn't Amanda sleeping with us? Well, where *is* she sleeping?—but had finally wound down and asked for his red stuffed horse and settled down in his bed.

Suki sighed. She turned as the door behind her opened, and Russ came out in a robe with his hair dripping from his shower and a toothbrush in his hand.

"Do you think it's too late to call Amanda?" she asked worriedly. "I've got the strangest feeling. I just can't relax."

Russ glanced at his watch. "Ten forty-five," he said. "Well, she's pretty keyed up too. She could be sleeping, but I doubt it." He toweled his wet hair and raised his eyebrows questioningly. "You're still dressed. Aren't you planning to sleep tonight?"

Suki looked at him, and swallowed, and turned back to the phone on the bedtable. "I don't see how," she said very quietly. She lifted the receiver, and started to dial.

"CHANGE THE 'G' TO AN 'N,' Susan Weems said.

Brian did. With the eraser in his left hand, he buffed carefully at the board, then reached up with his right hand to chalk in the new letter.

"See?" she said, looking up. "Now 'Go 'way becomes 'No way.' Like that. One letter changes the whole thing."

She watched as he stood back, his hands at his sides, the eraser and piece of chalk dangling loosely in his fingers. He was frowning with a concentration that almost frightened her, like a blind man insisting on seeing in the dark. "It's still not right," he whispered angrily.

The others had all gone out. Whatever it was that had happened on Country Club Lane, the result was as if someone had yelled Fire. Two detectives left saying that they were going to "drive right over." Others were rushing around, their voices tense and audible as they phoned in their offices and conferred in corridors. Timmy Steffins and his housekeeper had gone with Peter Barron and Detective McHugh to McHugh's office. Something else for him to identify, Peter had told them as he left the room.

Susan looked suddenly sad. "You know," she said, her fingertips sliding down the edge of the blackboard. "I never should have dropped out of college. There was this one course, teaching phonics to first graders . . . well, it wasn't that different from what we're doing now. We learned that people remember *vowels,* not consonants, when a word is new or they're trying to memorize a poem, whatever—" She stopped and stared. "Brian, what are you doing?"

He was in a sudden fury of activity. His lips were moving, she could hear him breathing, "Oh, goddammit. Oh *shit,*" as he frantically erased everything off the blackboard, making chalk dust fly, then started to write, pressing so hard that the chalk snapped— *"Jeezus!"*—and the ragged stub screeched horribly as he finished pounding out two new words. He stepped back, white-faced and staring, and said, *"That's* what I heard. I'm sure of it now."

Susan peered at the board. At the oversized letters, shakily written, spelling out the words, "NO RAY!" Her lips went dry. She couldn't swallow.

"You're sure?" she asked.

"Yeah, I'm sure." Brian's heart was thudding hard. "I also know a Ray with squarish features. Come *on!"*

AMANDA HUDDLED in the blackness of the closet, her blood pounding in her ears, her pain sharpening. She heard his footsteps race past where she hid, and she laughed bitterly in the gloom. He would be back; she knew she was trapped.

She thought about Toby, and grief and nausea welled up. Toby . . . Little Tubbs . . . what did he do to you . . . ?

Yards away he was moving around in the kitchen. Shoving things; yanking doors open. She held her breath as the footsteps paused, then came back to stand, motionless, in the door to the hall. He was listening, she knew. Could he hear the loud pounding of her heart? The footsteps started up again. She froze, then stared into the darkness. They were going away, heading back through the kitchen toward the back hall with all its closets, its stairs to the basement. Much at that end to keep him busy, she thought grimly. If I could move I would make a run for the front door. I would yank it open, which would set off the alarm and notify the police, and I would race out and maybe even make it ten feet down the driveway before he . . .

Forget it.

What if he didn't go down to the basement? What if he just did a quick search through the back hall closets, then circled around through the dining room and living room, just in time to catch me in my pathetic little hobble?

She tried to straighten her legs out before her, and pain ripped through the injured one as if she had been gored. She squeezed her eyes tight; her teeth bit almost through her lower lip. Resigned, going limp, she found a sleeve of one of Peter's jackets, buried her face in it, and felt the tears come. Peter, she thought, crying, I've never told you I love you. Well, I do, you know. I did in January, but was too proud and afraid to say so, and I never stopped loving you when we were apart, and tonight I thought my heart would burst with loving you, only why didn't I *tell* you, why didn't I just say the words—

The phone rang, on the hall table only feet away, and Amanda sat, stunned.

I could reach it, she thought wildly. Even crawling I could reach it and grab the wire hanging down. The phone rang again. She pushed the door open and blinked at the light, and through sheer frantic willpower got herself up on one leg, steadying herself—the phone rang—limping, hobbling, covering the short distance until she saw her hand go out to the receiver—

—and screamed at the form rushing toward her, grabbing her arm away with a shout of fury, shoving her hard, hard, against a protruding stair riser. She felt the knock at the back of her head like a bolt of lightning. Felt the world go gray as she toppled forward, felt herself lifted roughly, being carried, like a rag doll, over his shoulder.

". . . look like a suicide!" His voice. Angry. Dim. ". . . last problem gone and I'll be *free* . . ."

Pain. A distant fog, enclosing her, the kitchen he carried her through. Please don't carry me that way. I can't breathe . . . my leg . . .

". . . *prize* keys, the medical examiner's house . . . !"

She heard more as if from afar, an ocean receding as a man ranted above it. "See these? See these? *Look,* damn you!"

She opened her eyes despite lids of granite. Saw blurry keys he jangled cruelly before her face. Closed her eyes, felt them moving again.

". . . once was in this house . . . saw his maid . . . groceries . . . saw her hang up the car keys . . ."

The Jeep. Please God. No.

Key-click sounds. Tiny red light. White. Through the door. Down concrete steps. Garage. Jeep door yanking open. No! Please! Don't put me . . . Please God . . .

Once, she got her eyes open. Watched him bloodlessly as he adjusted her body behind the wheel; reached in and started the ignition. Saw two of him, out of focus, as he smiled good-bye.

". . . were *so* despondent about your failures . . . blamed yourself
. . . tragic . . ."

The car door slammed. Then another, far-off door slammed.
Amanda lay, crumpled, the world going darker. All doors closed, yes.
Engine going. Death billowing out, only takes minutes.

She closed her eyes, and an enormous tear rolled glistening
down her cheek.

And in the house, he let himself out the back door, locked up
carefully, and headed through the night to his car parked an acre of
woods away.

55

TIMMY STEFFINS peered around at Detective McHugh's office with its half-glassed walls, its desk and chairs and file cabinets. He tried not to appear too fascinated or excited because the adults in there with him were looking so serious. The man named Peter was pacing and looking more worried than anybody. The Bird was looking just plain mad. They had stuck her in the corner in one of the chairs and said, "Ma'am, why don't you wait here while we're talking to Timmy?" That had made him feel important.

"Okay, Tim," he heard Detective McHugh say, and he turned back again. The policeman was standing behind his desk. His eyes were tired and sharp and kindly all at once as he handed a newspaper across, and Timmy took it. It was a copy of the local paper, the latest edition.

"See that picture on the front page?" McHugh pointed. "Tell us if you see the man you saw go into Mrs. Hagin's house."

Peter came closer and exchanged glances with McHugh. In the photo, five men in their Brooks Brothers suits stood smiling for the camera at John Kirkley's lavish fund-raiser. McHugh gave Peter a nervous shrug. "One of the swankier lineups," he muttered.

"Yes," Peter said.

They both held their breath.

Timmy frowned. He put the paper down flat on McHugh's desk and hunched over it, peering carefully at each face one by one. His index finger went without delay to the face of Ray Herrick. "That's him," Timmy said.

There was a shocked silence. After a moment McHugh said, "First eyewitness identification," and smiled at the boy. "Good job, Tim."

Timmy beamed back.

Peter stiffened. A sick feeling of urgency went through him as he tried to picture Herrick terrorizing Amanda from her attic, creeping up on Emily Hagin, and . . . Kelly? He looked down, rubbed at his brow. Looked up again with a newly troubled expression.

"Eyewitness identification . . ." he said.

"I know." McHugh nodded unhappily and sank down into his chair. He checked that Timmy was still engrossed in the newspaper and said quietly. "Too often unreliable. Defense lawyers love to tear it to shreds, especially if . . ." He trailed off, knowing that they were both thinking the same thing. Especially if the only eyewitness you've got is a young child.

"You know this guy Herrick?" McHugh asked after a pause. "How much roughly does he weigh?"

"About one-seventy, as a matter of fact," Peter said, getting more frustrated by the minute and resuming his pacing in the small room. "Now, if I could just go stick him with a pin, we could see if his blood type matches our forensic findings. Unfortunately, it's illegal. Hey—do you suppose he's limping? Think we could get us a warrant sworn out so we could pull him out of bed and see if he's limping?"

"Sure. In Russia." McHugh's voice matched Peter's in its tone of drained sarcasm. Both men felt their spirits plunge. Police work was like that. Elation to despair. You think you've got something and then you think again and it caves in, and you know someone's going to come along and call it unsubstantiated. What they needed were more eyewitnesses, more observations and statements that corroborated. They had come up against a brick wall and it hurt.

In the distance they heard the muted whistle of the 10:48 to New York. It sounded very mournful tonight.

McHugh rose to his feet as the housekeeper came to reclaim Timmy, telling him it was time to go home. He was giving her a hard time, and in a piping voice was reading off the names in the caption of the newspaper photo. "Fourth guy from the left," he said now with his finger marking the place. "It says his name is Ray Herring!"

"Herrick," Peter said, trying to smile, placing his hand on the boy's shoulder.

There was a commotion in the hall. Through the glass wall, they saw Brian and Susan tearing around a corner and colliding with a detective who was also headed their way. Almost frantically Brian extricated himself and was the first one through the door.

"It wasn't 'Go 'way' I heard Friday night!" he half-shouted, trembling. "It was . . . 'No, Ray!' And Timmy's description sounds one *hell* of a lot like Ray Herrick!"

"He had it blocked," Susan cried, careening in behind him. "Now he's sure!"

"Aw*right!*" yelled Timmy Steffins, clapping Brian on the arm. "You heard him and I saw him. Guess that makes *two* of us, huh?"

Peter went pale. McHugh frowned as the arriving detective handed him a sheet of paper, saying, "Just copied this down from Harris out at Country Club Lane. Whoever did it is a real nut case. Thought he could pin it on the guy by leaving *keys*—well, read it."

McHugh scanned the sheet, his face tightening as his voice droned rapid fire. "Traces of wet shoe prints found near the pool and in a parquet hall. Tread uneven, suggests"—he swallowed—"a limp. Keys found on desk of owner's study, labeled Oh Jesus duplicates of keys from Hammond, Payne, Norwin, and Gartrell homes. Also a realtor's keybox key . . ."

He slammed the sheet down furiously on his desk. *"Keybox key . . . !"*

Peter started frantically for the door. "Joe," he said in a strangled voice. "If it's Herrick he knows where I live. Send cars to check on Amanda. The neighborhood patrol—"

"—can be there in a minute," McHugh said. He nodded and the detective ran out to radio them, just as another man stuck his head in and said there was a call for Dr. Barron on line four. "That Mrs. Pepper who found the busted stairs," the second man said. "She's crying."

Peter flew to the phone. "Suki?" he said, yanking it up.

Suki was indeed in tears. "I can't reach Amanda," she sobbed. "I called, and you both said she'd be there all night, but there's no answer, and I let it ring and *ring.*"

His voice deadly calm, Peter said, "We're on our way. You just tried her?"

"One minute ago! Peter, tell me as soon as you get there what the matter is. Promise!"

He did, and hung up, his face ashen. To the detective he said, "Tell the cars on their way to break into the house if they have to. Tell them to look everywhere for her. I'm going."

"I'm right behind you," McHugh said, escorting Timmy and a horrified-looking Miss Wrenn out.

Brian and Susan caught up to Peter as he bolted down the hall. "Please." Brian's face was pleading. "I want to come with you."

"Me too," Susan said in the same quavering voice. Her eyes were round with fear.

Peter looked at them both and nodded. "Come on," he said, and the three of them ran out.

56

THE ROAD WAS SLICK from the rain. Ahead of him, Peter saw the squad car with its siren screaming nearly miss a corner and fishtail sickeningly, then right itself and zoom up the winding lane. He swerved at the same corner, felt the car slide sideways, controlled it. In the seat behind him, a high-pitched squealing from Susan; and Brian's voice saying: "It's okay, it's okay."

This can't be happening, he thought feverishly. Even if some bastard had the keys to the alarm . . . what about the panic buttons . . . what about Toby? Maybe Amanda stumbled on her bad leg and fell, and was having a hard time getting to the phone, or maybe . . . He frantically searched his mind and came up with nothing. Nothing but a desperate, gnawing fear. Amanda, I love you. I want to spend the rest of my life with you. God, what has happened? Please, let it be nothing, let it be (. . . *there was no answer . . . I let it ring and ring . . .*)

Brian, now leaning over the back seat. Angry. Talking about Herrick. Always making real estate deals, that's where his main money was from. Always in some real estate office or another . . . they bowed and scraped . . . easy for him to steal a keybox key . . . probably easy for anybody . . .

"Stealing the key's one thing," Peter said low. "But *saving people's house keys over years?* Jesus, he must have a collection."

"Some sicko," Brian whispered.

They tore behind McHugh's car into the driveway. The first cruisers were already there, dome lights flashing. The front door was open, the alarm wildly ringing. The others had already broken in. Peter got out and hesitated, looking up at the house, at every window lit and the sounds of shouting, searching inside. Finding nothing, apparently. His mind flew back to something he had told Amanda earlier, and was now hearing again—his own voice playing back to him in a tight-throated, horrified fast forward: *He steals Kelly's tapes, and plants them in your car. Why? To make you drive into a tree and self-destruct. Much more convenient that way . . .*

Self-destruct . . .

"Peter? Peter?" At his side, Brian and Susan. Not running into the house like the others. Staring at him as if desperately trying to read his thoughts.

"Joe!" McHugh and the man with him were nearly through the front door. McHugh in the lit rectangle looked back.

"Over here!"

He raced madly across the gravel, Brian at his heels, horror making him forget as they tugged desperately on the heavy garage door. "Locked!" he yelled, stumbling back, looking around frantically as the others caught up. McHugh pulled his .38, aimed it, and blew the lock off.

All four of them heaved up the door and fell back, coughing, as deathly fumes billowed colorlessly out. *Please God,* Peter thought.

He gulped air and dashed wildly ahead. Behind him they were shining their lights and his heart stopped as he saw her, through the windshield, her head tilted back at an unnatural angle, her face turned away and pale as death.

"Amanda!" he screamed, losing his breath, breaking into racking coughs.

The others were coughing, too, he could hear but not see them in the fumes as his hands worked convulsively to get the Jeep door open. He reached in, coughing and gasping, and lifted her to him. His eyes burned from the exhaust, his chest muscles were nearly in spasm, his knees buckled as he carried her. "I've got her," he heard, and there was Brian facing him, hooking his arms under Amanda from the other side and helping to carry her toward the door and the night.

Susan wailed and cops came at a run. Two spread a blanket as, still coughing, gasping in the damp air, they dropped to their knees and lay her down on it. "Need light," Peter managed, and McHugh knelt too, his chest still heaving, his flash trained on Amanda's face.

Amanda's pale blue, cyanotic face. A quiet groan, almost of pain, escaped Peter as he brought his face close to hers, the fingers of his right hand going gently, automatically, to the side of her throat. He swallowed, and tears flowed as he said, "She's got a pulse."

But a pulse seconds from quitting, he realized. It was faint and thready, and she was getting bluer and her breathing was rapid, shallow and ineffective. Around him the walkie-talkies squawked and someone yelled that the EMS was on its way and he thought, *No time.* He grabbed her face between his hands. He got her mouth open, worked her jaw into position. He pulled in a gigantic breath of cool, damp air, clamped his mouth over hers, and blew hard, down her throat and into her lungs, watching her chest rise as a kid watches a balloon he's puffing expand. He released, pulled in more air and breathed her again, two good ones, two *damn* good ones, and was ready to do it again when he heard Susan stop crying next to him where she was kneeling and say, "Look! Oh, look at her!" And burst into tears again.

He looked. Felt bells, chimes, violins, and his eyes filling, too. She was pinking up like a newborn babe. And breathing, her chest going up again on its own, shuddering for an instant, stopping to lose ground to a cough, then pulling in a deep and wholly independent *gasp,* and coughing again, a smaller one this time, then up, down . . . aw*right,* as Timmy Steffins would say, breathing on her own, deep, gorgeous, I-want-to-live breaths, her eyelids fluttering, her lips beginning to move. She was struggling to speak, and he bent his head closer.

"Peter . . ."

He kissed her. "I'm here, babe. You're going to be okay." His voice roughened as he said, "Who did this to you?"

Her eyelids opened, swimming with tears. She reached for him, and in the barest of whispers said, "Herrick. He's the one . . ."

She faltered, and he lifted her to him and cradled her in his arms. Over his shoulder he heard McHugh straighten from a bending position and turn to give orders to the others. "Herrick! You hear that? Okay, find the bastard. Send out an APB and find the bastard!"

57

RAY HERRICK WAS HUMMING as he drove. He had switched the car radio to a good classical station and had found music to soothe his nerves.

He was in no hurry. On the contrary. He was taking this more scenic shore route home as a reward to himself for a job well done. Correction—a job *brilliantly* done. The time of severe stress and mental anguish had been handled to perfection and put behind him. I am free now, he thought. I am totally free. I can return to my old life with a clear slate. No one knows that the one person who could have destroyed me is in that garage right now, dying, or probably already dead. Five minutes, give or take. What difference does it make?

He looked out and marveled at the eerie beauty of the night. The dense fog of before had changed into a kind of opalescent, drifting mist, so lovely as it swirled before his headlights that he wanted to breathe it in, he wanted to *taste* it, like a celebration vintage. His manicured fingers went to the power switch by the door handle and pressed. With a whir the two front windows went down a few inches. Another whir and the rear windows went down, but just a bit, he reminded himself. Enough to let in this cool, tangy breeze without blasting the things on the back seat. He glanced over his shoulder to check on the zipped bag containing his wig, his polished-dark running shoes, the rest of his disguise. How good it felt to have those loathsome things off, to be back in his usual, comfortable attire . . .

When he glanced back he noticed a police car, parked at the head of a side road he was passing, but he paid it no heed as he drove on.

Which was why he was surprised when the cruiser pulled out and started coming after him.

At first, glancing in his rear view mirror, he thought it was just a coincidence. The fellow was finishing his shift and just happened to be leaving now, that was all. He knew he wasn't speeding; he was doing a leisurely thirty-five. But why didn't the patrol car *pass* him instead of following so close like that? He frowned, feeling the first faint pulse of fear. Because the road was narrow and winding? he wondered. Yes, that must be it. Well, I'll do him a favor by going faster. It's just like the damn cops to ruin your evening.

Herrick speeded up, and was surprised when the cruiser did the same. He was following close now—*tailgating! I thought you weren't supposed to do that!*—but otherwise not making a move. Not passing, not signaling, nothing, as if . . .

Herrick broke out into a sweat. As if the cop was *waiting,* somehow, watching and tailing but waiting as if ordered to until something else should happen and—*There! Yes!*—another patrol car roared out of a side road and pulled in behind the first, both now following him, and no mistake about it.

His throat went dry. His heart was pounding and perspiration was pouring off him. Something had gone wrong, horribly wrong. He didn't know what, couldn't imagine what, but they were after him, they were after him. The car just behind him was signaling now. Flashing his overheads on and ordering something through a loudspeaker that he couldn't hear. Pull over, must be, but *why?* Mistaken identity? he thought frantically. Of course not—his lighted license plate told them exactly who he was. What to do? What to do?

His hands gripped the wheel as he put his foot down hard, speeding now, taking the curves like a dragster because—he gritted his teeth—he suddenly had an idea. There was a bridge ahead. If he could make it over that bridge he could shake them. It was a dock area over there, with alleys and byways and a couple of deserted warehouses. He'd ditch this car and hide, rent something else later, have time to plan. If only . . . the bridge . . .

He was almost there. He gave a roar of anger and floored it. Shot onto the old washboard-floored expanse at a speed he knew they wouldn't dare, until, horror-struck, he saw the flashing dome lights of the roadblock waiting on the other side. In a mindless fury he slammed on his brakes. The car spun around and hit a side steel girder. In a blur he realized that . . . he was tilting . . . that the back of the car was lifting, lifting, as it poised for a moment on the edge of the bridge. He gasped, saw the front tip down, then screamed as the car sheared off the edge and slammed down onto the embankment below.

He felt the heavy dull crunch, felt his body flung around and the lightning pain as his face slammed into the dashboard. But even as the world grew dimmer and one eye filled with blood, he thought, At least I didn't go into the water.

Whereupon the car rolled down the rest of the embankment into the river, coming to settle in water only nine feet deep. He knew it wasn't deep, the car hadn't rolled down that far an incline. And he watched, horrified, his bloodied face illuminated as in a grotesque night carny show by the dials from his dashboard, screaming and screaming as water poured in through his partly open windows, filling the car, shorting out the electrical system so the windows and door locks wouldn't open, despite his pounding, his struggling; and then the lights went out, and the water level reached his face, his bulging eyes, and his screams became one last shrieking gurgle as he drowned, realizing in the last seconds that it was his car, not the water, that was killing him. *The one door I couldn't open . . . !*

It was his last coherent thought.

58

AT A FEW MINUTES AFTER MIDNIGHT, the police frogmen resurfaced, signaled, and the winch began cranking up its dreadful burden. On the bridge, Peter held Amanda very close as they watched. She was still pale, still trembling a little, but she had insisted on coming, and he had understood.

He squeezed her gently now, turning away from the men's shouts, the light beams sweeping the black water. "Pain better?" he asked, although he knew that it had to be. Seventy minutes ago she had been out of danger and he had sent the ambulance back. He had carried her into the house, laid her on a couch, and insisted that she take a painkiller. She did, and he had sat on the couch by her, calling the vet, calling a hysterical Suki to tell her what had happened, reassuring her. On both occasions, Amanda had wept—although Toby, carried down on a police stretcher, was feebly wagging his tail and seemed to have only a minor concussion.

The police had started to leave, except for McHugh and the officer with him who came in for a statement. Brian and Susan, drawn-faced, wandered in behind them and knelt over Toby.

McHugh had looked very somberly at Amanda. "You took a terrible chance," he said. "You almost died."

"I had to do it," she said weakly.

The officer's walkie-talkie had suddenly come alive, the room filling with an excited male voice saying that Herrick had been located. Amanda did not understand the following words of the garbled barrage, but the two policemen did, and McHugh looked up in astonishment. *"Eighty?* He's doing eighty on Harbor Road?"

Peter, watching Amanda's face, had not been surprised by her reaction to their having located Herrick.

Grim-faced, almost rigid with expectation, she had gotten herself back into a sitting position. She was waiting, he realized; probably seeing the reckoning of twenty years rushing toward her within the next few minutes.

McHugh finished getting his statement just as they heard that Herrick had gone off the bridge. "Oh boy," he said softly. "We gotta go." He put his hand on Peter's shoulder and smiled in tired triumph at Amanda. "You two make one terrific team," he said. "Hang on to each other."

Brian, kneeling by Toby, had stared after the departing policemen with a look of deep frustration. "Damn!" he exploded. "Now I'm sorry I left my car at Kelly's house. I want to go, too. I want to *see* this bastard get his!"

Susan had looked at him, frightened by the idea, and Amanda, very still, had looked at him and nodded. "I feel the same. I want to see . . . have to see . . . with my own eyes that it's over."

They had waited until the vet-van came for Toby, then drove down in Peter's car.

And now they stood on the bridge, Brian and Susan further down and closer to the men operating the winch. They had arrived just as the cable was fastened and grew taut in the black water. Amanda tensed. There was a grinding, cranking sound, and she stared as two rear wheels and then the underside of a car were rising up, like a slain and hideous monster being lifted from the deep. Hard to believe, she thought, that the source of so much grief and destruction was in that car now, dead, his body sodden and probably covered by water weeds, mud, river junk. The man who had killed her mother . . . and Kelly . . . she blinked tears and looked up at the night sky, clearing now, the fog drawing back like a curtain to let the moon sail out . . . the white, healing moon . . .

Wynken, Blynken, and Nod one night . . .

"Don't cry, Mandie." Peter held her closer. "It's all over. That's twenty years of bad memories getting washed away out there."

Amanda sniffled, nodded, and dried her eyes. She leaned forward a little and looked down the rail to where Brian stood with his arm around Susan. They were comforting each other, solemn-faced as they watched the creaking winch lift the car. Brian must have felt her gaze, because he looked over at her and smiled grimly. Then he seemed to remember something as his eyes went to Peter and he called out, "Hey—*how* long did you say Toby has to stay at the vet's?"

In unison, Peter and Amanda answered, "One week."

Brian seemed to have something else on his mind, but looked at Susan for reassurance before glancing over again.

"When he's back, can we play with him? I never had a dog."

Peter grinned. "Come every day. He gets lonely."

And Amanda felt a warmth and calm seep into her which she had never felt before. It was incredible, she thought. Love, friends, a future to build after all, and no more nightmares. She turned to Peter and felt his arms go around her.

"I've seen enough," she said. "Let's go back home."